THE SOUL OF THE RADIANT

D. S. KOGLER

Cover design by MiblArt

978-1-952033-05-6 (paperback)

978-1-952033-04-9 (ebook)

www.dskogler-books.com

Chapter 1

Warm light illuminated the room around Ev as the sun set on what might well prove to be the last day of her world's existence. Her eyes were fixed beyond the white wall of the city. There, the magical forest of lumine pines that ten years ago, on her first visit here, had glistened with orange and blue lights, now lay dead, dim, and silent. Despite her best efforts at repurposing the Masters systems to bring things back to the way they had once been, the world's decay had not only continued, but accelerated. There just wasn't enough left of those systems to salvage, and her attempts at manipulating weather directly had led to disastrous results. Ev liked to think that she'd managed to buy the world at least a little bit of time as her mentor, Syrus, worked diligently to hand the world off to someone who could care for it, but looking at how bad things had become, it was hard to say for sure if anything she'd done had actually helped.

Now, they were potentially only minutes away from the end. Syrus had already made the announcement warning everyone to be ready. Ev knew it was time for her to join him, but she wanted to at least spend a few more moments to take in what might well prove to be her last memory of Doxla.

The sound of familiar footsteps interrupted her solitude before an arm reached across her shoulders and gave her a comforting squeeze.

"Hey, it's going to be okay," Birdie told her. "Even if the world's destroyed, we've got this. This is what you've all been training for, right?"

"If you can call it training," Ev replied, eyes fixed on the horizon. "Syrus has barely let us explore beyond Doxla's borders. We've practiced using anther, but we have no idea what's waiting for us out there in the Cosmic Graveyard."

Birdie squeezed Ev's shoulder more tightly and smirked. "I know you're worried, but Syrus has faith in you, and so do I. Hell, if he thinks Helcant can keep it together out in that Cosmic Graveyard place, I *know* you can. You've trained under him longer than anyone."

Ev couldn't help but smile at that. She then pulled away from Birdie, moving toward the door. "Maybe. Hopefully we won't even need to find out. I suppose we do need to get going, though, don't we?"

Birdie joined Ev, and the two of them walked through the extravagant streets of Ars Summis toward the Lumine Tower at its center. Ever since Syrus had found a way to designate nepacs as Divine, the city had become a home to everyone dedicated to taking back the world from the Masters, of which there were many. Once Syrus had seen that it was impossible to prevent nepacs from stumbling across the ever-multiplying degradation of the world, he'd invited as many as were willing to learn to interact with the antherial systems that Doxla was built upon. At the moment, however, the city was nearly empty. Everyone who lived here knew what would happen if things turned out poorly today, and they had all returned to their home regions to prepare even before Syrus had made his announcement.

At the very top of the Lumine Tower, Ev stepped into the Masters' former control room. Syrus had removed all of its fancy aesthetics to help him concentrate, leaving it looking like an oversized metal dome with several circular desks arranged in the center of it. Each desk had a ring of glass along its inner edge that displayed various bits of information — most of it in the language of the seitti. In addition to Syrus, a number of people were already there waiting for her. The long list including her brother, Jax; her sister-in-law, Fauna; Jax's longtime friend, Gare; Gare's wife and daughter; Birdie's now-human friend, Umber, who'd taken on the permanent form of a middle-aged, brunette man; and Syrus's four other apprentices: the human, Tallis; the demon, Helcant; the demoness, Nictis, who looked just like a female Helcant; and the gold-tinted naga, Lylia, whose long, serpentine lower "half" coiled up into a ball beneath her.

"Nice of you to join us," said Jax, arms crossed.

"Don't give me that look," Ev shot back. "We're right on time. Zun-Roven's not even here yet."

"Zun-Roven has sent word that he will not be coming," Syrus announced. "He believes that, considering the current unrest among immortals now that so many of them have become human, he would better serve assisting with the evacuation should one prove necessary."

Gare harrumphed. "He's got a lot of confidence in us, doesn't he?"

"I would be doing the same in his place," remarked Syrus, "and I certainly hope you have taken the proper precautions as well."

"Of course I have," Gare snapped. "Everyone in our family's waiting with their town's anthermancer in case things *do* go wrong. I just don't get why everyone's so worried. We're ready, right?"

Syrus shook his head. "We most certainly are not. We're only doing this now because we're out of time. Frankly, I'm surprised the Masters haven't erased this world before now."

"So what's the hurry?" asked Gare. "If the Masters forgot about us, we can take all the time we need."

Helcant answered for Syrus. "Do your eyes not function? The world is dying! Even the Underworld has grown cold."

"And magic is failing," Umber added. "Those of us reliant on it for survival have been forced to become human. We are grateful that Syrus was able to grant us this transformation."

Tallis continued where Umber left off. "There's no point in putting it off, anyway. There's literally nothing more we can do. We've got one shot at breaking into their core systems, and we don't have any clue as to how to do it. Syrus's "hacking" thingy is our only hope."

"And it's a very slim hope," Syrus finished. "If only I could make a local copy of myself. Then I could go with you into the Cosmic Graveyard and we could work from there, but since this body is just a vessel, well . . ."

He trailed off, then started fiddling with the controls of the device in front of him.

Ev tried to ignore his comment about making copies of himself. He might not have been all-powerful like a seitti, but from her understanding, prifae like him were capable of utilizing multiple bodies at once, so it made a sort of sense that such an action would seem natural to him. Still, his past musings on the topic made her uncomfortable whenever he brought it up, and not just because of the constant reminder that he'd be leaving them behind should this fail.

Ev pushed the thoughts from her mind and stepped over to her own desk where she typed out a handful of commands on the machine. The upper display responded by showing her what Syrus's screen showed, and she watched as he entered the deepest level of the Masters' systems they'd yet breached. He wrote one final command, which popped up a new display floating above the desk, then stopped.

Syrus looked around the room to each of his assistants as he spoke, stopping his gaze when he reached Ev. "I will say this one final time. If we fail, I will no longer be able to help you. It will be up to you to survive in the Cosmic Graveyard until you are able to find a way to contact a member of the seitti. The Masters most likely own this entire region of the Graveyard, and it will certainly be sealed off from other regions. No matter how great your skill with anther, I guarantee you will not be able to break such a seal. You will have to find another path to salvation."

"Enough of this doom and gloom talk," interrupted Gare, his wife looking uncomfortable with his outburst. "Look, I get it. Everyone here knows what we're getting into. Even *I* know the plan. But all this talk of failure isn't helping anyone. If we have to do it now, then let's just do this thing already."

Syrus glanced over to Gare, then back at the other faces around the room. He sighed. With one hand, he produced a swirling shimmer and positioned his hand inches away from the new display.

"Very well. Do each of you have my key with you, in case this fails?"

Ev and her fellow apprentices all nodded as they produced small, rippling shimmers from their hands.

Syrus gave them a nod in return. "Then let us pray that with this, you will meet my world's creator and not your own."

He pressed the button.

Red letters popped onto the screen.

Ev's heart nearly fell out of her chest.

Helcant slammed his fists against a desk. "Curse it all!"

"Do not panic," Syrus ordered as he activated another small shimmer with his hands and spoke into it, sending a message out across the entire world. "All anthermancers, activate your portals, now! I am opening the world boundary. You must evacuate immediately! Everyone else, follow your anthermancers to safety. Take only blankets and what you need to survive."

Syrus removed his hand from the shimmer and spoke only to those around him. "I'm so sorry I couldn't do more."

"Don't be sorry," Jax replied. "You gave our world a chance. Even if it gets destroyed, at least *we* still have one."

"Get to the portals," Syrus told them. "It's truly been an honor to know you all."

Everyone but Ev, Birdie, Jax, and Fauna fled the room.

"Come with us," Ev pleaded.

"You know that I can't," Syrus replied. "My connection is with your world. If I—"

"At least come with us to the world's edge," Ev insisted. "If the Masters find you here—"

"There's nothing they can do to my true self," Syrus stated. "I will buy you whatever time I can. Now please, go."

Ev hesitated only a moment more before she felt Birdie tug at her to follow. She did.

In the adjacent room, a portal to the world's edge awaited them. The others had already gone through. Jax beckoned for Ev and Birdie to hurry before running through after them with Fauna.

On the other side, Ev found herself on the rocky shore that circled Doxla's oceans. Looking around, she spotted portals as far as she could see, with countless people of all races pouring through them and out through the tears in the world's boundary. Before her sat one such tear — the landscape beyond it shrouded in darkness.

Ev recalled the various anther fields Syrus had taught her, then plunged on through to the other side. Immediately, she felt her magic and strength leave her as the air of her world billowed past into the cold darkness. She also felt the anther all around her, and she channeled her will to create a region of warmth as large as she could manage. She then tried her best to tell the surrounding space to produce breathable air.

Whether by her efforts or not, someone must have succeeded. Lights from other anthermancers sparked to life around her. Ev joined in, producing a giant bubble of light that followed her as she moved and revealed a twisted, roiling gray landscape.

She ran deeper into the darkness, her sense of time distorted in the chaos until she felt it — a wave of heat crashing into her from behind. Looking back, Ev shielded her eyes against the blinding blaze erupting from each of the tears in Doxla's boundary.

It had happened. The Masters had returned, and they'd destroyed everything.

Ev stood frozen in place — a still figure in a sea of statues all processing the loss that they had all known was coming, yet none of them were ready for.

After a few minutes of standing in silence, Ev felt Birdie place a hand on her arm. "We need to keep moving. It's up to us to keep these people safe now."

Ev swallowed, then nodded. They'd need to search to find a place to make shelter. To do that, she needed to figure out how to make portals out here. Portals were one of few things that were supposed to work similarly to how they did within Doxla, so with just a little bit of work . . .

A bright light bathed the entire area. Her thoughts vanished as a terrible fear gripped her. Heart pounding, she forced her head upwards to see the source of the light.

There, high above them all, floated a lone figure in pearly armor.

The Master, Sylvra, tilted his gaze downward.

Before Ev could even blink, the wasteland around her vanished. The people around her vanished. Birdie and Jax vanished.

Everything disappeared in a blinding flash of white.

* * * *

Seemingly floating in an endless haze, Ev's mind felt trapped halfway between a dream and lucid thought. Slowly, the realization of what had transpired took hold in her, and with that realization came clarity.

Reality snapped back into focus, and Ev found herself imprisoned in an odd, barely-translucent bubble.

How much time had passed? Seconds? Hours? Days? She had no way of knowing.

Standing and pressing her face against the wall, Ev strained to see outside the foggy bubble. She spotted what she thought might be other prisons of a similar nature, though it was impossible to be certain.

Either way, there was hope. For whatever reason, Sylvra had chosen to imprison them instead of destroy them. Why? She didn't care. He had unwittingly given her a chance, and she was going to use it.

Ev placed her hand against her container. It felt like glass, but she could sense that it was something else entirely. Sylvra had clearly not expected any of them to know how to manipulate anther, because she could feel the raw components swirling within, completely unprotected from outside influence. The anther was not a continuous field, as she would have preferred, but the concentration of it seemed to be sufficient for her use.

Closing her eyes, Ev did as Syrus had taught her. She extended her will into the anther — the very fabric of reality that she would never have been able to touch if Syrus had not gifted her the ability to do so. Those packets of space and energy and their relationships between one another gave rise to the physical existence that she knew. Ev dove deeper and deeper into the interweaving pattern of the barrier's anther until she found a vital repeating relationship holding the entire thing together. With all her concentration, she willed a single instance of the bond to be rewritten into a "disease" of sorts. The bond would now spread her will to all adjacent similar connections before destroying itself.

Immediately, the entire shell of her prison disintegrated, and Ev dropped to the well-lit grassy ground below. Without even bothering to examine her surroundings, she rushed over to the nearest bubble and repeated the process. A confused young woman that Ev didn't recognize fell out. The woman stared at Ev with tear-filled eyes.

"Are you okay?" Ev asked.

"What happened?" the woman squeaked. "Where are we?"

"I don't know," Ev answered, "but we're getting out of here."

She then ran to another bubble, this one producing Jax upon its destruction.

"Jax!" Ev shouted, embracing her brother.

"Ev?" Jax said, frozen in place by Ev's sudden hug.

As soon as she let go, Jax looked around the area. "What the hell is going on? Did the Masters do this? Where's Fauna!"

Ev frowned, the sight of Sylvra hovering over them still burned into her mind. "It was Sylvra. I'd recognize his armor anywhere."

Jax stared into Ev's eyes, a hint of fear on his face. "We have to find the others and get out of here."

"You think I don't know that?" Ev replied, turning to pop another bubble.

Before she reached it, however, she heard a commotion going on some distance into the field of bubbles. She recognized two of the voices as Tallis and Helcant's, and breathed a sigh of relief knowing that they had also survived, and had also figured out how to break free of their prisons.

Deciding she'd leave them to hopefully do the same thing she was doing, Ev turned her focus back to the next prison and freed Fauna to Jax's relief.

Ev left the two of them to collect themselves as she tried more bubbles. Two later, she found Birdie. The moment Birdie touched the ground, Ev practically threw herself onto her as she tried to hold back tears.

It was starting to look like everyone who'd escaped Doxla really had survived. What Sylvra hoped to accomplish by imprisoning them, Ev didn't know. She wasn't sure she *wanted* to know. What she did know was that as long as they were all together, they still had a chance.

Birdie returned Ev's embrace, but released it shortly after, reminding Ev that there were more important matters at hand.

"Okay, that's everyone," Jax stated, trying to sound tough despite clearly not feeling it. "We need to go."

"We have to save as many as we can," Ev stated before turning her attention to the next prison.

"You said Sylvra did this," Jax protested. "If he comes back, we won't stand a chance."

"Jax is right," Birdie added. "If the Masters return and see that we broke free, I doubt they would try to merely contain us again."

Ev frowned, but before she could answer, the woman from before spoke up.

"You can't leave," she pleaded. "Please. My husband is still here. My baby . . ." the woman trailed off, unable to finish her sentence.

Ev looked to Jax and Birdie in turn and shook her head. "We aren't leaving. Not yet. If we escape by ourselves, then what's even the point? Where will we go? What are we even supposed to do? Live out the rest of our lives alone in a cave while the rest of Doxla stays locked in these jars?"

"Ev—" Jax started.

"No!" Ev shouted, but she knew he was right that they couldn't stay long. "Just give me five minutes. I'll save as many as we can, then we'll find Tallis and the others and see if we can figure out a way to escape."

Jax and Birdie exchanged glances but didn't say anything.

Fauna decided to speak up. "Jax, I think Ev is right. I'd feel awful if we were the only ones to get free."

Jax sighed, then relented. "Fine, but Ev? Please hurry. I'll go find the others in the meantime. I thought I heard Tallis and Helcant over there."

Ev nodded, smiling at Fauna, then went back to work breaking the floating prisons. Fortunately, they only took about thirty seconds each to shatter. It didn't take long for the woman to be reunited with her husband and son. The three of them huddled together as the parents did their best to console their child. Unfortunately, the time before Jax's return came and went all too quickly. Ev had only managed to break seven more free from their cages before he approached her again.

"Alright, it's time to go," stated Jax. He'd managed to gather up everyone else who was missing, along with another six individuals the others must have broken out.

"Not yet," Ev insisted. "There's barely more than twenty of us."

"And if the Masters return, there won't be any of us," Jax almost shouted. "Please Ev, let's at least try and find a way out of here before we try and save more people. Helcant said we can't make those portal things here. If that's the case, then we need to move. Now."

Ev growled, knowing he was right, but she was surprised to hear they couldn't make portals. Deciding to try it herself, she stretched out her hand to feel the anther around her.

There wasn't much of it, or more specifically not much that hadn't already been configured to be resistant to tampering. The only anther she could manipulate was from the microscopic particles left over from the cages she'd disintegrated.

Ev frowned, then looked back to Jax. "If I can get us a way out of here right now, then we stay until we free at least one hundred people."

"This is not negotiable," Jax said, agitated.

Birdie crossed her arms. "Just agree to it, Jax. The longer we argue, the less escaping we're doing." Birdie then looked to Ev. "I'm guessing you must have an idea, then?"

Ev smiled. "I might. Jax?"

"Fine. But any sign of the Masters, and we are gone. Agreed?"

"Deal."

Ev stepped over to another bubble-prison and placed her hand on it.

"What are you doing?" Jax asked. "I thought we—"

"Silence," Helcant hissed.

"The deal was to get out first!"

The naga, Lylia, put her hand on Jax. "That one requires concentration. This one requires patience."

Ev heard Jax sigh, but she did her best to drown out all distractions. Portals weren't particularly difficult to make when surrounded by anther, but she'd never tried to make one from discreet packets of anther as opposed to a continuum.

After a few minutes, though, she was able to remedy that situation. Rather than disintegrate the bubble, she split it open and reshaped it into a disk — its former occupant helped away by Umber as Ev converted the solid wall into a gateway that would lead as far away as she could imagine.

"There," she said, turning back to the others and gesturing to the portal. On the other side was the darkness of where they'd been prior to Sylvra's involvement. "Now, let's—"

Ev cut herself off when she realized she was no longer speaking to anyone.

Birdie, Jax, everyone — they had completely disappeared. Even the sea of bubbles around her had vanished.

Ev spun back around to the portal, but it, too, had gone.

She spun around again, looking for any sign of anything.

Panic started to set in, but she still had one more idea. Raising her hand, she attempted to interface with the particles of the shattered cages, but even those had vanished!

Ev could feel her heart racing. What the hell was going on?

A sharp clap from behind made her jump. Wheeling toward the source of the sound, Ev gasped.

There, only ten feet away, was Sylvra — standing seven feet tall, his armor gleaming, his silver hair combed neatly, and his lips pulled back in a sly smile — putting his hands together in a dramatic show of slow applause.

"My, my," he stated calmly. "While I certainly expected at least a few of you to be able to escape my prisons, I did not expect any of you to actually make a portal out of them."

Ev simply glared at Sylvra, her nails digging into her palms at the hatred she felt for this man. She wanted to scream at him, but she could barely even process the emotions she felt, let alone put them into words.

"Speechless, I see," Sylvra continued. "I can't say I blame you. I felt the same back when I was in the exact same position you are in now."

"What did you do with them?" Ev growled, barely registering what he said.

"If you mean the others who were with you, I have removed them," Sylvra stated. "They were clearly inferior to you. I did not want them getting in the way."

He took one step closer, and suddenly Ev felt herself surrounded by anther. She had no idea what this monster's game was, but she was going to make him regret playing it. She was sure she couldn't kill him, but that didn't mean she couldn't make him hurt. If she died, so be it, but he would at least once feel pain from the people he'd made suffer for so long.

Suppressing her inner rage enough to focus one final time on the anther around her, Ev pulled it inside her to make it easier to control. She braced herself for his move to stop her, but he only eyed her curiously.

Well, that would be his mistake, she thought, and she unleashed a chain reaction that spread in his direction, piercing through him with thousands of invisible strands that then expanded — slowly at first, then more rapidly, tearing Sylvra apart before combusting into a raging fireball that consumed him completely.

Ev was left panting. She knew this wasn't the end, but even something like him had to feel that.

Moments later, the anther around her vanished as Sylvra reappeared. She was ready for the worst, but Sylvra's expression was not one of anger. It was so much worse.

"My, my, indeed," Sylvra nearly whispered. "So much anger within you — and so much potential."

He chuckled before giving Ev a genuine smile. "I think you and I should have a little chat. It appears we have so very much in common."

Chapter 2

Ev found herself on the rocky shore that circled Doxla's oceans. Looking around, she spotted portals as far as she could see, with countless people of all races pouring through them and out through the tears in the world's boundary. Before her sat one such tear — the landscape beyond it shrouded in darkness.

Ev recalled the various anther fields Syrus had taught her, then plunged on through to the other side. Suddenly, the world around her shifted, and she found herself falling upwards! She felt her magic and strength leave her as she landed hard upon some dark, frozen surface. The only light around was from other anthermancers who had already passed through and begun creating light — the portal she'd come from seemingly having vanished, though she still felt warm gusts of air billowing around her from some unseen location.

Ev stood, then focused her mind on the anther around her to join her fellows in producing light for the area, as well as warmth and air. Even if a good bit of the latter was already swirling around her, there was no guarantee it would last.

Now able to see the area, she noticed that countless evacuees had landed in the region around her, and even more were still coming — appearing seemingly out of nowhere, but never from exactly the same location twice.

A hand grabbed Ev's arm. She turned to see Birdie, who was clearly concerned.

"Are you okay?" Birdie asked.

Ev nodded. "We have to get as far from Doxla as we can before the Masters show up."

Ev was about to say more, but she stopped herself. She quickly spun around, looking at the sea of darkness extending in all directions.

"Wait. Something's not right," she said. "Where *is* Doxla?"

Birdie blinked, then looked around, apparently having just realized there was no sign of it.

She drew closer to Ev. "Do you think the portals were only one-way?"

"Maybe," Ev answered, "but we *saw* what was on the other side. This isn't what we saw. I think we somehow ended up somewhere else."

"Somewhere else? So the portal didn't work right?"

Ev shook her head, but before she could answer, a scream rang out from behind them. The two exchanged glances, then quickly pushed their way through the crowd to the source of the distress. Jax joined them on the way, and they eventually reached a clearing — the other evacuees having retreated from a horribly charred corpse that had fallen from above.

Jax, his face white, barely whispered, "What the hell?" before looking up at where they'd fallen from.

The warmth and wind had stopped flowing from above. No further survivors — or anything for that matter — appeared.

"So that's it, then," Birdie stated after a moment. "Doxla's gone."

"We don't know that," Jax protested, but he was physically shaking.

The crowd around them began to murmur, quietly at first, but then one man shouted, "Cassie? Cassie! Where's Cassie?"

It was like a bomb went off. Almost immediately, the survivors began scrambling, shouting, crashing into one another as they searched for missing loved ones. Cries of adults and children alike filled the air. One large demon knocked Ev to the ground in the chaos.

Fortunately, she'd had the foresight to make her environmental manipulation permanent, so the crash didn't plunge them all into darkness. Unfortunately, it did nothing to stop someone else from stomping down on her cheek in the confusion.

Ev cried out as she felt blood dripping down her face, but with help from Jax and Birdie, she was quickly back up on her feet.

"We have to do something!" shouted Jax.

"Everybody stop!" shouted Birdie to no avail. "You have to stay calm!"

"*BE STILL!*" boomed a terrible voice, shaking the ground itself as a blast of wind rushed over everyone.

Most of the crowd froze, and Ev's heart nearly stopped at the roar, her fearing that they'd been discovered by the Masters. Her relief was immediate when her eyes landed on the source of the voice — Helcant, standing tall atop a large stone about a hundred yards away.

The demon continued, though thankfully he'd turned down his artificially heightened volume. "Much has been lost, and much more will be lost, but behold your surroundings! We are not safe here. Panic will only beget even more loss! We must be calm to survive.

"One hundred thousand have trained to tame this place. Find those with light and seek shelter among them. Obey the words of the anthermancers, and we shall yet persist!

"Do not let fear take hold! Have patience, for before all else we must organize! Only once we have found safety will the time for mourning be at hand."

Helcant hopped down from his rock, and Ev was relieved to see that the crowd, though still frightened, was no longer out of control.

"I need to talk to Helcant," she told Jax and Birdie.

"We'll go with you," offered Jax, and after he grabbed Fauna, the four of them made their way over to where Helcant and the other apprentices of Syrus were talking furiously among themselves. There, Gare and Umber worked to keep the crowd calm and at a respectable distance. Ev spotted Gare's family against the rock, his wife keeping their daughter close to her and away from the crowd.

Once the group drew near, the big man ran over.

"There you guys are! Do you have any idea what's going on? Where's Doxla?"

"We don't know," answered Ev. "For some reason, the tears in the world's boundary spit us way out here instead of where they were supposed to."

"Weird," remarked Gare. "I guess that worked out for us, though. I doubt the Masters will be looking for anyone out in the middle of nowhere."

"That's a good point," Jax said. "Syrus must have thought of that and made portals at the last minute."

That still didn't explain why they could see a different area than where they ended up, thought Ev, or why she had seen others in the Cosmic Graveyard outside of Doxla before running through. But, as odd as it was, she figured now wasn't the best time to dwell on it.

"Excuse me," she said, pointing to Helcant, "but I really need to talk to the others."

"Oh, of course," said Gare, moving out of her way.

Ev thanked Gare, then approached the other apprentices. Before she had the chance to speak, Tallis descended upon her.

"Ev, great, you're here. We're trying to get organized with the other anthermancers, but we're having trouble with Syrus's 'networking' idea. There are so many people that the way we practiced isn't working out. Do you think you can help Nictis with this while I—"

"I *know* what I'm doing," the red-eyed, black-haired Nictis hissed. "I require time to build an entire system from nothing!"

"I know that," returned Tallis, "but Ev—"

Ev interrupted Tallis. "Nictis and Helcant specialized in communication techniques. I'm not going to get in the way when we have other things that need doing."

Nictis glared triumphantly at Tallis before turning away from him to continue her work.

Tallis crossed his arms and frowned at Ev. "Well, we can't do much else until we get in contact with the other anthermancers. If you aren't going to help Nictis, then what are you going to do?"

"We can't leave these people out in the middle of nowhere. We need a place they can take shelter."

"You're going to look by yourself? Are you crazy? We need to coordinate with the others before we start wandering around the Cosmic Graveyard. We need a plan."

"No, we need to move now," Ev shot back. "Look, I'll mark this location so we can return easily. Then you, Lylia, and I can go look around the Graveyard so we're actually doing something useful."

"Uh-huh, great. And without Nictis's network working, how are we supposed to communicate if anything happens?"

Nictis growled. "Just make some nodes, fool! You were instructed to do so after making warm air! A network is unneeded to speak to individuals."

Tallis and Ev exchanged sheepish glances. They'd both forgotten that part of the plan. For the next few minutes, they — and Lylia as well — worked on building a small, shimmering bubble they could use to speak with one another from any distance away. Once finished, they absorbed the bubbles into their bodies.

"There; ready?" Ev asked Tallis.

"I still think this is a bad idea," Tallis folded his arms again.

"I'm with Tallis," Jax said, having observed the whole thing. "You should at least take Birdie and me with you for protection."

Birdie laughed. "And what are we supposed to do? We don't have magic out here, remember?"

"Maybe not, but I do have a sword," Jax protested.

Ev shook her head and patted her brother on the shoulder. "Thanks, but I think we can take care of ourselves. It's pretty easy to use anther to destroy things if you know how."

Lylia slithered up from behind. "We are ready."

Tallis sighed. "Fine. I guess I'm as ready as I'm going to be, too."

"In that case, we're going to need some room," Ev said.

Gare took that as his cue and started ushering people away.

"Alright everyone, back up! The anthermancers need room to do their stuff!"

Jax, Birdie, and Umber joined Gare in his efforts, and soon they had a nice clearing about twenty feet in diameter.

Once she was comfortable that they had plenty of room, Ev created what Syrus had dubbed an "anchor," a connection to this exact location so she could always know where it was relative to her to enable a swift return. Next, she crafted a large, impenetrable bubble around where she would create the portal. Like Tallis had said, there was no telling what would be on the other side, so it was better safe than sorry.

Ev then focused on a distance about ten thousand miles away, then connected the space between those two locations, opening up a portal that appeared to be embedded in solid rock. That was useless, so she tried again.

The second, third, and fourth all opened up into an endless void, but with her fifth attempt, she was just able to make out land in the distance after shining a brilliant light through the portal. Making a minor adjustment to the portal's end point, so that it was no longer high in the air, she removed the protective barrier and stepped over to Birdie, hugging her tightly.

"I'll be back soon. If anything happens, have Helcant or Nictis contact us immediately."

"You got it," Birdie replied, returning the embrace. "Be careful, Ev."

"Don't worry. I will," Ev replied, smiling as she let go of Birdie.

She gave a reassuring look to Jax, then stepped through the portal. Once Tallis and Lylia had joined her on the other side, she closed the portal, leaving them alone in a barren, ash-covered landscape.

****

"I'm telling you," said Tallis as the group crested a small hill, their footprints and Lylia's tail leaving trails in the soot all the way to the top. "Let's make a bunch of portals high in the sky and shine light from them. Weren't you the one saying 'we need to move now.'"

"And what if the Masters see all that light?" protested Ev. "I thought you wanted to play it safe."

"I wanted to coordinate so we aren't just running around randomly," Tallis returned. "Jax is the one who's worried about things attacking us. If you ask me, there's literally nothing out here, the Masters included."

"We concur with Tallis," said Lylia. "These lands have long been dead. Whatever machinations the Masters pursue, they would not be found here."

Outvoted, Ev relented. "Fine, but let's be careful with how we do it. Any light bright enough to light up the whole area could blind us if we look at it."

"Then don't look at it," remarked Tallis, already opening a portal in front of him. Ev assumed the other end was high above. "You never looked at the sun, did you?" he added.

Lylia joined Tallis and put up a dark barrier over his portal. "Our people had a custom where a chosen one would gaze upon the summer solstice each year. That one would be forced to live a year's time in darkness. The next solstice, the new chosen would slay the former, and the cycle would repeat."

"Wait, seriously?" responded Tallis, horror on his face.

"No, but its fun to see this one's expressions," replied Lylia, smiling playfully.

Tallis blinked, clearly unsure what to think of that. Ev couldn't help but be amused, even though she tried not to show it.

"Right," said Tallis, clearing his throat, "well, let's light her up and see what we've got here."

Tallis concentrated, and within moments the area around them was bathed in a decent light, though it only allowed them to see for maybe a mile into the distance. Tallis began tweaking the brightness of the light, but it didn't change the fact that it only produced a limited cone due to its position on this side of the portal.

Ev sighed. "If you're going to do this, you should at least do it right."

"Oh, really?" returned Tallis. "And how exactly would you do it differently?"

"For starters," said Ev, "I'd put the light on the other side of the portal."

She willed his light ball through the portal, allowing it to shine in all directions, then closed the portal and removed the dark barrier.

"I'd also move it much farther away to make it more like our sun back in Doxla."

Ev sent the light thousands of times farther than Tallis's portal had been, increasing its brightness as she did so. The effect let them to see as far as the hazy atmosphere would allow.

Tallis looked unamused. "Yes, well, I could have done that, too, you know."

"Then you can do it next time," said Ev. "Let's look around this place for now and see what we can find."

"What is that?" asked Lylia, pointing high up into the sky.

Ev and Tallis both looked where she was pointing, shielding their eyes from the light. Far above them — well beyond said light — was an enormous glassy structure that stretched off into the horizon. Beyond that structure sat a large yet very faint circular outline.

"Maybe it's a moon?" suggested Tallis.

"It might be another world," offered Ev.

"Do you think we should check it out?" he asked.

"Definitely," replied Ev, "right after we finish looking around this place."

Lylia slithered past Ev and looked out over the now bright landscape. "We are not certain there is much to see of this location."

Lylia was right. The entire area was nothing but barren hills covered in ankle-deep ash. Perhaps there was more further out, but there was absolutely nothing nearby.

"Welp," Tallis said, crossing his arms. "I'm all for seeing what that other place is. It can't be any worse than this."

"Please don't tempt fate," Ev stated as she put up another protective barrier before creating a portal to what she assumed would be close to their new destination.

After a few adjustments, the other side appeared next to the nearly upside-down ground of the other world.

"What the heck did you do to the portal?" Tallis asked. "You made it crooked!"

"That's just the angle that the other world is at," Ev said. "I can try spinning it if you give me a minute."

"We believe this is acceptable," stated Lylia, examining the portal. "We offer to travel first. We expect the transition would be simpler for us. We may then offer our assistance when these ones follow after."

"I guess that would work," said Tallis with a touch of uncertainty.

Ev removed the barrier around the portal, but the moment she did so, deadly-cold wind blasted out from it — nearly overpowering the warmth the group had generated to protect themselves.

Ev quickly placed the barrier back. "I guess that isn't such a good option after all."

"Oh, come on," remarked Tallis with a smirk. "If you're going to do something, you should at least do it right."

Ev frowned, but decided to hand the reigns over to him. "Alright then. Be my guest."

Tallis cracked his knuckles before willing a great deal more air into existence around them, making Ev's ears pop from the pressure. He then removed Ev's barrier once again. This time, the air flowing out of it was much more manageable.

"See?" he smiled victoriously.

"Yeah, yeah. That was a good idea," Ev replied.

Lylia slid up alongside Tallis, mischief in her eyes. "This one always does think best wind under pressure."

Tallis stared at Lylia. "Are you serious right now?"

Lylia giggled. "We believe we are mirthful, actually."

She then slid on through the portal, flipping over gracefully as she used her tail to anchor herself against the change in gravity.

"Come on through when ready," she cooed. "We shall gladly assist with the landing."

Ev waited for Tallis to go first and watched as he cautiously approached the edge of the portal. He tried sitting to scoot in — presumably hoping to attempt a graceful flip as Lylia had — but ended up tumbling awkwardly. Lylia was quick to grab him from the air and set him down gently, however, which left Tallis blushing.

Ev smiled at the interaction then stepped right through. She didn't even try to pull off a stunt she knew she would fail at, opting to let Lylia catch her just as she had Tallis.

"Alright," said Tallis, brushing the soot from the previous location off of himself. "Which way now?"

Without a word, Ev created another light high above and opened up several portals to the surrounding areas. She stopped when one of them revealed what appeared to be strange buildings of some nature.

"There," she pointed.

Tallis and Lylia looked at the buildings, then back at Ev.

"Works for me," Tallis shrugged.

Ev moved the exit of the portal closer to the city, and the three of them stepped through.

On the other side, they found themselves staring at a massive complex of rounded buildings stacked almost haphazardly atop of one another. They had clearly been carefully balanced, but the city still looked as if it should topple over at any moment. Large platforms wrapped around the entrances to each level of the towers, and suspended walkways stretched between structures. Behind the group lay a dead forest — the broken trees half buried in snow and covered in a sheet of ice. The city stretched up from a gigantic pit in the ground — the highest tower had to rise at least a thousand feet above them. Pulley systems and stairways connected the different levels, and pipes both large and small snaked throughout every inch of the snow-and-ice-covered metropolis.

"What kind of place is this?" asked Tallis after walking up to the pit's edge. "It looks like some kind of ugly Ars Summis."

Lylia joined Tallis at the edge. "We find this place fascinating. A civilization lost in ancient times once lived here — perhaps before even the Masters came into existence."

"Or maybe the Masters are why it ended," Tallis grumbled. "Syrus said the Cosmic Graveyard is where dead worlds go, but this one looks fine. Maybe the Masters made another world here too."

Ev spoke up now, scanning the city as she did so. "Or maybe other seitti decided they were done with the world and sent it here. The Masters didn't care about Doxla except when it suited them. Why would other seitti be different?"

Lylia appeared surprised by Ev's statement. "Syrus has told us that the Masters' behavior is atypical and unbecoming of seitti. We find it difficult to believe that we would so quickly stumble upon another world abused in such a way."

"Syrus also told us that most Divine were likely seitti," Ev shot back, "and how many of them tried to help us? What about Lux Rosa and everything she did to us? We *know* she was a seitti. Maybe there are seitti who actually care about normal people, but I have yet to ever see one for myself."

Tallis nodded in agreement. "Well said. The only one who even sounded halfway decent was that Aurum fellow Syrus said was his world's creator, yet Syrus admitted even Aurum doesn't care about us."

Lylia looked at Tallis disapprovingly. "We believe this one is twisting Syrus's words. We also believe that we came to this place with a purpose. Perhaps we should continue our endeavor?"

"You're right. Let's see what we've got here," said Ev as she led the way to a metal bridge into the city.

A sheet of ice covered the bridge and every surface of the city, but as the group approached with their field of warmth, the ice quickly began to melt away. The metal creaked and popped, reminding Ev that Syrus had warned her that increasing temperature too rapidly could destroy things. She altered her method of heating to be more gradual, then proceeded.

Looking over the side of the bridge, Ev could see that the pit went down at least as far below her as the tallest tower went above. At the bottom, the largest pipes appeared to go even deeper — stretching into dark holes for who knew how far. When she approached the nearest structure — a large rounded room that appeared to be some sort of dwelling — she noticed that the windows and door had been broken inward, and a number of dents and deep scratches marked the edges of the windows and the door.

Tallis rubbed his hand over some of the scratches. "Looks like there was some kind of battle here."

"Yeah," said Ev as she ducked into the very low doorway. Once inside, she created a new light so they could see better.

The interior was completely trashed. What must have once been furniture was now splintered wood and twisted metal. The only bits of the interior that remained undamaged were shelves and picture frames on the walls. Odd-looking skeletons were partially buried under the wreckage. Having never seen anything like them before, Ev stooped over to investigate.

In the meantime, Lylia slithered up to one of the frames. "What funny little people these were," she said, pointing at the image. "So round and plump, like large, fuzzy eggs."

Ev got up from her skeleton and stepped over the debris to see what she assumed were the former inhabitants. Lylia's description was rather accurate. The two large and one small individuals in the painting were indeed shaped like eggs — having very short, almost nonexistent legs. Their fuzzy faces reminded her of moles with their pointy noses and beady eyes, and they had long arms that reached almost to the ground.

"Such a funny shape," Lylia mused. "We must wonder how such mole people ever had children."

"Really?" asked Tallis. "Out of everything else here, that's what you wonder about?"

"This one does not?" replied Lylia, smiling slyly. "Perhaps we must explain why we wonder."

Ev cut that topic off right there. "We most certainly do not," she said. "What we must do is let everyone know we found somewhere they can stay."

"We've only checked out a single room," replied Tallis. "I know it seems pretty sturdy, but we should probably make sure this place won't fall apart if a bunch of people suddenly show up."

Ev didn't like the idea of leaving everyone out in the open, but she supposed Tallis had a point.

"Okay, but let's make it quick. We should also keep an eye out for anything to eat."

"Food?" Tallis repeated. "This place has probably been dead for ages. What kind of edible rocks do you think we'll find here?"

"I don't know," Ev snapped, "but in case you haven't noticed, the entire world is completely frozen. Even if it's awful, there might be something edible somewhere around here."

Tallis crossed his arms. "Well, if there is, we're going to need a lot of it. We had nearly a hundred thousand anthermancers last I checked, so we probably have millions of mouths to feed."

"We don't need much," returned Ev. "All three of us know how to duplicate things."

"Yeah, *we* do, but most anthermancers were only taught how to make light, air, water, portals, and heat," said Tallis, counting on his fingers.

"Then if we can't find a lot of food, we'll have to do a lot of teaching," said Ev, quite ready to get moving.

"Alright, fine," said Tallis, "but we really do need to be thorough. This place is probably ancient."

"We can give it a once over," said Ev, "but we should split up to make it faster. Once we're all satisfied, we should meet up back here and message the others. We need to see if we can find more cities like this. There's no way just this one will fit everyone who escaped."

"We shall accompany Tallis," said Lylia, swiftly moving alongside him.

Tallis blushed, and Ev raised an eyebrow.

"I was under the impression that we would *all* split up," she said.

Lylia giggled. "Oh, we shall, but observe how *cute* this one is when the cheeks redden."

Tallis went even redder, stammered for a bit, then quickly stepped out of the room without getting out a single coherent word.

Ev looked over at Lylia. "Do you just like messing with him, or do you actually, you know, *like* him?"

"Why can it not be both?" Lylia shrugged before slithering out of the room as well.

Ev shook her head, gave one look back at the skeletons on the floor, then stepped outside to begin examining the rest of the city.

* * * *

For the next hour or so, Ev made her way around the metal buildings. The warmth that she, Tallis, and Lylia generated quickly spread, melting much of the ice before it ever became an issue. The metal creaked loudly and often as it heated, but it appeared to hold solid. Traversing on foot still wasn't easy, however. Though they didn't appear rusted or frozen over, none of the pulley systems worked despite Ev's best efforts. She was sure the pipes connected to the machinery had something to do with it, but figuring that out really wasn't her top priority at the moment. Instead, she resorted to using portals to move about when there was no obvious path to whatever next happened to catch her eye.

After checking more rooms and platforms than she cared to count, she was satisfied that all was well. While they may have only covered a small fraction of the mid-level of the city, everything was consistently structurally sound. The only significant damage from whatever had occurred here was limited to doors, windows, building interiors, and a few of the pulley systems.

Unfortunately, Tallis had been correct about the food situation. There was nothing that looked even remotely edible to be found. On the bright side, Ev had discovered that nearly every room was well-stocked with oil. Even better, the room that she'd just entered was almost overflowing with coal. If the frozen trees she'd seen outside of the city could still burn, then that would give the non-anthermancers access to all the fire they would need for the foreseeable future.

Still, it was curious that the coal was all in this one room. Ev walked over to what appeared to be a furnace and noticed that many large pipes sprouted out from it. This coal had obviously been used for something. Perhaps heating? There was a large chamber above the furnace completely filled with now-melting ice. This was definitely something she'd have to investigate later. For now, however, she was satisfied that the city would serve as a decent shelter.

They could always find food elsewhere and bring it here.

As Ev made her way back toward the rendezvous point, a scratching sound caught her ear. The sound certainly wasn't like any of the metallic creaks caused by the heat. Curious, Ev approached one of the very large pipes that stretched all the way to the ground.

This pipe was definitely the source of the sound. Now that she was closer, it sounded like there was more than just scratching coming from it. Placing her ear against it, a sense of unease crept into Ev as she heard something that almost sounded alive — an odd mixture of steady buzzing and horrible growling.

Stepping quickly away from the pipe, Ev headed to the nearest railing to peer down and see if she could spot any possible source of the noise. She noticed movement near the pipe about a hundred yards below in the shadows. The figure moved to reveal . . .

"Tallis?" she called down to him, simultaneously relieved and annoyed. "What do you think you're doing?"

Tallis looked up and pointed to whatever he'd been fooling with.

"I think I have an idea what all these pipes are for!" he called back. "If I can just get them working again, I can find out!"

"We don't have time for that!" Ev yelled back. "We have millions of people who need shelter. Did you find anything that might make this place unsafe?"

"Only a bunch of broken railings," Tallis replied, "but we really haven't checked all that much yet. Shouldn't we at least go look at the bottom and make sure the supports are all solid?"

Ev shook her head. As far as she was concerned, everything here seemed good.

"These towers don't even sway all the way at the top. I think the supports are fine. Meet me back up here as soon as you can, and we'll go find Lylia. We need to—"

Ev jumped as Lylia dropped down beside her from out of nowhere. "This one called?"

Ev quickly recomposed herself. "We need to head back to show the other anthermancers how to find this place. We also need to warn them about the pressure so they don't accidentally freeze everyone when they open portals. Then we need to look for more shelter and anything we can find for food."

"We believe food should not be an immediate priority," remarked Lylia. "Safe shelter will be required within days, but food not for weeks. Besides, for what reason is this one concerned? We may always make duplicates of our own bodies for nourishment if we grow hungry."

"Please tell me that's a joke," said Ev.

Lylia tilted her head. "We certainly hope it to be so, but only time and desperation will reveal this."

Ev grimaced. After they went back, they *had* to find something edible out there.

Chapter 3

Ev slammed her fist once more against the smooth metal wall of her prison. After her encounter with Sylvra, he'd placed her in a well-furnished room devoid of windows or doors. There wasn't a trace of manipulable anther to be found, which left her completely powerless.

Finally accepting defeat, Ev slouched down onto the carpeted floor, but she refused to use any of the furniture provided to her by Sylvra. She also refused to partake of the pastries left on the nearby table, though after several hours of being left alone with their smell, they were very tempting. Her eyes shifted to the large tank of colorful fish where she watched them dart about. They were the only thing that offered any sort of distraction from her current situation.

A knocking sound from the far wall caught her attention. A moment later, a doorway appeared, and Sylvra stepped inside before closing the wall back behind him.

Jumping to her feet, Ev glared at him.

"My apologies for the wait," Sylvra stated. "The number of anther users from your world was unprecedentedly large. It took time to sort through them all, and I wanted to save you for last."

"What did you do with them?" Ev growled.

"I have yet to decide what I will do," Sylvra answered. "For now, they are safe and contained. But let us hold off on that topic. First, I believe introductions are in order."

"I know who you are."

"Then half the work is already done. I need only your name, and we may proceed."

Ev clamped her jaw shut.

Sylvra smiled. "Now, now. Neither of us gain anything from your being obstinate. I believe we have much we can offer one another."

"Can you bring back my home? Can you bring back the world you destroyed!" Ev felt herself tearing up, but she refused to allow herself to cry in front of this monster.

"The latter is already done. The former we can work on," Sylvra replied.

Ev paused. There was no way he was telling the truth.

Sylvra noticed her hesitation. "I've peaked your interest, I see. Unfortunately, I have nothing more to say on the matter to one I do not know."

This had to be a trick. It just had to. Still, on the off chance that he was telling the truth . . .

"Eveline. My name is Eveline."

Sylvra nodded, eyeing her in a way that made her very uncomfortable. "It is quite the pleasure to meet you, Eveline. Out of the seven thousand, nine-hundred and two individuals able to break their containment, you are by far the most talented. Only those four who were with you even came close. It would appear Rusalka was quite the effective and prolific teacher."

Ev's face went white. "How do you know that name?"

Sylvra chuckled. "All Divine were required to register their true name before they could enter Doxla. With only one registered Divine still active in yours, it was not difficult to determine who taught you about anther. Tell me, what name did they prefer in Doxla?"

Ev once again closed her mouth tight. She wasn't going to tell him anything about Syrus.

"My, my. Such paranoia. I assure you I mean no harm to anyone."

"Bull!" Ev spat. "You created Doxla only to use it. You turned people into immortals and spread war and hatred to make Divine feel like heroes. When we stopped being profitable, you left us to die! When we tried to escape, you attacked us and destroyed everything!"

A grin spread on Sylvra's face before he started laughing loudly, clapping his hands. "Yes! Almost exactly so. Congratulations on experiencing firsthand what it means to be born into a seitti-controlled world."

Ev couldn't believe what she was hearing. She'd always known Sylvra was a monster, but he was laughing about what he'd done. Laughing!

Sylvra calmed himself, putting on a patronizing smile. "Suppose I hadn't, though. Do you believe your world would have thrived? Or would it have fallen?"

"We did thrive! If you hadn't made the world rot when you left, we would have overcome everything!"

To her surprise, Sylvra's expression became genuinely sympathetic. "Yes. I believe that, as well. Unfortunately, neither of us were given that chance."

"What the hell are you talking about? You—"

"The world I was born in was also abandoned by seitti — left to rot just as yours was," Sylvra stated as he turned away from her.

"Sure it was. Don't lie to me. You *are* a seitti."

Sylvra produced a small chuckle, but he didn't smile.

"I am now, but I wasn't always. Like you, I found a way to escape my dying world." He turned his head to look Ev in her eyes. "Unlike you, I had to do so without help from so-called 'Divine.' I observed the seitti while they remained in my world. I learned of anther, found ways to manipulate it on my own, and I escaped. When seitti society found me, they offered to elevate me to become one of their own."

"So let me get this straight. You claim that seitti ruined your world, and then you turn right around and destroy mine?" Ev was seething.

Sylvra frowned for the first time. "You seem to misunderstand the situation. I did not destroy your world. I turned off its systems. Will it die now? Most certainly — likely in a matter of weeks. In that, however, I had no choice. Your Rusalka attempted to access systems that would jeopardize everything I seek to accomplish."

"Well, maybe if you'd actually cared enough to make Doxla sustainable, we never would have had to," shouted Ev.

Sylvra stared at Ev for a second before nodding in agreement. "Yes. That was certainly a failure on our part. Unfortunately, stable worlds are almost impossible to create where we are."

His eyes opened wide as if he had an idea. "Actually, that might be something you would be able to help us with."

Ev glared at him. "I'm not helping you with anything unless you save it."

Sylvra tilted his head.

"Save Doxla," Ev growled. "Restore it to how it was, and bring back everyone who was lost."

Sylvra smiled. "That is simple enough. As I said, it is already done."

Stepping past Ev, Sylvra gave a wave of his hand, and the wall before him grew transparent. Ev's eyes opened wide as she realized where she was.

Without thinking, Ev approached the wall and placed her hands against it. Outside was Ars Summis, teaming with inhabitants. Beyond the city's borders, the forest of lumine pines had been completely restored.

Sylvra drew closer to her. "Speechless once again, I see."

Ev snapped out of her trance and looked up at him. "This is a trick."

"It most certainly is not." Sylvra gestured toward the city. "This is Doxla, exactly as it was one hundred and twenty years ago from when yours ended."

"Mine? What do you mean, 'mine'?" Ev asked, once again on guard.

Sylvra stared out the window. "This Doxla is my newest attempt at creating my perfect world. Your Doxla served well as a template for its creation."

Ev backed away from Sylvra, scowling. "How dare you? This isn't my world. It's just another Doxla that *looks* like my world."

"And? Does that make it any less real? Does that make the lives of its people worthless to you?"

"What does it matter? You don't care. You didn't care about us; you don't care about them, either."

Sylvra smiled. "You are correct. Their lives have little meaning to me. That's why I ask if they have meaning to you. Do you wish the fate of your world upon them as well?"

Ev narrowed her eyes, then she laughed. She didn't know where he was trying to go with this, but she was done playing his games. "Are you seriously trying to blackmail me with the wellbeing of some place that I have no connection to?"

Sylvra shook his head. "Don't be absurd. I am not blackmailing you. I am making you an offer. Eventually, this Doxla will also fail. It is inevitable. When that time comes, I will move on to the next. If there are none to care for this one, then it will indeed meet the same fate as yours.

"It doesn't have to be that way, however." Sylvra extended his hand to Ev. "Your skills truly are impressive, Eveline. With further training, *you* could see to it that this world is cared for long after I have abandoned it. Until then, you can help me gain all that I can from its existence."

Ev almost laughed at the insanity of the proposal. Her? Work for *him?*

She jerked away. "Are you really so full of yourself that you think I'd *ever* help you after everything you've done to me? After all the people you've hurt?"

Disappointment spread across Sylvra's face. "No, I suppose not. It is a shame, though. After all, if you *were* to help me, you would be in a position to do a great deal of good, whatever your idea of 'good' might be."

He turned away from her and shrugged. "Oh, well. If you would rather do nothing to help this world, I understand. After all, this isn't 'your Doxla,' right? Perhaps you are more like a seitti than you realize."

Pointing his finger at the far wall, he created a portal leading to a grassy field before turning his head back to Ev. "Go on, then. Return to the other refugees. I will not stop you, nor will I punish you for your choice."

Ev stared at the portal. Was he really letting her go? She could see log cottages in the distance with people milling about them. She knew she couldn't trust him, yet nearly every fiber of her being told her to run through and not look back. Even if it was a trick, the mere chance of escape was incredibly enticing.

Yet, what he had said — he was right. If she left, she wouldn't be able to do anything. If she didn't help him, he would do to this world exactly what he had done to hers. If she stayed, she would likely be made to do terrible things in his name, but at least she could try her best to make things better where she could. It might not be her world, but these people did nothing to deserve the suffering her own people had gone through. And maybe, just maybe, the chance would come where she could put a stop to Sylvra's machinations once and for all.

Ev closed her eyes and clenched her fists before looking back to Sylvra once more.

"Alright. I'll help you. What do you want me to do?"

The portal vanished as Sylvra smiled. "What all Masters of Administrator designation do. Maintain order, maintain nature, see to it that this world is profitable, and in your spare time, you may work to prevent the world's decay when the time comes for us to leave. And just as a show of good faith, I will also allow you to visit your companions whenever you wish. No harm will come to them from me or any who serve me."

Ev blinked. A Master? He was actually making her a Master? And her friends, her family — they were safe?

"Of course, we will need to give you a new name," Sylvra added. "Eveline is fairly common among humans. What do you think about being called Evress?"

Ev looked Sylvra in the eye. Honestly, she didn't know what to think at the moment, but she didn't really see any other choice.

"If that's what you want. I don't care."

Sylvra chuckled. "Very well, then. Welcome to the team, Master Evress."

* * * *

The portal to Ars Summis closed behind Ev, leaving her in the middle of a green, flower-filled field. Sylvra had given her permission to see for herself what he'd done with everyone, and she had every intention of investigating thoroughly.

According to him, this is where he and the other Masters had imprisoned Birdie, Jax, and everyone else who had been with her. Though from what she could see, this place was hardly a prison.

Ev made her way to the group of cottages on the far end of the field. No one noticed her until she drew close, and even then, they didn't pay her much mind, though she couldn't help but notice they all seemed very much on edge.

She saw no sign of Birdie nor anyone else she recognized around the outskirts of town, so Ev made her way in deeper. As she passed by each cottage, she peered inside them.

Nothing. These people were all strangers to her.

Ev's hopes began to dim. She knew she hadn't been looking for long, but she couldn't help it, at least not until she picked up on a conversation that drew her attention.

"I'm telling you we shouldn't stay here. The anthermancers left. This is obviously a trap!"

Anthermancers? Perhaps these *were* the people she'd escaped the old Doxla with.

Ev walked over to the cottage where the conversation was happening and peeked in. Her heart nearly skipped a beat.

Inside was the woman she'd rescued from the bubble sitting in a chair with her toddler. Her husband was standing on the far side of the room, clearly upset.

They had been with her when everyone had vanished. Perhaps they knew where Birdie and the others had gone.

Knocking softly on the door, Ev opened it and placed one foot inside.

"Excuse me?" she said.

The man stared at her, but the woman jumped to her feet.

"It's you! You're the anthermancer who saved us!"

"Saved us?" the husband repeated. "All she did was let us out of that bubble. Now we're here, along with everyone else who wasn't. She didn't do anything; none of the anthermancers did!"

"Hush, Cole," the wife said. "This woman did everything she could to help us."

"Oh, is that why she's the only one who disappeared after we wound up here?"

"Cole, I'm sure she just ended up somewhere else. Not everyone ended up in this village."

The woman walked over to Ev, still holding her son. She did her best to smile.

"I'm sorry for the rude welcome. We do appreciate what you did for us. It's just . . ."

She trailed off as she used her free arm to wipe away some tears.

"I'm sorry. We're just so confused right now." The woman's voice shook a little as she spoke. "I'm Anna, by the way. And this is Rikki." Anna pushed her toddler up in her arm a little higher.

Ev gave back the best smile she could manage. "My name is Ev, and believe me, I understand. I didn't mean to bother you. I'm just looking for friends and family right now. We kind of got separated, and I wondered if you happened to know where they might be."

"You mean those other anthermancers?" Cole interrupted. "They all ran off. They left us here."

"What?" Ev replied, shocked.

"No, they didn't," Anna corrected, her tone somewhere between annoyed and upset. "They said they were going to look around. They even left the big one here with his family."

"The big one?" Ev asked. "Was his name Gare?"

Anna thought for a second, then nodded in confirmation. "I think that's what they said, yes."

Ev breathed a sigh of relief. She wanted to ask where Birdie and Jax had gone, but she also wanted to subtly tell Cole off.

"Well, if Gare's here, you can bet the others will come back. Even if he wasn't, there's no way any of them would abandon you."

Cole hacked up a mock laugh. Ev had to keep herself from laying into him at that point.

"Thank you, but I know they won't," Anna replied. "I admit that Jax character and those demons worry me a bit, but I . . ." she trailed off again.

Ev tried to give a comforting smile. "Don't worry about Jax. His wife will keep him in line. And I know Helcant and Nictis can be a little abrasive, but they really do mean well."

Anna looked only slightly comforted by those words.

Ev continued, "I don't suppose you'd know which way they went, would you? I haven't seen them in a while, and I just want to make sure they're okay."

Cole shouted from across the room. "You see? She's also trying to run away!"

Anna's face flashed red as she spun on him. "Cole, please, I don't need this right now! I know . . . I know they couldn't . . ."

Anna wasn't able to finish her sentence. She suddenly broke down crying, dropping to her knees and clutching her child.

Concerned, Ev knelt down beside her as Cole rushed over.

The man looked as if he truly regretted what he'd said but didn't know how to make it better. He joined Anna on the floor, placing his hand on her shoulder.

"Anna, it's okay," he said. "We don't need them. We'll make it through this together."

His words did nothing to help. Ev wasn't surprised.

Cole looked over to Ev, his expression stern. "I think you should go."

Ev stared Cole in the eyes before turning her attention back to Anna. "Are you going to be okay?"

Anna shook her head.

"We'll be fine," stated Cole. "You said you wanted the other anthermancers, right? Half of them went up the mountain. The other half went across the field. All of them went far away from here. You should join them."

Ev frowned at Cole. She'd decided she didn't like this man, but she did need to find Birdie and Jax.

"Which way did the black-haired woman and man with a sword go?"

"How should I know? I told you where they went. Just get out of here already."

Anna spoke up through her tears. "Both of them went to the mountain."

Slowly, Anna stood back up before walking out the door, with Ev stepping aside to give her room. Anna pointed to a mountain with a barren peak a few miles away.

"They left a few hours ago. They said they wanted to get to the top so they could see if there's anyone else around."

Cole growled from behind them, but to his credit he kept his mouth shut for once.

"Thank you," said Ev. "I appreciate the help." She looked back at Cole. "And don't worry. As bad as things are, your husband is right."

Ev turned back to Anna and smiled. "We're all going to get through this together."

Anna nodded and returned the smile, wiping away her tears with her free arm.

As rude as it may have been not to seek out Gare as she walked through town, Ev really wanted to talk to Birdie and Jax as soon as possible. To that end, the moment she was in the woods and out of sight of the cottages, Ev produced a small shimmer. It wasn't anther per se, but it was an antherial tool provided to her by Sylvra. With this, she would be able to create portals even without anther, which was good, because wherever this place was had zero free anther available to use.

Ev used the tool to create a portal in front of her that opened up to the top of the mountain. The pressure difference caused air to blast through the portal out on top of the mountain, nearly sweeping Ev off her feet as she stepped through. She closed the portal as soon as she was through, and her ears popped right after that.

Looking down the mountain toward the village, there was no sign of anyone approaching yet. Hopefully, they hadn't already come and gone. Ev realized she probably should have asked exactly how long ago it had been since the group had left, but it wasn't like she had anything better to do. Sylvra had told her she could have a full day to do as she pleased before her duties as Master would begin, and finding everyone was really all that she cared about right now.

Her wait wasn't long, thankfully. After only about another thirty minutes, she spotted movement far down below. Even from this distance, Birdie's raven-black hair was immediately recognizable. Jax's uniform, unmistakable. The two others were harder to recognize, but one was a woman — almost certainly Fauna — and the other was too large to be Tallis, so that meant he was probably Umber.

Ev's heart leapt at seeing that everyone was okay. Not only that, but there was no way Sylvra was trying to trick her. Without even talking to them, she knew they were real. Not because of any deep feelings or anything like that, but purely by the fact that they hadn't simply been waiting for her, and by the fact that her interaction with Anna and Cole told her that those two were the same people she'd saved from the bubble prisons not long ago.

Nearly skipping down the mountain, Ev rushed as quickly as she could to meet them. She sent several rocks tumbling as she hurried along.

The sound must have caught Birdie's ears, because a moment later, she was pointing up at Ev. Right after that, both she and Jax doubled their pace, with Fauna and Umber doing their best to keep up.

A few minutes later, they all reached a large, flat boulder at about the same time. As Jax climbed atop it, however, his expression made Ev pause, and she noticed he'd moved a hand closer to his sword hilt.

"Wait," he said, putting his other hand out to stop the others.

Birdie ignored and ran past him, embracing Ev so hard she nearly crushed her.

The next thing Ev knew, her shoulders were locked in Birdie's hands as Birdie stared concernedly at Ev.

"Where were you? What happened? Are you okay? Are you hurt?"

Ev reached up and gently removed Birdie's hands, holding on to them as she smiled back reassuringly. "I'm okay. Really. Are all of you alright?"

Jax stepped up behind Birdie, his hand now on his sword hilt. "That depends. How do we know you're really Ev?"

Ev blinked. "I—"

Fauna stepped up behind Jax. "Jax, please, calm down. It's obviously Ev."

"Is it?" he asked, eyeing her suspiciously. "Don't you think it's odd that everyone else ended up in that village, but Ev just so happened to show up at the top of the mountain we were heading to alone?"

Ev huffed. She couldn't blame Jax, but it was still frustrating.

"A woman in the town told me you'd all gone to this mountain."

"How'd you get here before us then? Portals don't work here. Tallis checked that." Jax stepped closer, but Birdie put herself squarely between him and Ev.

"Ev is better with anther than anyone else," said Birdie. "If anyone could find a way to make portals, she could."

Jax backed off, but he wasn't sated quite yet. "I will grant that, but that still doesn't explain why she disappeared."

"Well, why don't you ask her instead of jumping on her like she's an enemy?" Birdie growled.

"Indeed," stated Umber, who had now joined them as well. "That would seem to be the most logical course of action."

Jax's expression shifted. It was clear he knew he'd screwed up. He sighed, then took a step to get a better view of Ev.

"Alright, then. I'm sorry for jumping to conclusions, Ev. After you opened that portal, we all ended up in that village. Where did you go?"

All eyes were now on Ev. She wasn't sure how to explain the situation, but she knew she had to. Even if they hated her for what she'd agreed to, she had to at least come clean.

"After I opened the portal, Sylvra captured me," she said, unable to look at any of them.

"What?" they all said in unison.

Ev shook her head. "He took me to a new Ars Summis. He told me—"

"Wait," Jax interrupted. "Did you say a new Ars Summmis?"

Birdie shot daggers at Jax. "Don't interrupt. What happened next, Ev?"

"He told me . . ." Ev felt tears forming in her eyes. "He told me that if I worked for him, he wouldn't hurt you."

Ev forced herself to look at Birdie. The expression on her face was frightening, and Jax's was hardly better.

"Ev," he said, "tell me you didn't. Tell me you didn't agree to work for him!"

Jax took a step toward her, but Birdie put out her arm to stop him. Her face was almost one of stone as she addressed Ev.

"What does he want you to do?"

Ev shook her head. "He said he wanted me to help him maintain order. He wants me to make his new Doxla profitable for him."

"*New* Doxla?" Jax repeated, incredulous.

Ev continued, tears now streaming down her face. "He said he's going to do to that Doxla what he did to ours, but if I help him, he'd give me the chance to save it."

"And you *believe* him?" erupted Jax.

"What do you want me to do?" cried Ev. "If I do nothing, he'll erase you all! He'll destroy another Doxla! If I help him, you'll be safe. Maybe that Doxla will be safe, too."

Jax shook his head, disgust written on his face.

Umber looked between Jax and Ev. "Perhaps it is not my place to interject, but I believe Ev has made the best decision afforded to her."

Jax glared at Umber, but Ev was grateful for his support.

Birdie sighed and shook her head. "I can't believe I'm saying this, but I agree. At least now you have a chance at stopping him. If you can gain his trust, maybe you can do what Syrus couldn't."

Jax's face lightened at that remark.

"I don't know," said Ev. "I don't think he'll ever trust me. He knows what I think of him. Besides, if I try anything, there's no telling what he'd do to all of you."

"It doesn't matter what happens to us," said Jax. "If you get the chance to bring him down, you take it."

Ev looked pleadingly at Birdie, hoping she'd understood why that was too risky.

Birdie's expression softened as she sighed once more. "Whatever you do, just promise me you'll be careful. If you really think the only way to stop the Masters from doing more harm is to join them, then that's what you need to do."

Ev nodded, her appreciation for Birdie as great as it had ever been.

Jax frowned and shook his head again. "Whatever. I'm going to the summit. We need to see if there are other villages around."

"Do you want me to help?" Ev asked. "I can probably—"

"We're good," replied Jax, not even looking back.

Fauna looked apologetically at Ev but said nothing as she followed after Jax.

"Don't mind him," said Birdie. "You know how he gets sometimes."

Ev nodded.

"We'll take care of things here," Birdie continued, "but if you ever need anything, you know I'll always be here for you. Jax will, too, even if he doesn't always show it."

Ev hugged Birdie again. She didn't want to let go. Right now, she wanted to let herself be swept up by the comfort and leave behind the fate her future self now faced, but she knew the moment couldn't last forever.

Reluctantly, Ev let go and pulled out the portal tool. "I promise I'll visit as often as I can. I'm so, so sorry for doing this."

Birdie shook her head. "If it was anyone else, I'd have my doubts, but you're Ev. You're *my* Ev. I trust you, and I know you'll always do what's best."

"Thank you," said Ev, wiping her face dry.

She activated the portal that led back to Ars Summis, and with one final look back at Birdie, waved goodbye.

It was time for her new life as "Evress" to begin.

Chapter 4

The Cosmic Graveyard quickly proved to be a terrifying place when explored alone. There was nothing but silence there, and all was still. There wasn't even a hint of a breeze, leaving only the sounds of Ev's own breath and the crunching of snow beneath her boots.

After sending back word to Helcant regarding the first city they'd discovered, Ev, Lylia, and Tallis had decided to split up to scout the rest of the world more quickly. Since then, Ev had quickly shifted her search to primarily be one for food. Finding additional habitation proved to be a simple enough task, but no place so far had anything that even *looked* edible. Most cities remained in relatively good condition, however, so Ev regularly sent back the locations of them to Helcant and Nictis. Yet, with each new discovery, Ev's thoughts leaned more and more towards there having been a good reason this world had been sent to the Graveyard. No matter how far she went from the initial city, the scene was the same — doors and windows smashed, homes ransacked, and skeletons everywhere. Something terrible had happened here; that much was abundantly clear.

After about an hour of searching, Ev found what looked like a another farm. Hoping this one would prove more productive than the others she'd found, Ev stepped through the portal and waited for the ice and snow to melt. To her disappointment, but not surprise, the land had been destroyed. The few surviving plants, withered and frozen solid, broke down into an ashy goo as the heat freed them from their icy prisons.

Frustrated, Ev went back to searching for yet another farm. A few minutes later, she spotted something she hadn't seen before through one of her portals.

Intrigued, Ev stepped through to find a massive metal structure. Unlike every other building or city she'd encountered here, this one was built directly on solid ground. As she scanned the area, she notice there were a few of these large buildings along with several odd machines scattered about and numerous icy lumps sticking out of the rapidly-melting snow.

Ev took three steps toward the nearest building when her foot met with one such lump she hadn't spotted, causing her to fall face-first into the slush.

Sputtering, Ev wiped the crud from her face and pushed herself back up to her feet, then turned to see what she'd stumbled over.

A chill ran down her spine as the snow melted to reveal the remnants of a terrifying corpse. It looked similar to the pictures of the chubby mole people she'd seen in the cities, but far more grotesque. It appeared rotten — even moreso than a revenant — and what was left of it seemed to be held together with bits of metal and strange tubes. One of its arms and a good portion of its torso was missing, as was about half of its head. The arm that still remained ended in wicked, jagged metal claws. It's remaining eye stared up at her coldly and almost seemed to follow her as she moved.

Ev shivered, then turned her attention back to the large building. It's side had been torn open. A large number of similar creatures had made their final resting place at the opening.

Reluctantly, Ev approached the hole and peered inside, shining a light through the gap to help her see. More corpses were scattered around the room — strewn about more of those large machines. At the center of the room lay a large pile of the skeletal remains she'd grown used to seeing, and around them were a number of holes that looked to go deep into the ground. She was curious where those holes went, but at the same time, wasn't sure she wanted to see what was down them.

A crash behind her made her bang her head on the opening as she jumped. She almost tripped over another of the corpses as she scrambled to see the source of the sound.

There was nothing there. She scanned the area intently until she saw a large icicle crash into the ground near the far corner of the building.

Ev almost laughed from relief. She didn't know why she was so on edge. As Lylia had said, this world had been dead for ages. Still, there was something about the horrid creatures around her that she couldn't shake, and without any real reason to stick around here, she had no intention of doing so.

Ev retreated away from the building and out toward a nearby field, well away from the grotesque bodies. This area had been explored quite enough. Whatever the place had once been, it didn't look like a place where food would be, or where anyone could settle. She'd move on to another area, but first . . .

"Hello, Helcant?" she said, speaking through the anther.

"Ah, Ev," Helcant's voice resonated inside of her. "Have you discovered yet more shelter?"

"I found . . . something," Ev answered hesitantly, then she cleared her throat. "We've found lots of cities, but we haven't found anything for people to eat. It's like everything that could have been edible has been destroyed. I'm starting to think we won't find any food on this world. Maybe we should start looking elsewhere."

"Elsewhere? That is dangerous. A stroke of luck you had finding a safe world so soon. What if you find one who's nature would kill you for entering it?"

"That's what the barriers are for," Ev replied, trying to hurry the conversation along. "Anyway, I feel like things would go faster if I had some help. Is there anyone over there who isn't busy?"

"All are busy," replied Helcant. "All anthermancers are scouting or protecting survivors from the cold. Jax and Birdie are trying to keep order. Food can wait some days. We must have more shelter now."

"You said yourself we were lucky to find a world we can live on. How long do you think it will take for us to find a source of food? If people think they're going to starve, there'll be panic. Please, I'd just like someone to watch my back out here."

A loud sigh vibrated through Ev's skull from the other end of the conversation. "Very well, I shall see if any are willing to assist. Do not expect much, however."

"Thank you," replied Ev.

She shifted uncomfortably as she waited for a response. She could almost swear the dead things by the buildings were staring at her from beyond the grave.

Fortunately, Helcant responded after only a few minutes. "I have found a volunteer. Do not move. I do not wish my portal to injure you."

A moment later, a portal opened, and to Ev's surprise, Umber stepped through.

"Umber? You volunteered?"

The portal closed behind him.

"Helcant stated that you do not wish to be alone. I know I can do little without control of anther, but I can assist you in that small matter. Besides, I do not seem to be all that helpful in maintaining order among the survivors, and unlike the others, I am intrigued as to the nature of this place."

Ev did her best to hide a frown. Even after ten years, she didn't really know Umber all that well. She'd hoped Birdie or at least Jax would have joined her, instead. Also, she certainly did *not* want Helcant telling people that she just didn't want to be alone out here, even if it was true.

"Well, thank you," she said. "I appreciate it."

Ev lifted her arm and focused a hundred thousand miles away. After quite a few tries, she eventually found another world. Unfortunately, after spending about thirty minutes exploring it, Ev concluded that one to be a dud. There weren't even signs that anyone had *ever* lived on that barren rock. A few more worlds later — still nothing.

"This is infuriating," complained Ev. "Why can't we find anything?"

"I do not know what you expect to find," stated Umber. "Are not the worlds of the Cosmic Graveyard ancient? Surely everything must have rotted away."

Ev shook her head. "No. Syrus said there's a chance that we could find seeds or plants that froze long ago. The cold could have preserved them. I've even found some, but there's something wrong with the plant life where we're settling. It all crumbles when it gets warm."

Umber contemplated that. "Perhaps we have found nothing because the worlds we are exploring are all close together. They may have met similar ends."

"We've traveled nearly a million miles away from where we started. I'd hardly call that close."

"Is that far on the scale of worlds?" Umber asked. "Syrus said there is a boundary to this region of the Cosmic Graveyard, but we have yet to encounter it, so perhaps it is not."

Ev put her hand to her chin. That was a good point. Aside from the mole people one, all of the worlds they'd visited were practically indistinguishable. Maybe trying farther out *would* help.

"Alright, let's see how far we can go, then," she said, and she focused on creating a portal to as far away as she could imagine — a million times the distance they'd already traveled.

Just prior to the portal's formation, Ev felt a jolt through her consciousness, as if the anther fought back against her control.

The portal appeared nonetheless, revealing yet another world in the distance, but something was off. This portal appeared glassy. It was similar to the glassy structure over the mole people's world, except that structure was almost completely transparent. The portal before her was cloudy.

Anything new out here deserved caution, so Ev backed away before removing the protective barrier around the portal. When nothing happened, she picked up a nearby stone and tossed it.

The rock bounced off the portal with a loud *clack!*

Umber approached the cloudy surface and examined it. "Intriguing. Do you believe this is the boundary?"

"Possibly?" Ev said before placing her hand against the strange wall.

"If it is, would that mean you know the limits of the region we may explore?"

Ev thought for a bit, then shook her head. "Not yet, but I might have an idea. Give me a moment."

After performing a few quick tests on the properties of the surface, Ev closed the portal and sat down. Working as quickly as she could, she constructed a new tool that would be able to detect similar boundaries and report back to her. Holding the shimmer above her head, Ev willed it to activate. It pulsed briefly, then projected a large, glowing orange cube around them.

"What is this?" asked Umber.

"This is what our region of the Cosmic Graveyard looks like. There," Ev pointed to a small blue line floating about a third of the way out from the cube's center. "That's how far we are from the settlement, so we can use that not only to see the size of the region, but also see where we are in it."

Umber appeared impressed. "Incredible. And to think that even this is but a small fraction of the full extent of the Cosmic Graveyard."

Ev had to admit that she was proud of herself. Still, she frowned as she looked around the cube. That tool should have detected any boundary she couldn't create a portal through, so she'd hoped it would have found any other worlds the Masters might have created. As of now, she saw nothing. Either she was wrong about what her tool could detect, the Masters' worlds were too small to see at this scale, or no other such worlds existed. If the latter was the case, then that meant there might be no hope of ever finding relief from this awful place.

Ev supposed that might not be so bad. With enough time, she and the other anthermancers could potentially transform the mole world into a decent place to live. However, she did *not* want to spend the rest of her life cannibalizing duplicated bits of her own flesh to survive.

"Alright, then," she said. "Now that we know how much we have to work with, let's get back to searching for something we can eat."

* * * *

Now able to use her giant cube as a reference, Ev felt much more comfortable traveling around the Cosmic Graveyard. Sure, she was still going in blind to every new location, but having any sort of map at all was nice. Plus, she could mark the locations of where she and Umber had already been. That might not have truly been that useful of a feature, but it at least gave her the sense of making some sort of progress out in the void.

It also seemed that Umber had been right about needing to travel farther in their search. Since taking that approach, Ev had discovered an ocean world, a desert, a giant network of caves, and many traces of ruined civilizations markedly different than the mole people's. There was still no sign of food — though admittedly they only explored each area for about thirty minutes before moving on — but at least she had more hope of success now.

Then, they found it — a world covered in trees. As Ev stepped through the portal, her heart nearly skipped a beat at the sight of rows upon rows of neatly lined trees. Frozen balls of some sort of blue fruit hung from their branches. Even the leaves somehow still clung to these trees. Either the plants were extremely hardy, or this place must have frozen in a flash.

"We found something!" Ev exclaimed, running ahead of Umber.

Looking up into the thorny branches, Ev took a rock and tossed it at one of the lower clusters of fruit.

The rock connected, and several pieces of fruit landed on the wet ground in a series of thuds.

Ev picked up one of the pieces of fruit and smiled as she examined it. It was shaped like a teardrop and possessed a rough, seemingly thick skin. She dug her nails into the skin and peeled some back, taking in its aroma. The scent was a combination of sweet and pungent — not exactly appetizing, but it was the first thing they'd found that seemed even remotely edible.

Ev moved to take a small bite when Umber stopped her.

"Miss Ev. Perhaps it would be wiser if I were to try the fruit."

"I just want to see how it tastes."

"This is fruit from another world. We know nothing of its properties. It may prove deadly at even a taste."

"Well, someone has to try it, and I don't want anyone else risking their health for it. Besides, this is clearly an orchard. How bad can it be?"

"You are our most skilled anthermancer," Umber chastised. "I have little purpose as I am, and I should not have even survived the destruction of Doxla.

I only did so by becoming human. I can see no greater purpose than to use my new humanity to safeguard others, nor can I see anything I may lose from doing so that I would not have already lost."

Umber stretched his hand out to Ev, palm up. Ev pulled the fruit away.

"Don't be ridiculous. You have more to live for than to test for poisons."

"So do you," Umber replied, gesturing with his hand to give the thing over.

Ev sighed and gave him the fruit. "Fine. But just one tiny bite. Not that I think anything will happen, but if it does make you sick, there's not much I can do. None of us can use anther to heal people."

Umber gave a look of surprise at that revelation, but nodded in agreement.

To Ev's annoyance, he then proceeded to take a decidedly *not* small bite and swallowed it.

"That was not tiny," she scolded.

"Your definition of 'tiny' was not specified."

Ev growled in exasperation and snatched away the fruit before tossing it into some nearby bushes. She then marked the location of the grove on her map and made an anchor so she could return quickly.

"Let's just see what else we can find. If they have one kind of fruit here, they probably have others. But you don't get to test any more," she said, pointing a finger at Umber. "Just in case something here is toxic, we need to know which fruit caused it."

"If I cannot test more fruit, then we should return with more volunteers."

Ev was just about to retort when she heard Helcant speaking in her head.

"Ev, return now! We are being attacked!"

"Attacked? By who? Is it the Masters?"

"Monsters!" Nictis yelled, and Ev could hear horrible, gurgling screeches coming through the message.

Monsters? That was impossible. Nothing out here could still be alive, unless . . .

Ev looked up at the fruit above her, freshly unfrozen from the heat she'd brought here. A twinge shot through her stomach.

"Oh, no," she muttered before turning her head back to a concerned Umber. "We need to get back. Now."

****

Ev and Umber reappeared a short distance from the town. The moment they stepped through the portal, they could hear the screams.

The two of them rushed to the edge of the city's pit only to be greeted by the sight of hordes of terrible creatures scaling the pipes and attacking anyone they could reach with their wicked claws. Ev recognized the creatures as the same monstrosities she'd seen earlier. They spewed clouds of purple gas from tubes dangling from their flesh. From what Ev could tell, the gas had little to no effect on anyone, but she wasn't going to chance it.

"Stay here," she ordered Umber.

"I would like to assist."

Ev didn't have time to argue. This was her fault. If only she'd listened to Tallis and done a more thorough investigation. Now, she had to stop this catastrophe before anyone got hurt. With a wave of her hand, she opened a portal to where one of the mole monsters had managed to corner a small family. The top half of the creature flew screeching out of the portal, leaving a trail of black liquid in its wake.

Ev took a step back, held her breath, and charged through — launching herself into the air on the other side before landing between the family and the lower half of the monster she'd just split in two with her portal. The moment her feet touched the platform, she created a blast of air to blow away the gas surrounding her.

The family stared at her in disbelief as Ev adjusted the portal to allow Umber to more easily pass through. In the meantime, she scanned the area for any sign of Birdie or Jax. She saw nothing, but she did see her fellow anthermancers doing their best to fight off the creatures by burning them to a crisp as survivors escaped through portals to who knew where. By making use of barriers for protection, the anthermancers were doing well at holding off the beasts, which gave her hope that her haste in finding shelter wouldn't end in complete disaster.

Umber approached from behind. "What should I do?"

Ev didn't answer, instead trying to contact Helcant.

"Helcant, where's Birdie? Where's Jax?"

"We have other concerns now, Ev," Helcant replied, sounding frantic.

Ev growled, then looked out again at the chaos. There were thousands of these creatures already, more crawling up from the pit below, and no end in sight. The anthermancers might be keeping them at bay for now, but if they couldn't put a stop to this soon, there was no telling how many they'd lose.

"Ev, look out!" Umber shouted.

Ev turned in time to see the upper half of the creature crawling back through the portal with surprising speed. The monster screeched a gurgling shriek and sped towards her.

Ev put up a barrier around the creature, then surged the temperature of its prison upwards until only a metal skeleton covered in a sticky black tar remained.

"Wh-what are they?" a man behind her whimpered.

Umber investigated the lower half of the creature. "I have never seen anything such as this before."

"We don't have time to wonder what they are," Ev stated, wracking her brain for any ideas on how to stop them from climbing the pipes before they were completely overwhelmed.

"To defeat a foe, one must understand the foe," replied Umber, squeezing a part of the creature between his fingers. "Perhaps there is a weakness we can exploit. This flesh does not appear to be natural."

"And how do we know what 'natural' is in this world?" Ev retorted, but then it hit her. "Wait a minute."

She rushed over and made a rip in space to slice off a chunk from the creature. Black liquid poured from the cut as Ev picked up the piece of flesh. She tried to see if she could use the communication network to find other anthermancers, but it didn't seem like it was ready — or at least, it wasn't ready for everyone to use just yet.

"Helcant, I need to know where Tallis or Lylia is at. Can you locate their communication nodes?"

"I told you, we—"

"I think I know how to stop these things, but I need their help."

There was a pause on the other end before Nictis answered. "Do not move. I will create a portal to take you to them."

"Thank you," replied Ev before turning to the others. "Stay back! A portal is about to open. Umber, do what you can to get as many as possible to safety until I can fix this."

Umber nodded, and a moment later the gateway appeared. On the other side, Ev saw Tallis and Lylia in the middle of an absolute swarm of mole monsters doing their best to keep the monsters' numbers down. Ev jumped through the portal, blew away the purple gas, then opened up a massive slice in space that removed the heads of every creature in her way.

To her shock, the now headless bodies spun around and charged toward her, using their oversized arms to run in lieu of their stubby legs.

Ev put up a barrier that they all crashed into, then put up another barrier around herself as another mole monster barreled toward her from the side.

The monster swiped its claws uselessly against Ev's shield, but she didn't have time to deal with this.

She created two more barriers on either side of her attacker and slammed them together, splattering black goo and bits of metal across the scenery. She then created one more barrier and used it to swipe the other monsters still in her way off the side, sending them back to the bottom of the pit.

Deciding to leave her protective barrier up, Ev hurried over to Tallis; Lylia had dropped down to a lower level to aid another less-experienced anthermancer.

"Ev? What are you doing here?"

"I know how to get rid of these monsters, but it requires looking for physical patterns. Do you think you can make a tool that can recognize the stuff those monsters are made of?"

Tallis blinked. "I think so, but it would take time."

"Do it," Ev ordered. "I'll put together something that will get rid of them once and for all."

A scream from the level above caused both of them to look up.

"I've got that," said Ev. "Just get that tool ready. Here."

She tossed him the chunk of flesh she'd picked up and hopped through a portal leading to the upper level. There, she found another mole bearing down on a trio of children cowering at the back of one of the rooms. Ev opened another portal at the monster's feet and dropped it off high in the sky, letting gravity take care of it. She blasted the smoke from the room, then rushed over to check on the terrified kids.

Ev breathed a sigh of relief to see them unharmed, but when she looked around for their parents, her heart sank. She had been too late to save one of them, and the other — he was still breathing, at least.

The three children started sobbing.

"It's okay, it's okay," Ev said, desperate to believe her own words but knowing full well she could never make what had happened be okay. "A friend of mine is making a power that will make those bad things go away forever. You'll be safe soon."

"What . . . what . . . what about mommy?" the smallest one sniffled.

Ev felt her throat tighten. "Your mommy's going to watch over you from far away now. Her soul is with the seitti."

"W-what's a seitti?"

Ev tried her best to come up with an answer. It took all of her effort not to let her voice crack.

"A seitti is a very powerful person — more powerful than even the Masters. If your mommy's with them, she'll always be able to see you, even if you can't see her. Understand?"

The little one nodded her head, then buried her face in the shirt of the oldest. The oldest then clutched his two siblings, a look of terror on his face.

Ev spun around to see another mole clawing its way through the window. A new level of hatred for these creatures welling up within her, Ev trapped the monster in a barrier. She focused on converting all antherial fields within the barrier to zero. A moment later, the mole — and the window it was stuck in — vanished without a trace.

Ev looked back at the three kids. She felt awful leaving them. She felt awful knowing this could have been prevented if she'd just listened to Tallis and checked more, but she had to put together her half of the tool if she was going to end this.

"Stay here and take care of your father. I promise you'll be safe."

Their eyes pleaded with her to stay, but she couldn't. Instead, Ev placed a barrier around the whole building, then headed back down to where Tallis waited.

"Please tell me you're done," she said as entered into his protective bubble.

"I'm trying," returned Tallis, "but if you're about to do what I think you're about to do, I need to make sure I've got it exactly right."

Ev growled in frustration but said nothing more. Instead, she focused on constructing her half of the solution.

Tallis was right, after all. She'd rushed in finding shelter, and look what that had cost. If either of them made a mistake with this, they could end up doing a lot more harm than the mole monsters ever could.

After a minute, Tallis shoved a shimmering wisp into her face. "There," he said. "I can't promise it's perfect, though. You'll want to test it before you use it for real."

"You think I don't know that?" Ev almost shouted.

She took the shimmer and absorbed it into her body where she combined it with her own tool already inside of her. The process took another full minute to make sure the two tools would work together properly, but then she was ready.

She focused on the nearby platform covered in black goo. In an instant, the goo vanished, and the platform remained.

Ev then picked up the piece of flesh beside Tallis and held it at arm's length.

Tallis balked. "Wait, you aren't—"

The piece of flesh vanished. To Ev's admitted relief, her hand was still there.

"I had to test it, didn't I?"

Tallis looked concerned, but Ev ignored him. She next turned her attention to a group of survivors being ushered to safety a few platforms away. A pair of mole monsters pursued them. Two seconds later, the creatures were gone — only broken metal skeletons and tubes remained in their place. The survivors were unharmed.

Ev looked to Tallis. He still looked uneasy, but he nodded.

Taking a deep breath, Ev raised her hand high above her head and closed her eyes. She didn't need to do that, but it helped her concentrate on the sheer scale of the world around her.

With one final push of her will, the gurgling shrieks of the moles turned to silence; the crash of metal against metal echoed around the city as the remains of the creatures fell lifeless.

Tallis scanned the now-still city, awestruck.

"Damn," he whispered.

When he turned back to Ev, he looked pensive, as if he was afraid to say anything to her after that. Truthfully, Ev wasn't entirely sure how *she* felt at the moment. Yes, she'd ended the slaughter, but she'd also caused it. Because of her, she had to resort to a desperate action that could have killed literally everyone if she'd gotten something wrong.

Ev lowered her arm and took several deep breaths. Tallis approached her slowly.

"Hey, you okay?"

Ev nodded. She didn't exactly feel up for words.

Helcant's voice chimed into her head. "The beasts are all dead! What did you do?"

"Tallis and I got rid of them," she replied.

Ev could practically hear the demonic grin in his voice. "Insanity! With such skill, you would be a match for the Masters."

"Unlikely," said Ev.

"Nonsense! If we can but find a world of theirs, you could match them in combat while others steal their systems!"

Ev exhaled heavily. She didn't want to even think about that right now.

Nictis spoke next, but it sounded like she was addressing all anthermancers. "We have word that all dangerous beasts have been slain. Return to the cities and continue making shelter."

Once Nictis finished her announcement, Ev addressed Helcant again. "There, the problem has been dealt with. Now tell me where Birdie and Jax are."

"Why should I possess this knowledge?" Helcant replied.

"Helcant, find them!"

Helcant went silent. Ev stood stock-still as she awaited his response. A minute or so later, he finally replied.

"Jax and Birdie are both in the seventh quarter."

"The what?" Ev asked, relieved to hear they were both okay.

"The seventh quarter. This city is large. We named the sections while you were out gallivanting."

"I was out finding food," Ev shot back annoyed. "And for your information, I found some."

Helcant paused. "Truly? Real food?"

"We aren't sure if it's safe to eat yet, but yes. Now give me a portal to this 'seventh quarter.'"

Helcant obliged.

Ev looked back at Tallis before stepping through. "I'm sorry. Do you think you can handle things in this area."

He nodded. "Yeah, I got this."

Ev smiled, then remembered the children in the room above her. "There are some kids one level up I put inside a barrier. Could you do me a favor and take care of them?"

Tallis nodded again.

"Thanks," she said, and she stepped through before closing the portal behind her.

Chapter 5

Ev examined herself in the mirror and took in the sleek black armor she'd been provided. She'd been placed in a fancy room near the heart of Ars Summis for the time being, but that arrangement would only be temporary.

Sylvra stood next to her. "My apologies if it doesn't suit you. I will have Amethine create something more to your tastes once you have demonstrated mastery of the laws and systems you must uphold."

"This is fine," Ev stated plainly.

"Hardly," replied Sylvra. "This armor belonged to Shodin, an Enforcer found abusing her authority. You have stated clearly that your decision to join me hinges on protecting the inhabitants of this world. I would not want an armor with such a history to be associated with you. Besides, you will be an Enforcer for a short time only. I hope to see you join the Administrators soon enough."

Ev said nothing. Enforcer, Administrator — to her, a Master was a Master. There was no way Sylvra would actually let her touch his core systems, regardless of what title he gave her.

"Come," said Sylvra. "There is much we must do today. You must meet Amethine, Crovos, the Enforcers; and of course you must choose a permanent home for yourself. I also have a small task for you to attend to. Once all of that is done, you may then begin your studies."

Ev looked warily at Sylvra. "What sort of studies?"

Sylvra chuckled. "Oh, we have some documents detailing the rules that nepacs, Divine, and even Masters must follow. You will have to learn these rules by heart. After that, Crovos will take you under his wing and teach you the proper way to use our systems. I'm certain that your Rusalka only ever taught you how to affect things by manipulating anther directly. While such skills are certainly impressive and necessary at times, that is not how we usually do things here. Such an approach is inefficient and far more likely to involve mistakes, and that is something that none of us can afford."

After a few moments, Ev stated, "Syrus."

Sylvra looked at her. "I beg your pardon?"

"He called himself Syrus. If you're going to refer to him, at least use the name he preferred."

Sylvra smiled. "As you wish. Now, let us walk."

"Why?" Ev asked. "Can't you just teleport us?"

"I can, but I would prefer to show off our newest member to the Divine of Ars Summis." He motioned with his hand to follow.

Begrudgingly, Ev obliged. They had barely made it out of the door before Sylvra stopped.

"Oh yes, and before I forget, here."

Ev simultaneously felt both a number of antherial tools and some sort of powerful enchantment manifest within her body.

Disgusted that he would do that without any warning, Ev glared at him. "What did you do to me?"

"You now have the full suite of Enforcer tools to use at your discretion, as well as the enchantment of the Masters. All Divine will recognize you as a Master on sight, and you are impervious to harm. Unlike other enchantments, it is impossible to remove. I have also taken the liberty of configuring some of the tools for you. Once you learn to control them, you may adjust them to your liking."

Sylvra continued walking. Ev followed, looking at her hands. She could hardly believe this was happening. Why this monster would give her any sort of liberty was something she just couldn't wrap her head around. He had to have some ulterior plan for her, but she couldn't for the life of her figure out what it might be.

As for the tools, it wasn't until they stepped outside into the noonday sun that she saw any effect from them. There, it was immediately obvious. All around her, the crowd of Divine had two names floating above each of their heads — one in Doxlan, and one in, well, it wasn't always consistent. Some of the lower names she recognized as being written in Seign — the language of the seitti, but most of them were in characters that were completely alien to her.

Sylvra must have noticed her expression. He spoke to her in her mind. "Now, now, a Master should never appear surprised. I trust you are familiar with at least some of the languages before you."

Ev looked back at him. "I know how to read Seign. I don't know the others."

"Seign was the preferred language for the Divine of your Doxla. The world was advertised in a region of seitti space where that language was common. We do not announce ourselves in the same place twice, however. Most Divine here natively speak the language of Runish."

Ev noticed that people had stopped to stare at the two of them. When she responded, she did so quietly. "Am I supposed to learn that, too?"

"It might be beneficial, but it is far from necessary. As long as you know at least one."

Sylvra resumed his stride. Ev walked briskly but at an even pace to keep up with him, trying her best not to look out of place. There were literally hundreds of Divine on this one street — more than she'd ever encountered in her entire life prior to this day. If she hadn't seen them out her window prior, it would have been unbelievable. All kept their distance from them, however, so thankfully Ev didn't have to speak to any of them.

After some time spent walking and receiving countless stares, they reached the Radiant Gardens, and from there the Supremacy Plaza beneath Lumine Tower. While there were certainly a fair number of Radiants in the garden, the plaza was completely empty. This told Ev that either no Radiants had reached the rank of Supreme yet, or none of them were interested in the place. She did notice that inside, however, the decorations were much different than in her Doxla. The place appeared much more toned-down in terms of technology, suggesting both that Syrus's theory that Divine wished to escape technology had been correct, and that the Masters had learned that from their time in her Doxla.

Indeed, the only bit of otherworldly technology in the area was the central lift, which she and Sylvra took up to the second-highest floor.

As soon as they stepped out of the elevator, Ev spotted two extravagantly-dressed individuals resting on ornate couches — a woman with crimson colored hair who reclined obnoxiously while sipping a drink from a crystal glass, and a man with curly black hair and a short beard who sat upright and stared out the window. Neither of them wore their signature armors, but Ev knew exactly who they were from the statues and paintings that decorated Ars Summis.

As Sylvra approached, both of them stood in greeting. The woman, Amethine, tossed her glass to the floor where a fake fire elemental appeared, cleaned the mess, and vanished again in the span of two seconds. For the brief moment here eyes were on Ev, Ev felt like a piece of livestock under appraisal. Crovos also gave her a once-over, though his gaze was more of curiosity than anything else. Ev also noted that unlike the others, a hint of exhaustion lingered in his eyes.

"Friends," stated Sylvra with arms opened wide. "Allow me to introduce our newest member, Evress."

Amethine sniffed, purposefully not looking at Ev as she spoke. "A bit young, isn't she? Are you sure she has the maturity to take on such a role?"

"I did not take interest in her for her maturity," replied Sylvra with a smile. "I took interest in her ability. She is a natural. If you are not careful, she may one day surpass even you."

"Is that so?" Amethine replied, looking at Ev once again with a smile so venomous it would have slain vipers. "In that case, I look forward to seeing what you can do."

Ev met Amethine's gaze without flinching. "Just give me the chance, and I'll be more than happy to show you."

Crovos stepped between the two of them before either could say more, his hand extended. "It is a pleasure to meet you. I've been looking forward to the day another would join our number. As capable as we are, there is only so much we can do with just the three of us."

Ev looked at the offered hand and, after a moment's consideration, shook it. "What about the Enforcers? Don't they help at all?"

Amethine sniffed again. "You clearly don't understand how things work around here. Enforcers *enforce*. That is all they do. Everything else, *we* are responsible for. *We* run this world."

"I'm afraid that is true," said Crovos. "Amethine manages everything involving bringing Divine to the world and making sure we profit from them, while I am responsible for Doxla's upkeep and all systems outside of Ars Summis."

"Is that so?" Ev looked up at Sylvra. "What do you do, then?"

Sylvra smiled. "I'm certain that with your education, you are aware of the unsanctioned nature of our endeavors here. I am responsible for ensuring that our work proceeds uninhibited. *Your* job will be to keep the natives happy and assist Crovos in securing a future for those natives beyond our exodus."

"In other words, you want me to help nepacs turn a blind eye to what you're doing to them," said Ev.

Sylvra ignored the bite in her remark. "I want you to be in charge of the Enforcers. They are not like us. They are outsiders who often forget their place and require reminders from time to time. In fact, that is the exact task that I have for you at this moment."

Ev raised an eyebrow as Sylvra turned his attention back to Crovos and Amethine. "I will allow you to return to your duties. Thank you for your time."

Crovos and even Amethine bowed their heads before vanishing from the room.

"Now, then," stated Sylvra, his gaze intently on Ev. "You despise us Masters, correct? I am afraid there is nothing I can do about Crovos, Amethine, or myself, but from this day onward, you will have jurisdiction over who is granted the role of Enforcer and who is not — provided that you are able to discipline the current Lead Enforcer, of course. Should you succeed, only I will retain the authority to veto your decisions."

Ev narrowed her eyes. "In other words, you'll still have sole authority over the Enforcers."

Sylvra chuckled. "I know you don't believe me, but unless you make decisions that threaten our ambitions, I will not override them. Now, aren't you interested in the prospect of permanently banishing a Master from Doxla?"

Ev shifted a little. She had to admit, as unbelievable as the offer was, it was an enticing one.

Sylvra continued. "Xaltus, like all Enforcers, is not one of us. He condoned the actions of the former occupant of your armor, and thus is also culpable."

"You keep saying 'not one of us,'" interrupted Ev. "What does that mean?"

Sylvra's tone grew serious. "Xaltus has not experienced the loss of his world of origin. He cannot sympathize with nepacs."

"And you can?" spit Ev.

"I do not empathize with them, but I understand fully the pain that they and their descendants will in time endure. I have felt it. I remember it — even if I have long since moved on."

Ev kept her gaze on Sylvra. There wasn't a single word he spoke that she trusted, but he had yet to say anything that sounded like a lie. He was even open about his disconnection from the people he harmed. As much as she tried to resist, she couldn't help but feel a faint glimmer of hope that she really would be able to make a difference here.

"You will find Xaltus in the remote city of Ellinquin," Sylvra continued. "Divine rarely frequent the location, so he believes his abuse of the citizenry has gone unnoticed, but it has not — nor has his usage of raw anther without my permission. I will give you the tools necessary to banish him, but I want you to do more than that. I want you to defeat him in battle and humiliate him. Show yourself as a purveyor of justice to the people and make an example of him to the other Enforcers. Do you understand what I desire of you?"

Ev nodded. What choice did she have?

"Good," Sylvra's smile returned. "Then let us get you prepared. You should know exactly what you are dealing with."

* * * *

The portal closed behind Ev as she approached the outskirts of Ellinquin. Within her body swirled dozens of antherial tools and even concentrated anther — a gift Sylvra had instructed her to use only defensively, though frankly she was surprised he had given it to her at all, even if it was obvious to her that he'd done something to it before giving it to her. Even with those tools, however, she wasn't sure she could do what had been asked of her. This would be her first real combat using anther as a weapon, and her opponent would be an actual Master.

At first assessment, the city appeared to be a prosperous one — perched high atop a green hill in the cold, northeastern region of Doxla's main continent. The buildings were all in good condition, and for a place seldom frequented by Divine, so were the roads leading in and out of it. It wasn't until Ev set foot in the city proper that she realized something was wrong. The townsfolk all appeared on edge, and the moment anyone spotted her they hurried about their business or ducked into nearby buildings. None of them dared make eye contact with her, or even look at her face, for that matter. She could only assume they recognized her armor and were intimidated by the sight of an Enforcer.

Finding Xaltus proved easy. With the tools Sylvra had provided, she could see the outline of his form even through buildings halfway across the city. She focused her sight on him, making it look as if he was only about thirty feet away. He was clearly sitting at the moment, so rather than go directly to him, Ev opted to walk and allow as many as possible to see her, as per Sylvra's instructions.

About halfway to her target, Xaltus stood up. With only his outline visible to her, it was difficult to see what he was doing, but something about his movements made her uncomfortable.

Quickly making a portal, Ev jumped through to just outside of the pub

Xaltus was in. Xaltus's outline swung its arm. The sound of a crash and a woman's cry reached her ears, followed by whimpering.

Ev no longer had any hesitation regarding what she was doing here. Now, it took all of her restraint not to charge in there at once. His form lumbered toward the door, so she waited for him to come to her.

The door opened. Xaltus, clad in white, spiked armor, stepped outside, dragging a heavily bruised woman along behind him.

Ev glared at him.

Xaltus stopped the moment he saw Ev, his eyes narrowed into slits.

"Who the hell are you?"

Ev ignored the question. "Let go of her."

Xaltus sneered. "Listen here, Cupcake. Sylvra's on thin ice already for replacing Shodin with some scrawny nobody who thinks she can wear that armor. You'd best tuck your tail between your legs and run along, or I'll bring this whole operation crashing down."

Again, Ev ignored him. She activated several of the tools Sylvra had given her. The first removed all of Xaltus's antherial tools from his possession. The second removed his invincibility, and the third siphoned his anther away from him, though Sylvra had warned her that it would not be able to steal his raw anther unless she could either touch him or separate it from his body some other way.

Xaltus erupted in response, throwing the woman violently into a table. "How dare you! Do you have any inkling who I am? No one disrespects me!"

Xaltus lunged at Ev, his armor glowing with an iridescent shimmer. Ev's eyes opened wide as she realized he was attacking with anther, and she dodged out of the way of his swing — his arm carving out a rip in space beside her.

The Enforcer leered at Ev. "Once I'm finished with you, I'll tell AnAnCol that Sylvra broke our deal. You'll never work with the organization again!"

Ev jumped back from another swing. Sylvra had said she was invincible from ordinary damage, but she didn't dare chance it against anther.

Xaltus leapt over his newest tear in reality and swung again. Ev dropped to the ground to avoid the strike, then rolled out of the way of another blow that slammed straight into the dirt.

Seeing her opportunity, she aimed a kick directly at Xaltus's face while channeling her own anther to magnify the force one hundred fold.

Xaltus went flying down the street and landed over thirty yards away.

Remarkably, he stood up, though blood poured from his mouth and nose.

"You will regret that!" he sputtered, spraying flecks of red all over his armor.

Ev noticed him close his eyes and fist, and she realized he was reconfiguring his anther. For what, she didn't want to find out. Fortunately, she already had her own antherial attack ready.

She leapt through a portal that she created a few feet in front of Xaltus and unleashed the same attack that she had against Sylvra.

Xaltus screamed as his left arm disintegrated before exploding. He still wasn't down quite yet, however.

From his other arm grew a shimmering triangular blade. Ev jumped back as he swung, but the blade stretched out as it moved, slicing deep through her armor and chest.

Ev fell backwards, clutching her wound. She pulled her hand away to see it covered in blood, but the pain vanished in an instant — presumably due to healing from the enchantment Sylvra had given her.

Xaltus stared in disbelief.

"How? That should have shattered your Heart and banished you from Doxla!"

Ev stood up, focused on her anther, and created a blade similar to his. "I don't have a Heart, Xaltus. I'm a nepac, and I won't let you hurt anyone else!"

Xaltus's eyes widened as Ev lunged at him. He lifted his blade to block hers, but she dispelled her weapon before impact, catching him off-guard as she instead unleashed her disintegration attack upon his other arm.

His right arm also exploded, and Ev felt the anther he'd been using disperse around her. She activated Sylvra's tool once again and absorbed it. She then lunged forward and placed a hand on his chest, activating the tool a third time to drain the remaining anther from within him.

Xaltus was now helpless.

The disgusting Enforcer stumbled backward, bleeding from his head and the cauterized stumps where his arms used to be. His face was so red from rage it nearly blended in with the blood. "I swear you will regret this! Sylvra will pay for betraying me! I'll turn all of AnAnCol against him!"

"About that," said Ev as she took a step closer. "I don't care. And from what I can tell, neither does Sylvra. He told me to tell you he knows about Hecaton and how much you stole from them. What was it? Thirty thousand prestige?"

Xaltus's face turned white.

Ev spat. "You are filth. You pose as a hero and treat these people like tools for your own sick pleasure. If there is a hell for seitti, I hope you burn there, and if you ever do anything to hurt Doxla again, it will be *you* that AnAnCol comes for."

In all honesty, she didn't know anything about AnAnCol or Hecaton other than that AnAnCol was some sort of seitti organization that Sylvra worked with. All things considered, it was probably a criminal organization, but that didn't mean anything to her. Ridding the world of this creature was the only thought on her mind now.

Ev swiped her blade clean through Xaltus's torso, causing his body to vanish in a flash of white as his Heart dropped to the ground. Ev picked it up, then felt for the banishment tool that Sylvra had given her. She activated it, and the Heart disappeared as well.

Her job done, Ev first checked to see if she really had healed from her injury. Fortunately, she had. She then looked around the street at the frightened townsfolk. The spatial rends were already mending, so that was good. The woman that Xaltus had thrown still cowered behind the upturned table, so Ev approached to check on her.

The woman backed away at Ev's approach, but she stumbled over a chair and clutched her side, clearly injured.

Ev hurried over to the terrified woman and knelt down.

"Let me see where your hurt. I know I don't look it now, but I used to be a cleric."

Confusion appeared on the woman's face, but she said nothing.

Ev removed her gauntlets before lifting the woman's shirt to her ribs. It was obvious by sight alone that they'd been broken. Ev then tried channeling healing magic through her hands when she realized she couldn't.

Right. When she'd left the old Doxla, she disconnected from the magic systems that the Masters had put in place there. Well, perhaps she could use one of the tools Sylvra had given her instead.

"What's your name?" Ev asked as she focused on the tools inside of her.

The woman hesitated. "Milly."

"That's a nice name, Milly."

The two then sat in silence as Ev sifted through her antherial tools. Before long, she found one that connected to this Doxla's magic system. Thankfully, it then proved a simple matter to give herself back her alignment with healing magic, reactivate her favorite spells within her, and restore her "proficiency," which was the strength of her connections to those spells and healing magic as a whole.

Ev placed her hand gently on Milly's side and worked on healing first her ribs, then the rest of the injuries on her. When she was done, she backed away to give Milly space.

"There. Better?"

Milly touched her side, then her face, then nodded.

Ev smiled. "Don't worry. I've banished Xaltus from Doxla permanently. He won't be coming back, and no Enforcer is ever going to do the kinds of things he did ever again. If they do, they'll answer to me."

More confusion. "You? A-aren't you Shodin?"

Ev smiled and shook her head. "Shodin's gone, too. I'm just using her armor until Sylvra gives me my own."

A glimmer of relief also appeared on Milly's face. "So, Shodin's gone."

Ev nodded.

"And Xaltus."

Ev nodded again.

Milly hesitated before asking, "And Nereid?"

"I don't know who that is," Ev admitted, "but it sounds like I need to pay them a visit too? Have they also been hurting you?"

Milly immediately clamped up.

"It's okay," Ev prodded. "I promise I'm not like any of them. You won't get in trouble if you tell me. As of today, I've been tasked with cleaning up the Enforcers. I won't let any of them get away with abusing their positions."

Milly looked unsure, but she eventually nodded. "He did."

"Then he's next on my list," she smiled, then she helped Milly up to her feet.

Milly looked quizzically at Ev. "I don't understand. Didn't you say you," she nervously twiddled her fingers together before finishing, "didn't you say you're a nepac?"

Ev blinked. Crap. She had said that. She was sure that was something Sylvra wouldn't want getting out.

"I'm a nepac in the sense that I don't have a Divine's Heart. I still come from outside of Doxla, like other Divine," she said, not exactly lying.

"No Heart? Why?"

"Oh, well," Ev searched for an answer, "it means that I can't be banished by the other Enforcers. That way I can do the job Sylvra wanted me to do. Only he can banish me."

Milly twiddled her fingers. "So, does that mean you're a Master?"

"Yes, I am," Ev said, surprised to realize there was a touch of pride in her response.

Milly seemed a bit more relaxed now, though she was definitely still on edge.

"I didn't know the Masters could change," she stated with a hint of suspicion, "but, perhaps that might be a good thing."

She twiddled her fingers again. "Um, may I ask you your name?"

"It's . . ." Ev paused.

Milly looked at her expectantly.

"It's Evress," she answered at last.

Milly nodded, then bowed. "Well, thank you, Master Evress. I wish I had more than words, but I don't know what a nepac like myself could give to a Master."

Milly's words still had a hint of distrust in her tone, but that was understandable.

"You don't need to give me anything. Believe me, my only goal is to stop the suffering of nepacs. If I can do that, I'll be happy."

With that, she opened a portal back to Ars Summis and waved goodbye. Then, Evress stepped through to Lumine Tower.

Chapter 6

Two days had passed since the mole monster attack. Ev's stomach rumbled as she eyed the boxes of fruit in the middle of the warehouse. Umber sat in the corner, wanting to help but unable to do much given his injuries and sudden illness.

"Maybe we just aren't preparing it right," Ev said meekly as Gare picked up another box to carry it away.

"We don't really have many options, Ev," replied Birdie. "We've got fire, and that's it. Everything anyone has eaten from that place has made them ill."

"Don't sweat it," said Gare, stopping at the door. "At least you found something that's almost food. There's gotta be something else out there we can actually eat."

There was a loud hiss to her side as steam leaked from the rattling pipes. Tallis's persistence in figuring out the technology of this city had yielded a good amount of progress in getting things working again. Ev was amazed and, admittedly, a tad jealous after her own failure on the food front.

"Yeah," said Jax, leaning against the wall with his arm wrapped in bloody bandages. "At the very least no one's died from them yet. We'll just try again."

"How can you say that?" said Ev, her eyes watering from frustration. "Look at Umber. Look at your arm. Look at all the people who got sick! How many people did we lose when the monsters attacked? How many more were injured? It's my fault we got ambushed. It's my fault people are sick. I should have checked more! I should have been more careful with the fruit!"

"Oh, lords," Jax muttered, then a bit more loudly. "You know, if you really think it's your fault, then how 'bout you stop dwelling on it and do something to make it better."

Birdie dropped the box she'd picked up and stomped toward Jax.

He spread his good arm innocently. "What? She had no reason to think that frozen monsters lived miles underground. She didn't make those idiots break into the warehouse and steal those fruits before we knew if they were safe. If she wants to blame herself for morons getting sick, then she should at least be proactive about it."

"How about I get proactive on your—" Birdie started.

"No," said Ev before she started toward the exit. "He's right. I got us into this mess. I need to get us out of it."

"Ev, wait," pleaded Birdie, but Ev was already out the door.

Ev heard Jax shout, "Ow!" before Birdie's footsteps caught up to her.

"Ev, I know you feel guilty, but none of this is your fault."

"It doesn't matter," said Ev, not wanting to get into it.

"Yes, it does."

"No, it doesn't!" shouted Ev. "We have a hundred thousand anthermancers who could have been searching for food, but instead they were gathering poison because I thought we could eat it. Now, half of them are sick, and the other half are still looking for shelter for the twenty million people who still don't have any."

"No, half of them are not sick," retorted Birdie. "Almost all of them played it safe like *you* suggested. We still have thousands who are out looking for another source of food right now. You found something in a day, right?"

Birdie cocked her head and smiled. "I know they're not you, but I'm sure a thousand of them will be able to find something soon."

Ev shook her head vigorously. "You don't get it. That fruit wasn't supposed to be poisonous. It was in an orchard. It was meant to be eaten, but it made us sick."

Birdie raised an eyebrow but waited for Ev to finish.

"Those monsters sprayed purple gas everywhere. If that wasn't poison, I don't know what it was, but it didn't affect anyone other than making some people cough."

"Where are you going with this?" Birdie asked.

Ev shook her head. "Umber told me he was worried that plants from other worlds wouldn't be edible to us. I think he was right. Our bodies aren't adapted to survive in any of these worlds. What the natives used as food is poison to us. What they found toxic is just a nuisance."

Ev looked Birdie in the eyes. "We need to find another world like Doxla."

Birdie tilted her head. "Well, that sounds good on paper. Any idea how we might do that?"

Ev shook her head again. "I don't know, but there has to be some way."

A voice called out from behind Ev. "Why can we not search for the actual Doxla?"

Ev spun around. "Lylia? How long have you been there?"

Lylia giggled. "Not long. So, what does this one say? Is it not a good idea?"

Birdie crossed her arms. "I feel like finding the actual Doxla would be harder than finding another world like it. Besides, wasn't Doxla destroyed?"

"We don't know that," chimed Lylia, placing her arms behind her back. "We just know that people stopped coming through the portals."

"And the last one through was a charred corpse," added Birdie.

"Many trees can survive flames that humans cannot. Even if the land was scorched, the ground may yet hold palatable treasures."

Ev and Birdie exchanged glances. Lylia had a point.

"Okay," said Birdie, "but that still doesn't answer how we will find it."

"Actually," said Ev, "I might have an idea for that."

She turned to Lylia. "Are you still helping Tallis figure out those steam pipes?"

Lylia smiled. "The warmth is quite pleasant, but we have grown bored with it. Tallis pays little attention to us while playing with the machines."

"In that case, do you think you can help me for a bit? Doxla had a barrier that blocked most antherial tools, right? If that barrier's still there, maybe my mapping tool can find it the same way it found the boundaries of the Cosmic Graveyard. We just need to figure out why it didn't find it the first time I used it."

"Hopefully," remarked Lylia, "it is not because the barrier is gone."

"Yes, hopefully," said Ev. She really did hope this wasn't a wild goose chase. "Do you think you can help me?"

"Certainly," said Lylia, smiling.

"Well," said Birdie, arms crossed. "Sounds like you two have a plan. Guess I'll just go back to cleanup duty, then."

Ev looked back at Birdie. "I'm sorry. I just don't know how you can help me until we find something."

Birdie shrugged, then smiled. "Don't worry about it. I know I'm useless with anther. Let me know if you find anything, though. I'd like to see exactly what happened to our home."

Ev nodded. "We will."

She then headed off with Lylia to find a place where they could work in private.

****

The room that Ev and Lylia found to work proved quite cramped at first with Lylia's serpentine bulk, but after Lylia coiled up, what had once been cramped became merely cozy, instead.

Once they had set up their work area, Lylia extended a hand to Ev. "May we examine this one's method of mapping the Graveyard before we begin?"

"Of course," said Ev, floating a swirling shimmer over to Lylia.

Lylia accepted the shimmer, and while she investigated it, Ev did the same with her own copy of the tool. If Doxla's barrier still existed, then the tool should have already spotted it, unless — and this was her hope — the barrier was different in nature. The mere fact that Doxla's barrier was breakable while the Graveyard's border wasn't told her that this wasn't a far-off hope.

"We see some problems with this one's creation," stated Lylia after a short while.

Ev perked up. If there was a problem, she was eager to hear it. Fixing known problems would certainly be easier than trying to guess the different properties of Doxla's barrier.

"We see that this one draws the borders proportional to their actual size. It may be that Doxla is too small to see."

Ev responded, "Doxla is nearly five thousand miles in diameter, and that's not even including the Underworld and Netherworld."

Lylia tilted her head. "How large is the Cosmic Graveyard?"

Ev opened up her map of the Cosmic Graveyard — the orange cube filling the room — and pointed to the tiny blue sliver she'd shown to Umber when she first created it. The sliver was only about as long as her thumbnail. "This is how far away we were from the mole city when I made the map."

"And that would be . . . how far?"

Ev tried to remember how far apart she'd made her portals. She recalled they'd been a hundred thousand miles or more each, so . . .

"Oh," she said sheepishly.

Lylia lifted the shimmer up again. "We also see that this one has colored all detected borders the same. We imagine orange against an orange backdrop would be difficult to see."

Ev felt herself blushing as she worked to address both of the issues Lylia had brought up. After about five minutes, she felt confident that her improved tool was ready.

"Okay, let's try this again," she said.

She reactivated the tool, causing it to pulse briefly. Ev then reopened her map. This time, a number of blue regions appeared — scattered randomly about the cube.

"This can't be right," Ev stated. "Why are there so many?"

Lylia pointed a finger at each dot as she mouthed her count silently. "We spy a total of nine circles."

"No way," said Ev. "The Masters can't have that many worlds here."

Lylia tilted her head. "Perhaps they do not. Perhaps they are all abandoned worlds as Doxla was."

Ev felt a sick sensation in the pit of her stomach. If that was true, then the Masters were even bigger monsters than she thought.

Ev spoke using the communication node she'd created earlier. Nictis and Helcant had finished setting up their communication system, so she was able to address or find whoever she wanted.

"Helcant, Tallis, Nictis, could you come see me?"

Helcant was the first to respond. "We are busy, woman!"

"I think Lylia and I found Doxla."

"What? Doxla?"

"And the other worlds created by the Masters."

Not a moment later, Ev heard Helcant shouting from outside the room.

"Watch your portals, fool!" he said.

"Watch yours," returned Tallis before the both of them — followed by Nictis — burst into the room.

Tallis pushed past Helcant and stepped into the glowing cube — not that there was much room to be outside of it.

"Alright so what do we have here?" His eyes landed on one of the blue dots. "Is this what you found?"

Ev nodded. "It's one of them."

Helcant entered the cube as well. "This is not finding Doxla. These blues have no differences. This wastes our time!"

Nictis hissed at Helcant. "Quiet your complaints. The blues are few in number, though they are far more than one would expect."

Ev nodded, then moved toward the center of the map and pointed at one of the blue dots. "Lylia thinks there's a chance that Doxla might not have been destroyed. If she's right, then we'd have access to food that we know is safe. We just need to investigate each of these points and hope that one of them really is Doxla."

"And if they aren't Doxla," said Tallis, "does that mean they're other worlds of the Masters?"

Ev shrugged and shook her head in apology. "I don't know, but someone put up barriers in those locations."

Nictis suddenly rounded on Ev. "Your method of location. How did you find these?"

Ev was taken aback by the sudden aggression. "I searched for any barriers that blocked portal creation."

Nictis's eyes narrowed as she stepped closer to Ev. "How did you perform such a search?"

Lylia quickly slithered between Nictis and Ev. "The method was safe. The Masters would not notice Ev's probe from behind a world's barrier."

"How can you be sure of that?" demanded Nictis. "I sensed odd anther usage not long ago. If it was you, then the Masters will have felt it, too."

"We are still here, are we not?" Lylia responded. "We believe this is proof enough."

Nictis leered past Lylia to Ev but thankfully backed off. Ev wasn't sure how well she could handle confrontation at the moment.

"So, now what?" asked Tallis, giving Nictis a sideways glance. "Should we check them out?"

"That's what I was thinking," said Ev. "There are five of us, so maybe we could split into groups of three and two."

"No, no, no," chided Lylia. "Birdie wished to travel as well. That would make six. We should form three groups of two. Each group can investigate three regions."

Helcant spoke up again. "Why can you not investigate them all yourself? We have much work to do."

Surprisingly, Nictis disagreed with Helcant. "We have all systems ready for other anthermancers to organize on their own. We should learn our true predicament so that we may well plan our future steps."

"We do *not* have all systems ready," replied Helcant.

"They are ready enough," returned Nictis. "Besides, I wish to see these other worlds for myself."

Helcant growled. "Yes, if honesty is required, so do I. Very well, we shall assist in this. I shall go with Nictis."

Lylia wrapped an arm around a blushing Tallis. "We shall go with this one."

With the groups decided, Ev went ahead and, after thinking about it for longer than she probably should have, marked the locations on her map.

Three of them she marked red, three yellow, and three green. After that, she closed her map and handed copies of both it and her mapping tool to the others.

"Alright then," she said. "Three groups of two it is. Helcant and Nictis, you can check out the three red locations. Lylia and Tallis, you go to the green areas. I'll take Birdie with me to the yellows. Once we're done, we should all meet back here. Be careful if you encounter any solid world barriers. We don't want to do anything that might let the Masters know we're still out here."

Helcant scoffed. "Of course we will move with caution. We shall wait until we have a plan of victory before launching our revenge upon the great deceivers."

"We should be careful in general, too," added Tallis. "If those mole things were still alive out here, there's no telling what else might still be lurking in the dark."

Ev winced at the reminder. "Right. Take care everyone. I'll see you here when we get back."

The others agreed and created their portals, all of them heading off deep into the Cosmic Graveyard.

* * * *

Back at the warehouse, Ev approached Birdie as she helped Gare lift a particularly large crate of fruit. She waited for them to dump the contents through the nearby portal before speaking.

"Hey, Birdie."

Birdie let Gare take the empty crate.

"Hey, Ev. That was fast. Any luck finding Doxla?"

"Actually, I think we might have," replied Ev.

Gare stopped in his tracks and looked back.

Surprise appeared on Birdie's face before a big smile broke out. "Wow. I guess I should have seen that coming, huh?"

Ev brushed off the compliment. "We don't know for sure if we've found it, but we found a few locations that look promising."

"Well," said Birdie, placing a hand on her hip. "If you want someone to come with you to check it out . . ."

Ev smiled. "Yes, please. There are three locations I'd like to look at. Tallis, Helcant, Lylia, and Nictis are investigating the others."

Gare put his box down on the floor and approached. "Yo, do you really think you found Doxla? Can I go, too?"

"Uh, sure?" said Ev, not really expecting that. "But, you know we don't know for sure if we've actually found it."

"I know," he responded, "but if there's even a chance, I'd like to go. I want to see if we can find my old ax, just in case any more strange creatures show up. I was pretty useless last time. I had to hold them off with whatever was lying around, and they got really close to getting past me to Ronda and Marin. I don't like the thought of not being able to protect my family."

Ev lowered her eyes and rubbed the back of her hand.

"Yes, Gare," Birdie enunciated loudly. "Ev already said you could come."

"It's alright," said Ev, looking back up at Birdie. "We should probably ask Jax if he wants to come, too."

Gare rubbed the back of his head. "Uh, that might not be such a good idea."

Ev was confused. "Why not? Did something happen?"

Birdie answered for Gare. "Let's just say he and I aren't on the best of terms at the moment."

Ev sighed as she looked over at Birdie. "Really? I was only gone for like thirty minutes."

"Yeah, well, I only needed five," Birdie replied.

Ev shook her head. That was something she'd have to deal with later. For now, she needed to fix at least part of the problems she'd caused for everyone else.

With a wave of her hand, Ev opened a portal to just outside of the first location on her list.

On the other side, she found herself face-to-face with a massive, seemingly endless reflective wall.

Gare approached the mirror. "What the heck is this?"

"Don't touch it!" Ev yelled as she dashed in front of him and spread her arms. "This looks like the outside of Doxla's barrier, so it's probably one of the Masters' worlds."

"Doxla's barrier?" repeated Gare. "So, is it Doxla, then?"

Ev turned around and gave the wall a once over. If it was Doxla, then there should be tears in the side, unless the Masters closed them again for some reason.

After a bit of investigating, Ev concluded that this was almost certainly a different world. Unfortunately, the only way to be sure would be to interact with the barrier. If she wasn't careful, and if this *was* one of the Masters' worlds, then she might alert them to her presence by doing so.

Ev shook her head and walked back to the others. "We should check out the other places first. I don't want to do anything that might bring more danger to everyone. If they all look like this, then I'll need to talk with Tallis and the others about what we should do."

Birdie crossed her arms and tilted her head. "We're following you on this. Whatever you think is best, we'll do."

Ev didn't respond. Instead, she just opened another portal to the next area. As soon as she found a good exit point, she found herself staring. Without even passing through, there was no mistake.

They'd found it.

"What is it?" asked Birdie.

"It's Doxla," Ev answered.

She stepped through the portal to find herself before another mirror-wall. Unlike the other one, this one had very clear, very large tears in its side — each spaced about three hundred yards apart from one another.

Ev approached the nearest tear and spotted several charred, now-frozen corpses on this side of the barrier. On the other side, the only remains were ash and bones. As terrible as the sight was, it didn't surprise her. What did surprise her, however, was the fact that the she could hear the sound of ocean waves still slapping against the rocky shoreline.

Gare stepped over the bodies behind her. "This is awful. To think these folks were so close to safety . . ."

"Why are there so many?" Birdie asked, her tone catching Ev's attention. "Only one fell through the portal where we were. Why are there so many here? Why are there *any*, for that matter? Shouldn't they have all ended up with the survivors?"

Gare scratched his head. "Huh. Now that you mention it, that is weird. Maybe Syrus's portals broke?"

Ev scanned the bodies. Gare's hypothesis didn't make sense. Even if they had broken, the last person through the portal had been a corpse, so whatever had killed these people happened before the portals stopped. With how far away from the tear they were, they all should have made it through.

Actually, now that she thought about it, even the idea of portals didn't make any sense. With everything that had happened since Doxla's fall, Ev had forgotten about how strange it had been to suddenly appear in the middle of the Cosmic Graveyard. She *knew* she'd seen others outside of Doxla before she'd been transported away, yet Jax and the others had all been transported as well. Did Syrus only send some people to safety? No. No, that couldn't be right. But, if not, then what the hell was going on here?

"Hey," Birdie said, snapping Ev out of it. "You okay?"

"No — I mean, yes, I'm fine," Ev replied.

Birdie gave her a look saying she didn't believe her.

Gare, thankfully, came to her rescue by tromping right through the world's border. "Well, no point in staying out here. From the sound of things, the Masters didn't completely destroy Doxla. Though, the sky sure doesn't look right."

Ev and Birdie both followed Gare and looked up. The sky was completely black — no sun, no moon, no stars, no light whatsoever.

Gare then pointed at the black wall housing the tear to the Cosmic Graveyard. "And was that wall always there? I thought when we ran through here before, there was open sky on the other side of those rocks."

Ev looked at Gare. "The sky we lived under was an illusion. This is what the border of our world actually looks like. I guess the illusion is gone now."

Birdie looked around the area. "You don't think they're still here, do you? The Masters, I mean."

Ev shook her head. "I doubt it. If they didn't come looking for us in the Graveyard, I can't imagine they'd wait for us here."

"Yeah," said Birdie, "I guess that's a good point. So, where to now?"

"Can we head back to Maristol for a bit?" asked Gare.

"Really?" remarked Birdie.

"Why not?" returned Gare. "It's where my ax is, and last I checked, there was decent food there, too. At least, as decent as we could manage with the drought, anyway. I'd bet it's still got some, assuming the place is still standing."

Ev shrugged. "Sounds good to me. Just give me a moment to find it."

Thankfully, raw anther flowed in through the rip in the boundary. That would make working here easier, but just in case, Ev pulled a good bit of it into herself — more than enough to take care of whatever she might need to. She then opened a window high in the sky at the center of Doxla — directly above Ars Summis — and shined a bright light through. From there, she searched until she spotted the Crystal Desert. That let her get her bearings. From there, it was a simple matter of locating the Windy Mountains, and after that,

Maristol.

"Wow," said Gare, "it's all still here. Are we sure the Masters actually came back?"

"Gare?" said Birdie. "The. Sky. Is. Gone."

"There aren't any lights on anywhere, either," said Ev. "If there were survivors, there should at least be a few lamps down there. Hold on."

With a quick flick of her wrist, Ev closed the window she'd created and opened the way to the outskirts of Maristol. With all of the skeletons where they were now, she wasn't looking forward to what waited for her on the other side.

* * * *

Walking through the streets of Maristol was like an eerie dream. Ev had spent nearly the first half of her life here, and had visited many times in the years since. To see it like this — dark, silent, and abandoned — it reminded her of the nightmares she'd had after Dezeroth had attacked it so long ago.

Even though they were sure there was nothing here waiting for them, the trio stuck close together as they made their way to Gare's old home.

"You know," said Gare, "I kind of wish you'd dropped us off a little closer. This is right creepy."

"I've seen worse," said Birdie. She paused before adding, "Where is everyone?"

"What did you expect?" asked Gare. "If the Masters came back, of course everyone's gone."

"No, I mean, where *is* everyone? Back at the world edge, there were at least skeletons, but here, there's nothing. Don't you think that's a little odd?"

Ev stopped and looked around. Now that Birdie mentioned it, she was right. Even if most of Marisol had evacuated, there had to have been at least a few who stayed behind.

Ev shivered. There was just something about all of this that sat very uneasily with her.

"Let's just hurry up and get Gare's ax and see if we can find some food," she said.

Eventually, they reached Gare's big old fancy home — still standing as if the end of the world hadn't happened less than a week ago. Gare ran inside, and after a few minutes of clanging about, he returned fully clad in armor, ax in one hand and a little doll in the other.

Ev looked at him. "Are you sure it was your ax you wanted to come back here for?"

Gare grinned. "What? As long as we're here, I figured I could at least get Marin's dolly. She's not taking all of this too well, you know. I know she says she's too old for it now, but maybe having something familiar will help a bit."

Birdie looked bothered by something, but she wasn't looking at Gare. Ev responded instead.

"It's fine, Gare. Is there anything else you need."

"Not right now," he answered. "It's weird, though. This stuff is a lot heavier than I remembered it."

"The Masters probably removed all of their systems," Ev said. "That includes the ones that made people stronger from fighting a bunch."

"Seriously?" said Gare. "That sucks. I know you guys had said something about that before, but I never realized how much it actually made a difference."

Birdie looked around the area, seemingly on edge. "Well, now that you've got your stuff again, we should see if we can find what we really came for."

"There's a bakery just around the corner," said Gare, leading the way with his ax over his shoulder.

Around the bend, a flash of movement darted into a nearby building, and Birdie immediately brandished a dagger.

"What was that?" asked Gare. "Is there actually something still alive here?"

"It could have come from the Cosmic Graveyard," said Birdie, on guard.

Gare readied his ax as best as he could with one hand. "Well, whatever it is, it ran into the bakery."

"Great," muttered Birdie.

"Relax, you two," said Ev, stepping ahead of them.

With but a thought, she formed a barrier around the group. Birdie and Gare both eased up, but they kept their weapons ready nonetheless.

Ev squeezed her barrier tight to let them through the doorway without breaking it. To her utter delight, she spotted bags of flour up on the shelf in the back.

"Look!" she exclaimed. "We found something! Wait here."

Ev split the barrier in two, leaving half around Birdie and Gare and taking the other half with her. On the other side of the counter, she spotted movement once more. Shifting her light to get a better look, she finally got a good look at the creature hiding behind the counter.

"Aww, you poor thing," she exclaimed, lowering both of the barriers as she squatted low to the ground. "Come here, puppy. It's okay."

"Puppy?" she heard Gare say before he clomped over behind her.

The small brown dog shivered as it wagged its tail weakly. When Gare appeared, however, it wagged a bit harder and gingerly stepped closer.

"I know that dog," said Gare. "He belongs to Mason."

Birdie sheathed her dagger. "Why the hell is there a dog here?"

"I don't know," Ev said tiredly. "I have no idea what's going on anymore, and I don't really want to think about it right now."

By now the dog had made his way all the way to Gare, who was presently giving him a good old pat.

"I'll make an anchor to this place so we can come back later," Ev continued, and she worked on doing so.

"What about Boof?" asked Gare. "Should we take him with us?"

"Boof?" Birdie raised an eyebrow. "You mean the dog?"

"Of course I mean the dog. We can't just leave him here."

Ev thought about it for a moment. She didn't want to leave the dog either, but they still had one more location to check out. Sure, they'd found food and Doxla, but she had to see what that last place was. She had to know what else was out there, be it good or bad.

"We'll come back for Boof later," she said.

"Oh, come on, Ev," said Gare. "We can't just leave him alone here in the dark."

"We won't," said Ev, and she went about searching for a bowl.

When she found one, she placed it on the ground and used the anther she'd stored inside of herself to generate enough water to fill it.

Boof made a beeline for the bowl and started lapping it up. While he quenched himself, Ev produced another light that also generated warmth. She then put up a barrier at the door in case there was anything else out there that wasn't as friendly as Boof.

"There," she said. "That should take care of him until we're able to come back."

Gare scratched his head and sighed. "You know, it would be a lot easier if you could just make food like you can water."

The statement of the obvious was not appreciated. "Yeah, well, for your information, food is a lot more complicated than water. Heck, *air* is more complicated than water."

Gare looked back at Ev sheepishly. "No, I figured as much. I was just thinking out loud, sorry."

Ev sighed. "It's okay. We've still got one more place we need to go see, though."

She hunched over and gave the dog a little pet. "You stay here, boy. We'll be back soon."

* * * *

At first glance, the final area looked like another world with a solid barrier. On closer inspection, however, Ev noticed something was off. Against her better judgment, she approached the barrier and placed her hand on it.

"Uh," said Gare, "are you sure you should do that?"

"Something's weird," said Ev. "Look, you can see through it. It's like the barrier's only halfway there."

As reflective as the surface was, Ev could clearly see a rocky landscape on the other side. Sure, she was also standing on a rocky landscape, and the surface was still reflective, but she could definitely see through to the other side. In fact, she could see through so well that she could see a frozen-over body of water about a hundred yards away.

"The anther in the barrier's degraded," said Ev, removing her hand. "Whoever made this hasn't maintained it in decades, at least."

Birdie approached the world's border as well. "Another abandoned world; do you think the Masters are responsible?"

"If they own this region of the Graveyard, then probably."

Now Gare approached. "Well, if it's abandoned, do you think we should check it out?"

Ev thought for a moment, then nodded. "Yeah. What we saw in Doxla didn't make any sense. Everyone at the border was dead. Everyone everywhere else disappeared without a trace, but nothing else had been touched. Maybe if we see what happened to this world, we can figure out what happened to ours."

With that, Ev traced her finger in a wide circle along the border, cutting through it. The circle complete, she placed her hand in the center and made it vanish, allowing them inside.

As they made their way down to the frozen water, Ev couldn't help but feel that the place looked very similar to the border of Doxla. She supposed that made sense, though. If the Masters made this world, too, they likely gave it a similar edge.

"So, how should we do this?" asked Gare. "A world's a pretty big place to explore with just the three of us."

"The same way I explore everywhere out here," said Ev before opening up a series of portals to different points in the sky above. She didn't know how big the place was, but she felt it was a safe bet to assume it was similar in size to Doxla.

The portals open, she shined light through them to illuminate the very dead, very cold landscape behind each of them.

"What are you hoping to find?" asked Birdie.

"I don't know," said Ev. "A town, maybe? I'd like to at least see if the same thing that happened to Doxla happened here."

"Well," said Gare, "there weren't any bones waiting for us, so that's a little different."

Birdie looked toward Gare. "That might be because these people didn't try to escape before it happened."

Ev nodded in agreement. She then closed her portals and opened many more. The first batch had been too high up to make out any settlements. These new ones would be lower, but she'd need more to cover the same area.

"Let me know if you see any big cities," she said. "Be careful not to fall through."

The three of them went around peering through the makeshift windows. Ev spotted a few small villages, but she was looking for something bigger.

Gare was the first to find something.

"There's a place. It kind of looks like Ars Summis."

Ev and Birdie joined him, and Ev's jaw nearly dropped.

Birdie looked directly at Ev. It was obvious they were thinking the same thing.

Immediately, Ev opened her higher-elevation portals again. This time, she took a closer look at the shape of the land and waters.

"It can't be," said Ev in disbelief.

"What?" asked Gare. "What is it?"

"This is Doxla," replied Birdie.

"That's impossible," scoffed Gare. "We just came from Doxla. How can this be Doxla, too?"

"I don't know," said Ev, "but look."

She pointed at the various landmarks. "See? It's the Sea of Rezin. There's Tyranor's Domain. There's Loch Porifera."

"Which means that actually was Ars Summis," said Birdie.

Ev stood speechless for a moment, then dispelled all of her portals before opening the way to this Ars Summis. If there was anywhere that answers might be, that would be it.

On the other side, the streets were dark and abandoned as expected. At first glance, everything appeared identical to the Ars Summis of her world. As they explored, however, Ev couldn't help but notice subtle differences. The signs here were all wooden and painted, unlike the advanced displays of light back home. The lamp posts and benches were all significantly less ornate. At the center of the city, there were no Radiant Gardens or a Supremacy Plaza. There was, however, still the central tower of the Masters. At the top of Lumine Tower, every trace of the Masters' tools had been removed. The top room was simply an empty metal shell.

Gare shook his head in disbelief. "Can someone please tell me what the heck is going on?"

"I think it should be obvious," said Birdie, frowning. "We weren't the first."

"The first what?" asked Gare. "Doxla? But why? Why would the Masters make more than one Doxla?"

"If I had to guess," replied Birdie, "it was easier than making new worlds every time. The Masters only ever cared about becoming rich on prestige. Of course they'd go the route requiring the least effort possible."

"That's not it," said Ev, not looking at anyone in particular. "There's something else going on here."

"Like what?" asked Gare.

Ev didn't know, but she had every intention of finding out. Seeing that her Doxla wasn't the first, but only one of who knew how many — something just clicked inside of her.

Ev started searching for towns — any towns — and as soon as she found one, she hopped through.

A quick search revealed that the same fate had befallen this place as her Doxla. The inhabitants had all vanished without a trace, but the skeletal remains of livestock and other animals littered the ground; trees and buildings still stood, though long dead and with heavy disrepair respectively.

Ev moved on to another town. Then another. Everywhere she went, she found the same scene. Wanting to confirm that the same thing truly had happened here, she went back to her Doxla — to Roehelm, specifically — and indeed, only animals remained.

"Any ideas?" Birdie asked, standing close to Ev.

Ev stared out at the empty city. "They're taking them. The people — they're taking them."

"The Masters?" Gare asked. "Are you sure?"

Ev looked at Gare. "If they wanted to kill them, they would have. We saw what they did at the border, but they didn't do that. Not here. Not in the other Doxla. It's like they want us for something."

Gare processed his thoughts for a moment. "That's unsettling. I can't even imagine what the Masters would want with nepacs."

Honestly, neither could Ev, but she couldn't think of any other explanation for what they'd seen today.

Inside her head, the voice of Tallis interrupted her thoughts.

"Ev, where are you? Everyone else is back, and you won't believe what we found."

"Did you find Doxla?" Ev asked.

"Yes! But, something was off about it."

"Did it look older than it should have?"

"Uh, yes. How did you—?"

"How many did you find?" asked Ev.

"How many . . .?"

"How many Doxlas?"

Tallis went quiet for a moment. When he spoke again, his tone had changed. "We found one Doxla and two smaller worlds kind of like it. The rest of the locations all had solid barriers that we avoided. Why? How many Doxlas did you find?"

"We found two," Ev said. "An older one, and the one we used to live in."

Another bout of silence. "I think you should come back and tell us exactly what you found."

"Yeah," she replied. "We're on our way."

Ev looked back at Birdie and Gare. "Are you ready?"

Birdie nodded.

Gare picked up his ax and Marin's dolly. "Ready."

With that, Ev lifted her arm and opened the way for their return.

Chapter 7

"I don't care who you are," Evress stated to the furious Enforcer up in one of the chambers of Lumine Tower. "I made the rules absolutely clear, and you broke them. You're gone."

The Enforcer opened her mouth to protest, but Evress didn't give her the chance. In a flash, the now ex-Enforcer disappeared — banished from Doxla.

For almost three months she'd been dealing with this now. Her reshaping of the Enforcers was perhaps the only reason her friends and family still spoke with her, though she hadn't seen them in a while. The last time she'd visited them, things hadn't gone well with Jax, and with how busy she'd been, she hadn't worked up the nerve to go back again quite yet.

Evress sighed and turned to Crovos — the only Administrator-level Master that she actually trusted. Sylvra was an enigma who only cared about business, whereas Amethine was a heartless viper with no hesitancy about asserting her authority, but Crovos had been genuine with Evress from the start — at least as far as the others would allow him to be.

"You'd think by now they'd have learned that being part of AnAnCol doesn't protect them," Evress stated.

"Though I sympathize with the goals of AnAnCol, it is undeniable that its members often believe themselves untouchable, at least in my experience," responded Crovos.

"Just what are AnAnCol's goals, anyway?" Evress asked. "What do they have to do with Doxla?"

Crovos shook his head. "I wish I could give you answers, but that is something Sylvra wishes to tell you himself when he feels the time is right."

"Well, he's sure taking his time, isn't he?"

Crovos shifted uncomfortably. "For what it's worth, I believe he will provide you with your answers soon. In the meantime, perhaps we should continue with our lesson?"

Oh, right. She'd forgotten about that. When one of her new appointees had informed her of what that particular Enforcer had been up to, she'd seen red and completely forgotten about what she'd been doing prior.

"Oh, of course. Sorry about that. I just—"

Crovos waved his hand dismissively. "You have nothing to apologize for. It's honestly refreshing to see AnAnCol members being held to the same standards as everyone else. I wish this could have happened sooner, but I know that Sylvra would not have been able to defy them in the past."

"Really? Why not?" Evress asked.

Again, Crovos shook his head. "I am not privy to the details, but I know that he has slowly become more influential in AnAnCol. I believe he also has discovered some way of finding out information that other members of AnAnCol would prefer to keep secret, though any guess as to how would be but speculation. Anyway . . ." Crovos trailed off as he gestured toward the screen that he and Evress had been working on.

"Oh, right," said Evress, trying to remember where they'd been before she got distracted. "So, you said each point in the grid represents a line across the world, right? Then if the point is active, there is degradation. Is that correct?"

"Exactly," said Crovos. "With a three-dimensional grid, we can pinpoint and correct any new degradation that occurs immediately. The difficulty lies in maintaining the repair system itself. I've tried for centuries, but nothing works perfectly. The central problem is that any system we use to repair degradation can also degrade, and the technique I just described can fail if multiple points degrade simultaneously."

Evress thought for a bit. Her goal was to find a way to preserve Doxla for eternity — or at least close to it. What Crovos was talking about clearly couldn't work indefinitely, but maybe if she combined it with something else, it would be possible. She had an idea, though she was sure that Crovos would have already tried something so obvious.

"How do you restore damaged regions?" she asked. "I know you maintained the old Doxla up until you left. The world fell apart after that, so you must have some way of resetting things to a pristine state."

Crovos smirked, though his expression appeared somehow sad. "I know what you are thinking, child, but I am afraid that is not a solution. While we do have a blueprint of Doxla and a way to recreate parts of it — or even the entire world, when necessary — the blueprint is stored in Sylvra's mind. Sylvra must use that blueprint directly. There is no way for us to automate its usage to restore the world at regular intervals. This is not his choice, mind you. Even if we were to extract it, the blueprint would also degrade in the Cosmic Graveyard."

Evress sighed, but she wasn't surprised. She did find it interesting that the blueprint for Doxla was somehow kept in Sylvra's head, though she didn't see how that knowledge helped her.

"I guess if it was easy, you would have already figured it out," she remarked.

Crovos nodded solemnly, but gave her a reassuring smile. "Don't worry. With every iteration of the world, I have managed to improve my techniques. Now that I finally have a partner, perhaps we will soon see a Doxla that can last as long without any Masters as it does with them."

A small smile appeared on Evress's lips. Of all of the Masters, Crovos was the only one she felt actually cared about nepacs and Doxla as a whole. Sylvra, though he had so far stayed true to every promise he had made, she could not bring herself to trust. He was hiding something — that she was sure of. As for Amethine . . .

A derisive "Tch" met her ears from behind. Evress and Crovos both turned to face the scarlet-haired devil herself — somehow scowling and smiling contemptuously at the same time.

"You're *still* trying to teach this girl how to play with your toys? Really, now. If she is as good as Sylvra says, I'm sure she can figure it out on her own. You have more important work to do, Crovos."

Crovos puffed out his chest. "Leave us, Amethine. If you are so concerned about productivity, perhaps you should keep your nose to your own business."

Amethine sniffed as she lifted a hand to her chest. "Oh, Crovos, you should know I don't associate with children unless my job requires it. I am here because Sylvra desires a report on the girl, and he asked me to relay that to you."

A frown appeared on Crovos's face before he turned to Evress. "In that case, we should not keep him waiting. I—"

"Oh, no," interrupted Amethine, wagging her finger. "He only wants to speak with you, Crovos. Don't worry, I will keep the girl company until you get back."

Crovos's frown deepened, but he ultimately sighed and complied. "I will return shortly. In the meantime, please look at how repairs are carried out. Depending on the nature of the degradation, it can be rather complicated."

Crovos turned back to Amethine before leaving. "Let her work. I will inform Sylvra if you cause trouble for her."

With that, Crovos vanished, leaving Evress alone with the witch. Not once had she had even a decent experience with Amethine, and this time looked to be no exception as Amethine eyed her like a cat eyed a mouse.

"What's that look for?" Amethine asked. "You should be more gracious in the presence of your superiors."

"I'll keep that in mind for whenever I see one."

Amethine's eye twitched as she held her not-at-all pleasant smile on her face. She slowly approached Evress and ran her hand over Evress's console, completely shutting down what she was looking over.

"Do you want to get in trouble?" Evress asked. "Because I have no problem reporting you to Sylvra."

"Oh, yes, do that," replied Amethine, practically leaning over the console. "That's exactly what Sylvra wants you to do."

Amethine tapped several buttons and erased one of Evress's other projects.

"Hey!" Evress yelled, pushing Amethine off and having to hold herself back from decking her. "When I—"

"When you go crying to Sylvra, boo-hoo," said Amethine, rubbing one hand over her eye mockingly. Her expression then quickly turned to a venomous scowl. "Go ahead, child. Go cry to Sylvra so he can save you from the big bad lady and show you that he's your new best friend. You'll trust him more and he'll trust you more, and you'll be a nice happy family. That's what you want, isn't it?"

"What I want is to do my job without being harassed by a jealous old cow."

"Right. I'm so sure you do. I'm sure you aren't at all looking for a way to betray him after he left your world to die."

Amethine raised a pointed finger and drove her long nail into Evress's chest. Instinctively, Evress reached up to slap the hand away, but to her shock she found she suddenly couldn't move. The next thing she knew, Amethine had her pressed up against the wall — enveloped in some constrictive antherial field. Amethine had actually *attacked* her?

Furious, Evress tried to break free, but the more she struggled, the tighter the field became. Fury turned to concern, then to panic. She tried to tell Amethine to stop, but at that point she could hardly even breathe.

Amethine slammed her hand on the wall next to Ev's face as she hissed. "Do you think I haven't been watching you? Do you think I haven't noticed you poking around in systems you have no business touching? You're a spoiled brat who doesn't appreciate what's been handed to her on a silver platter. Crovos and I had to *work* for our position. We had to prove our loyalties. Yet here you are: a little girl who thinks she's special just because she can control a little bit of anther.

"Well, let me make one thing clear to you, child. Just because Sylvra is making you an Administrator doesn't mean you are my equal. You are a rat looking to bite the hand that feeds you, and the moment you even take one nibble, I will gladly crush you beneath my heel."

Amethine stood back and released Evress, who collapsed to the ground, choking.

Evress felt Amethine's hand grab her chin and force her head up to look Amethine in the eyes. "Do I make myself clear to you, Rat?"

Evress couldn't find the words to respond. She was trembling. From fear or rage, she couldn't tell, but thankfully, Amethine seemed satisfied with the situation.

She stood up and smiled haughtily down. "Good. Then remember. I *will* be watching you."

In a flash, Amethine was gone, leaving Evress to finally catch her breath. She felt tears coming to her eyes, but she refused to let herself actually cry. If Amethine had wanted to intimidate her, well, she had, but she'd also told Evress that Sylvra so far had every intention of following through with his promises. Even if she couldn't find a way to expose Sylvra to seitti authorities, the possibility of saving Doxla as an Administrator seemed more real every day.

If she was honest with herself, she was beginning to lean more towards that option anyway. She had no reason to believe other seitti would actually be able to stop Sylvra or even try to save Doxla from its doomed existence in the Cosmic Graveyard. She would, of course, keep her options open, but right now, it seemed like embracing her role as Master was truly the best course of action. If she could rise to the point of finally being able to put Amethine in her place, then that would be a nice cherry on top.

Back at her console, Evress spent the next fifty or so minutes trying her best to recreate the project Amethine had destroyed. Working on it a second time went much faster than the first — so much so that she'd essentially finished by the time Crovos returned.

He approached Evress jovially — a mood unusual for him. "Sylvra requests your presence, Evress. He has something important he'd like to discuss with you."

"Oh? What's that?" she asked, having mostly recovered from her encounter with Amethine.

"I believe it would be best for him to tell you," Crovos replied. "Do not worry. It is something I believe you will be pleased with."

With a slight smile, Evress nodded. "Alright. I'll see you later, then."

Evress opened up a portal to near the top of Lumine Tower where Sylvra always held his personal meetings.

Up in Sylvra's office — a small room with a single large desk and giant window behind it — Evress's heart sank as she saw Amethine standing off to one corner smiling a fake sweet smile that only she could manage.

Well, Evress wouldn't give her the satisfaction of her attention. Ignoring Amethine completely, Evress greeted Sylvra with the usual stoic demeanor.

"Crovos says you had something to tell me."

Sylvra smiled but remained seated. "Indeed I do. I have been most impressed with how quickly you dismantled and reformed our list of Enforcers. Though I cannot say I entirely approve of all of the changes you've implemented, you have certainly succeeded in the most important task of all — establishing confidence in the Masters among nepacs. Your name in particular has been whispered far and wide.

"Furthermore, Crovos has informed me that you have made rapid progress in understanding the theory behind much of what he works with. I also have noticed your aptitude in learning how to use the tools we have presented to you.

"Now, as a reward for your talent and effort," Sylvra said as he at last stood, "I would like to officially make you an Administrator."

Sylvra offered Evress his glowing hand. "Take my hand. You are ready."

Evress eyed the hand with suspicion but only hesitated for a moment. She stepped up to Sylvra's desk, reached for the hand, and grabbed it.

Immediately, a plethora of new antherial tools flowed into her, as did yet another enchantment.

Sylvra released his grip and smiled. "Congratulations. You are now not only impervious to harm, but to aging, starvation, thirst, and suffocation as well. You are truly a Master now, and a Master deserves a unique outfit that identifies them."

Sylvra motioned to Amethine, who manifested a suit of emerald green armor. The armor looked like it would fit Evress perfectly. It lacked a helmet, but it came with a matching green tiara fitted with a golden topaz in the center.

"You should try it on," Sylvra prompted. "I have already taken the liberty of updating your summon-armor tool to work with this new outfit."

After another look over the armor, Evress activated the tool. The tool lifted her an inch off the ground for a brief second as the armor vanished from its spot in the corner only to reappear wrapped around her body. Instinctively, Evress gave her self a once over. It was certainly more comfortable than the other armor had been. She didn't have a mirror on hand to see how she looked in it, but her first impression was that it did suit her better than that old black one.

"Yes, much better," stated Sylvra before he dismissed Amethine.

Amethine bowed her head to Sylvra, but glanced menacingly over towards Evress just as she vanished from the room.

"Now then, Master Evress, I have a special task for you. Consider it your final test before I grant you permission to access seitti systems beyond this world."

Evress's eyes opened wide. "Wait, what? You'll let me access seitti systems?"

"If you complete this task, I will grant you *limited* access," Sylvra stated, sitting down once more. "I want you to see the world of the seitti. I want you to see what they are capable of and what they have done. I will, however, limit the range of your investigations and will not allow you to establish any sort of contact with beings outside of Doxla. Perhaps one day that restriction will be lifted, but that day will not be today."

Evress relaxed her shoulders. Of course. She really should have known better than to think he'd trust her with something like that.

"What do you want me to do?"

Sylvra smiled. "I want you to maintain the status quo. As we speak, a group of Divine are meeting with a clan of immortals in an attempt to broker peace. This is unacceptable. Go to Loch Porifera and banish the guilty Divine. Give them three years' banishment. Do not give them a chance to speak. Announce that they were reported by Oakman as soon as you arrive. If Oakman shows any sign of remorse for reporting them, banish him as well. Before you send them away, accuse the guilty ones of trying to gain power with an alliance. As for the immortals, learn where they come from and report that to me. If any have learned of what lies beyond this world, erase them permanently. For the remainder, I will announce a quest for other Divine to destroy their villages. When they revive, they will not seek peace again."

Evress felt her muscles tense as Sylvra spoke. It took a conscious effort not to let her hands ball into fists.

"Let me see if I understand," she said while trying to keep her voice level. "You want me not only to stop people who are actively trying to make the world a better place, but make future conflict even more likely?"

"If that is how you choose to see it, then yes."

"And how exactly am I supposed to see it, if not that?"

Sylvra turned in his chair to look out the window. "There is an understood balance in this world. The conflict that exists between mortals and immortals is kept in check by the Divine. If this balance is disrupted, there is a very real chance that the entire world will fall into chaos."

Evress scoffed. "Do you honestly believe what you're telling me? Do you really think that making peace can bring war?"

Sylvra turned back to Evress. "I know it can, but my beliefs are irrelevant. You have been given a task to carry out. Will you do it?"

Evress frowned, then sighed. She didn't have to answer. They both knew that she didn't have a choice.

* * * *

Deep beneath the surface of Loch Porifera, Evress stepped carefully along the wet, spongy cavern floor. The tunnels were ankle-deep in water with deeper pools scattered throughout. Wherever she stepped, the floor compressed several inches, making movement difficult. The only light in the tunnels stemmed from skull-sized, glowing bulbs protruding from the sides of the tunnel walls, but that was plenty sufficient for her. With her enchantments, darkness was no longer an obstacle for her. The constant drip-dripping from the ceiling and the naturally sound-absorbent walls, however, made it impossible for her to hear the voices of the people who met less than one hundred yards away from her at the end of the tunnel. She hadn't teleported directly to the meeting, choosing instead to approach from the side so that she could at least eavesdrop on the conversation before making her move. She knew it wouldn't happen, but a part of her desperately hoped that perhaps these Divine really were trying to ally with the immortals to make a power grab.

From what her tools told her, one of the Divine possessed low-level magic-sensing, so Evress activated both an invisibility and magic-cloaking enchantment before she got too close. As she approached the edge of their cavern, she moved more slowly so as not to disturb the water too much.

There, Evress identified Oakman — the guy who had allegedly reported this gathering to Sylvra, and took note of how many others were present. She counted a total of six Divine and nine immortals — four of whom were winged water imps that stood about four feet tall; the rest were scaly, almost fish-like humanoids called pisceans. The pisceans possessed pointy teeth, webbed feet and hands, and an overly bulky upper chest area, as well as a spiny dorsal fin running down each of their backs. It was one of the pisceans who spoke as Evress approached.

"You still do not offer us assurances," the female piscean hissed at one of the Divine. "What you ask makes us vulnerable. We will not expose ourselves to even more slaughter."

The man, whose name above his head read "Lance," responded. "I know it's risky, but if you want the cycle to end, you have to try something new. It will take years, and it won't be without incident, but just look at the gobbols. They are immortals that have made peace with humans, for the most part."

"You do not understand, Divine," returned the piscean. "We were made what we are. We were assigned roles to play long ago, and humans see those roles as holy decrees. Gobbols were decreed as neutral, but we as monsters. None will ever see past this."

"You're wrong," said a female Divine named Roxy. "We aren't supposed to say anything about where we come from, but I assure you, your appearances mean nothing to Divine. The only reason so many side with mortals is because you are stronger than them, and you can't die. We have to protect them because they could die out entirely if we didn't. If you show Divine that you want this war to end, well, I can't promise they will all support you, but many will."

The other Divine all nodded.

A second piscean looked to the first. "Perhaps an attempt would be desirable. What more can we lose but a single year of endless strife?"

The imps murmured from behind the others, seemingly in agreement.

The first piscean looked from Roxy back to Lance. "Very well. We shall speak with our clans of this. We will attempt to aid Divine who come here, so long as they do not attack us."

Lance nodded. "And we will spread the word. You will see. This is just the beginning of peace in Doxla."

The Divine extended his hand, and Evress knew she had to act. She hated it. She hated removing the invisibility enchantment. She hated stepping loudly through the water toward them. She hated the look of surprise the Divine gave her — they recognizing her as a Master due to the enchantment Sylvra had placed on her. After spending years brokering peace between humans and immortals back in her Doxla, she now had to brutally break apart the seeds of that very same peace.

"Y-you, you're a Master," stammered Lance, and the immortals present all backed away the moment the words left his mouth. "Why are you—?"

The one called Oakman splashed away from the others and addressed her. "Master Evress! I'm the one who sent the message to Sylvra."

The other Divine all spun toward Oakman. "You did what? Why?"

Oakman faced his comrades. "You know the rules of this place. We are to protect the humans, and that is all! We were expressly told not to make alliances with immortals."

One of the imps in the back flitted up into the air. "Betrayal!" he shouted as he lodged a spear of water at Oakman.

Oakman took the hit and clutched the wound at his side.

"No! Wait!" Roxy shouted as she jumped between them, arms outstretched. She looked directly at Evress. "Please listen, we aren't here to make an alliance, we just—"

"Shut up," Evress muttered, her throat tight.

Roxy looked at her in confusion. "What did—?"

"I said 'shut up'!" Evress shouted.

The woman took a step back, now frightened. "Please, just listen. We—"

"I know why you're here," said Evress.

Moisture ran down her cheeks. Whether from the dripping ceiling or her own tears, she couldn't tell. She didn't care. It had been a mistake to listen in. She should have just gotten it over with as soon as possible like Sylvra had told her to. At least then this wouldn't have been so painful.

Standing as tall as she was able, Evress did her best to steady her voice. "You seek an alliance with immortals to gain an advantage over other Divine."

"No! We—"

"For that, you are hereby banished from Doxla. Do not return if you intend to repeat your offense."

"You can't—!" Lance shouted, but he didn't get to say anymore.

With a bright flash, he and all of the Divine save for Oakman vanished without a trace.

Evress then turned to the immortals. To her surprise, they stood their ground.

The lead piscean hissed at her. "And what will you do to us? Break our bodies? Take away our immortality and end our suffering?"

"Go home," Evress told her. She just wanted this to be over.

The piscean eyed her suspiciously. "You jest poorly. Is that what you seek? To torment us with words before taking away our breaths?"

"My task was to banish the Divine. Now, please go. I need to speak with this one." Evress turned her head toward Oakman, who looked nervous at being called out.

The immortals still stood their ground. "Or perhaps we should remain, instead. It is not every day we have the opportunity to spit upon the whims of a Master."

Evress spun on them. "I said *GO!*" she shouted, activating a powerful water spell that blasted them all into the tunnel at the far end of the cavern.

Before they were out of sight, Evress used a spell that Birdie had taught her long ago for hunting monsters. Upon an imp and piscean each, she placed a tracking enchantment. It could last for days and across many miles and would almost certainly give Sylvra the location of where they lived.

She then turned her attention back to Oakman and approached him.

Upon seeing her face, Oakman was clearly nervous. "You see? I told you they were breaking the rules."

"I'm well aware," replied Evress as she stared at the man. "What I want to know is why. Why did you report them?"

Oakman face became one of confusion. "Isn't that your rule? We are supposed to report anyone disturbing the balance of the world."

"Of course you are. After all, isn't that how all worlds are supposed to be? Managed by seitti — making sure there's always enough conflict to keep things interesting."

Oakman looked like he didn't know how to respond. "Um, yes? I mean, if a world is boring, there's no point to it, is there?"

If looks could kill, Oakman would have dropped dead on the spot. Without saying a word, Evress teleported to the surface of the lake — appearing atop a large spongy hill near its center. Sylvra had told her not to banish Oakman, but Sylvra hadn't said anything about making sure the Divine got out of there safely. Using the tools Sylvra had given her, she located Oakman's position from afar and cast a monster-lure enchantment upon him.

Evress didn't bother to wait and see what happened to Oakman. She needed to get back to Sylvra so she could give him the information he wanted and put this awful task behind her. Before she could return, however, Crovos suddenly appeared beside her.

Evress refused to look at him. "What? Did you come to make sure I did it?"

Crovos answered quietly. "No. I know that you did."

"Then why are you here?"

Crovos looked out over the lake before answering. "Because I still remember the first time Sylvra had me do the same thing. I couldn't understand why he wanted me to do it. I couldn't understand his goals, but I do now. I wish he would have explained it to me, but I know why he didn't. He wanted to test me, just as he is testing you."

"Testing me for what?" Evress rounded on Crovos. "To see if I'll hurt people just because he wants me to? To see if I'll become as big of a monster as he is? Well, guess what? I won't. I'm only doing this because I don't have a choice. It's the only way I can make sure this Doxla survives after he's done with it. Once I do that, I'm done. I won't serve him anymore, and you can tell him that."

"Doxla won't survive, Evress," Crovos said, looking sadly into her eyes.

"W-what? No. He told me I could save Doxla. He said I could find a way. He said we can make a system to keep it alive!"

"You can't. You've seen it in our lessons. It's not possible for a world to survive in the Cosmic Graveyard indefinitely. Unless one of us remains here to maintain it, the best we can do is slow its decay so that fewer will die before Doxla's purpose is achieved. That is what he wants you to help me do."

Evress stared at Crovos in disbelief. She'd been lied to, and he'd known it all along. She'd served as Sylvra's puppet, and for what?

"I'm sorry that I said nothing sooner," Crovos continued. "It required all the convincing I could manage to persuade Sylvra to let me tell you now, but I don't want you to feel the same disappointment that I felt when I first learned the truth."

Evress turned away from Crovos, her teeth clenched. She couldn't believe she'd fallen for it. She'd known she couldn't trust Sylvra, yet she had anyway. Now she was helping him hurt this Doxla just as much as he'd hurt hers. Jax had been right. It had all been a waste, and in her fervor to try and make things better, she hadn't even been looking for a way to actually defeat Sylvra.

Crovos attempted to rest his hand on Evress's shoulder, but she jerked away. He spoke to her nonetheless. "You may not believe me, but I know the pain you feel. I know the anguish, the frustration, the betrayal, but I also know what lies beyond that."

Evress turned her head to meet Crovos's eyes.

"As difficult as it may be to imagine, all of this is to serve a higher purpose. Every world Sylvra has created was made with a single goal in mind. He does not take joy in people's suffering. It is but a necessary evil to ultimately make the realm we exist in a better place."

"A better place?" Evress nearly spit. "How is making people suffer making things a better place? How is turning people into immortals just to be vilified making the world a better place!"

"It is not my place to say," Crovos answered. "I only want you to be aware that Sylvra does have his reasons. If you wish to know them as well, you must ask him yourself."

Evress narrowed her eyes. "Oh, I will. Believe me, I will."

Chapter 8

Atop the tallest tower in the mole city, which the survivors had decided to name Steam Town, Ev held a small apple in her hand as she leaned against a thin railing and watched the people milling about down below. Three months had passed since they'd first found this place, and most were adjusting to the situation surprisingly well. Some went to and from their jobs, some watched the children, some carried food or water back to their homes, and many of them simply mingled or meandered about aimlessly. Expedition groups had even managed to rescue some of the surviving animals from Doxla. Most were being kept for their meat, but a few were kept as pets. Thanks to the ability to duplicate things, food was thankfully no longer an issue. As far as most were concerned, the biggest problem was the growing group of outspoken individuals who insisted on returning to Doxla to resume their lives there. While Ev doubted the Masters would return to Doxla yet again, she still didn't want to chance it, and neither did most from what she could tell. This world they could live in, perhaps indefinitely. There was just one thing on her mind that troubled her.

The sound of footsteps climbing the stairs alerted her to Jax's approach. She turned to meet him and forced a smile.

"Hi, Jax, thanks for coming."

Jax was slightly out of breath from the long climb. "Is there a reason you wanted to talk all the way up here? You know there are plenty of other places we could speak in private, right?"

"Yeah, I know," said Ev, turning back to the city, "but just look out there. Life is completely different, but people are adjusting to it."

"Maybe some of them are," said Jax, "but most are just scared and confused. A lot of them don't have anything to do, and it's driving them crazy."

"I know," said Ev again, "but we're still adapting. I think with time, we can make this our new home."

"Come on, Ev," Jax said impatiently. "What's the real reason you wanted to talk to me, and why did you say you didn't want Birdie or Umber to find out?"

Ev gripped the apple tightly and glanced at it with her eyes. Turning to Jax, she tossed the apple toward him.

He caught it, looking confused.

"What are you holding?" she asked him.

"Uh, an apple?" he asked, examining it.

Ev suppressed a sigh. "Yes, it's an apple, but where did it come from?"

Jax made a face that said he was getting impatient. "What does—?"

"Where does it come from, Jax?"

"I dunno. A tree? Ev, just tell me what's going on."

Ev shook her head. "That's what I'm trying to figure out."

"Uh-huh," said Jax, holding the apple up, "and an apple helps, how?"

"Please just answer my questions, Jax," Ev said. "I don't want to say what I think is going on until I'm sure of it."

Jax frowned, but gestured for her to continue.

"When we escaped from Doxla, we ran through the a tear in the boundary to the Cosmic Graveyard. You were behind Birdie and me, right? What did you see when we ran through?"

"There was a lot going on, Ev. Could you be more specific?"

Ev tried her best to remain stoic as she nodded. "Did you see Birdie and me vanish when we ran through, like we teleported. Did you see anyone vanish?"

"Uh, no? I saw you run through. It was a portal, right? That's kind of how portals work."

Ev eyed the apple in Jax's hand. That was the answer she'd expected. It was also the answer she'd hoped he wouldn't give. After hearing that, there was really only one conclusion.

Jax crossed his arms. "Are you going to tell me what's going on, yet?"

Ev turned away from him and looked back down at the people in the city. She couldn't tell Jax what had happened. She couldn't tell anyone. She wasn't sure how they'd react. She wasn't even sure how *she* should react. Instead, she gave the best answer she could — something she knew must be true, but she withheld the part she had to keep to herself.

"Syrus didn't send everyone here," she said. "He left people. He left them so the Masters would find them and think they were the only ones who escaped. Everyone here — he saved them just so we'd try and finish his work. He wants us to defeat the Masters. That's the only reason we exist."

"That's ridiculous," said Jax. "I mean, okay, maybe some people got left behind. I'll even buy that Syrus might have left them on purpose, but do you honestly think he did it only so we'd be able to fight the Masters? I think he would have said something instead of just leaving us in the middle of nowhere with nothing to go on."

"Would he have? He didn't even tell us he'd do that. He didn't want us to know. He wanted us to figure it out. I just don't understand why he saved so many of us. He must have wanted us to teach everyone how to be anthermancers."

"Or," said Jax, "hear me out, here. Maybe he just wanted us to do exactly what you just said and survive."

Ev looked back at Jax. Of course he'd think that.

Jax continued. "I know he hated the Masters and wanted to bring them down, but he also cared about what happened to Doxla. Maybe he did hope that we would try again to beat the Masters, but even I know that wasn't his only goal. Come on, Ev. What's got you thinking like this? If it's because we survived and others didn't, then you need to snap out of it. Of course not everyone made it. We knew that would happen before Syrus ever pushed that button."

"Yeah," said Ev, knowing this conversation couldn't go any further. "You're right. I think it's just the stress. Sorry for worrying so much."

"Hey, it's okay," replied Jax, tossing the apple back to her. "We're all stressed, but you don't need to keep it bottled up. Take it easy for a while. Birdie and I can take care of those idiots trying to get people to go back to Doxla."

"Yeah, thanks," said Ev, looking again at the apple in her hand. "I appreciate it."

Jax smiled and headed back down the stairs. Once he was gone, Ev walked to the far side of the platform where a small box waited for her. She'd collected it from Doxla on one of her return trips. Opening up the box, she peered down at another apple she'd left there a week ago.

Ev gripped the apple already in hand tightly as she closed her eyes in a grimace. Jax had answered incorrectly. This one hadn't come from a farm. It hadn't even come from Doxla. She knew what Syrus had done. She knew why he'd done it. She knew that he'd created her — an empty shell with no point to her existence other than to finish what he'd started.

And she knew that she would never forgive him for it.

* * * *

A few days after her talk with Jax atop the tower, Ev found herself pulled into a meeting to discuss the future of their little colonies. They had a nice-sized room specifically for these meetings, but they didn't usually have this many people in there at once. Jax, Tallis, and Helcant were at the center of the discussion, literally — as they were standing closest to the middle of the room. Gare and Umber both stood against the wall by the door — Gare with his arms crossed and Umber mimicking him. Nictis stood quietly in the back of the room near Lylia, the latter of whom was busy filing her nails. Ev stayed off to the side near Birdie where they kept to themselves while the others spoke.

"Perhaps some people could move to one of the other Doxlas," Tallis suggested. "I don't think the Masters are likely to go check on any of them."

"You know," replied Gare. "That's not a bad idea. Folks could grab their stuff from home and rebuild. I doubt they'd complain much about that."

Jax huffed and looked back at Gare. "You clearly haven't been talking to them much, if that's what you think."

"Fools, they all are," said Nictis. "Reckless and thoughtless, they endanger themselves and all of us with their desires."

Lylia looked up from what she was doing. "Why do we not just destroy Doxla? None can return if there is nothing to return to. We could have a bonfire!"

Jax looked mortified at the suggestion, but Nictis supported the thought.

"Agreed," she said. "These children must learn the seriousness of our predicament. Let us act now, before they grow more emboldened."

"You can't be serious," said Jax.

"I do not jest," replied Nictis, staring at him.

"Jax is right," said Birdie, speaking for the first time since the meeting started. "The Masters didn't destroy Doxla. If they do come back and see it gone, they'll know we're out here somewhere. It wouldn't be much better than trying to make it our home again."

Tallis chimed in again. "I still say another Doxla is our best bet of appeasing them. I think what a lot of them don't understand is that even if they return, the world isn't the same anymore. There is no sky, no moon, no stars. Maybe if they see that, we can convince them that a different Doxla isn't any worse than the one we came from."

"Again," said Jax, "you aren't going to convince them. What we need is to make sure all the anthermancers understand that this is a bad idea. No one can go there without an anthermancer's help."

Helcant almost shouted. "You are wrong! What we must do is remove the danger altogether! If the Masters are gone, we will be free to do as we please."

"Uh-huh, great idea," said Jax. "And how exactly do you propose we do that?"

Helcant grinned. "Three Doxlas have we seen thus far. Several worlds with barriers have we seen as well. Surely one such hidden world must be another Doxla. The Masters will be there. An attack from us would be unexpected."

"Are you insane?" replied Jax. "We wouldn't stand a chance."

Helcant chuckled and manifested a swirling shimmer in his hand. "Do not forget, Brother of Miss Ev, that we now control the very power that they possess."

Jax's eye twitched at that remark. "Maybe you've forgotten just what the Masters are. They are seitti. It's impossible to kill them. Besides, there's no way for us to break through one of those barriers without them finding out, and we don't even know if any of those other worlds actually *are* another Doxla. We could be throwing away our lives for nothing."

Helcant's tail twitched as he stared down Jax. Jax returned the stare with neither of them blinking.

The standoff ended when Tallis spoke up. "Actually, I think I might know a way around that last bit."

All eyes turned to Tallis, who shifted nervously.

"I, uh, I might have done some work on my own—"

"We helped, too!" Lylia chimed.

Tallis blushed. "Okay, we might have done some work together. We think we've figured out a way to peek inside the systems of the other worlds without being detected. If it works, we can see if the systems are the same as the Doxla that we knew. That's really all we'd be able to see, but I think it would be enough to go on."

Jax narrowed his eyes. "Uh-huh. And what if it doesn't work?"

Tallis answered, "Well, we'd know right away if it didn't and could pull back. It's not a big disruption, and would probably look like a natural case of degradation, if even that."

Jax crossed his arms and shook his head. "I don't know. I don't like it. Besides, we still don't have any way to deal with the Masters."

"Of course we do!" exclaimed Helcant. "We do as Syrus did. If the Masters are there, their systems will be fully connected. We need only reach their main terminal, and we can bring swift justice upon them."

"And risk everything even trying to do that," Jax added, clearly irritated. "I'm sorry, but look around you. We have everything we need here. What we need to do is focus on making sure no one does anything that might attract the attention of the Masters. Besides, didn't Syrus say that the whole reason the Masters use those terminals in their worlds is to hide their activities from other seitti? Maybe if we use enough anther out here, we can attract the attention of other seitti that way."

"Or maybe we'll just attract the Masters," said Gare. He looked at Jax apologetically and shrugged. "Sorry, bud, but I gotta agree with Tallis and Helcant. I'm not saying we should make a move right away, but you gotta admit, it does feel like our days our numbered out here."

Jax shook his head, then sighed loudly. "Alright, you know what? Let's take a vote. This isn't what we were supposed to discuss, but it looks like that's where we are. So, everyone against risking everything to take on the Masters, speak up. I'm against it."

"As am I," stated Nictis. "Such a battle would invite destruction."

Birdie agreed. "We still haven't even finished settling in to life out in the Graveyard. We should hold off on doing anything reckless until we're more prepared."

Jax looked around, waiting for someone else to agree with him. At last, his eyes landed on Ev, but she didn't give him the agreement he sought.

"Alright," he said, "looks like there's just three against it. I guess everyone else thinks we should, then."

"Of course we do!" exclaimed Helcant.

Tallis rubbed his shoulder. "Actually, I don't. While I think we should at least check it out, I feel like this isn't something we should decide on our own."

Gare grunted. "Yeah, I suppose that's a good point. I think we should do it, but maybe not until we've talked to the other groups."

At that, Ev finally couldn't hold her peace any longer. "What's the point?"

Everyone looked at her. She glared back. "Who cares what other people say? It doesn't matter. None of this matters. If we don't stop the Masters, then everything we've been through was pointless. Our lives in the Cosmic Graveyard would be meaningless. We'd grow old, we'd die, we'd disappear forever, leaving nothing behind. Any children born would have the same fate — a meaningless existence that would eventually end when the Masters one day realize they didn't find all of us."

Ev could feel Birdie's eyes on her, but she pretended not to notice.

Umber nodded in response to Ev's speech. "I concur. A life without purpose is not one worth living. I can imagine no greater purpose than one that would be felt even by the overseers of reality itself."

Jax growled, clearly frustrated. "Look, I get that you want to do this, but Tallis is right. We shouldn't—"

Ev cut him off. "How many people have already died out here, Jax?"

Jax paused. He clearly hadn't expected that question.

Ev turned to Lylia before he could respond. "What do you think we should do?"

Lylia shrugged. "We believe an attempt would be fun."

Ev turned back to Jax. "There you go. You wanted a vote. You got a vote. Five for and four against. If you want to talk to the other group leaders before we launch an assault, go for it, but I'm going to check out those barriers."

"Oh, no you aren't," said Jax. "It was not 'five for,' and you can't go off on your own to do something that could get us all killed, regardless."

"I'm not going on my own. Tallis or Lylia will come with me."

Tallis put up his hands. "Don't look at me. I'm not getting involved in this."

Lylia hopped out of her coiled position and slid over. "We will go. We are curious as to the nature of these hidden worlds."

"No one is going anywhere," Jax said loudly, stepping between Lylia and Ev.

Birdie then stepped between Ev and Jax. "Jax, I've got this."

Birdie then proceeded to grab Ev by the arm and tug just hard enough to let Ev know she was serious about Ev needing to follow. Ev begrudgingly obliged, but only because she knew that dealing with this now would be easier than later.

Once they were out of the room and out of earshot, Birdie instructed Ev to make a portal to the forest at the outskirts of town.

"Why?" Ev asked.

"Because it's obvious that you know something that you don't want anybody else to know. If we go to the woods, then you won't have to worry about anyone overhearing."

Ev sighed, then opened the portal. On the other side waited a crystal-clear lake surrounded by a forest of purplish brambles; the brambles reached up and over the entire area forming a spiked canopy. At the center of the lake was a small temple built atop a small island. A white stone pathway stretched between the island and the shore, though it was presently submerged several feet beneath the water.

It only took a moment for Birdie to realize where they were. "This isn't near town. Did you just take us to the Throne of Ascendance?"

Ev closed the portal and sat on the shore near the pathway. She picked up a small stone and skipped it across the water as she waited for Birdie to say her piece.

Birdie sighed, then sat down as well next to Ev. "Ev, talk to me. You've been acting strange ever since we found Doxla. What did you learn, and why did you not want Jax to tell me you talked to him?"

Ev frowned and threw another stone, harder this time. Of course that idiot wouldn't be able to keep quiet.

"It's just that Syrus sacrificed people so we could get away, is all," Ev said.

"Mm, nah-ah. Try again," said Birdie as she pointed to her temple. "Master of perception here, remember? You'll have to try harder than that to fool me."

Ev shook her head, stood up, and walked further down the shore.

"Ev!" Birdie shouted.

"What?" Ev spun back around. "What do you want from me? Can't you just trust that if I don't want to say something, I have a good reason for it?"

Birdie rubbed her forehead, and Ev knew that she wasn't going to get out of this that easily.

"You know that goes both ways, right?" said Birdie. "You say you want me to trust you, but you can't trust me? I'm sorry, but I don't want to hear it. Remember my othermind and how you told me 'no secrets' after finding out about that?"

Ev turned away from Birdie. Yes, she remembered. She knew she was being a hypocrite, but she just couldn't bring herself to tell Birdie. If she said she was upset because she'd found out that Syrus had created her artificially, how would that make Birdie feel?

Birdie continued speaking. "Now, considering what you asked Jax the other day, I'm guessing this has something to do with those bodies we saw outside of Doxla's border."

Damn it, Jax. Why couldn't you have kept your mouth shut?

"So, what did Syrus do that's so bad? I thought I'd figured it out, but if you're this upset, I'm guessing I must have missed something."

Ev lifted up her head at that and looked back at Birdie, genuinely curious. "What do you think happened?"

Birdie lifted her hands up in a dramatic shrug. "Well, I *thought* Syrus must have made a bunch of decoys of us for the Masters to find.”

“Oh,” said Ev, hoping for a way out. “Yes, that’s basically what I thought.”

“Basically isn’t exactly. How is your idea different?” Birdie pressed.

“It’s really not important.”

“Ev,” said Birdie, hand on her hip. “We can go back and forth for a year. Just spit it out, please.”

“Alright, fine!” Ev yelled, picking up another rock and holding it in front of her. “You want to know what happened? *This* happened!”

Ev held out her other hand and produced a copy of the original rock within it. She then threw the original to the ground, shattering it.

Realization set in on Birdie’s face. “I see.”

Tears welled up in Ev’s eyes as she finally let her emotions come to the surface. “‘I see? *I see*’? How can you be so calm? We aren’t even the real Ev and Birdie. We’re just copies! He made us!”

Birdie sighed, then looked over sympathetically. Silently, she approached Ev and reached out to her. “Give me your hand.”

Ev looked at Birdie’s hand for a moment before obliging.

Birdie took Ev’s hand and gripped it tightly as she looked Ev in the eyes. “Well?”

“Well, what?” asked Ev.

Birdie tilted her head. “Can you feel my hand in yours?”

Ev sighed and tried to pull her hand away, but Birdie held on tighter. “You didn’t answer my question.”

“Of course I can,” said Ev.

“Good. I feel yours, too. You seem pretty real to me.”

Ev pulled her hand away again, and this time Birdie let her.

“That’s not what I mean, and you know it,” she said, using a sleeve to wipe the wet from her cheek.

“You mean you’re worried about being created by Syrus and not being the Ev born in Doxla.”

Ev shook her head, crossing her arms across her chest. She felt awful about the words about to leave her mouth, but she had to say them. Birdie had pushed her to this.

“We’re just tools he created.”

“That’s nothing new for me,” Birdie stated.

Ev pulled her arms tighter. “I know, but that’s different.”

“How?”

Ev looked up at Birdie. "He didn't create you — the original you, I mean — he didn't create you completely. The Masters made the shade part of you. You still had a soul."

"Did I?"

"I mean, of course you did. You . . ."

Ev trailed off as Birdie smiled sadly and shook her head. "You know, I used to think that, too. I believed that up until the day I defeated Lux Rosa. She was right when she said I was soulless, but not because Syrus created me. When I walked through Ars Summis that first time, I finally realized just what kind of creatures the Masters are. I didn't really have time to think about it then, but I've thought about it plenty since.

"Tell me, from everything you know about the Masters, do you honestly think they would go through the trouble of creating people with souls? Assuming that such a thing even exists, I don't. Not anymore."

Ev opened her mouth to say something, but she stopped herself. She'd never even considered that possibility. Hearing Birdie say it out loud, it made sense — a horrible, twisted kind of sense.

Birdie waited for a minute before she added, "Even if they did give us souls, do you feel any different now? Maybe we aren't actually the copies. Maybe we are, and Syrus gave us new souls as well.

Ev looked down and turned away from Birdie. She shook her head and started walking back toward the path across the lake. "No. Maybe. No. We are the copies. We appeared far away from Doxla — coming out of portals that we never entered."

Birdie followed behind and reached for Ev's shoulder.

Ev jerked away. "Don't. Please."

Birdie backed away.

"I'm sorry," said Ev. "I just—" she laughed sadly. "Oh, what am I saying? You felt the same way before, didn't you?"

"I did," said Birdie, "but then I realized it doesn't matter. The people I care about are here with me now. If I did ever die, then I'd be leaving them behind anyway. Sure, it's nice to think there's something more waiting for me, but it's this life that matters to me, not some other one that may or may not come. Even if I'm wrong, and we do — or at least did — have souls, that doesn't change that."

Ev processed that for a moment, then nodded. After thinking on it further, she turned back to Birdie and hugged her tightly — an embrace which Birdie returned.

"Thanks," she said after letting go. "I think I just need more time, is all. But, I also think I needed that."

Birdie smiled. "Don't worry. Believe me, I understand." She looked over at the temple in the middle of the lake. "So, is there a reason you wanted to come here?"

Ev sniffed and wiped her eyes again. "Yeah. I wanted to see if we can figure out how Divine become Radiants. Since this is where it happens, I think its our best shot."

"I'm guessing this means you still plan on breaking into a new Doxla."

"If one exists, yes," said Ev as she turned her attention to the submerged bridge.

While she could have simply made a portal to the other side, Ev was curious as to whether the Masters had actually destroyed the underlying systems governing Doxla or if they had only shut them down.

Using a bit of anther, she attempted to induce degradation and was both surprised and relieved to see a small shimmer appear before her.

The Masters truly were confident that no one remained in the Cosmic Graveyard. Either that, or they wanted to limit their own usage of raw anther as much as possible to reduce the likelihood of drawing attention to themselves. Either way, this was exactly what Ev wanted to see.

Reaching inside the shimmer, Ev felt around for a mechanism that would control the bridge. The systems were indeed more-or-less still there, but she could tell they'd been damaged. Still, she was familiar enough with the whole thing to figure out how things should be, so it only took a moment to find the bridge mechanism. She had to power the mechanism with her own anther, but she soon had the bridge lifted up out of the water.

"You know, you really are good at that stuff," remarked Birdie.

A small smile crept onto Ev's lips, admittedly proud of herself for getting the bridge working so quickly. "Well, I have been practicing for ten years now."

Across the bridge waited the temple. The great stone doors were shut tight, but another foray into Ev's artificial degradation pushed them open. Her hopes of finding how to mark an individual as a Radiant were now quite high.

Inside, the temple was constructed of pearly white stone. Marble pillars stretched up to the ceiling, and enormous stained glass windows lined the walls. At the center of the temple waited the Throne of Ascendance. Divine who sat there were granted the title of Radiant, but only if they had passed the requisite trials beforehand.

"Odd choice of decoration," Ev remarked, looking at the windows.

They all portrayed various Radiants with wings extended. While that made sense, she didn't understand why they had such windows in a temple blocked off from the sun.

As if she could read Ev's mind, Birdie offered, "The area around the temple is usually magically illuminated. It probably looked better before the world ended."

"Ah," said Ev before walking the rest of the way to the throne in silence.

There, she once again reached behind the surface of the world to tug at the strings the Masters had put in place to give the illusion of magic and mystery for the Divine. At first, it seemed like the process of making a Divine become Radiant was a rather intensive one. The throne had all sorts of checks built into it to ensure that hopeful Divine had indeed earned the right to ascend. However, after digging deeper, Ev found a single mechanism that would mark anyone found worthy with what she assumed was the status of Radiance. It took a bit longer to be sure that indeed was the case, but after about half an hour, Ev removed her hand from the degradation and smiled at Birdie.

"Found it."

"Great," said Birdie. "So, what does that mean?"

"It means that if we find another Doxla, I should be able to make us all Radiants without us actually becoming Divine, and I can combine that with Lux Rosa's techniques to maximize our strength and abilities. We'll be able to fight without drawing attention to ourselves like we would if we used anther, and the Masters won't even be able to track us. I'll have to work fast once we're there, but I have a plan."

Birdie crossed her arms and tilted her head. "You know, Ev, you don't have to do this. We really can just live in the Cosmic Graveyard. We can train more anthermancers. We could probably even have better lives than we ever did in Doxla."

Ev met eyes with Birdie. "Maybe some people can, but I can't. Umber told me he shouldn't be alive. He should have died with Doxla, and because he didn't, he's willing to lay down his life in pursuit of his purpose.

"Now that I know what Syrus did, I know that's true for all of us. None of us should be alive. The only reason we are is because Syrus wanted us to stop the Masters. Even if I can't forgive him for hiding that from us, I will do everything I can to at least make sure what happened to us never happens to anyone again. So many families have been broken, so many lives ruined. So many people are hurt and scared, and this isn't even the first time this has happened. The Masters have to be stopped, no matter what."

Birdie sighed. "Ev, I know how you feel, and I know that Syrus hoped we would find a way to contact seitti civilization, but that doesn't mean he wanted us to risk everything to fight the Masters. I'm sure he'd be happy if he knew that we'd found another way to survive on our own, even if we did end up living the rest of our lives in the Graveyard."

"Maybe he would be happy, but I wouldn't. I have to do this, Birdie. Please understand."

Birdie sighed again, looking defeated. "Okay. If you're sure this is what you want, then I'll support you."

"Really?" said Ev, her heart lifted by those words.

Birdie nodded. "I just hope you know what you're doing. Last time didn't exactly work out so well for us."

"Things will be different this time. The Masters will likely still be in the new Doxla, so they'll have more systems connected to the seitti realm, and they definitely won't expect us. We can do this."

"If you say so," Birdie said. "I trust you, Ev."

"Thank you," said Ev, "but Birdie? Please don't tell anyone else about what Syrus did."

"Don't worry. My lips are sealed," Birdie said. "Just promise me that you won't do anything reckless without telling me first."

"Deal," said Ev, and she opened a portal that would take them back home.

Chapter 9

Back at Lumine Tower, Evress burst into Sylvra's room.

Sylvra stood in response to her entrance.

"Ah, you're back," he stated. "I trust the problem at Loch Porifera has been dealt with."

"It has," growled Evress. "The Divine were banished, and I placed tracking enchantments on the immortals."

"I suppose that is good enough," remarked Sylvra. "I will transfer ownership of the enchantment from you to one of the Enforcers. You should be proud of a job well done. Although, it seems you are not. Is there a problem?"

"Yes, there's a problem! You lied to me! You said if I worked for you, I could save this Doxla. You said I could stop it from decaying when you were done with it!"

"I never said that," replied Sylvra. "I said you could see to it that it is cared for after it is abandoned. I never said it would last forever. I said you could work to prevent decay, but I never said you would succeed."

"You're a monster," Evress spit. It took all of her restraint not to attack him then and there. "You're sick. Do you get some kind of pleasure from making me hurt people? Well, guess what?"

Ev ripped off her stupid tiara and lobbed it across the room. "I'm done being your puppet! Do what you want to me, but I will *not* help you hurt anyone anymore!"

Sylvra tilted his head, a look of obviously feigned shock on his face. "My, my. It seems you still harbor some resentment toward me. Don't tell me that after everything I've done for you, you still hate seitti."

"What you've *done* for me?" Evress nearly shrieked. "You destroyed my home! You spread war and suffering and left it to die, and then you tricked me into helping you do it again! Hatred doesn't even begin to describe what I feel toward you."

Sylvra chuckled, a maniacal grin on his face as he clapped dramatically.

Unable to take it any more, Evress willed her anther into a devastating attack, only to find that all of it had vanished from within her.

"Now, now. You know that I gave you that anther. I'm sure you also noticed that it wasn't truly raw. I configured it to obey my will from any distance prior to giving it to you, so of course you can't use it against me."

Evress broke down. "Why? Why are you doing this? What do you want from me!"

Sylvra slammed his hand down loudly onto his desk, drawing Evress's attention. He stared icy daggers at her as he stated, "This. This is what I want. I want you to suffer. I want you to hurt, to hate, to despair. I want you to feel these emotions down to your very core. Embrace them. Remember them forever, for this is the pain that countless others have suffered at the hands of seitti. Then, know that this is what I aim to prevent."

"Prev— *prevent?*" Evress could barely get the words out. "Y-you—"

"You say I destroyed your world, but as I have stated before, I did not. The only ones I killed were those near the border during your escape. I needed the others who escaped to have reason to fear and hate me. If I showed mercy to all of them, some might have come to the conclusion that I am not, as you say, 'a monster.' As for those who did not try to flee, they remain unharmed. They have been placed in a small world to be reeducated. This was your world's fate from the beginning."

"You lie!" cried Evress. "You abandoned us! You left us to Apollyon. You left us to starvation. If it wasn't for Syrus and Birdie, we'd all be dead by now!"

Sylvra shook his head. "I'm sorry to disappoint you, but that is not the case. When we left your world, we left behind a mechanism that would detect if Apollyon's rampage spread too far. If it had done so, we would have returned sooner and ended it ourselves. As for starvation, we calculated how long it would take before your world could no longer sustain itself. We, in fact, were very nearly about to return prior to your attempt to break into my core systems. That was very naughty, by the way."

"Are you serious?" Evress stated, finally regaining some of her composure. "Do you honestly expect me to believe you after you lied to me?"

Sylvra narrowed his eyes. "Once again, I did not lie. If you do not believe me, then ask yourself this: Why did I not end your world when I abandoned it?"

"Because there were still Divine there," Evress glared at him. "You were still getting prestige from it."

"I gain no prestige from any of my Doxlas," Sylvra stated. "All prestige earned is funneled into the AnAnCol network. If I earned it myself, my activities could be tracked, so I donate it to support our common cause. In exchange, they make it possible for me to continue my work."

"And what work is that? To torture worlds for your own sick amusement?"

Sylvra sighed, shook his head, then stepped out from behind his desk to approach Evress.

Her instincts told her to back away, but Evress held her ground.

Two feet in front of her, Sylvra looked Evress in the eyes as he raised a hand — his middle finger pressed against his thumb.

"Let me go back to your first question of 'why am I doing this?' I believe the best way to answer that is with a story."

Sylvra snapped his fingers, and the world around them changed.

Evress found herself atop a tall, grassy hill. Wildflowers bloomed in the midday sun all around her. A warm breeze lifted her hair and brought with it the sweet smell of a ripened orchard. At the bottom of the hill sat a dirt road leading to a small town in the distance. A lone traveler led a horse and cart toward the town. A young, blond-haired boy dragged a stick through the dirt not far way, and Sylvra stood next to Evress as he swung his arm out in presentation of the view.

"What you see before you is a picture of long, long ago — a picture of the world in which I was born. Everything around you has been created from my own memories. I once stood atop this very hill and watched this very salesman cart his wares into town. I was but a child then," he motioned toward the boy. "At the time, I believed my world was the extent of reality. Then, one day, seitti revealed themselves to us."

Before Evress could respond, Sylvra waved his hand. The scenery changed. The sky had turned orange, and the small town had become a walled city. Young Sylvra had become a featureless shadow. At the center of the city sat a large structure that Evress immediately recognized as a Radiant's citadel.

"Some of my people had found ways to make themselves immortal," Sylvra continued. "Most methods involved using what my people called 'magic' to transform themselves into more powerful but oft disfigured forms. Through that same process, we learned how to do something else that the seitti couldn't ignore. We learned how to create artificial life. We began reshaping the world into our own vision. That is why they came."

The entire hill instantly populated with immortals of every type, from artificial fiends such as gargoyles, shades, elementals, and even dragons, to corrupted beings such as revenants and demons. There were even races she didn't recognize, but what caught Evress's attention the most was the shadow of young Sylvra coming into focus as a winged lightning imp.

Evress found herself at a loss for words. The world he was showing her — the world he claimed he'd been born in — it couldn't be what he was suggesting.

Sylvra scowled and waved his hand again, this time shifting the entire landscape to a scorched, still-smoking field. The bodies of countless humans and immortals littered the ground. The putrid scent of burning flesh reached her nostrils, making her recoil. Only a handful were still breathing. One of them was the imp — Young Sylvra — clawing his way out from under a horse that had fallen on top of him. With both wings clearly broken, Young Sylvra limped over to the body of another female imp. He bent down and wept as he clutched her in his arms.

Evress shook her head. No. This wasn't possible. How could Sylvra be so cruel to immortals if he had suffered as one himself?

"We were not immortal in the sense that you know," Sylvra stated, his voice genuinely pained. "We did not age, but we could easily be killed. At first, the seitti responsible for our world attempted to eradicate us. As a world officially recognized as under their care, they could not do so themselves without penalty, so they turned the remaining human population against us to keep their own hands clean. When it became clear that would not be sufficient, they reached out to other seitti for assistance, except by that time their goals had clearly changed."

Sylvra didn't bother waving his arm, but the scene shifted once again. Then again. Then again and again, rapidly. Some showed conflict, some showed peace, some showed futuristic cities, and some showed broken ruins. In all of them, the small silver imp stood watching, fury etching deeper into his face with every new vision.

The real Sylvra turned toward Evress, fire practically burning in his eyes. "They saw an opportunity for profit and received approval to use our world to train new seitti in various methods of conflict resolution and governance. The clashing approaches brought chaos, which in turn brought more seitti. The cycle continued for centuries until the inhabitants grew so weary that most of us merely complied with whatever new instructions the seitti gave us. Eventually, the seitti realized that the only remaining conflict was between themselves. All but the original owners of our world left it, and our creators saw no further use for us. They could no longer profit from us, and the other seitti had transformed our world into something unrecognizable. It was far from the vision our creators had originally planned, but they could not change it back without scrutiny, so they abandoned us. They placed our world in what they call the Preserves — essentially a museum for seitti."

The world around Evress stopped changing, leaving her standing in a city almost identical to Ars Summis. By now, she was numb. Yes, Sylvra could be lying. He could have conjured these scenes from nothing, but she couldn't help herself. Even for someone like him, this was too extravagant to be simply all for show.

The crowd around her was almost exclusively comprised of immortals now. They all stood watching a large screen. On the screen was another group of immortals standing next to a massive ball of anther.

"Unfortunately," Sylvra stated angrily, "our creators never bothered to prepare our world for existence in the Preserves. They opted out of the recommended protections for the world, and they neglected to remove everything the other seitti had brought with them, including antherial tools. The astute among us had already learned of anther and its properties, and those who lacked caution attempted to use it to travel to other worlds. In doing so, they unleashed the cosmic horror known as 'sentiments' upon us. By the time we'd learned how to stop it, only a handful of us remained. Our world was all but dead, and I was left with only a singular desire urging me to press on."

A ruined landscape appeared around Evress — devoid of all life save for the silver imp, who trudged through a muddy graveyard. As he walked, flashes of nightmarish creatures and mutilated bodies appeared and vanished around him. At last, Young Sylvra stopped at a small grave — the name on the tombstone long since worn away. Placing his fingers atop the stone, Young Sylvra gave it a gentle caress before backing away and pulling out a small ball of anther. With eyes matching the real Sylvra's, the silver imp activated the anther. A brilliant flash later, Evress found herself standing with Sylvra back in his office.

Once more, Sylvra looked Evress in the eyes. "That was the end of our world. That was the end of my home — the original Doxla."

Sylvra waited a few seconds for Evress to say something, but no words came to her. If Sylvra spoke the truth, then her world — it had only ever been a replica.

Tired of waiting, Sylvra continued again. "My final act was to trigger a chain reaction that erased Doxla from existence. Shortly after, I was found floating in the void, and I was interrogated. I told the seitti why I'd done what I did. They offered empty apologies and made me into a seitti for my centuries of experience and mastery over anther. As for my world's creators, they received a slap on the wrist for what they had done to us. *That* is why I am doing this."

Evress at last managed to find her voice. "What's that supposed to mean? If everything you said is true, then you must realize that you're doing exactly what the seitti did to you. You're recreating your old world just to abuse it again and again. That doesn't explain anything!"

"You are only looking at the immediate impact," said Sylvra as he walked back to his desk and sat down. "My ultimate goal is to make every nepac understand the true nature of seitti society. When they die, they will carry that pain to their next life. They will carry the teachings I give them. Not all will become seitti, but some will, and those that do are less likely to forget their roots and become the heartless monsters that most seitti turn into. I find it to be a sweet, poetic justice that the world that seitti so mistreated be the one to produce these new seitti that will work to undo their corrupt empire.

"If I could, I would raise all nepacs to understand these truths, but I cannot. Only AnAnCol has the connections to ensure that nepacs born in the Cosmic Graveyard are given the chance to become a seitti in their next life, and their price per soul is not cheap. That is why I must play host to Divine for as long as I am able. The more prestige I funnel to AnAnCol, the more nepacs I can fast track to becoming seitti. Should any nepacs prove particularly promising, I take them under my wing as fellow Administrators. That is how I found Amethine, Crovos, and now you."

Evress blinked. "Crovos? He and Amethine are nepacs?"

"They are." Sylvra leaned forward in his chair, eyes still locked on Evress. "They understood the importance of what I am trying to accomplish. The future of entire worlds hinges on ensuring that new generations of seitti are better than what most are now. I hope that you can understand that as well."

"Y-you," Evress stammered, "you're insane."

"I assure you, I am not," returned Sylvra. "I have almost two millennia of experience with seitti society and access to the entirety of their collective knowledge. What I am doing has been proven to be successful, especially when partnered with organizations such as AnAnCol. If you refuse to take me at my word, then you can go and see for yourself. I promised you that I would give you access to seitti knowledge, and I will. Once I do, immerse yourself in it. Ask Crovos for assistance if you must and take all the time you need. If you decide that you cannot be a part of our endeavors, then you may remove the enchantments I placed upon you and live out the rest of your life in peace. Should you instead realize that I am justified in my efforts . . ."

Sylvra reached down and picked up Evress's thrown tiara, then teleported it back atop her head.

". . . then I look forward to a continued partnership. Do keep in mind that everything you have heard here today has been shared in the deepest confidence. You are to tell no one. Not the Divine, not the Enforcers, not even your friends in the other world. I assure you, you do *not* wish to break my trust on this matter."

Evress swallowed. What if he really was telling the truth? Even if he was, could she actually be a part of something so heartless?

She supposed at the moment, it didn't matter. She needed to leave. She needed to process what Sylvra had told her, and she needed to see for herself if seitti truly were as cruel as he claimed. Based on her brief exchange with Oakman at Loch Porifera, however, she feared that the truth would indeed be so.

"Come," Sylvra said, and he transported the two of them to the main control room.

Evress then watched as he tapped a few buttons on the console. He then placed his hand on the display that popped up and appeared to channel a bit of anther into it. This then opened up a new display, which he worked on for about a minute before turning off the whole thing. Evress couldn't be completely certain, but she was pretty sure that she'd just witnessed Sylvra access his core systems. It was definitely similar to what Syrus had done in his final attempt to do so.

"There," stated Sylvra. "Now you may see for yourself the true nature of seitti."

With that, Sylvra motioned with his hand that she was dismissed, and without a word, Evress teleported herself away.

✳ ✳ ✳ ✳

For the next eight days, Evress locked herself inside her room at Lumine

Tower as she threw herself into the world of seitti. Thanks to her privileges as a Master, she could use her personal terminal to manifest food and drink whenever she desired. She'd never indulged in such excessive luxuries prior to then, but if it meant not having to talk to anyone, she'd take advantage of it.

It was the first time she'd interacted with an external seitti system — a task that proved confusing at first, but after eventually caving to frustration and asking Crovos for a brief moment of assistance, she found herself exposed to a virtual library of knowledge beyond what her wildest imagination could have conjured. Her personal terminal showed her page after page of whatever information she asked of it. How so much knowledge could exist in one place was beyond her, but considering what seitti were capable of and how long they must have existed, it wasn't surprising.

Everything Sylvra had said proved true, so much so that she would have doubted the veracity of her discoveries had she not also found information directly condemning Sylvra's actions. Yes, his claims that a former life of hardship and suffering led to more compassionate seitti seemed to hold water, but that was not the end of the story. Many who were mistreated ended up cruel and dangerous, not just to their own creations, but to seitti society as a whole. Those who ended up as such were removed from their society, but never before notable damage had been done.

Sylvra's words of hoping new seitti would "work to undo their corrupt empire" took on a different meaning with that knowledge. He didn't simply hope for responsible seitti to make positive change. He wanted to reshape the seitti world entirely — with compassionate seitti to care for worlds properly, and cruel ones to damage the civilization that he hated so much.

The deeper Evress dug, however, the more she was inclined to believe that his goals might be justified. Again and again, she found reports of worlds abandoned by their creators or worlds made only to be used as playgrounds for the beings that existed in a realm free from the consequences of their actions. One of the few things she couldn't find was a report resembling what Sylvra had described regarding his home world, though she chalked that up to the overwhelming number of other incidents that kept coming no matter how deeply she searched.

Another omission Evress found strange was the lack of info on the process of transforming individuals into seitti. She also found next to nothing relating to AnAnCol, government, or laws, which led her to believe that even if everything she saw was legitimate, Sylvra was still somehow manipulating what she could find on her own. That thought pushed her to dig even deeper to try and find what he wanted to hide from her, but most of what she found was ever more evidence of despicable behavior by seitti.

On the ninth day of her self-imposed solitude, Evress prepared to dive once more into her research when a knock drew her attention. It was the first time anyone had disturbed her since getting help from Crovos, and she was curious, if wary, to see who it was.

Upon making her way from her bedroom to the front door, Evress slid it open to reveal Crovos in rather ordinary, and in fact dirty, clothing. If she hadn't known his face, she would have mistaken him for an ordinary nepac. While certainly preferable to any other Master, Evress still did not wish to see him.

"Let me guess," she said. "Sylvra sent you to talk to me."

"On the contrary," replied Crovos, his voice calm. "Sylvra asked me to let you be."

"Then why are you here?" Evress asked.

"I will tell you, but not where others may overhear. May I come in?"

After a moment's thought, Evress stepped aside to let him enter. With all of her family and friends trapped in that little world Sylvra had placed them in, she had no need for furnishings that would accommodate guests. This left her main room completely empty aside from bookshelves, which she'd filled with various books and curios that reminded her of her old life. As such, there really wasn't any place for him to sit down aside from the floor, so he merely stood as she shut the door.

"There. Privacy. Now, what do you want?" Evress asked again.

"Have you found the answers you seek?" asked Crovos, completely avoiding her question.

Evress frowned. "To most of them. Others seem to be conspicuously absent. It's obvious Sylvra doesn't want me to learn everything like he said he did."

Crovos nodded solemnly. "Yes, I fear that is the case. I suspect he has hidden things even from Amethine, though she certainly is privy to more than I am."

The remark took Evress aback. "What are you talking about? I thought you and Amethine were equals."

"We are, in a sense," said Crovos. "We both have our responsibilities, and our responsibilities do not overlap. Neither of us can command the other, and we both take orders from Sylvra. However, because she must interact with

Divine outside of our world, she has been given far more freedom in what she is allowed to learn and do than I have been."

"So you know he's hiding things from you, but you still serve him?"

"As much as I hate that innocent people must suffer, I take solace in the knowledge that we are making a difference, however small, in a civilization essentially comprised of gods. Though, to be honest, I have grown weary of my role. Sylvra is obsessed with his ambitions and Amethine cares nothing for either Divine or nepacs — only how to profit from them. At times I have felt that I am the only one who cares about the wellbeing of the people of this world, which is why I don't want you to turn your back on us. I don't know how much longer I can continue on if I am the only one who strives to make the world a better place in the short time that we are allowed to do so."

Evress studied Crovos's face. As much as she hated that he'd also played a role in deceiving her, he did seem genuine.

"I'm not going anywhere," Evress said. "If I leave, he'll just find someone else who doesn't care, won't he?"

Crovos nodded. "Most probably, yes. It is good to finally have someone else here who understands that feeling."

Evress shifted uncomfortably. "Is that all you wanted to say?"

"Not quite," replied Crovos. "I'm sure you've noticed my traditional garb. I would request that you change into something similar. I want to show you something, but you will not want anyone to recognize you as a Master where we are going."

"I'm not going anywhere until I find out what AnAnCol does with nepacs' souls to turn them into seitti," Evress said, opening the door again and waving him out.

Crovos tensed up but stayed put. "I'm afraid you will remain here for a very long time, if that is the case."

"Why is that?" Evress asked, eyes narrowed.

"Please close the door, and I will answer," Crovos said, looking worried.

Evress complied, then waited.

Crovos breathed a sigh of relief. "Thank you. You really should not mention AnAnCol where others may hear, especially now that you have replaced so many Enforcers with Divine who are not part of it."

"Is that so?" Evress asked, crossing her arms. "Why not? Just who are they?"

Crovos shook his head. "I honestly know very little. All I know is that they are an organization that hopes to reshape seitti society according to their own vision, which I cannot fathom could be any worse than it already is. That said, Sylvra guards the details of their plans almost as much as he does his true name."

"And? Don't you think that's suspicious?"

"Of course I do, but I have no more choice in aiding him than you do. Now come, let us forget about AnAnCol for now and let me show you what I came here to show you."

Evress sighed in exasperation. She supposed she might as well.

"Hold on," she said, and she went back to her room to change into the clothes she'd had before being made into a Master. In a way, it was kind of refreshing to return to them.

When she got back, she crossed her arms. "Now what?"

"I want to take you to a small town in eastern Apex. Are you ready?"

"As ready as I will be," Evress replied, and Crovos teleported the two of them to the middle of a wooded trail.

The trees here were a mixture of two types. Most were tall and thin with green bark. They towered overhead and were bare of leaves aside from at the tops, which branched out into fluffy white plumes. Those of the second variety stood a bit shorter and possessed thick, twisty branches that weaved extravagant knots surrounded by dark green leaves. A strong minty scent wafted through the forest as numerous furry critters skittered amongst the fallen leaves.

"Do you like it?" Crovos asked.

Evress nodded. She had to admit, it was nice being back out in nature for a change.

"I'm glad. Do me a favor and start patting yourself down with dirt. Your clothes are too clean."

Evress raised an eyebrow, but did as he requested. In the meantime, Crovos worked to manifest a large cart with his antherial tools. Moments later, crates of fruits, vegetables, and grains appeared atop the cart, followed by a large horse in front that reared back and whinnied at its sudden appearance from nowhere.

"Did you just create a horse?" gasped Evress in disbelief.

Crovos laughed. "Of course not. This is Mac. I keep him in a field on the other side of Doxla. Poor boy still hasn't gotten used to teleporting even after three years."

Crovos gave Mac a pat on the shoulder and offered him a carrot. Evress couldn't say she particularly condoned moving a horse around without warning like that, but at least Crovos wasn't making horses out of nothing.

Once Crovos had finished outfitting Mac and hooking him up to the cart, he pat the side of the cart with his hand.

"You might want to sit," he said. "We're a few miles out from our destination yet."

"I'm perfectly capable of walking," replied Evress. "You still haven't told me what we're doing here."

"You will see," said Crovos as he tugged Mac's reigns to get him moving. "By the way, I don't believe I ever asked, but what was your name before you took on the moniker of Evress?"

"Eveline."

Crovos nodded. "A good name. Mine was Corvid, though I request that you refer to me as Jack until we return."

Evress gave Crovos an odd look, but she had to admit he was gaining her curiosity.

The two of them walked in relative silence for the next hour before coming to a village deep in the woods. The tall, thin trees had been cleared from the area on this side of a small stream, leaving only the large, twisty trees still standing. Almost the entirety of the village's buildings sat up in the branches of the trees, though a few larger structures that seemed to be for housing animals had been built on the ground at the outskirts of town. Wooden platforms had been put in place to connect the buildings and make ramps leading up into the branches. What caught Evress's attention the most, however, were the inhabitants.

"An avian village?" she asked, eyeing the short, half-bird people flitting about the trees and tending the animals on the ground.

The avians stood like humans but were covered in feathers. Their arms were wings with small hands at the end, and their legs ended in talons. They had beaks instead of mouths, and the tallest of them had to have measured four feet at the most.

One of the locals — a red-eyed, black-feathered individual — flitted over to Crovos. When he landed, he looked over the goods on the cart before eyeing Evress suspiciously.

"Jack," the avian squawked. "You are early this season, and you bring a guest. This is an unusual occasion indeed."

"Well, as you can see, the harvest has been quite generous this time round,"

Crovos gestured toward the goods. "I didn't see any point in it going to waste by leaving it out in the field for wild animals. Unfortunately, I injured my back in the harvest and needed help from my niece. I assure you she is trustworthy."

The avian looked Evress over again, seemingly satisfied. "If you have Jack's affirmation, then we welcome you to our village. What is your name, young one?"

"It's Eveline," Evress stated after pausing for a moment to be sure not to say "Evress."

The avian bobbed his head up and down. "Welcome, Eveline. You need not be nervous. No harm will come to you here. I am the head of trade in our little town of Branch Haven. My name is Corvid."

Evress's eyes widened as she glanced toward Crovos, who gave a knowing nod. She looked back to Corvid and cleared her throat. "Oh, I didn't expect to meet you so soon. It's a pleasure."

Corvid cocked his head slightly, then put it back again as he addressed Crovos. "Well, we were not prepared for this visit, but if you wish to get started, I will see to it that two more places are readied at the table."

"That would be appreciated," Crovos said as he bowed his head.

Corvid returned the bow and flew off.

Crovos then turned to Evress. "I hope you don't mind helping me unload these wares."

Evress stared at Crovos and asked quietly, "How?"

Crovos smiled sadly and answered in nearly a whisper. "I am from Sylvra's second successful attempt at recreating Doxla. The first is the one where he transformed humans into immortals. It is where Amethine was born. Yours, mine, and this one are all copies from a point in time after the creation of immortals. Therefore, another version of me and my village has existed in all of them."

Crovos tugged on the reigns to lead Mac toward the largest ramp up to the trees. Evress followed right beside him.

"But, that means you're a copy of someone else! Doesn't that bother you?"

"I admit the revelation, when made known to me, was not one I adjusted to quickly," Crovos answered. "However, I have realized that I am my own person, and we are all equally alive. Still, though I have moved on from my old life, I find solace in helping my old village from time to time, even if it is no longer my own."

Evress suddenly felt guilty that she had hardly visited Birdie or the others since becoming a Master. Even if they'd had their differences, she'd been given a life of luxury, while they all toiled away in some tiny village.

"Come," said Crovos a bit louder once they reached the bottom of the ramp. "Help me carry up these crates. The people of this village are very good cooks."

Silently, Evress picked up a large crate of apples and hauled it up after Crovos into what appeared to be a supply room. It took quite a few trips — made doubly so by Crovos's "hurt back" — but with her Master's enchantments, the job was easy enough. Several avians gathered around to watch in the meantime, which was awkward, but not something that bothered her too much.

When they were through, Corvid had returned.

"You have a strong lass, there," the avian quipped. "I see why you brought her. She is more than welcome at our table."

"Yes," remarked Crovos, "I am quite proud of her. She's always wanted to help people, and I'm trying to show her that she can help immortals to, so long as she doesn't try to help where she isn't wanted."

Corvid nodded in understanding. "Yes, the situation between humans and immortals is unfortunate, so much so that I would advise a young lass such as yourself to avoid seeking them out. If you want to make a difference, just remember that anything you do to show immortals you don't view them as monsters will help more than you can know. I'm certain you will have many opportunities in the years to come."

Evress looked back at Crovos. So that was why he had brought her here.

"Now, however," continued Corvid, "I would like to invite you to sit at my table. I hope to show you that not all immortals are to be feared."

"I would be honored to join, as usual," said Crovos before turning to Evress. "I know my niece had some discomfort about remaining here, but I hope now that unease has been lessened."

Corvid and the other avians also looked at Evress. She did not appreciate Crovos putting her in this spot, but at the same time, he was right. If he could get away with helping immortals here and there, then so could she.

"You know what?" she said, standing tall. "It has. I'll be happy to stay, and you can bet this won't be the last time you see me, either."

Crovos gave her a genuine smile, and the two of them followed Corvid back to his home.

Chapter 10

Deep in the bowels of an endless network of caves, one of the other worlds sat buried. Ev extended her mind deep into the world barrier, feeling the structure of the systems within. Very little of what she saw looked familiar, suggesting to her that this world was also not another Doxla.

Her focus was interrupted by the sound of rocks tumbling from a hole in the ceiling behind her. Immediately, Ev withdrew her touch from the barrier and spun around, on guard.

To both her relief and frustration, the figure that appeared from the hole was that of Lylia, hanging upside down as she lowered herself to the ground.

"Why were you up there? You nearly gave me a heart attack!" Ev shouted.

"We finished early and were curious regarding these caverns," Lylia answered. "We find it strange for an entire world to be buried below ground."

Ev huffed. "Whatever. Wait, you said you're finished? You checked both of them?"

"Mm-hm," replied Lylia absently as she looked around the cave before freezing and turning to Ev. "Oh, wait, no. We only looked at one."

"You—" Ev stopped herself. "Why did you only look at one?"

"Well, this one said our goal is to find a new Doxla. One is all it took for that goal to be accomplished."

"Wait, you found a new Doxla?" Ev nearly jumped in excitement. "Which world is it?"

"The one floating in the middle of nowhere."

"The one . . ." Ev trailed off.

Great. That was the only one she'd hoped it wasn't, but she could work with that.

"Okay, thank you, Lylia," Ev said, then she opened up a connection to Helcant. "Helcant? We found it."

"Most excellent!" Helcant hissed from the other side. "I shall begin my task of misdirection so that Birdie and Umber may begin gathering equipment without scrutiny. Where should they meet you?"

"Here is good," Ev said. "We'll need to work through portals until we can build a ring around the border where we can stand. Thanks for covering for us.”

“Please work quickly,” said Helcant. “I know not for how long Nictis will be deceived.”

“Don’t worry. We will,” Ev replied before she sighed and smiled to herself. She knew the odds were against them, but at least they’d have one more chance to make a difference.

She turned to Lylia, who’d by now slithered closer. “Thanks again for helping me with this.”

“This one needs not repeat herself,” Lylia responded. “We are absolutely tickled at the prospect of becoming a Radiant.”

“We won’t know for sure if we can do that until after I’ve really examined the systems behind the barrier.”

“Have some faith, oh young one,” Lylia replied as she placed her hands together in what Ev assumed was supposed to be mimicking the appearance of a wise sage. “The systems appeared very familiar to us. This endeavor should be well within our capabilities.”

Ev sighed. “I hope you’re right. Even if the systems are identical, this is going to be a lot of work. I just hope we can get it all done before we’re found out.”

✳ ✳ ✳ ✳

For nearly two days, Ev and Lylia were able to work without interruption. That all came to a halt when an unexpected portal opened up on the platform they’d built next to the new Doxla they’d discovered. Out of the portal stepped Nictis and a very livid Jax.

“Ev! What the hell do you think you’re doing?”

Ev turned to face her brother. “I already told you. The only thing that matters is stopping the Masters.”

“That’s not your call to make! The other anthermancers agree that it’s too dangerous. I won’t let you do this.”

“I don’t care, and you can’t stop me.”

“Are you even listening to yourself? If that world is another Doxla, then the Masters are probably there right now. As soon as you do anything to it, they’ll know.”

“That’s why we’re preparing,” Ev returned. “This will be our final chance to put an end to this."

Nictis approached Ev, her tail twitching like Helcant's. "Enough of this nonsense. We did not survive this long to perish because of a foolhardy child and her whims."

"Would this one prefer death of age?" Lylia chirped.

Nictis growled at Lylia. "This does not concern you."

"Oh?" replied Lylia. "But we have contributed as much as any other. It is unfair to assign responsibility upon only one when many are involved."

"How many?" Jax asked, his eyes narrowed.

As if on cue, another portal opened up, and Helcant, Birdie, Tallis, and Umber all poured on through.

Helcant scrambled forward. "Apologies, Miss Ev. I gathered the others as quickly as I could when I saw Nictis come here."

Nictis hissed. "Helcant. I suspected you were involved."

Jax, on the other hand, looked surprised. "Birdie? Tallis? I thought you said you opposed doing this!"

Birdie shrugged. "What can I say? I was created to slay Divine. Can't get any more divine than a Master."

"Yeah," said Tallis as he rubbed his arm sheepishly. "Besides, Ev had some good arguments."

"Oh, really? Like what?" asked Jax as he turned his head back to Ev.

Ev stood up tall as she answered. "Like the fact that the Masters have done this before. The fact that they are clearly doing it again. The fact that they didn't come looking for us — meaning that we're the first to ever escape from them, and we might be the last. Syrus gave us a chance no one else has ever had. The Masters won't expect us. We can get in. We can reach their terminals, and we can expose them for what they are."

"How can you be sure?" returned Jax. "For all you know, the same thing will happen again. You won't be able to access their core systems or whatever, and we'll lose everything."

"Yeah, we might," responded Ev.

"Then—"

"But if the Masters aren't stopped, countless more will meet the same fate. What makes us any more important than the people of the new Doxla? What makes us more important than the people of the countless Doxlas they'll make after they're done with this one?"

"You don't know they'll make—"

"Then when, Jax?" Ev stared at her brother. "When will they stop? How many will it take before the Masters are satisfied?"

Jax hesitated before answering. Ev could see from his expression that she was beginning to sway him.

"Ev, think about this," Jax pleaded. "Millions of survivors are out here. Our families — your family, is out here. We'd be risking all of their lives if we did this. Are you saying their lives don't matter?"

Ev shook her head. "I already told you what matters. If you want to stay here, I won't blame you, but this is bigger than family. It's bigger than a few lives. The Masters are beings who see entire worlds as tools and playthings, and we might be the only people to ever have a chance to stop them."

Ev looked Jax straight in the eyes. "I'm taking that chance. What are you going to do?"

Jax clenched his fist and growled. "Damn it, Ev. Why do you have to be so stubborn?"

"Because I know I'm right, and so do you."

Jax cursed and stomped away from Ev.

Nictis looked at Jax with concern. "Surely you are not swayed by these words."

Jax turned his attention to Nictis. "What am I supposed to do? Stop her?"

As he spun back toward Ev, she knew she'd beaten him. "Fine. If you absolutely insist on doing this, then I'm going, too."

"You're all fools," hissed Nictis before she growled. "I suppose I have no choice but to follow, however."

"Guess that's it, then," said Jax. "We'd better make sure we have a good plan moving forward, though."

Manifesting several antherial shimmers around her and pulling out a book about Radiant abilities from her bag, Ev smiled. "Don't worry. We already do. As long as we make sure we're well prepared, we can win this."

* * * *

For the next three months, the entire group dedicated every moment of their spare time to training, preparation, and appointing trustworthy anthermancers to take their places after they'd gone. They did their best to keep their plans under wraps so as not to cause a panic, but Ev knew that at least a few people must have figured out that something was up. Even so, no one tried to stop them, and when the day of action finally arrived, it was too late for anyone to protest.

Everyone met on the platform at the border of the new Doxla, including Jax, Nictis, and . . .

"Gare?" Ev asked, surprised to see him step through Nictis's portal. She was even more surprised to see Fauna and Gare's family step through right behind him.

"Hey, Ev," Gare said. "I heard you were planning to strike back against the Masters. Sounded like something I'd like to get in on."

"But, what about Ronda and Marin?" Ev asked, looking at his wife and daughter.

Gare shrugged. "From what I've gathered, this little trip will be all or nothing, right? If I stay here and you guys fail, there wouldn't be anything I could do against the Masters anyway. At least this way I can hopefully do something to help keep them safe."

A hint of sadness lurked behind Gare's eyes as he looked back toward Ronda and Marin, the former of whom nodded in approval of his words.

Fauna approached Ev. "We all understand why you have to do this. I'd go myself if I was any kind of fighter, but I'm afraid that's more Jax's trade than mine."

Fauna gave a slight smile, and a tinge of guilt crept down Ev's spine, but she pushed it away as quickly as it came.

Jax took a spot next to Fauna. "I still think we should try and get more people involved — at the very least more anthermancers."

Ev reminded Jax of their earlier conversation. "We're the only ones that Syrus trained to use the Masters' terminals. The only reason to involve anyone else would be to use them to cause a distraction, which we've got covered anyway."

"I know," replied Jax. "That doesn't mean I have to like it. So, how will we be splitting up? Should it be me, you, and Birdie in one group?"

"No," returned Ev. "We need at least one immortal in each group in case this Doxla's like ours was. It will be me, Birdie, and Lylia. You can go with Helcant and Umber."

"Not a chance," said Jax. "I'm worried about you, Ev. I made a promise fifteen years ago that I'd watch out for you, and I'm going to keep that promise."

"Fifteen years ago I was still a child," said Ev. "In case you haven't noticed, I can take care of myself now."

Birdie stepped in to diffuse the situation. "It's alright, Ev. I can go with Helcant and Umber."

The statement shocked Ev. "What? But—"

"Don't worry," said Birdie, cocking her head. "I'm not planning on dying anytime soon. I'll be there at the rendezvous point no matter what."

"But . . . are you sure?"

"Positive," replied Birdie before she addressed Jax. "I'm counting on you to watch her back, but you'd better listen to her if she tells you anything."

"Yeah, yeah, I know," said Jax before adding. "Thanks."

Birdie nodded before moving to join Umber and Helcant. Ev was admittedly a tad irritated about the switch, but she knew the important thing was that they were still moving forward.

Once that was settled, Gare approached Ev as well. "So, uh, I guess I should go with those two?"

He pointed to Tallis and Nictis.

"That's right," Ev nodded, "but first, could you tell us what abilities you'd like to have? We'll only have a moment after making you into a Radiant to give you them."

Gare slapped a hand to his forehead. "Oh, right! I'd forgotten Jax had said something about that. Well, I don't really know what sorts of ax abilities Radiants can have, so maybe whatever ones you think are best."

"Okay, well, let's go work on that real quick; then we can grab our stuff and head out."

For the next fifteen minutes, Ev worked with Gare, Jax, and Tallis deciding on what abilities to give Gare, with most of that time spent explaining to Gare what each would do and how to use them. He honestly didn't seem all that enthused about the new abilities, but they gave them to him nonetheless.

Once that was out of the way, the group put on their armor and weapons. Most outfitted themselves with the highest quality plate armor they'd been able to recover from Doxla. The exceptions to that were Lylia, who'd found a bejeweled, naga-specific mail armor that covered the entirety of her snake half as well as her human torso, and Tallis, who'd donned one of Syrus's outfits under the optimistic hope that their Radiant class properties could be restored. For weapons, Ev had brought a bow, some arrows, and a dagger; she'd discarded her healing rod as she doubted it would be useful once she had Radiant class healing abilities. Jax, of course, had his sword, and Lylia carried a tower shield and lightweight spear. The other groups were similarly outfitted. None of them had any enchantments on their equipment, but the tools that she, Tallis, and Lylia had crafted would take care of that as soon as they stepped past the world border. In addition to all of that, they were each outfitted with backpacks stuffed with food and canteens of water.

"Alright," Ev said once they were done putting everything on. "Everyone ready?"

Helcant cackled gleefully. "Four hundred years have I been ready. Let us delay no longer. Retribution will finally be served!"

Jax sighed and placed his hand on the hilt of his sword. "Guess I'm as ready as I'll ever be."

His wife approached him from behind, turned him around, and wrapped her arms around him. "Be careful, Jax."

Jax returned the embrace and whispered something to her. Fauna then looked at Ev. "You be careful, too."

"I will," Ev responded.

Out of the corner of her eye, Ev could see Gare finishing up his goodbyes with his family. When they were done, Ronda and Marin made their way back to the portal home. Fauna shared one last kiss with Jax before she, too, went to the portal. A few final words were exchanged, and the portal was closed.

It was time.

Ev stepped up to the world border and turned to face everyone. "Okay, we'll only get one shot at this, so I just want to make sure we're all clear on the plan. Once we activate the portals, we'll have five minutes to create some degradation, mess with the world's systems, and get to a safe location. After that, the portals will close on their own, and we won't be able to use anther or degradation any more. If we try, I'm certain the Masters will be able to find us. Since the portals are random, we could end up anywhere in the world, so we allow three weeks to meet up at the Shrine of Merius. All of the other Doxla's had one, so it should exist in this one, too."

"If this really is another Doxla," remarked Jax.

Ev shot him an annoyed look. "If it's not, then we meet near this world's equivalent of Ars Summis. It should have one. Either way, we have three weeks to find each other and figure out the exact situation. Remember, we don't know what's over there, so stay alert and look for opportunities that we might be able to use to draw out the Masters when the time comes to finally strike."

Umber spoke up from off to the side. "We should be wary of the words we speak. Divine were forbidden from speaking of the realm beyond Doxla's borders and were swiftly punished for it. I suspect the Masters are able to listen for such words."

"They are," said Tallis, "but only for Divine. Even if we're not from this world, we're still nepacs. We should be safe."

"Exactly," said Ev, "but Umber brings up a good point. We shouldn't say anything about where we're from unless we're certain that there are no Divine around. Now, is everyone clear about what we need to do?"

Helcant twitched excitedly. "Of course we are! Let us cease our prattle and attack already!"

Lylia giggled. "So antsy-pantsy. We have not even wished one another luck yet. Oh, Tallis~" she called in a sing-song voice as she slithered over to him.

Ev smiled briefly, but then she approached Birdie to also say goodbye.

Birdie placed a hand on her hip. "I guess this is it, huh?"

"Yeah," Ev replied. "I wish you were coming with me instead, but . . ." Ev trailed off.

"But the only thing that matters is that we're going at all, right?"

Ev averted her eyes from Birdie's and nodded.

She could hear Birdie sigh. "Well, while that might be true for you, it's only almost true for me. Don't get yourself killed Ev, and try to keep Jax alive, too. Don't ever tell him this, but I kind of like the guy."

Ev smiled a little at that and nodded. She then embraced Birdie one final time before moving on to bid well-wishes to the others who weren't accompanying her. Then, once all was said and done, she stepped up to the world border.

"Alright," she said. "Let's do this. Helcant, Nictis, let me know once you're in position."

The two other teams then disappeared through portals to faraway locations so that they could enter from three sides of the world at once. Seconds later, Ev heard confirmation from both of them.

Immediately, Ev tore open a hole in the world border and activated a ball of anther that scattered across the surface of the border, which opened up countless other holes. On the other side sat a rocky shoreline exactly like the one from her Doxla. She pulled as much anther into herself as she could — hoping against hope that she could carry enough to succeed, then she charged through.

"Let's go!" she shouted.

Not ten steps in, Ev activated another tool that would open countless portals randomly across a third of the entire world. Hundreds appeared in her immediate vicinity — all of them tailored to form only in open air a few inches above a solid surface of some kind. This led to quite a few of them leading to the treetops, but there were still plenty of viable options for them. The hope was that the chaos would help them escape notice by the Masters, but the downside was that the tool required a heavy amount of anther to use — over half of what she'd brought with her. Thankfully, her proximity to the opening to the Cosmic Graveyard meant she could recover most of that even as she headed deeper into Doxla.

"This way," Ev yelled as she ran towards the nearest safe portal, which led to a snowy tundra next to an icy lake.

On the other side, Ev doubled back behind the portal and ran for another — this one leading into a rocky canyon. Before she reached it, a hairy frost wyrm lunged at her from beneath the snow.

Caught by surprise, Ev was thrown to the ground as the wyrm reared back to attack again.

With a mighty roar, Jax charged at the twenty-foot serpent and struck it with his sword. The blow barely left a scratch but succeeded in drawing the wyrm's attention.

"Keep away from it!" Ev yelled. "We can't beat it until I've connected us to the systems!"

"Well, hurry up, then!" Jax yelled back.

The wyrm screeched before blasting icy breath in Jax's direction. He dodged in time, but the wyrm took aim and prepared again.

Its attack was interrupted by a swift crack to its head by Lylia's tail. The naga swiftly positioned herself between the wyrm and Jax — she and the creature matching one another almost exactly in size and stature.

Ev had hoped to hop through at least one more portal before stopping to work, but it seemed that she didn't have much of a choice anymore. Upon tearing open a piece of degradation, Ev activated the other tools she'd brought with her and set about marking the three of them as supreme-ranked Radiants so that she could then instill them with Radiant class strength and abilities.

In the meantime, Jax and Lylia held off the wyrm. Any time it attempted to spray ice, Lylia's tail whipped around to smack it. If it lunged at Lylia, she'd guard with her shield while Jax struck. If it attacked Jax, they'd reverse their roles.

After about thirty seconds, Ev had done it.

"Jax! It's finished!" she called.

Jax grinned. Leaping away from the wyrm, he drew back his sword as it began to glow. With a mighty swing, he let loose a giant golden arc that cleaved the wyrm cleanly in two.

Jax sheathed his sword as he looked to Ev, grin still on his face. "You know, I kind of always wanted to be able to do that."

Ev merely grunted in response as she continued working. Now that she'd started, she needed to finish. She next worked on making Lylia a Radiant, then at last herself. The change upon completion was immediate. She could feel the strength of a Radiant coursing through her as the weight of her armor became but an afterthought.

Even then, she had more work to do, but Jax was getting impatient.

"What's taking so long? I thought we needed to move quickly."

"I still need to enchant our weapons and armor. Just give me a moment."

Before she could even start on the enchantments, however, a terrible screech reached her ears.

"*YOU!*"

Ev, Jax, and Lylia all turned to see a crimson-haired woman clad in a silvery purplish armor. Ev's heart sank into her stomach at the recognition of who stood before her.

Amethine's face was pulled back in a terrifying mixture of absolute hatred and sadistic pleasure. "Don't think I don't recognize you, brat. I've heard your sickening voice enough to recognize you anywhere. When Sylvra finds out what you've done, he'll have your head, and I'll be the one to give it to him!"

In a flash, Amethine vanished and reappeared inches away from Ev. Instinctively, Ev put up an antherial barrier just in time to block the attack.

Amethine's glowing hand crashed into the barrier, sending shock waves rippling across the snow.

"Ev!" Jax shouted as he sent another arc tearing through the snow directly at Amethine.

The arc collided in a shower of golden sparks, but when the light cleared, Amethine's armor hadn't even been scratched.

A sickening smirk appeared on Amethine's face as she stared at Ev from across the barrier. "It seems your little boyfriend is upset. Looks like you aren't the only one who needs to be put in her place."

Amethine stretched out her arm in Jax's direction. Whatever she was preparing to do, Ev wasn't going to give her the chance. She'd already been found out anyway, so using more anther couldn't do anything to make the situation worse.

As quickly as she could, Ev focused on forming another portal right through Amethine's torso, but nothing happened!

Before she could try again, Jax had already been lifted into the air and was screaming in pain as his armor cracked under some invisible pressure. The screams quickly turned to gasps as blood started dripping through the cracks.

Without thinking, Ev dropped her barrier and threw a full-force punch at Amethine. The Master must have expected it, because she caught Ev's wrist mid-punch and started squeezing.

Jax, thankfully, dropped back to the ground, but now Ev could feel her own bones cracking under Amethine's vice-like grip. Pain shot up her arm as she tried desperately to use her free hand to pry off Amethine's fingers, but no sooner did she attempt to reach out then she found herself completely paralyzed by an invisible force.

"What's the matter?" cooed Amethine. "Still haven't figured out how to use your own power?"

The Master twisted her grip; Ev cried out as she felt the bones in her forearm snap. Through the pain, however, she could also feel the anther within Amethine. If she could only analyze it, maybe she could break free.

"Brats like you deserve to suffer," Amethine sneered. "Oh, but don't worry. I won't make it hurt too much. I just want to hear you beg. Go on. Admit how worthless and spoiled you are, and how you never did anything to deserve what's been handed to you."

Ev whimpered. She didn't know what this crazy witch was talking about, but if she humored her a little, she might be able to buy enough time.

"I-I'm sorry. You're right. Please . . . just let the others go," she begged.

"It's too late!" Amethine twisted her grip once more, and Ev nearly passed out from the pain as her forearm bent backwards. "If you cared about them so much, you wouldn't have brought them here. I warned you what would happen if you crossed me, and now you're just going to have to deal with the consequences."

Just a little more, Ev thought. Though it was almost impossible to focus on Amethine's anther through searing pain, she was fairly certain she'd at least figured out how Amethine was holding her. If she could just ignore her screaming arm for even a moment, she was sure she could find a way to get past Amethine's defenses.

"I'll tell you whatever you want," Ev squeaked as she activated a minor healing spell that acted as an anesthetic. "I'm worthless. I'm a fraud. Is that what you want to hear?"

With a chilling smile, Amethine released Ev's arm and took a single step back.

"Desperate pleas from a spoiled brat who's finally realized who her superior is. At least you'll die knowing your true place in life — an immature, filthy little rat."

Amethine formed an antherial blade in her hand, and Ev knew she had to act now. With every last bit of concentration she could muster, she configured the anther in her free arm to break free of Amethine's constraint as she lunged and drove her fist straight into this vile woman's nose.

The look of shock barely had time to form on her face before Amethine went flying to the ground several feet away. At first Ev wasn't sure if she'd actually succeeded in breaking through Amethine's defenses, but when Amethine looked up again, Ev knew that she had. Whatever injury Ev had caused seemed to have vanished, but the copious amounts of blood plastered across Amethine's face told Ev that she now had a way to hurt a Master.

Amethine roared and jumped to her feet as she wiped the blood from her eyes. "Cursed brat! I'll tear you apa—aaagh!"

Amethine was cut short by a giant tail wrapping around her legs and slinging her far into the air. She spun head over heels screaming like a banshee before crashing through the lake ice a good hundred feet away.

A smug-looking Lylia stood tall in the snow. "That one needed to cool off."

Ev winced at the pain coursing through her arm, but she'd have time to deal with that later.

"We need to go, now," she called to Lylia. "Grab Jax and follow me!"

With lightning speed, Lylia slithered over and scooped up Jax before joining Ev near the rocky canyon portal. Just before they passed through, an explosion followed by a scream erupted from the lake.

Ev looked back to see Amethine floating in the air and looking as if she was conjuring some invisible attack. Whatever she was doing, Ev didn't want to find out. She created a large, pitch-black barrier that completely blocked the portal just as she jumped through to the other side. Once in the canyon, Ev looked for another portal that seemed promising and created yet another to take the group straight to it. She then dispelled the temporary portal as the three of them entered into a dark cave filled with glowing pink and blue crystals.

From back in the canyon, Ev could hear Amethine shouting threats and obscenities, and she knew they weren't safe yet.

Ev led the way deeper into the branching paths of the cave, but she couldn't find any other portals.

"I know you're in here!" Amethine's voice echoed through the tunnels. "There's no escape! I will find you, brat! You are marked, and I'm coming for you, now!"

Amethine must have been able to detect the anther usage. If that was the case, then Ev wouldn't be able to make any more portals to get away. She had to find another one that already existed before they all closed.

As the group turned another corner, at last they spotted one. On the other side was a raging inferno, but it was the only choice they had. Ev jumped through first, then Lylia — carrying Jax — followed right behind her.

They found themselves in the middle of a large brimstone path overlooking a lake of lava. The heat was intense, and the smell of sulfur filled the air. They'd clearly wound up in the Underworld. With any luck, they were near one of its exits. If not, then they could be about as far from Ars Summis as possible.

Not fifteen seconds after they'd passed, the portal closed, and Ev breathed a sigh of relief. With any luck, the Masters wouldn't be able to figure out where they'd gone, but Ev wasn't about to risk that they would.

"We need to get as far away from here as possible," she said.

Lylia looked at Ev with concern as she held out Jax in her arms. "Not to invoke an argument, but perhaps this one should aid her brother first. These injuries are not minor."

Ev cursed to herself. They needed to get to safety first.

"Once we're out of sight. There," she pointed to a pathway hidden in the crags about a hundred yards away.

They moved as quickly as they could. Once they'd arrived, and Ev was sure they'd have at least some chance of getting away should they be followed, she finally took a look at Jax. No sooner did she inspect him, however, than the blood drained from her face. Not only was he unconscious, but the edges of his helmet had been crushed into his skull. Lylia was soaked in his blood.

"Jax! No, hold on!" she cried before turning to Lylia. "Get his armor off of him!"

Lylia went to work at removing his armor's straps while Ev focused her healing into her own broken arm so she could then help get the rest off.

The Radiant spell was amazing. Ev could even feel it resetting her bones without causing any pain.

As soon as that was done, Ev took her dagger and cut through the remaining straps of Jax's armor. She and Lylia then removed all of the metal and the padded gambeson from Jax's body. The padding had been torn to shreds where the armor had cracked and pressed into him — it was almost as if he'd been crushed by invisible spikes — and she needed to remove it from his wounds before she healed him. Because of that, it turned out to actually be a blessing that she hadn't had time to enchant the armor, as she and Lylia were able to easily bend and rip the plates where necessary. Ev worked as quickly as she could without accidentally injuring him further. Jax was still breathing, but with how much blood he was losing, she knew she didn't have much time. The moment his wounds were all clear, Ev activated her healing magic, which enveloped Jax in a soft light.

Not long after, Ev finally breathed easily again with Jax looking as good as new — aside from being covered in his own blood, that is. He was still unconscious, but she knew he'd be fine.

"Thank you," she told Lylia. "You saved all of us back there."

"That was fun," Lylia smiled back. "We were able to not only see a Master bleed, but throw one for a quite a loop. We are encouraged that we all may indeed succeed in our endeavors now."

Ev gave a small smile back. Lylia had a point. Even if they'd fled, they had actually battled a Master and survived.

Lylia lifted up high on her coils and looked around. "It would seem that we all are rather far from our destination, however. Might we suggest that we see about finding the locals so that we might find our bearings?"

"Yeah," Ev nodded. "We should see if we can get some replacement armor while we're at it. I'm not about to try enchanting it with anther, and I'm pretty sure Jax's isn't viable anymore."

Lylia looked herself and her sparkling armor over and sighed. "Such a shame. We rather liked this outfit."

"I don't think we'll be able to replace yours down here," Ev said.

Lylia blinked then giggled. "Yes, that is a fair point."

"I'll wake up Jax," Ev said. "I don't think the Masters are able to tell where different portals went, but just in case they can, we'll want to move quickly."

Chapter 11

Happy with her choices, Evress submitted her list of towns and other areas that needed more protection from Divine to the kiosks of Ars Summis. By presenting the task as a monthly quest with monetary rewards, she hoped to encourage Divine to travel to the more remote regions of Doxla. Since Sylvra had disallowed her to slay monsters herself, this was the best idea she'd been able to come up with to keep monster damage down to a minimum.

Satisfied, Evress leaned back in her chair to relax for a bit. Research into what areas were underserved had been simple enough, but deciding on appropriate rewards for clearing each area and putting the systems in place to make sure Divine actually did so had been a bit more challenging. She didn't have long to rest, however, before her display started beeping and flashing.

Sitting up, Evress saw three warnings that she'd never seen before show up on the screen. Before she could analyze them, countless other warnings exploded. Evress touched one of the warnings, which brought up a circular map of Doxla. The border of the map was absolutely covered with red, flashing dots. A few seconds later, the rest of the map erupted in dots as well. Further investigation revealed that the dots were seemingly all locations of spacial disruption, suggesting anther usage. "Spacial disruption" also told her the anther had likely been used to make portals, but to what end, she couldn't guess. She set to work trying to find the source of the problem, but there were so many dots that she had no idea where to begin. She tried opening up a one-way window to the location of one of the dots, but she saw nothing that looked suspicious. Before she could investigate further, Sylvra — clad in his pearly armor — appeared beside her.

"We have a problem," he said.

"Is it rogue Divine?" she asked.

"No," Sylvra answered, surprising Evress with the sternness in his voice. "The disruption began with a tear in the world border, and I have seen the culprits for myself."

Sylvra touched one of the other dots, which opened a view of a mossy, craggy landscape. When Ev saw Birdie, Helcant, and Umber in the middle of the rocks, she audibly gasped.

"Capture them quickly, but be wary of Amethine," Sylvra warned.

"Amethine? Wh—?"

"She did not wait for me to explain the situation and may seek to harm you. Unfortunately, she was right that we do not have time to discuss this further. If we do not capture them now, we may not have the chance to. They have just now accessed Doxla's systems, and I do not expect they will do so again until they are in position to do significant damage. Just know that the invaders are not who they appear to be. I will explain more soon, but suffice it to say that your Syrus was very clever. Now, go."

Evress swallowed. She wasn't sure if she could trust Sylvra, but she was sure that she could apprehend her friends without harming them . . . whether they really were her friends or not. Before she had a chance to respond, Sylvra teleported away.

That was just as well. Considering who was causing the problem, she'd much rather her deal with this than Sylvra anyway. She manifested her emerald armor to show that she meant business, then teleported to the location that Sylvra had shown her. There, she approached Helcant, who was still hands deep in degradation.

"Are you insane?" Evress asked Helcant.

Helcant jumped back, immediately on guard, but when he spotted Ev's face, he stopped and stuttered.

"E-Ev? Why are your clothes such? We do not have time for foolishness!"

"This is my new armor," Evress answered while maintaining a safe distance. After Sylvra's warning, she, too, was going to be cautious. "What are you doing here? I told you that we can't fight the Masters. Just let me do my best to help this world where I can."

"What treachery is this?" Helcant spat, getting into an offensive position. "You are not Ev! You are a deceiver!"

Birdie jumped between them — her face one of utter disbelief.

"Helcant, stop!" she cried.

Helcant rounded on Birdie. "Stand aside! You heard her words!"

"Keep doing what you were doing," Birdie commanded, looking back at him. "I'll talk to her."

Helcant hesitated, then went back to work on the degradation. Evress raised a hand to attack.

"I said stop!" she yelled.

"Tell me something," said Birdie, now facing Evress. "Are you really Ev?"

"Of course I am! Birdie, you said you trusted me. You said you trusted that I was doing what's best! Was that a lie, or are you not actually Birdie?" Evress frowned as she prepared to attack Helcant. "Sylvra said you aren't who you seem to be. In case you are, I'm giving you one more chance. Stand down."

Helcant backed away from the degradation and grinned. "You are too late, deceiver! I have finished! We are Radiants now!"

Evress lowered her hand slightly, baffled at the announcement. "You . . . what? Why?"

Umber called out from behind the others. "Birdie, we must go. We do not have much time."

"Go, then," stated Birdie.

"Are you a fool?" began Helcant. "You must also—"

"Go!" Birdie yelled back.

Umber and Helcant hesitated only half a second before running toward a nearby portal. Evress once again raised her hand, this time fully intent on stopping them, but Umber and Helcant vanished behind a wall of trees that appeared out of nowhere. It took Evress a second to realize what had happened, but when it clicked, she yelled at Birdie.

"Why are you doing this? Don't you realize how much trouble you're causing me? Illusions or not, you won't get away from Sylvra."

Birdie stared at Evress. Her eyes were full of concern.

"From what I'm hearing, you work for him now. I'm sure you have your reasons, but we've seen what he's done. Ours was not the first Doxla he's destroyed. He's harvesting people, Ev."

Evress's eyes opened wide. "You knew? How?"

Birdie's concern gave way first to surprise, then a frown. "So, you knew as well. Yet you still joined him."

"I had to! You don't know what's really going on, but I do!" Evress was growing frustrated. "Birdie, if that's even who you are, what are you doing here? How did you get out?"

"I didn't. I'm not the same Birdie you escaped with, and you're clearly not the same Ev I came here with."

Evress shook her head. "That's enough! It doesn't matter who you are. I have a job to do. Birdie, I'm sorry."

Evress prepared to imprison Birdie, but another wall of trees appeared before her. Before she could give chase, she heard Birdie's voice whisper in her ear, "I'm sorry, too."

Evress ignored the illusory voice and activated an ability to dispel even Radiant class illusions.

The trees disappeared to reveal Birdie sprinting toward the same portal that Helcant and Umber had run to. Evress had a clear shot at her target, but before she could act, she felt a sharp, searing pain in her back before suddenly being flung to the ground several yards away.

Evress coughed up blood, then received a powerful kick to the jaw that somehow broke through her Master's enchantments and sent an agonizing shock down her spine. Fortunately, her injuries healed themselves as quickly as she'd received them. Unfortunately, her attacker wasn't done, as she felt herself lifted up and slammed hard into the ground — no longer able to move. Amethine stood over Evress, holding an antherial blade and practically frothing at the mouth.

"You stupid brat," she growled. "Did you think you're still a common nepac? Did you think I couldn't track you down? There's no escape from me. I'm going to kill you, and all your precious friends will follow!"

Evress closed her eyes as Amethine drove her blade downward, but the attack never came.

Cautiously, Evress opened her eyes once more to see Crovos struggling to hold back Amethine's arm.

"Amethine, calm yourself!" Crovos yelled.

"She's a traitor!" Amethine screamed.

"She is not! I observed everything!"

"I don't care what you observed! I saw her with my own eyes. Now, move!"

Amethine blasted Crovos with an invisible force from the side and sent him careening into the crags. Once more she bore down on Evress, but once again the attack halted.

Amethine stood frozen in place, clearly struggling but unable to even move her mouth.

Sylvra — having appeared suddenly — stepped calmly around Amethine, placed his fingers around her blade, and shattered it into nothingness with his grip. The pressure that Evress had felt holding her down vanished, and she took several deep breaths as Sylvra offered his hand to her and helped her back to her feet.

Sylvra turned to Crovos. "Go back to Lumine Tower and protect it. I must speak to these two."

Crovos nodded, gave Evress an apologetic look, and disappeared.

Sylvra then turned his attention to Amethine — his expression stoic as he released her.

"I take it by your presence here that you failed to capture the three individuals you went after."

Amethine was red in the face as she thrust a finger at Evress. "This wretch protected them! She helped them get away!"

Evress wasn't about to sit there and take Amethine's accusations. She'd put up with that witch's abuse more than long enough.

"I had nothing to do with whatever happened where you were! I was about to capture Birdie *here* when you attacked me! You're the reason anyone got away. Don't blame your failures on me!"

"You lying — gck!"

Panic appeared on Amethine's face as she started clawing at the armor over her throat. She struggled to get out even a single sound, and it was clear she couldn't breathe.

"My dear Amethine," said Sylvra coolly as he walked a slow circle around her. "You have repeatedly ignored my warnings not to mistreat Evress, and the moment you believed she was to blame for something horrible, you did not even wait for me to finish speaking before you jumped to action. Moreso, I did tell you to capture the invaders, but from your actions here, I assume you attempted to kill them instead. Perhaps worst of all, you attacked Evress, preventing her from capturing her own targets and forcing Crovos to abandon his post to intervene, which in turn left Lumine Tower open to invasion."

Sylvra released his hold on Amethine, leaving her gasping on the ground and still clutching her throat.

"Now the portals have closed," he continued, "which means there are potentially six anther users who are not registered and are thus *untraceable* running amok in Doxla. Do you have even the slightest inkling of how much damage they could do if they are left unchecked?"

"No," Amethine growled, "it was her. I saw her."

"You saw a *copy* of her!" Sylvra exploded.

Amethine's eyes opened wide in shock — her face pale — but Evress barely noticed.

Evress stared at Sylvra and barely managed to squeak out, "A copy? There's a copy of me?"

Sylvra turned his head toward Evress, but his expression was unreadable. "I would not have believed it had I not seen it myself, but yes. This is a development that you and I must discuss. As for you," Sylvra addressed Amethine once more, "I will not warn you again. Evress is one of us. Mistreat her again, and you will no longer be. Do I make myself clear?"

"Y-you can't replace me," Amethine stuttered, rising to her feet. "No one else knows how to lure in Divine like I do!"

"You forget who taught you," stated Sylvra with eyes narrowed. "Do you believe I cannot teach another?"

Amethine swallowed but said nothing.

"Return to Ars Summis. Once I have spoken to Evress, we must plan for how to tackle this little incursion."

Amethine glanced at Evress, lowered her eyes, bowed, and vanished.

Sylvra sighed, then looked at Evress. "I'm certain you have many questions. In truth, so do I. Let us see if we cannot help each other understand what has taken place here today."

****

"How?" Evress asked quietly as she stared out across the landscape. "How can there be another me? Was that a different Birdie, too?"

Sylvra had taken Evress to a small floating island in the sky. He said he'd wanted to take her to a new location unassociated with Amethine's attack or her confrontation with Birdie, but honestly, she didn't care. Birdie had said she wasn't the same Birdie, so she was inclined to believe Sylvra's claims, but she still didn't understand how it could have happened.

Sylvra, standing next to a worn stone pillar that was part of the ruins on the island, answered. "I admit that I haven't checked in on your friends as I do not have an easy way to track nepacs in any world, but I would assume that yes, the one you call Birdie was not the one that you occasionally speak to during your time off. As for how it is possible, I believe the obvious answer is that your Syrus is responsible."

"But how? When? Wouldn't I have noticed that?"

"That depends on many factors," replied Sylvra. "If you are the original, you are less likely to have noticed, but even if you are not, Syrus could have hidden the action through various means."

Evress was taken aback. "W-what? Are you saying I might be the copy?"

"It is a possibility, but since you were not aware this happened, I find it unlikely. Most probably, either Syrus created copies of you prior to your attempt to take control of the previous Doxla, or he made copies of you as you fled your world. Either way, his intention is clear."

Sylvra met Evress's eyes before he continued. From the look he gave her, she wasn't sure she wanted him to.

"Syrus predicted that I had other worlds, so he made copies of you and your friends for the purpose of continuing his efforts to take control of one of said worlds. The entire evacuation of your Doxla was all to hide this fact, so that I would believe you were the only ones to escape with any grasp of anther, when in truth he had already hidden your copies elsewhere in the Cosmic Graveyard."

"He — no," Evress shook her head. "He wouldn't. No, you're wrong! There must be some other explanation."

"Do you have another explanation for this, then?"

Sylvra created a little bubble showing a rocky shoreline along the world border. A hole had been torn into it, and several portals were scattered about. In the middle of it all, Evress saw another version of herself in silver armor with Jax and Lylia accompanying her.

No, it couldn't be. This had to be fake!

"I record every incident where Doxla's systems are altered or damaged," stated Sylvra. "This happened only ten minutes ago. I have other recordings as well. Would you like to see them?"

Evress shook her head once more. She could hardly breathe. Hearing Sylvra say she'd been copied was one thing, but seeing for herself that it was true — was Sylvra right? Had Syrus actually used her and her friends as bait just so these copies could carry on his work?

She felt sick — betrayed. Tears started to form in her eyes, so she turned away from Sylvra so as not to show them. She needed space. She needed time to process this. She walked away from Sylvra, and to his credit he didn't follow her.

Staring blankly at the ground far below, Evress tried to think of when Syrus could have done the deed. She tried to fathom how he even could, and then she remembered that he had indeed mentioned on multiple occasions his desire to copy himself. It had been months; she'd completely forgotten, but now it seemed so obvious. Of course he would have copied them, but without asking? Without even telling them, and just to leave them to die?

Angrily and through streaming tears, Evress slammed her fist into a nearby pillar and shattered it. It took all of her effort not to let out a scream.

After taking several deep breaths, Evress heard Sylvra finally walk up behind her.

"This is what I am trying to prevent," Sylvra stated. "Few seitti see the lives of others as more than pawns in a game. It seems to me that even your Syrus is no different."

"He's not a seitti," she blurted, though she didn't know why she said it. It's not like that knowledge made her feel any better.

"Is that so?" Sylvra asked, apparently intrigued. "May I ask what he is, then?"

Evress shook her head. "He's just a stupid prifae."

"Interesting," remarked Sylvra. "I don't suppose you happen to know his true appearance, would you?"

"What does that matter?" Evress practically growled, not wanting to talk about Syrus at all right now.

"In the last region that we operated in, there were only a few races called 'prifae' that had access to seitti technology. If I know which race he is from, I may be able to identify the seitti responsible for giving him access to your world to begin with."

Honestly, Evress didn't care, but she also didn't see any reason to hide it.

"He had four arms and tentacles. He also had two legs. You don't need to guess about his seitti, though. Their name is Aurum."

"I see," said Sylvra as he walked to the edge of the island. A few moments later, he continued his thought. "Yes, there is only one 'Aurum' associated with prifae where we last advertised. Once we have dealt with this little problem we've found ourselves saddled with, I will see if I can pull a few strings to make Aurum's — and in turn Syrus's — life difficult as punishment for what Syrus did to you."

Evress lowered her eyes. "That's not necessary."

Sylvra put his arms behind his back and walked away from Evress. "No, I suppose it isn't. We can always decide what to do about Syrus and Aurum at a later time, regardless. For now, we must learn all that we can of whatever plan Syrus's creations are following."

Evress looked back up at Sylvra. "And how are we supposed to do that?"

Sylvra turned to face Evress. "While Amethine failed to capture her targets and enabled yours to escape, I succeeded in imprisoning the third group. If you pretend to be the Eveline that they entered Doxla with, then perhaps you may be able to extract that information from them without resorting to unsavory tactics."

Evress found the thought disgusting, but a part of her was inclined to agree. The fact that Syrus had left her to Sylvra's mercy without even telling her — she never would have believed it possible. But, he did, and that was something she would never forgive. He'd used and betrayed her, and from what the copy of Birdie had said, it sounded like the copies knew exactly what they were and didn't care. They didn't care that Syrus had abandoned her — that he'd abandoned everyone that Sylvra had captured. They were all just as guilty, each and every one of them.

"Alright," Evress finally said. "I'll do it."

Sylvra smiled. "I'm glad to hear it. I do prefer nonviolent solutions whenever possible. Do be careful, though. To prevent any suspicion, I will remove your anther from you beforehand."

"I'll be fine," responded Ev.

Sylvra's smile widened. "And I'll be watching."

Chapter 12

"This is stupid," complained Jax — stuck wearing very broken armor that the group had managed to bend back into a wearable state, though with several straps now cut, it didn't all stay held on very well. "We have no idea where we are in the Underworld. For all we know, we're heading further away from the surface."

Ev, tired of his whining, responded. "If we're going away from the surface, then we're heading toward the Netherworld, and there are plenty of gateways to the surface down there. Regardless, I'm not making more portals, or do you think you'd fair better against Amethine if you have a round two?"

Jax grumbled but otherwise dropped the subject, which was quite the relief. The heat in the area was nigh unbearable without Jax's complaining, and with his pack of supplies having been crushed by Amethine's attack, that left them even shorter on water than they would have been otherwise.

All around them, jets of fire erupted periodically through holes in the brimstone. Bubbles of sulfuric gas burbled up through the magma in the hotter, open regions, while hordes of dark, flaming beasts lurked in the shadows of the cooler tunnels. With their Radiant strength and dwindling water supply, the group elected to keep to the darker areas whenever possible. As a paladin, Jax was the most suited to take on the demonic creatures with his light magic, so Ev and Lylia let him take the lead in most battles, which he was happy to do. The fights almost seemed cathartic to him.

As the group stepped out of one such tunnel and into a particularly spacious cavern, Ev spotted what looked like a great city surrounded by magma off in the distance. A network of paths weaved across the molten rock and connected the city to various tunnels around the edge of the great chamber.

"Finally," Ev said, relieved to see some sign of civilization.

Lylia slithered up close to Ev. "This should prove interesting. We are curious as to the nature of the inhabitants of this Doxla."

"We might be finding out sooner rather than later," Jax warned, drawing his blade as he faced a large formation of brimstone not far away to their right.

Ev could hear shuffling coming from behind it.

"Put that away until we see who it is," she said to Jax. "We don't want to act like we're a threat."

"High level demons can be dangerous to even Radiants," Jax returned quietly. "We can't take any chances."

"It doesn't matter. If they are demons, we could use their help," Ev shot back before stepping closer to the rocks and calling, "Please come out. We don't mean any harm."

The sound of boots against stone behind her made Ev spin just in time to see a trio of sword-wielding demons leap out from behind a large rock by the tunnel's exit. They sprinted forward with flames erupting from their bodies.

Before they could reach the group, Lylia sprung out from a coiled position and slammed her shield into two of them — sending them flying into the hot magma. The third and easily the largest attempted to stab her with his sword, but Lylia pulled away almost as quickly as she'd struck.

Ev didn't get to watch that particular confrontation any further, however, as her attention was pulled away when an arrow clipped her shoulder from behind.

"Ev!" Jax yelled, and he pulled back his sword to unleash his golden arc attack.

"Wait!" Ev shouted, tackling him before he could finish.

The two of them crashed to the ground, and Jax yelled at Ev. "What do you think you're doing?"

"Don't hurt them! We need to talk this out. Agh!"

Ev clutched at a flaming arrow that had just penetrated her armor on her lower side. Fortunately, it hadn't gone deep. While her armor was weak without any enchantments, it was still high quality, and when combined with her Radiant durability, it protected her well enough. Still, if they wanted help, they'd need to deescalate the situation as soon as possible.

Upon seeing Ev struck again, Jax jumped back to his feet, but Ev was faster.

"I'm fine, and I've got this," she called as she pulled out her bow.

Ev nocked a single arrow and drew it back. The arrow began to glow white, and dozens of glowing green bolts appeared around her. The demons behind the brimstone must have noticed, because they ceased their attacks and scrambled away. Once Ev was certain she wouldn't hit any, she released her arrow.

It and the entire volley of green bolts rained upon the demons' cover, blasting holes clean through the rock with violent explosions and leaving little more than rubble remaining. Two of the demons bolted down the path toward the city and left a trail of fire in their wake. That left only one taking cover behind what little remained of the brimstone, the one Lylia was presently toying with, and the two still scrambling to crawl out of the magma. The latter two now seemed hesitant about doing so after seeing Ev's attack, however.

Ev called out to her serpentine companion. "Lylia, will you please stop antagonizing that one?"

Lylia gave a half glance back at Ev and sighed. Her opponent took advantage of the distraction and struck her with a blast of fire, but Lylia shrugged off the attack and countered with a strike of her spear. The blow knocked the demon's sword clear of the battle, and Lylia followed up by wrapping around the demon and constricting him tightly.

The demon screamed curses and insults — especially repeating the words "traitor" and "quisling" — but neither words nor flames did anything to loosen Lylia's vice-like grip.

While Ev was distracted, the sound of an explosive blast reached her ears. She turned to see Jax pointing his glowing sword at the demoness from the rubble, who from her position must have tried to run for the cave entrance. The blast had sent the demoness to the ground, but she thankfully appeared mostly uninjured.

"You don't need to attack if they're running away," Ev stated.

Jax answered without turning or lowering his blade. "If they run away, they'll just bring stronger reinforcements. We shouldn't have let those other two escape."

"We'll be fine," replied Ev. "We just need to show them that we aren't their enemies."

Ev put away her bow and approached both Lylia and her still struggling captive. "May I borrow your spear?"

"Certainly," Lylia smiled as she tossed the weapon over.

Ev caught it. "Thanks."

Spear in hand, Ev approached the two demons who'd fallen in the molten rock. Kneeling as close to the edge as she could manage, she offered them the spear's shaft.

"Grab on; I'll pull you out."

"Do you think us fools?" the male demon spat. "'Tis obviously a trick!"

"Well, if it is, it's not a very good one," returned Ev with a smile. "I think if we meant any harm we'd have an easier time with you stuck where you are."

The two demons exchanged glances before the female one reached out and grabbed the pole. With a tug, Ev pulled the demoness back onto solid rock before doing the same with the other.

Once they were both safely ashore, Ev spoke to them again. "You see? No tricks. My name is Ev, and we're here because we know what the Masters did, and we want to stop them before they can do it again."

That got her new acquaintances' attention.

The male narrowed his eyes. "What exactly do you speak of, outsider?"

Ev put on a more serious tone. "I know that you used to be human. I know they tricked you into becoming demons so Divine could have an enemy to fight against. I also know that this isn't the first world they've done this to, and if they aren't stopped, it won't be the last."

Both demons backed away, visibly nervous.

"Watch your words!" the male hissed. "The Masters will hear, and we will all be destroyed!"

Ev smiled reassuringly. "I don't think they will. The Masters can listen in on Divine, but they can't hear the words of nepacs unless Divine are nearby."

"What nonsense do you speak? You are a Radiant! We witnessed your attack!"

"Let's just say," Ev gestured to Jax and Lylia, "that the three of us found a way around the rules that the Masters put in place, and we aren't the only ones. I can tell you more, but I'd rather we officially end the little conflict that we just had. Do you think you can help calm your friend down? Lylia here will be happy to let him go if she knows he won't attack again. Maybe we can talk more after that."

The demoness growled, but she complied and called to the one in Lylia's coils.

"Belphor! Cease your struggles. Let us hear what these outsiders have to say."

Belphor, clearly exhausted, reluctantly put out his flames. After receiving a nod from Ev, Lylia then released him.

"So his name is Belphor," Ev stated. "What are your names, then?"

The male demon spoke again. "I am Abeleth the Depraved, and this is Meredith the Cleaver."

Abeleth then pointed to the demoness still held at point by Jax's sword. "That is Pyrene the Burning. If you come peaceably as you claim, then call your swordsman away."

"Jax," Ev stated, "that's enough."

Jax gave a sideways look back at Ev before sheathing his sword. He still kept his eye on Pyrene, but Ev was fine with that.

Meredith spoke to Ev again — now somewhat more relaxed but still suspicious. "Do not believe you have earned our trust, Radiant. We have only just received word that Divine have attacked a nearby village. What proof do you have that you are not of their ranks?"

"Did the Divine attacking the village have a naga with them?" Ev asked.

As if on cue, Lylia slid over to Ev and reclaimed her spear with a smile.

Meredith eyed the giant snake lady for a moment. "I suppose that is convincing evidence. Very well. You claimed you broke the Masters' rules. Speak more of this."

Ev answered, but she tried to keep things simple. "We are nepacs, but we aren't from this world. When the Masters were done with our world, they destroyed it. Because of the help of a sympathetic Divine, we survived. We learned that the secret to the Masters' power is something called 'anther,' and in the void between worlds, it is plentiful. We used it to come here and make ourselves Radiants, and once we get to Ars Summis, we'll use it to put a stop to the Masters forever or die trying."

Abeleth's tail twitched. "You insult us! Do you expect us to believe such fantasy?"

"You saw all those portals earlier, didn't you?" Ev countered. "Those gateways leading to other parts of the world? We did that. When we made ourselves Radiants, the Masters could sense that we broke their systems, and they attacked, but we used the portals to confuse them and escape. They'll be watching for us to use anther again, but the next time we do, we'll be where they're most vulnerable."

Abeleth scowled, but Meredith looked on with interest.

"Long have we known the true colors of the Masters," she said. "If what you say is true, it brings me great joy to see their sins return upon them."

Abeleth rounded on Meredith. "You must jest! Surely you do not believe such outlandish tales."

Lylia laughed. "Oh, but this one does speak the truth. We can offer proof with our own Radiance. Although, it occurs to us that we are not sure how to manifest the wings of a Radiant. Ah, but we know. Allow us to demonstrate another way."

Ev had a feeling she knew what Lylia was about to do and nodded her approval. The demons all watched in awe as Lylia pointed her spear at the nearby cavern wall and unleashed an incredible bolt of light. The attack blasted a giant hole clean through the rock deeper than they could see. Lylia giggled at the look of utter shock on Abeleth's face.

"S-such is impossible," he stuttered. "A naga cannot possess such an ability."

Ev stood up tall next to Lylia. "They can if they are made into Radiants."

Meredith's surprise turned to laughter as she exclaimed, "Then it is true! We must inform Queen Ibilis at once."

Ev blinked. She must have heard Meredith wrong. Though Ev had personally only once ever seen her, Ibilis was the name of the Demon Queen from *her* Doxla.

Abeleth looked wary but he agreed. "I do not see how what they claim is possible, but neither do I see any other explanation for a naga capable of a Radiant's attack. Belphor, Pyrene! We shall escort these three to the capital. Queen Ibilis will decide what to make of them."

So, she had heard correctly. If this world had a Queen Ibilis, then it likely had another version of every other immortal as well — including Dezeroth and his undead hordes. Syrus wasn't the only one willing to make copies of people, it would seem, not that Ev was surprised that the Masters would do something like that. Did this Doxla also have another version of herself? She supposed it depended on what point in time Sylvra copied this Doxla from.

Ev glanced back at Jax and Lylia to see if either of them had made the connection. From Lylia's expression, she certainly had. Jax was a bit harder to read, but he seemed to be deep in thought about something.

"Why do you appear worried?" Abeleth asked. "Is it because you are not what you claim and know of Queen Ibilis's power? Know that if you do not speak the truth, you will not leave the city alive. Radiants you may be, but we are many, and we have slain Radiants before."

Ev faced Abeleth, not about to let him mistake her thoughts for concern. "We look forward to meeting with your queen. The Masters are strong, but they aren't invincible. The more powerful our allies, the greater our chance of success."

The sound of a horn blew in the distance, interrupting the conversation.

"What was that?" Ev asked.

"The Divine have attacked!" yelled Abeleth. "Conter Sul has been breached!"

Belphor erupted. "We have been deceived! These three were but a distraction."

"Don't be an idiot!" Jax yelled at him. "We have nothing to do with that. Ev, we can't be here. We can't be spotted by other Divine. If they report us to the Masters—"

"Where are we supposed to go?" Ev shot back. "We don't have any water, and if we make portals again, we can expect more than just Amethine to come after us this time. We need their help as much as they need ours."

"You aren't seriously suggesting that we barge into the city to fight Divine, are you? Odds are everyone will think we're invaders, too, and I'm pretty sure the demons can handle themselves."

"Maybe they can," replied Ev, "but historically speaking, experienced Divine don't start fights they aren't sure they can win. Even if the demons do win, the Divine will do a lot of damage before they're through."

Jax wasn't swayed. "Think, Ev. If the Masters learn that we're here, we're finished."

Lylia lost her usual jovial tone. "Jax is correct. Even if we all flee before we are caught, the Masters will know we were here. They will show no mercy to the local residents to learn what they can of us."

Ev cursed. They were right, of course. The only thing that mattered was stopping the Masters. Perhaps they could find another village with water before they all died of thirst.

The sound of an explosion from the city reached the group. Jax placed his hand on Ev's shoulder.

"I'm sorry, but this city will recover. Immortals always revive. We won't."

Ev nodded. "Yeah. I know. Let's go."

The group turned to leave when Meredith scurried after them.

"Wait!" she shouted. "The words you have spoken — they are true, are they not? If you would aid us, we shall aid you in turn."

Abeleth yelled after her. "That is not your decision to make. Queen Ibilis —"

"Be silent, Abeleth," Meredith shouted back. She turned her attention back to Ev again. "If we take you to the royal armory, you can hide your true selves behind masks. You can blend in with the Queen's elite guard."

"Sorry," said Jax, "but we can't risk it. Besides, Lylia would stand out like a sore thumb."

"That is not necessarily so," remarked Lylia. "If this world is like our own, there is a tribe of naga that have made the Underworld their home. It is not inconceivable that one would visit the demon capital."

"That's right," Ev spoke her thoughts out loud, "and with the right enchantments, we can be given temporary alignment with the fire element to complete the illusion. If we could keep the weapons and armor afterward, we'd have an excellent cover after leaving the Underworld."

"Aid us, and you may keep whatever you desire," stated Meredith.

Abeleth looked like he was about to object, but instead he sighed, "You have the strength of Radiants. If you assist us, then I, too, will offer you my aid."

Ev nodded, then turned to her companions. "I say we do it. Any objections?"

"Not a one!" said Lylia.

Jax didn't seem completely convinced, but he agreed nonetheless.

"Then come quickly," said Meredith. "We must escort you to the palace before the invaders get there."

* * * *

The demons escorted Ev and company to the gates of the large city where they were greeted with hostility. After some convincing from their escorts, however, they were not only allowed in, but given further escort by the guards to the palace.

There, both Ev and Jax received new suits of black, spiked armor. The suits came with protective masks that hid all but their eyes. Lylia also took the opportunity to upgrade her armor, though only for the human-like part of her. Once they were properly outfitted, they found new weapons with fire enchantments to help with the ruse.

As they finished up, one of the guards said to them, "We place much trust in you, outsiders. Were it any less than the word of the Queen's niece and nephew professing your intent, you would not be standing here today."

Ev looked up at the guard in surprise. "Her niece and nephew?"

The guard motioned with his head to a grinning Meredith and stern Abeleth.

"You two are related to Queen Ibilis?" Ev asked.

"Not by blood," replied Abeleth. "Our stepfather is the Queen's half-brother. Our mother was but one of many wives he took before we became demons."

Jax donned his mask and headed toward the door. "That's all very interesting, but if we're going to do this, we need to do it now. It's already been thirty minutes since the horn blew."

"We feel the vibrations of battle drawing nearer," remarked Lylia. "We all will not have far to go to meet the Divine."

Ev turned to the guard. "We just need fire-alignment enchantments to complete the disguise."

Abeleth stated, "Pyrene is capable of such."

Ev nodded and turned to Pyrene. "Then we'll need you to stay nearby and out of sight to make sure we stay enchanted."

An explosion rocked the room.

"Damn it," said Jax. "I told you we need to hurry. They're already at the palace!"

"We're ready," Ev said as she put on her own mask and grabbed a healing rod to extend the range of her spells. "Let's send these Divine back where they came from."

The group ran out of the armory and towards the battle, which had already reached the palace courtyard. At the opening to the outer yard, nearly ten Divine had taken cover. Large statues littered the area and provided cover for the guard, but dozens of demon guards had already been wounded or killed in the area. Still, the elite guard had managed to halt the progress of the Divine up to this point, though it was clear that their defenses wouldn't hold for much longer.

Jax sounded nervous from behind his mask as they surveyed the area from the second floor balcony. "This is a bad idea. They must be Radiants if they've made it this far on their own."

Ev kept close to Jax. "We don't know that this is all of them, and even if it is, you can see that some of them are staying back."

"Those are probably healers and support," Jax replied.

"Then they're who we need to defeat first," said Ev.

"Obviously," stated Jax before turning to Pyrene. "How long will your enchantment last?"

"Five minutes," she replied.

Jax thought about that for a second. "Alright then. You'll need to come with me. Ev can always pull back if her enchantment wears off, but I might not be able to."

Ev turned her head to Jax. "We shouldn't split up. We should fight together."

"We should end this quickly," Jax countered. "Lylia and I will flank their backs. When you see my golden arc, that will be your signal to rain your arrows down."

Ev growled, but she knew Jax had more experience with this kind of battle.

As soon as Ev was enchanted with fire-alignment, Jax and Lylia took off with Pyrene back into the castle halls to make their way to the Divine.

While she waited for the signal, Ev snuck across the balcony to get closer to the invaders. Though they were on the ground, it was obvious they were watching the balcony closely, as they unleashed magic bolts at the balcony's structure itself any time they were fired upon from above. The destruction of the balcony brought the upper defenders down to the ground, and it furthermore made it difficult to traverse the upper level. Fortunately, there were multiple openings to the balcony from the second floor halls, which Ev used to work her way to a position near the Divine. Even more fortunate — the damage the Divine had done to the upper floor provided her with a crack in the wall from which she could observe without fear of being spotted.

About two minutes passed before a golden arc — enchanted to now be ablaze with fire — ripped through the ground floor's wall. Ev knew that was her signal, but most of the Divine had backed up out of her range in response to reinforcements to the guard within the yard. If Jax and Lylia were on the other side, however, then her chance would come soon enough.

A second arc of fire came, but she still didn't have a shot. Then, instead of the Divine doing as she'd predicted, they turned and pressed back in Jax's direction!

She didn't have a choice now. Ev jumped out from behind her cover and dropped to the floor below — trusting that her Radiant's strength would protect her from the fall.

It did, thankfully, and she rushed forward to take a clear shot at the entire group of Divine.

Drawing back an arrow, it once again glowed white with energy. The bolts that appeared around her, however, were this time made of fire.

When Ev released her bow, dozens of flaming bolts rocketed toward the Divine. Several of them hit, and even those that didn't struck the ground with fiery explosions. She doubted they would do much, as anyone with half a mind attempting to assault this place would have brought all the flame protection they could manage, but the force of the explosions should at least have done a little damage.

The attack drew the attention of the Divine back to her, and Ev jumped behind a large statue of a dragon as a powerful spell encased the area around her in ice.

The surviving guards, perhaps emboldened by Ev's attack, rushed forward to follow up with their own spells and sustained heavy injuries in the process.

Ev switched her focus to healing and pointed her stave at as many injured as she could. Unfortunately, she didn't have any group-healing spells since she hadn't expected to be supporting many allies, but with her now immense supply of magic and ridiculous healing speed, she was able to mostly keep up with the injuries even if she could only heal one at a time.

Her support seemed to make a great difference, however. With their injuries healing completely and almost immediately after occurring, they pressured the Divine even harder. With her support on this side and Jax and Lylia backing the guard on the other, the Divine found themselves squeezed between two forces they couldn't keep up with and were soon overwhelmed. The first to fall was a healer at the center of the group — pierced by Lylia's light beam through the chest — followed by a spellcaster who seemed to be responsible for maintaining enchantments on the others. After that, their rout was swift. With Jax leading the charge from the other side, it only took about sixty seconds before the last of the Divine had been slain. Their bodies vanished to leave only their glowing Hearts behind.

Ev ran out from her cover toward the others to aid the demon healers with the remaining injuries.

"We did it!" she exclaimed to Jax when she got there.

"We did," returned Jax. "I don't know if those guys were Radiants or not, but if they were, they must have been low-ranking."

Lylia picked up one of the spherical Hearts and tossed it between her hands a few times. "These were indeed low-level Radiants. One may tell their status from the appearance of the Hearts."

A loud crash in the distance interrupted the conversation.

One of the guards shouted, "The Stone is in danger!"

Jax sighed through his mask. "Looks like this isn't over."

The group joined the guards as they rushed off toward the palace throne room. When they arrived, the main entrance had been blocked by the Divine. Two bulky soldiers stood in the doorway while a pair of mages cast spells from behind them. Ev didn't see a healer, but she was sure there must have been one hiding out of sight. Beyond the doorway, a larger group of Divine had engaged who Ev assumed to be the Queen and her personal guard. Behind the Queen was the throne itself, which had been built against a pillar topped with an enormous blue stone that produced an endless stream of water.

Queen Ibilis was able to keep the Divine from approaching her with waves of blue, cursed fire, but her guards had clearly lost their healer while the Divine had not.

Jax addressed Pyrene. "We need that enchantment back, now."

Pyrene reapplied the fire-alignment to Jax and Ev.

"Alright, there's not many at the gate. I'm pretty sure I can take them out. Cover me!" Jax yelled as he charged headlong past the demon guards and into the Divine blockade.

Ev ran with Jax a short distance before stopping and taking aim at one of the mages. Her arrow stuck in the mage's armor but didn't go deep, but it did succeed in interrupting whatever spell he was casting.

The second mage blasted Jax with ice just as he unleashed his own magic burst from his hand at the ceiling above the Divine. The ice froze Jax's feet in place while Jax's explosion brought rubble down on the enemy soldiers. Jax prepared to use his golden arc when he was picked up out of the ice by Lylia and lobbed at the Divine.

Canceling his arc attack, Jax instead thrust his blade straight through the chest plate of a Divine soldier who'd been caught off guard between the falling rubble and sudden attack. With a fiery burst from Jax channeling his magic through his sword, the Divine vanished.

The second large soldier retaliated with a swing of his ax, which managed to break through Jax's armor behind his knee and cause Jax to buckle. Before another attack could come, however, Lylia wrapped her tail around the soldier and literally crushed him as she skewered one of the mages with her spear.

The other mage retreated, but by now Ev had reached the entrance to the throne room as well.

She tapped Jax with a healing hand as she pulled out a dagger and rounded the corner. As she'd expected, there was a healer taking cover by the wall.

The healer drew a short sword and attacked, but Ev was able to parry the blow easily.

Out of the corner of her eye, she saw a beam of fire explode against the surviving mage's stomach, which knocked him to the ground before he could attack again.

While Ev let Jax deal with him, she leapt forward and caught the healer's sword in her hand mid-swing.

She felt her gauntlet crack from the impact, but Ev herself was unharmed. The healer opened her eyes wide in shock and tried to back away, but Ev pushed forward and stabbed the Divine in the chest.

The healer dropped her sword but didn't fall as she stumbled backward and quickly began healing herself. As impressive as the healer's tenacity was, it wouldn't be enough to save her.

A part of Ev felt bad as the Divine vanished from a final strike delivered by her own sword. Most likely, these Divine all thought they were fighting for what was best for the world, but that didn't change the fact that they were wrong. Besides, getting split was merely an inconvenience for beings like them. They would lose their strength, sure, but they'd revive instantly far away from here.

With the central blockade removed, demon soldiers stormed into the chamber and quickly overpowered the remaining Divine. Before long, only a pile of Hearts remained, which a few soldiers carried off to some unknown location.

As the soldiers cleaned up, Meredith and Abeleth approached Ev, Jax, and Lylia. Meredith was practically giddy, and even Abeleth looked pleased with the situation.

Meredith spoke first. "Wonderful! This truly is the beginning of the time of reckoning for the Masters!"

Abeleth looked at Meredith. "Nothing that transpired today matched the power of the Masters. These three have been true to their word; that is all."

"Their word," growled Meredith, "is that they have obtained some of the Masters' power for themselves and can slay those deceivers at Ars Summis. We must aid them in whatever manner they require."

A booming female voice interrupted their conversation.

"Meredith! Abeleth! Is it true that you brought outsiders into the palace?"

Meredith and Abeleth jumped as they turned to face Queen Ibilis behind them.

Now that the battle was over, Ev could see the Queen more clearly. She looked exactly like the one she'd seen back in her Doxla — taller and slightly darker-skinned than most demons, with glowing blue eyes and long white hair draped over her black and silver armor.

"My Queen," began Abeleth. "We have found those responsible for the strange gateways that appeared across the kingdom. They have come from another world and seek to dethrone the Masters!"

Queen Ibilis narrowed her eyes. "Is that so? And you believe their claims?"

Abeleth and Meredith exchanged glances.

Ev removed her mask and approached Ibilis. "Your Majesty, we—"

"Humans? You brought *humans* here?"

"Now hold on—" Jax began, but Ev cut him off.

"Yes, we're humans, just like you were centuries ago."

Ibilis studied Ev carefully. "A wise woman would have claimed to be brigands. Of course, a wise woman would never have come here. Why did you help us against the Divine? Do you expect some sort of reward?"

"We did it because you needed help and so do we," replied Ev.

Ibilis smirked. "Of course."

Jax spoke up again. "Listen, we just want some water and equipment to help us get back to the surface."

"Not anymore," said Ev as she looked sideways at a surprised Jax. "Amethine attacked us almost instantly when I used anther. The others were probably attacked as well. For all we know, we might be the only ones left."

Ev turned her attention back to Ibilis. "We're going to attack Ars Summis. I know how to break in. I can even kill the guardian, but I need help distracting the Masters so I can get to the central tower. That's the only place that they can be truly hurt. If I can get there, I can defeat them."

Ibilis scoffed. "You are mad. I do not care if you are the ones who made those gateways. What you say is nonsense. Why would the Masters be any more vulnerable at their tower?"

"They aren't physically," replied Ev, "but that place is how they connect to this world from their realm. That's their weakness."

Ibilis sighed — her eyes surprisingly tired — and looked up at Lylia. "And what of you? Are you also filled with such blind assurance?"

"Oh-ho, not at all," replied Lylia with a smile. "We know the odds are unfavorable, but it is either this, or we all live in hiding for the rest of our lives. Such a fate would be so boring."

"Boring," Ibilis repeated. "Yes, that it is. Sometimes I feel that death may have been preferable to what we were given. I truly cannot understand how others do not grow weary of it all."

"It doesn't have to stay the way it is," said Ev. "If you want things to change, we need your help. We need to spread the word to other immortals to watch for more portals to open, because when I get to Ars Summis, I will open countless of them around the world. All of them will lead to the City of the Divine."

"And what then?" asked Ibilis. "Would you have immortals storm the city?"

"Lylia and I both have some of the same power as the Masters. One of us can create the portals and disable the protections around Ars Summis while the other breaks into the tower. We won't be able to do that without something to keep the Masters busy, however. That's where immortals would come in."

Ibilis studied Ev's face. "You ask much of us, human. I will not grant you this request."

Ev stammered. "W-what? But—"

"I have long ceased caring what fate befalls the world beyond this city. My purpose is to defend the Stone of Chiron. All else matters not to me. Should any others of the demon clan choose to aid you, that is their business. I will grant you water and equipment in gratitude for your aid, but that is all I will give you."

Ev closed her gaping mouth. She supposed she shouldn't have been all that surprised. The Ibilis from her world hadn't helped Syrus against the threat of Lord Grandis, either.

"Thank you," she managed to get out. "We appreciate anything you can give us."

Ibilis merely turned away and dismissed the group with her hand. Meredith and Abeleth then escorted them from the throne room. Once they were away from Ibilis, Meredith spoke to them.

"Do not despair. Queen Ibilis has decreed that all who desire may aid you. We shall spread the word on your behalf. We shall eagerly await these portals that you have spoken of."

"Thank you," returned Ev. "Be sure you tell everyone only to act if the portals lead to Ars Summis. I don't expect we'll need to, but it's always possible we might have to open up random portals to escape from the Masters again should we be caught."

The two demons smiled.

"All shall know," said Abeleth. "Now, let us see to it that you receive all that you require for your journey."

Chapter 13

Sylvra released Evress from his field of imprisonment and dropped her into the middle of a vast, grassy field. She recognized the area as the "prison" world that he'd taken her to back when she'd first escaped from Doxla. As she hit the ground, Gare rushed to her side, while Nictis and Tallis stayed back and eyed Sylvra warily.

"Ev! Are you okay?" Gare asked as he helped her up.

Evress brushed the grass off of her broken armor. Sylvra had helped her find a suit that looked like the one her copy had been wearing, and the two of them had roughed it up to make it look like she'd been involved in a battle. They didn't need a backpack as Sylvra had taken the weapons and supplies of the others already, so they'd expect him to do the same to her. He and Evress hadn't had too much time to rehearse, but she'd memorized the key points Sylvra wanted to press and what to avoid.

"I'll be fine," Evress answered. "I was able to heal myself before I got captured."

Sylvra called out from his position floating above them all. "I repeat my earlier offer to you. Tell me how many of you exist, and you will be treated well. Refuse, and you shall remain in this empty place forever."

Nobody said anything in response.

"Then live with the regret of your choice," Sylvra stated before vanishing.

The four of them all stared at the place Sylvra had been for several seconds before Gare broke the silence.

"I really don't like that guy," he said.

"Forget about him," said Tallis. "We need to find a way out of here."

"What is this place?" Evress asked, acting like she didn't know. "It looks like a field."

"Yeah, it's a field," said Gare, "but it's a *big* field. We've been walking since we got here, and there's literally nothing but grass."

"It can't go on forever," Tallis said. "It's got to be one of those other worlds that we found."

Evress tried not to show her surprise at that remark. Just what had these copies been up to?

Nictis joined in the conversation. "It is pointless to keep walking. We shall never reach the end on foot, and certainly not before Sylvra returns again. We must devise a different solution. Only cleverness will save us." She turned to Evress. "Ev, inform us of what happened. Where are Lylia and your brother?"

That was the question she'd been waiting for. Shaking her head, Evress lamented, "I don't know. When Amethine attacked, I made more portals so they could escape, but then Sylvra appeared and caught me."

Tallis looked at Nictis. "Sounds like they're still free then. Well, at least half of us still have a chance."

"A chance?" Evress repeated. "What chance? Maybe if it was just Amethine, they'd stand a chance, but you saw what Sylvra is capable of."

"Whoa, whoa," said Gare, "what's all that talk about? You're the one who said we should do this. 'Nothing else matters,' right?"

"Indeed," said Nictis, walking over to Evress. "I opposed such reckless action, but you convinced these fools to proceed nonetheless. You convinced even your brother, yet now you declare hopelessness?"

Nictis grabbed the front of Evress's armor by her collar and pulled her forward. "I do not want to hear such from you. If your words are truly what you feel, then you never deserved to be Syrus's protege."

Nictis shoved Evress away and started off in the opposite direction.

"Now hold on—" Gare started, but Nictis interrupted him.

"Silence, large one!" she shouted as she grabbed Tallis by the wrist.

"Hey, what—?" he began.

"You and I shall devise our own escape," she growled. "The girl wishes to admit defeat. Such a mindset is useless."

Tallis gave an apologetic look back at Evress as Nictis dragged him away. That was not the response Evress had been hoping for. She started after them, but Gare stopped her.

"Best let Nictis let off some steam," he said. "Besides, it sounds like you've got some heavy thoughts on your mind. If you want to share, I've got an ear. It's not like there's much else I can do here, after all."

With a sigh, Evress turned to Gare. She expected he'd be the least likely to know the details of the copies' plan, but there was something she was sure she could glean from him.

"Why did you come here, Gare?" she asked.

Gare shrugged and smiled. "Well, it's not like that Sylvra fellow gave me much of a choice."

"No, I mean, why did you come to this Doxla with me, really?"

With a mighty groan, Gare plopped himself into a sitting position on the ground with one hand over his knee. He motioned for Evress to join him, which she did.

"It's like I said," he told her. "This whole mess is all or nothing. Sure, I could have stayed back with Ronda and Marin, but if you guys failed, well, there's nothing I'd have been able to do when the Masters came looking for the rest of us. At least this way I thought I could maybe help a little. Turns out I didn't even get the chance, huh?"

So, Syrus had made copies of Ronda and Marin, too. Evress had to wonder just how many more were out there. They had to be somewhere in the Cosmic Graveyard, which suggested there were definitely more anthermancers with them, which was one of the things that Sylvra wanted to know. She did feel a little bad about probing; after all, it was possible that not all of the copies were aware of what they were. Still, Syrus had betrayed them so that these copies could live, and she now had a chance to really make a difference. These copies could ruin everything if they started a revolt in the new Doxla. Their assault was pointless anyway. If there was one thing Evress had learned about Sylvra, it was that he was the only one capable of accessing his core systems.

"Yeah," said Evress with a hint of genuine sympathy. Still, she had a job to do. "I guess none of us did. It was a stupid plan, anyway."

"Nah, Ev," replied Gare. "I mean, sure, it was a long shot, but we all knew that. But just think about it. We've still got Jax, Birdie, and everyone else still out there. It was your plan that kept them from being captured, and it's your plan that will win this. You just need to believe in those guys. They've beaten folks like the Masters before, right?"

"Yeah, I guess so," Evress said, starting to feel awkward. "But there's only five of them now. How are they supposed to pull it off on their own?"

Gare didn't look confident as he answered. "Well, I mean, they do still have two anthermancers. It sounded like that's really all they need, right?"

They only need two anthermancers, Ev thought. That didn't tell her much, but if her copy had the same mind as her, maybe she could take a guess at their strategy. The only thought that came to her immediately was the idea that one anthermancer might cause a distraction while the other broke into Sylvra's control room, but that seemed too desperate to be right.

There was one way to find out. "Do you think two is enough?"

Gare shrugged. "Beats me. I don't know enough about any of how that anther stuff works. Do you think it's possible? Like, is there even a chance it might work?"

Evress shook her head and answered honestly. "I don't know. I think it depends on if it's even possible to access Sylvra's core systems. Even if it is, though, the odds of getting to them with just two anthermancers are incredibly slim."

Gare stretched and stood up before brushing off some grass that had gotten pinched in the crevices of his armor. "Right. Well then, sounds like we need to find a way out of here to improve those odds, wouldn't you say?"

Before Evress could respond, she heard Sylvra's voice in her head.

"Agree to help them. I will prepare a scene for you not far from here. Use it to escape. Get them to lead you to where the others are — both those in the Cosmic Graveyard and those in Doxla, but do nothing to compromise your identity."

A knot started to form in Evress's stomach. The thought of tricking Gare into revealing the location of his family didn't sit well with her. Still, she knew she had to do this. She just needed to keep in mind that these people were merely copies of the people she cared about. For all she knew, they might not even be real people at all. Syrus wasn't a seitti, after all; perhaps it wasn't in his power to make real copies of people.

Evress forced a smile onto her face as she stood up. "You know what? You're right. We shouldn't give up just because things look hopeless. Maybe if we keep walking, we'll find something we can use."

Gare clapped Evress hard on the back. "That's the Ev I know! I'll go get the others."

"I'll come, too," Evress said.

Tallis and Nictis weren't far away. They were arguing in hushed voices, but they stopped as Evress and Gare approached.

"Guess what?" Gare called to them. "We're all getting out of this place!"

"We are?" asked Tallis. "How?"

"I have no idea," replied Gare with a smile before clapping Evress on the back again, "but Ev's feeling herself again, so now we've got twice as much knowhow behind us."

Nictis scowled. "Tallis and I know just as much as Ev about anther."

"I know," replied Gare with a goofy grin, "but seeing as how I know less than nothing, I figured I probably cancel one of you guys out."

Nictis appeared unamused by Gare's remark, but Tallis seemed happy enough.

"So, what's the plan, then?" Tallis asked.

Evress shrugged. "I don't really have one. Without anther, we're stuck here."

"Obviously," Nictis interjected.

Evress frowned. "That's why I think we should keep walking. I know it's not likely that we'll find anything, but we definitely won't find anything just staying here."

"Thank you," said Tallis, shooting a look in Nictis's direction.

Nictis growled. "Very well, but we are naught but wasting energy."

The small group traveled in the direction they'd been facing when Evress first arrived. The open field really did extend as far as the eye could see — seemingly forever. Evress kept her eyes open for whatever "scene" Sylvra had prepared, but it wasn't until two hours later that she saw it.

"What's that?" she pointed to a patch of gray in the distance.

Upon closer inspection, the gray turned out to be a large amount of ash with clumps of mostly human bones protruding from it. Most of the bones were only partially intact and looked as if large portions of them had simply vanished from existence.

"Holy hell," said Gare. "What the heck happened here?"

Evress simply shook her head before stepping into the ash. She needed to find what Sylvra had left her to use to escape; presumably it was a patch of—

"Anther!" shouted Tallis.

Evress turned to see him holding half of a skull.

Nictis approached him cautiously. "Impossible. Anther should float freely unless it is willed to remain in place."

"If you don't believe me, then see for yourself," Tallis shot back as he tossed the skull to Nictis.

As soon as the skull landed in her hands, Nictis's eyes opened wide, then she frowned.

"No. This must be a trap. The Masters would not have left anther here carelessly."

Evress picked up a piece of femur and felt the anther for herself. "Maybe the Masters didn't think there was enough here to do anything with. There's not very much."

"And how much is required to break through a world barrier?" Nictis shot back. "It makes no sense for them to have let *any* remain."

Tallis tossed a pelvis clear of the ash and picked up another bone. "Maybe not, but it's here, and it's our only chance at escaping. I for one plan to use it."

"I'm with Tallis," said Evress. "We can escape, regroup, then try and meet up with the others."

Gare scratched at his head before adding his thoughts. "Not to be a downer, but won't the Masters know if you guys use that stuff? I mean, I assume that's how that Sylvra guy found us the first time."

"That's a good point," Tallis said. "Once we start, we'll have to move quickly."

"We should make a plan, then," said Evress. "We don't have any supplies, so we'll need to restock before trying again."

"That concern is minimal," stated Nictis. "Our true challenge will be escaping pursuit. We will not have time to create complex tools to misdirect our pursuers."

"Maybe we don't need to," Evress offered.

The others looked at her.

"We're the only ones here, right? That means the Masters couldn't find any of the others. *That* means the Masters aren't able to follow where portals go, even if they can detect where they are created. They clearly can't even detect when anther is used in the Cosmic Graveyard, so as long as we make a portal the moment we break through the world barrier, we should be safe."

Tallis looked from Evress to Nictis. "You know, hearing it out loud, that almost sounds too easy, but it does seem about right."

Nictis growled. "This does not bode well with me. Something is amiss. I know this."

"Bah," said Gare with a dismissive wave, "you worry too much. What would the Masters even get from allowing us to escape, anyway?"

Nictis growled again, but she didn't have an answer.

"Alright," said Tallis. "Let's do this, then. I'll start by making a portal to the edge of the world. Ev, you need to break through the border while I close the portal. Once we're out, Nictis will make air and warmth while I make another portal. Gare, you keep an eye out for any of the Masters. If they show, we all protect whoever's currently working. We should be able to at least get one of us to safety."

Evress nodded. "Sounds good to me," she said, but truthfully, she didn't know how to break through a world's border on her own.

"Oh, yeah it does!" shouted Gare.

Nictis frowned. "This is a mistake. Mark my words".

"Just do your job," Tallis ordered before gathering up more remnants of anther from the bones.

Where Sylvra had gotten the bones, Evress wasn't sure she wanted to know, but she also siphoned what she hoped would be enough anther. As she worked, Sylvra's voice entered her head once more and gave her instructions on how to break the world's barrier.

"Okay. Everyone ready?" asked Tallis.

The rest of the group nodded.

Tallis jumped straight to work on his portal. Once on the other side, Evress did her best to follow Sylvra's instructions, and was relieved when a hole in the world appeared. Tallis closed his portal and jumped through Evress's tear. Gare and Nictis followed right behind, with Evress taking up the rear. She began working on closing up the tear, but before she could finish, she heard Gare shout.

"Above us!"

Evress looked up and froze in shock.

Sylvra pointed the palm of his hand at Nictis as he spoke. "My, my. How frustrating."

In an instant, Nictis vanished in a cloud of dust.

"Nictis!" shouted Tallis as he completed his portal.

Sylvra spoke in Evress's head again. "She lives. Do not hesitate. Run."

Before she could react, however, Gare had already tackled Tallis through the portal. Sylvra dropped down before the portal as if to pursue them, and Evress knew she had to put on a show.

Rushing from behind, she attacked Sylvra with an invisible force from the side that sent him flying away. She then dove through the portal and closed it, leaving them in freezing, absolute blackness.

Without Nictis's ball of warmth, the cold was so intense that it felt like Evress's exposed skin was on fire. Thankfully, warmth quickly returned — light following shortly after — as Tallis created his own glowing ball.

"Come on," urged Gare as he pulled Tallis to his feet. "He might be right behind us!"

"If he can follow us here, then he can follow us anywhere," Evress stated.

The two of them looked at her — both with genuine fear on their faces. Tallis clenched his jaw, clearly upset about what had just happened. It was enough to make Evress realize that, copies or not, they felt all the emotions that their original counterparts would.

The three of them stood in silence atop a barren black mountain as they waited for Sylvra to arrive, but he never did. Of course he didn't; he really couldn't follow them, and he wanted Evress to find the other copies, regardless.

After a few minutes, Evress spoke again. "Come on. We should head back home, regroup, and resupply. We'll need to move quickly so we can act again while Sylvra still thinks we're scared."

"No," replied Tallis.

Evress looked at him in surprise, and Tallis locked eyes with her.

"Like you said, we should move quickly. We should go back to our Doxla to get more weapons and supplies, but then we should attack again immediately. Going back to the settlement will only waste time."

That wasn't what Evress wanted to hear. She needed to find their settlement, but she also had to stay in character with what her copy would likely say.

"Yeah," said Evress. "You're right. The sooner, the better. Going now is our best chance at catching the Masters off guard."

"Then it's settled," said Tallis. "I'll work on finding the old and new Doxlas again, while you recreate all those tools you'd prepared for us last time."

"Oh, right," Evress replied, hoping she didn't sound nervous.

She could only guess at what her copy had created, but she did have some ideas. Before that, however, she had a suspicion that she could still locate where the other anthermancers were hiding. Syrus's plan had been to create a communications network, and she knew how to create a node for it. If the copies had succeeded in making it, then she should be able to connect to it as well, and she could find the other anthermancers that way.

So, while Tallis worked on locating Doxla again, she searched for the network that she hoped existed. When she found it, she connected her node and—

Evress nearly gasped at what she found. She had to turn away from the others so as not to show her surprise. The number of others connected to the network was more than she could count. Just how many copies had Syrus made? And why weren't more of them involved in the assault on Doxla?

She supposed it didn't matter. Now that she knew where the others were hiding, she needed to quickly create the tools she imagined her counterpart would have created. Based on her conversation with the copy Birdie, one of the tools had to be something that would allow her to make nepacs into

Radiants. Unfortunately, that wasn't something she knew how to do, but maybe with the right excuse, she wouldn't have to.

Instead, she focused on creating the few tools she was sure the other Ev would have made. Once she was done, she looked back at Tallis.

"Okay, all ready. You?"

"For the past five minutes," he replied coldly.

The way he answered made her uneasy, but she was nearly done with this charade.

"Hey," she said, trying to break the tension. "We got this. We beat Lux Rosa, right?"

"Hell, yeah, we did," yelled Gare, and Evress was relieved to see Tallis relax a bit.

"Yeah, we did," he said. "Alright, I'll open up the way."

With that, Tallis created a portal that led to a massive reflective wall that Evress assumed was the border of Doxla. The large holes that had been torn in the wall told her she was correct.

"Give me a moment and I'll take us to Roehelm," Tallis said.

A few minutes later, he did so, and the three of them went to work looking around the icy landscape for supplies.

Weapons were easy to find — the armory was right where it had always been — but food was a bit more problematic. Pickings were scarce, and despite the frozen landscape, most of what was left had rotted. This suggested it had taken a while for Doxla to freeze over.

Seeing Roehelm in this state, Evress began to have doubts that she was following the right path. She knew that one day, the new Doxla would end up exactly like this, but — she had to remind herself — if she didn't help Sylvra, the world would meet the same fate regardless. At least this way, she could alleviate some of the pain along the way, and maybe help train future seitti to follow a better path.

For some reason, Tallis was being very particular with the food they found — insisting that it be in good condition. Evress didn't push it, and Gare seemed happy enough to not be rushing back to the new Doxla, so they went at Tallis's pace. Eventually, the group was able to find something up to his standards, which he quickly duplicated until it filled his pack. With that, they were ready to go back to the new Doxla. With any luck, Tallis or Gare would let the location of the others slip early on, and Evress could be done with all the pretending.

Once at the endless mirror that was the border of the new Doxla, Tallis turned to Evress.

"You have all the tools ready?" he asked her.

"All except the one that makes us Radiants," she said. "That didn't work out so well last time."

"Good call," said Gare. "It'll probably be harder without it, but I'd rather face monsters without magic than run into that Sylvra guy again."

"Agreed," said Tallis. He paused slightly before adding. "You sure you've got everything? Even the sky dimmer? You sure made it awfully fast."

"Well, I have made it before," Evress replied, hoping she wouldn't have to use whatever the "sky dimmer" was before she learned where her counterpart was hiding in Doxla.

"I suppose that's a good point," returned Tallis. "There's just one problem with that. You haven't."

Evress blinked. "W-what—?"

"There was no 'sky dimmer.' Isn't it strange that you didn't know that?"

Evress swallowed.

Gare looked with concern back and forth between Tallis and Evress.

"I suppose you also don't know where we're supposed to meet up with the others, do you?"

Evress felt a knot forming in her stomach. "I mean, of course I do."

"Then where is it?"

Evress swallowed again.

"Hold on," interjected Gare. "Just what is going on?"

"That's what I'd like to know," Tallis answered. "Nictis suspected something was up with Ev. I didn't believe her until she was the only one Sylvra killed. Looks like she was right. The only reason we were let out was so we could lead the Masters to the others. Stop me if I'm getting anything wrong," he said to Evress.

Evress frowned. "No, you're not wrong."

Gare stuttered. "E-Ev? What are you saying?"

"That's not Ev," said Tallis. "It's an impostor."

"You're the impostor!" Evress shouted, pointing a finger at Tallis. "You're just a copy Syrus created when he left the rest of us to die!"

Tallis looked taken aback by that statement, but he recovered quickly. "Nice try. Do you honestly think we're stupid enough to believe that?"

"What's wrong?" Evress prodded, not believing for a second that Tallis didn't know. "Did you think the Masters would kill us all and you fakes would be the only ones left?"

"We aren't copies!" Tallis yelled. "I don't know what you think you can get out of us by saying that, but it won't work."

"Don't lie to me!" Evress returned. "I know what happened. I was there, and I survived!

"You're not Ev; you're an impostor!" Tallis shot back.

"Is that so?" Evress growled and stood up tall. "Then tell me how I know about Lux Rosa. How do I remember when Waylen died on that ship? How do I remember riding the roc to escape from Dezeroth, or when Gare helped Jax slay a dragon, or when you pinned Dezeroth to the ground with earth magnet after he betrayed us?"

Tallis stood his ground, but it was obvious he was shaken. "Th-this is a trick. You found Ev and—"

"And what? Not even Sylvra has the power to read minds. Do you think I'd just tell him my life story?"

"N-no," said Tallis. "Ev would never help the Masters!"

"A lot has happened," Evress replied sadly, "but I've made my decision. I know Sylvra's power, and I know his goals."

"Which are what, exactly?" Tallis asked.

Against her better judgment, Evress told them all she'd learned about Sylvra's plans, about AnAnCol, and about seitti society in general. If Sylvra didn't want them to know, he could deal with it after they were captured, but if there was any chance of concluding this situation without fighting, Evress wanted to try it.

Gare was the first to respond to the news. "Whoa, wait. You're telling me that Sylvra's trying to turn nepacs into seitti? Aren't seitti like, gods?"

"No," replied Evress. "They just think they are."

Tallis glared at Evress with clenched fists. "And that makes it all okay? That makes everything he's done to us *okay?*"

"Of—"

"Even if what you're saying is true, so what?" erupted Tallis. "He causes centuries of suffering just so a handful of lucky nepacs get to become seitti who, for all we know, end up just as crooked as any other. I don't care if it does work. I don't care if he makes 'good' seitti. The people he's hurting have nothing to do with any of that! It's wrong, and the Ev I know could see that in an instant!"

"Then I guess I'm not the Ev you know anymore."

"Clearly," he growled as he positioned himself to attack.

Instinctively, Evress formed a barrier around herself to protect against whatever he might throw at her, but to her surprise he instead opened a pair of portals — one between himself and her, and the other blocking her view from Gare.

Cursing, Evress opened her own portal to behind where Tallis had been, but it was too late. He'd already vanished off to who knew where, and he'd taken Gare with him.

Evress let out a shout of frustration. If only she'd opened a hole in Doxla's barrier, she could have alerted Sylvra to where they were, and maybe he could have prevented their escape. As it was, not only had she failed to learn where the others who'd broken into Doxla were, but she'd let the ones he'd already captured escape. The only silver lining was that she'd been able to locate where the other anthermancers were hiding in the Cosmic Graveyard. With any luck, Tallis and Gare had gone back to them. Though she dreaded Sylvra's reaction to her failure, delaying now would only make things worse.

Evress made her way to the world border and cracked it open. No sooner did she step through, than Sylvra's voice once again entered her head.

"What happened?" he asked, not at all pleased.

Evress grimaced. "Tallis figured out who I was and ran away with Gare."

In a flash, Sylvra appeared before Evress. "How much did you learn from them?"

Evress had to force herself to meet his eyes. "I only found out where the other anthermancers are hiding in the Graveyard."

"How many?"

Evress swallowed. "There are thousands. More than I could count."

"I see," replied Sylvra. "Then it is good that you found them. It would have taken me some time yet to unearth them on my own. Let us go and put an end to that threat so we may concentrate on the one immediately before us."

"What are you going to do?"

"*We,*" Sylvra stated loudly, "are going to capture them as I did the others and strip them of their anther. I will decide on further steps once I have seen for myself what the true natures of these copies are. Come. Let us deal with this matter quickly."

* * * *

Evress opened up a portal high above a strange-looking city illuminated with antherial light. She and Sylvra both peered down upon the place that the anthermancers had made into their home.

"Is this all of them?" Sylvra asked.

Evress quickly used the node she'd created to check.

"No," she answered. "They seem to be scattered across a very wide region."

"How wide?"

Checking again, Evress shook her head. "It's hard for me to tell. The node I made only lets me see the location of one other anthermancer at a time, but it seems like they are all within a few thousand miles of this place."

"Give me the node," Sylvra demanded.

Not wanting to risk getting in any more trouble, Evress removed the shimmering sphere from within her and handed it to Sylvra.

Sylvra examined the node and harrumphed. "I hate having to use anther on a large scale, but it would seem I have no choice here."

Evress swallowed. "What are you going to do?"

She received an annoyed look. "I already told you what our goal is, though I see now the matter was far more urgent than I had imagined."

"What do you mean?"

"This many anther users is bound to draw the attention of the Graveyard's overseers — perhaps even as soon as within the next century. Now, allow me to concentrate."

Obediently, Evress stepped back and observed as Sylvra did something with the node before crushing it into oblivion. He then continued to focus on something she couldn't see — likely creating some antherial tool — before he looked back and beckoned her closer to the portal once more.

"As unfortunate as it is that we failed to locate those who have already infiltrated Doxla, your efforts were not in vain. I have counted more than forty million individuals in the world below, as well as a few others scattered about the Cosmic Graveyard."

Forty million? Syrus had created *forty million* copies of people? The news left Evress completely speechless.

"Seeing this, I feel it safe to conclude that it is actually fortunate that your counterparts launched an assault. Thanks to them, their existence was made known to us, and thanks to you, these copies will be a threat no longer. In fact, they will now aid us in further accomplishing our goals."

Sylvra smiled at Evress, who said nothing. She was still processing the fact that Syrus had not only betrayed her, but had betrayed *forty million* people!

"I see that you are distressed, perhaps by the revelation of the scale of Syrus's crimes?" Sylvra continued, finally regaining Evress's attention. "Do not be. As you will see, I am not like Syrus. I value the lives of all Doxlans, copies or not. I am more than able to accommodate them in a world where they will be safe and of no threat to anyone. Should any of them show promise as future seitti, I will see that they receive souls of their own."

Evress blinked. "So the copies — they really are soulless?"

"They are but empty constructs gifted with the intelligence of actual beings — an intelligence copied from the originals they resemble. Syrus did not and does not have the power to grant them souls as I do."

Evress supposed that was comforting in some strange sense — knowing that Syrus hadn't actually created real people. It also meant that, if she ever needed to, she could fight against the copies of her friends without remorse. At least, she hoped she would be able to.

"Now then," said Sylvra, "let us conclude our business here."

With only a look in the direction of the city from Sylvra, every individual below vanished. A moment later, all of the lights that the anthermancers had created were also extinguished.

"It is done," said Sylvra. "I look forward to evaluating these specimens at a later date, but for now, we must prepare. I will return us to Lumine Tower. Rest if you must; I am sure these revelations have not been easy for you."

"Thank you," said Evress. "Some time to think would be good."

"Then time you shall receive," Sylvra replied. "I must make an announcement to Doxla explaining the situation, then deal with repairing the damage that the sight of those portals would have caused. There is also the matter of significant amounts of anther flooding the world, and it will take some time to make certain that no Divine have taken any for themselves once we remove it. For that reason, I will have Amethine assist me."

"What about Crovos?"

"I will task him with searching for the others still within Doxla. I will inform him that you require space, but I ask that you assist him should he request it. However, should you help him, you must not use anther to search for the copies. For all the damage they have caused, I do not yet deem them a threat worth the risk of searching for them in that manner. Such an action would not only show vulnerability to the Divine of our world, but your copies would detect that we are searching for them, and they may respond with desperation. The last thing I desire is to escalate the situation further without need."

"If Crovos needs help, I'll help him," said Evress. Right now, Crovos was one of the few people she wouldn't mind sharing her thoughts with.

Sylvra smiled, and the two of them returned back to Lumine Tower.

Chapter 14

After the battle at Conter Sul, the journey through the Underworld became far more comfortable. Abaleth had elected to join Ev's party as a guide back to the surface and acted as a mediator any time the group stumbled across other demons. That way, none of them had to reveal who or what they were — aside from Lylia, of course. They had also been provided skeletal hell-horses to help them move much more quickly, with Lylia requiring two to carry her. It was a sight to behold seeing her hold onto and coordinate both of them at once.

After a few hours upon the tireless steeds, the group found themselves in another large magma-filled chamber with another town full of demons — this one built up against the side of the chamber rather than the center. Neither the town nor the chamber were as large as Conter Sul, but that was to be expected. After a quick stop to restock on water, the group headed toward the far side of the chamber.

"We are nearly there," said Abeleth. "Beyond this tunnel lies one of the exits of the Underworld."

"Nearly there" was an understatement. The great stone pillars that marked the exit were only about a hundred yards away. Ev could even make out some of the ornate carvings of demons etched into the pillars' sides.

Abeleth continued. "Only the volcanic caverns shall remain between you and the surface. The path is easy there. As long as you but climb upwards, you will not get lost."

"Thank you," said Ev. "You've really helped us a lot."

Abeleth grinned. "I shall aid in all ways that I can against the Masters. Futile or not, I have dreamed of this day for centuries."

"You know," offered Jax, "you could come with us. We could probably use help convincing Tyranor to help us."

Abeleth's smile faded. "I fear such would be pointless. Dragons are fiends. They were created by the Masters and do not share our hatred of them. No, I believe I would most aid you by spreading your word throughout the Underworld."

"I think you're right," said Ev. "The Underworld is a big place. The more people spreading the message, the better, especially if you can somehow get Dezeroth on our side."

Abeleth looked unsure about that. "I will try, but I make no promises. Dezeroth is not known for understanding."

"That's an understatement," Jax muttered under his breath.

"That's alright if you can't," said Ev. "Any help at all is good. Besides, we might not need him. If we convince Tyranor, we convince all dragons, and I think I know how we can get through to him."

"I wish you the greatest of luck," said Abeleth as he stopped before the entrance to a particularly large tunnel. "This is where we part ways. I certainly look forward to the day of your summons."

Abeleth started back toward the demon town when a shimmering light in the center of the chamber caught everyone's attention. The light shaped itself into a giant sphere, then to Ev's horror, the face of Sylvra appeared within it looking straight at her.

She and the rest of the group froze.

"Greetings," Sylvra spoke. "I regret the disturbance I am sure this announcement will inevitably cause, but an urgent and dangerous development has arisen in Doxla.

"A Divine has broken the most sacred rule of our world and has attempted to claim it for himself. This Divine brought forbidden magic to Doxla and shared it with a group of nepacs that he has indoctrinated to his cause. He has tricked them into believing that he will make them gods should they serve him. This Divine, and most of the nepacs loyal to him, have been apprehended and banished from Doxla. However, some nepacs remain unaccounted for.

"The unnatural gateways you all inevitably saw not long ago were this Divine's attempt at protecting his nepacs from capture. Unfortunately, his attempt was successful for the six nepacs I will now show you."

Sylvra's face vanished from the ball of light, only to be replaced by images of Lylia, Helcant, Umber, Birdie, Jax, and finally Ev, in turn — each of them wearing the armor they'd had when they first breached the boundary of Doxla.

"What the—" Jax began, but he was interrupted when Sylvra reappeared once more.

"The magic gifted to these nepacs has the potential to cause great harm should it be misused. The woman last shown to you is particularly dangerous. As Masters, our first responsibility lies with repairing the damage caused by those gateways so that life may go on as usual. That is why I am declaring an official quest to slay or report these nepacs.

"Any Divine who can do either will immediately be elevated into a Supreme Radiant. Supreme Radiants who succeed in this endeavor will be granted the role of Enforcer. Nepacs — immortals and mortals alike — will be pardoned of any and all past crimes and granted eternal protection, as well as access to one hundred acres of any land they desire. Should multiple individuals assist in stopping this threat, all will receive the full reward promised. Thank you for your time, and may your efforts restore safety to Doxla quickly."

The light — and Sylvra's face — vanished, leaving Jax and Ev speechless. Lylia, on the other hand, burst into giggles.

Jax spun on her. "How is this funny? He just posted a bounty on us to the entire world! How does he know what we look like, anyway?"

Lylia smiled at Jax. "Does this one not see? Sylvra's announcement validates our efforts. We are indeed a threat to the Masters!"

"Well, that's great, isn't it, except now *everyone* will be after us."

Abeleth called back to them with a huge grin. "Everyone? No. The Master, Sylvra, has made a dire mistake. His words were chosen wisely, but we immortals have lived long enough to know the true meaning behind his sayings. All immortals know now you have power he fears. Some may be enticed by his offer, but far more desire only his fall."

"We all now also know how many have escaped his grasp," Lylia observed.

"That's right," said Ev. "There's still six of us he's searching for."

"Wait," said Jax, looking down, "but that means the people he didn't show . . ."

Ev felt a twinge of guilt as she looked at Jax.

Her brother clenched his fists. "That bastard got Gare."

Lylia's smile faded. "We did not consider that. We, too, have lost much today."

Turning away from Jax and toward Abeleth, Ev stated, "That's all the more reason to make sure we succeed. Abeleth, about the dragons — How would they respond to Sylvra's message?"

Abeleth pondered that for a moment. "I cannot be sure. They have never cared much for anything beyond being left alone. I cannot see them being swayed either way by Sylvra's words."

"I see. Thank you," said Ev.

Abeleth nodded and galloped away, and Ev maneuvered her hell-horse back closer to Jax and Lylia.

"Are you sure we should do this?" Jax asked, looking her in the eyes. "If the dragons are loyal to the Masters, we'll be in big trouble."

"I know it's a risk, but dragons have never been known for deceit. If they are loyal, they will tell us, and we can retreat back to the Underworld."

"Assuming dragons are the same in this world as ours," said Jax.

"We expect it to be so," offered Lylia. "All evidence suggests this world is exactly as our own. It is truly uncanny."

"It is," said Ev, "but that makes it easier on us. Even if they won't fight, we need the dragons. Otherwise, it will take two weeks to get to the Jesimine Peaks with the hell-horses."

"You know we could just go straight to the Shrine of Merius with plenty of time to spare, right?" said Jax. "We shouldn't risk losing anyone else."

"I know," replied Ev, "but if we can capture some zodiacs at the Peaks, we could travel almost a thousand miles in a day. We could contact any tribe of immortals on the main continent and still make it back in time for the rendezvous."

"What's with your obsession with recruiting immortals all of a sudden? That wasn't part of the plan, and it's dangerous. All we need is for one group to report to the Masters, and they'll be right on top of us."

"I know," returned Ev, "but we didn't understand what we were getting into when we started. This world is full of Divine. They'll help the Masters, so we need more allies to even the odds. Besides, bringing a bunch of immortals to Ars Summis is exactly the kind of distraction we need to draw away the Masters' attention, or at the very least help with the Divine in Ars Summis."

Jax sighed and shook his head, clearly unhappy with the whole thing. "I guess that is a good point."

"Thanks, Jax," Ev replied.

Jax looked back at her but didn't say anything. He didn't have to. They both knew it was risky, but they also knew they had to try.

* * * *

The journey back to the surface was long but straightforward; the group just needed to keep heading uphill, exactly as Abeleth had told them. Ironically, the further upward they climbed, the darker things became. The unnaturally warm glow of the Underworld faded away, leaving only cool, dark stone. The occasional lava flow was the only source of light provided to them in the tunnels. Of course, they were more than capable of using their magic to make light on their own, so the darkness was more of an inconvenience than anything.

Eventually, the long journey through the tunnels reached its end, and the party found themselves aboveground once more. Night had fallen by that time. Combined with the thick clouds of ash and smoke that blocked out the sky, that left the surface of the mountains nearly as dark as the caves below. All around them were active volcanoes belching out fire and oozing molten rock from their sides. Soot covered the ground as far as the eye could see. The red and gray was broken up by occasional patches of blue and white where giant glowing stones pushed up through the ground. These stones were quite cold — simply passing by them was enough to cause Ev to shiver.

"So, which way do we go?" asked Jax.

Ev wasn't completely sure, but she had an idea.

"Tyranor is supposed to live atop the largest mountain here. If we climb to the top of the one we're currently on, we should be able to see it."

The volcanic slope was rather steep, but there was a path that looped around the mountain at a shallow incline. The trio followed that path past hissing geysers and across streams of lava. They more-or-less ignored the slow magma golems, and the stone-skinned death lizards posed little threat as well. While Ev had never been all that invested in the thrill of battle, the ease with which they were able to dispatch these should-have-been-terrifying foes gave her a glimpse into why the Divine of her world would have grown bored with it upon achieving high levels of Radiance.

As they climbed, Ev could feel unseen eyes upon her. She was sure that dragons were watching them from somewhere, but if they were, they were well hidden. She was honestly surprised none had approached them yet, but considering how much she and Jax looked like demons with their current equipment and steeds, perhaps the dragons merely thought they were a group of immortals leaving the Underworld for some inconsequential reason.

Regardless, as soon as they reached the crest of the mountain, their destination was immediately obvious. On the far side of the mountain sat a smoldering wasteland. Beyond that was another row of mountains, and beyond even that — a single conical volcano that towered above all else they could see.

Jax sighed at the sight. "Are you really sure you want to do this? Even on hell-horses, that mountain looks at least half a day away."

"Jax brings up a fair concern," said Lylia. "At the very least, we all should find a place to rest before we seek out Tyranor. It might be embarrassing if we try to speak with him while only half awake."

"Then we find shelter," said Ev, growing annoyed at having to constantly defend this decision. She then nudged her steed forward without another word.

About halfway down the mountain, the sound of clattering rocks drew her attention. She expected to see yet another death lizard clambering after her, but what she found was a massive mound of ash shifting as a great scaly head lifted up from beneath it.

Ev held tight to her reigns and tried to appear calm — something made infinitely easier by the fact that the skeletal steeds didn't seem to care at all about the giant dragon now towering over them. She saw Jax reach for his sword, but he thankfully kept it sheathed. Lylia seemed almost as relaxed as the hell-horses.

The dragon lowered its head closer to the group and snorted hot breath over them. As it inhaled again, its glowing eyes briefly opened wider in surprise before narrowing menacingly.

"Humans," the dragon growled, rearing back as if he was about to strike.

"Wait!" Ev called, quickly pulling off her mask and helmet.

The dragon hesitated, and Ev seized the opportunity to dismount.

"We aren't here to cause trouble," she called as she took a single step forward. "We need help from King Tyranor."

The dragon growled and looked more closely at Ev before speaking. "Your unusual company grants you one chance to speak. State your business with Tyranor. Choose your words wisely."

Standing up tall, Ev told the dragon the truth. "We would request that King Tyranor stand with us against the Masters — if not in battle, then at least by aiding us in reaching those who will."

The dragon leaned his face down close to Ev. Even after everything she'd been through, she couldn't help but feel slightly intimidated by the hot breath blowing over her.

After another moment of studying Ev and her companions, the dragon let out a guttural sound that Ev could only assume was the dragon equivalent of a chuckle.

"So, you are the fools who defy the Masters. You will find no aid here.

Leave."

Ev didn't budge. "We will not leave until we have spoken with King Tyranor."

"Tyranor is dead," the dragon snapped.

"He . . . what? How? When?" Ev asked.

"He was slain by Divine on the eve of the waxing moon. Unless you intend to wait for his revival, you have no business here."

"But, no, there must be someone we can talk to," pleaded Ev. "There must be some other dragon to speak for Tyranor when he's gone."

"There are none," the dragon replied. "I grow weary of conversation. Begone. I shall not grant you the chance again."

"Come on, Ev," Jax called quietly from behind her.

Ev clenched her fists. This was too important to walk away from just because Tyranor was dead and this dragon refused to be helpful.

She glared up at the towering being and defiantly stated, "No."

A mighty claw slammed into the stone beside her as the dragon raised its wings and bellowed a deafening roar. Jax jumped from his horse and drew his sword, but Ev held out a hand to stop him.

"Is that supposed to intimidate me?" she asked the dragon. "I know you saw Sylvra's message. He sicced the whole world on us for a reason. He fears us. He knows we can stop him. We can put an end to his reign — to his endless crusade of pitting Divine against immortals. King Tyranor is dead because *Sylvra* made it a quest for Divine to come here and slay him. Was Tyranor the only one? How many others died when they came?"

The dragon growled but made no further move.

"You said you are weary of conversation, but aren't you more weary of being hunted for glory? Aren't you weary of your only purpose being fodder for Divine?"

"Enough!" the dragon roared. "Your words ring true, but words will not slay the Masters."

"Believe me," said Ev, "we have much more than words on our side."

"Yet words are all that I hear."

A thoughtful rumble gurgled from the dragon's throat as he examined Ev one final time.

"Still," continued the dragon as it finally relaxed, "your words are strong. I will aid you, but I give no more than you give me."

Ev wasn't sure what the dragon meant, but they didn't have time for a long side quest. "We don't have very much. What do you want us to give you?"

"You have shared with me your voice. I offer mine in exchange. You desire aid in reaching those who might stand with you against the Masters. Knowledge to that end I now grant to you.

"Speak to the harpies and water elementals. The latter especially will likely resist your efforts, but both can spread your words quickly if you can convince them. Beyond this, you may find your greatest allies among those who serve the Masters."

Ev gave a brief glance back at Jax, who simply shrugged.

"What does that mean?" Ev asked the dragon.

"I have heard tales of Divine that defy the Masters' decrees. While most have been purged from Doxla, a few may yet reside."

The dragon pointed with his head to a faraway mountain. "Seek out the hermit, Dogan, east of the northernmost volcano. He would know more."

Ev considered that for a moment. Contacting harpies and elementals wasn't a bad suggestion, but it wasn't what she needed.

"We appreciate your advice, but is it possible for you to help us travel north? Or do you know someone else who could help us?"

"No," the dragon growled with narrowed eyes. "Your intention is noble, but your war is folly. No dragon will willingly serve you as a lowly mount. The only reward for us would be a true death by the Masters."

"You're wrong," protested Ev. "We can do this. If we don't—"

"I have spoken," the dragon said in a raised voice. "Now, leave."

As much as she didn't want to back off, the edge in the dragon's last words told Ev there was nothing more to be gained from pressing further.

Begrudgingly, she gave the dragon a small bow before turning and climbing back atop her hell-horse.

The dragon turned away and stomped up to the top of the mountain where he spread his wings and took off into the sky.

"I hope you're right about dragons only speaking the truth," said Jax after a moment.

With a huff, Ev directed her mount in the direction the dragon had pointed.

"Let's just go," she said. "It's a long way to the Jesimine Peaks."

"Ev, come on," said Jax. "I know you want some zodiacs, but if something goes wrong, we'll be a month away from where we're supposed to rendezvous. Hell, it will take us at least two weeks to get there even if we go straight from where we are now."

"We need to gather more allies," retorted Ev, "and zodiacs are the fastest way to do that."

Jax squeezed his forehead, took a breath, and responded. "If you really think it's that important, then why don't you take the dragon's advice?"

"I'm *not* getting help from Divine," Ev answered.

"You?" Jax frowned. "How about *we?* We're in this together, Ev, or are you so obsessed with your crusade that you've forgotten that?"

"This isn't a crusade! We're the only ones who can stop the Masters. If we don't, maybe no one ever will!"

"That's beside the point," Jax replied as he looked over to Lylia. "What do you say? Should we trust the dragon?"

Lylia smiled. "We think that's a lovely idea. Truthfully, we were not enthused about the prospect of traveling to the Peaks. Cold is . . . well, cold."

Jax turned back to Ev. "Sounds like you're outvoted."

"This isn't up for debate!" Ev returned. "Divine can communicate with Ars Summis from anywhere. If we talk to the wrong ones, we're as good as dead!"

"Then go talk to the harpies and elementals instead," said Jax. "You'd trust them, wouldn't you?"

Ev frowned. "How are we supposed to do that? Harpies live northwest of the Forest of Fae. That's got to be at least a week away. We'll never make it back to the rendezvous in time. The Shrine of Merius is in the opposite direction."

Lylia piped up. "Don't wind wyrms live near the harpies? We could use them instead of zodiacs. We also seem to recall that water elementals make their home in the lake along the northern border of the Forest of Fae."

Jax smirked as he lifted his chin up, acting like he'd won. "Is that so? Sounds like all the more reason to head there. You still get a mount that can fly, and you don't have to travel all the way to the Peaks."

"Fine," Ev supposed that was a fair argument, "but no Divine. We stay away from them."

"I agree that you two should stay away from them," Jax said. "We can't risk you getting caught, but I can take that risk."

"Don't be stupid. We need to stick together."

With a sad smile, Jax shook his head. "You two are anthermancers. You can actually stand against the Masters. You can stop them. Me? You saw what happened when I tried to attack Amethine."

Ev protested. "That's—"

"—the truth," Jax finished for her. "I might be able to help you fight off nepacs and Divine, but when the real battle starts, I'll be useless."

Jax looked northward. "If the dragon was telling the truth, then it might be worth finding that Dogan guy. If we could actually find more Divine like Syrus here, that might be the edge we need. Hell, just Syrus by himself kept our Doxla going long enough for us to have this chance."

"Jax, I . . ." Ev searched for an argument, but couldn't find one. Everything Jax said was completely sound.

"Okay," she said at last. "Just promise me you'll be careful. I know I said nothing else matters, but—"

"Hey, I'll be fine," Jax replied with a smile. "I'm a Radiant now, right?"

Doing her best to return the smile, Ev replied, "Yeah. I guess you are."

After a moment's thought, she added, "Once we get the wyrms, we'll come back for you. Meet us on the east side of that northernmost volcano the dragon mentioned."

"I'll be there," said Jax, "but if I'm not, don't wait for me. Do what you have to do."

Ev nodded and looked to Lylia. "Are you okay with this?"

"Of course!" chimed Lylia. "This plan certainly is preferable to more snow."

"Okay then," said Ev as she looked back to Jax once more. "We'll be back for you soon."

Jax nodded, and they parted ways.

* * * *

Since the lake was on the way to the harpies, that was Ev's first destination. The journey there was straightforward — only taking eight days' time — what with most of the travel taking place across open fields. Ev wasn't entirely comfortable being out in the open, so she stayed close to cover whenever possible, but it did mean the hell-horses could run at full speed for the majority of the journey.

Upon finally arriving at the lake shortly after noon, Ev took a look around. Camped by the water a decent distance away was a caravan of what Ev had to assume were Divine on some sort of quest. She didn't see any water elementals, and she didn't want to stick around if it risked getting caught.

"We should keep going," she told Lylia. "I don't see the water elementals."

"That's because they're below water, silly!" chimed Lylia. "We both came all this way. Let us at least try to speak with them."

Ev sighed. "Fine, but not here. Let's go through the woods to the other side of the lake."

After dismounting from her ride, Ev led her hell-horse through the underbrush around the lake, making sure to refill on fresh water while she had the chance. The woods here were far more beautiful than any she'd seen back in her Doxla — flowers blossomed and berries grew on every plant she could see. The place was alive with gorgeous butterflies flitting about and small birds chirping in the trees. The only disconcerting sight were the occasional blue-petaled flowers with eyeballs at their center. The eyes followed her as she walked, but they seemed harmless enough.

Once she was confident they were far enough away to not be noticed even should they step out onto the lake shore, Ev turned back to Lylia.

"Okay, now what? How do we get them to come out?"

Lylia shrugged. "We don't know. Elementals tend to guard important places. Maybe if we find what they are guarding, they will speak to us."

"Or more likely attack us," Ev replied.

"Yes, that does seem more likely," Lylia smiled. "Well, perhaps we can try something."

Ev raised an eyebrow. "What do you have in mind?"

Still smiling, Lylia handed her spear to Ev and slithered waist-deep into the water. There, she called out, "Elementals! We are here!"

When there was no response, she began slamming her tail into the water before calling again. "We wish to speak with you!"

The display shocked Ev. Though she wasn't entirely sure how she felt about it, she was fairly certain that *wasn't* the right way to get the water elementals' attention.

"Maybe we should try something else," she called to Lylia.

Soaking wet, Lylia looked back and smiled. "Give us another minute. We have not tried for long."

"I—" Ev stopped herself and sighed. It wasn't like she had any better ideas.

Deciding to just let Lylia do her thing, Ev leaned back against a tree and looked off into the distance at where the caravan should be. From here, she could barely make out the wagons as tiny specks, and the people not even that.

Good. If she couldn't see them, they couldn't see Lylia's splashing.

Her attention was brought back by the sound of an angry female voice shouting, "You disturb our water!"

Jerking her attention back to Lylia, Ev saw a ghostly blue figure floating above the lake.

Lylia spread her arms wide. "Greetings! We come seeking the aid of your people."

"These waters are sacred!" responded the elemental. "Remove yourself or perish!"

Lifting her hands up innocently, Lylia backed away toward the shore. "Of course, of course. We did not intend harm. We only wish to speak with you."

Not wanting the chance to pass her by, Ev rushed to the waters edge but stopped when another elemental rose up from the water and pointed an icy spear at her.

"Please," Ev said to the elemental. "Just hear us out. We need your help to stage an assault against the Masters."

"We know who you are, and it matters not," replied the spear-wielding elemental. "We protect the lake. That is our purpose."

By now Lylia had retreated all the way back onto the shore.

"But are you happy with that purpose?" Ev pleaded with them. "Don't you want to do something that actually makes a difference?"

Neither elemental responded as they melted back into the water and vanished.

"Wait!" Ev called, but they were gone.

She kicked the sand. "Great! Just perfect!"

"Our dragon friend did warn us they would not be easy to speak to," Lylia said.

Ev spun on her. "Yeah, well maybe it would have been easier if you hadn't pissed them off by splashing in the lake!"

Lylia looked taken aback, but she quickly frowned. "What idea did this one have for speaking to them? We saw none. At least we succeeded in that."

Ev huffed and turned away. "Whatever. Let's just get out of here. This was a waste of time."

Ev tromped back into the forest to her waiting hell-horse. She heard Lylia moving behind her, but she didn't look back, and neither of them said anything to the other. With a tug on the hell-horse's reigns, Ev started back the way they'd come. It would be faster than continuing the rest of the way around the lake through the forest.

She hadn't made it far, however, before a pink fairy no taller than her boots flitted up in front of her face. The surprise almost caused Ev to yelp.

"Wait!" the tiny winged woman shouted. "I heard what you said about attacking the Masters. Our queen would be very interested in talking to you. We've always wanted to make them pay for turning us into these tiny things."

It took a moment for Ev to process what the high-pitched voice told her, but when she did, she felt her mood lift just a tad. Perhaps it hadn't been a waste of time to come here after all.

"Where is your queen?" Ev asked.

"Queen Holly Joy is actually on her way to my village as we speak! She has rallied our fiercest warriors to stand against the awful Divine who wait at our doorstep. I'm sure if you help drive them away, she'll be more than happy to help you in turn."

"You want us to fight Divine?" Ev asked.

The fairy nodded excitedly.

"I don't know," Ev replied. "I'd love to help, but if we're found out, the Masters will come for us."

"Oh, don't worry about that," the fairy said, flitting upwards slightly. "We fairies possess excellent illusion magic — our queen especially so! We can hide who you really are. Come on!"

The fairy darted deeper into the forest a few feet before stopping. "Oh, my name is Belle Sweet, by the way. What's yours?"

"Um, Ev, and behind me is Lylia," Ev replied.

Belle Sweet smiled widely and gestured for them to follow her. "Great! Let's go. Queen Holly Joy will be at my village any minute!"

Belle Sweet flew even farther away, stopping just before she was out of sight.

Lylia leaned over Ev's shoulder to whisper, "We are uncertain we should trust that one. Fairies in our Doxla lived comfortably with Divine until their forests burned."

With a dismissive wave, Ev replied, "We're more than capable of handling ourselves against some fairies. They can't contact the Masters, anyway."

"Perhaps not, but they may reveal us to Divine who can."

The suggestion gave Ev pause, but she couldn't risk alienating potential allies, especially if those allies could bring illusion magic to the table.

"We'll be fine," she replied. "We should at least see if she's telling the truth about her queen coming here."

Lylia let out a very slight groan, but she followed behind Ev nonetheless. With their hell-horses right behind them, they made their way through the colorful forest with its weird eye-flowers until they arrived at a small clearing surrounded by tiny houses.

"Here we are!" exclaimed Belle Sweet. "It looks like we got here before the queen, but that's okay. Now we can surprise her!"

With that announcement, fairies of every sparkling hue began appearing from the trees and houses and surrounded Ev and Lylia. Despite her confidence in her abilities, Ev couldn't help but feel unease.

"So," she began, trying not to look nervous, "how long will it be until Queen Holly Joy arrives?"

"Oh, not long at all, I'm sure!" replied Belle Sweet. "She's supposed to arrive sometime this afternoon, and it's after noon, right? Perhaps a delicious treat would help the time go by."

"Yes," said Lylia as she slithered menacingly toward Belle Sweet. "Perhaps a delicious fairy treat would sate our hunger."

Belle Sweet laughed nervously as she inched away from Lylia. "Eh-heh, yes. We shall fix . . . berries! Yes, just wait right there while I go find some."

"Lylia," Ev hissed. "What do you think you're doing? They might really need our help."

"*We* thought we were here to seek *their* help," returned Lylia. "We do not need to speak with their queen to accomplish this."

Ev was about to rebuke Lylia when she noticed the stares from the fairies all around. Their eyes were on her as much as the plants' eyes had been, though they were quick to turn away whenever she looked at them.

Her unease slowly growing, Lylia's caution started to seem much more reasonable. "Maybe you're right. We do need to keep moving. I'll tell Belle Sweet that we can't wait."

That seemed to satisfy Lylia, as she gave a subtle nod before turning a wary eye back to the other fairies.

Try as she might, however, Ev couldn't find Belle Sweet anywhere. After a minute or so of searching, she gave up and motioned for Lylia to follow as she approached a group of fairies loitering near their hell-horses.

"Excuse me," said Ev, earning nervous stares from the fairies. "I'm sorry, but we really can't keep waiting here. Can you tell Belle Sweet that we're sorry for leaving, but we'd still appreciate her help if she'll give it."

The high-pitched voice of Belle Sweet rang out from behind them. "Wait! Please don't leave yet!"

Ev sighed, turned around, then froze.

On either side of Belle Sweet, two heavily armored individuals appeared from nowhere, but they faded from Ev's vision as her eyes focused on the man in blue-tinted armor directly before her.

Belle Sweet floated in front of Crovos; her hands clasped together earnestly as she added with a sly smile, "I'm *so* sorry that you didn't get to meet the Queen, but at least my new friends will get to meet *you*."

Chapter 15

After about a week of processing her thoughts, Evress felt she finally knew what she had to do. All this time, Sylvra had only ever told her the truth. The world of Divine — of seitti and the various species that lived among them — they truly viewed nepacs like her as only tools to be used. Even Syrus, who had been her mentor to the point she'd almost thought of him as family, ultimately proved to be exactly the same. He'd only ever cared about stopping the Masters, and he was willing to play chess with millions of lives to do it — even her own.

The others needed to know. Her friends needed to know what Syrus had done. She'd put off speaking to them for a long time. Jax in particular had barely given Evress the time of day since she'd joined the Masters, but maybe if she told them what Syrus did, they'd understand that siding with the Masters really was the lesser of two evils.

After changing into her old clothes, Evress used the tool that Sylvra had given her to travel to where her friends and family — the original, *real* Jax, Birdie, and everyone else — now lived. Once there, she made her way to a small cottage on the outskirts of the small town that most of the people she knew had ended up living in. The sun had only just risen, so she hoped Birdie would be home. Out of everyone she knew, she felt Birdie would be the most likely to listen to her.

The cottage sat empty, but Evress smiled at the small flowers growing outside of the window. She'd brought them to Birdie from the new Doxla as a reminder of their old home after learning that this place didn't have nearly the diversity of wildlife that their world had before. It was good to see they were thriving here.

Well, if Birdie wasn't home, then it wouldn't hurt to go for a walk in the woods behind the cottage. As bland as the forests here were, Evress found them more relaxing than the ones in Doxla. There were no monsters whatsoever and certainly no chance of running into Divine. It really was a nice break to get so far away from what her life had become. Though she had been anxious about talking to Birdie and the others, the stroll among the trees helped her relax. As she listened to the insects chirping merrily, she realized that the life Sylvra had thrust them all into wasn't really all that bad. Maybe everyone would be willing to hear her out after all.

After a nice hour or so in the forest, Evress worked her way back to Birdie's cottage where she found Birdie facing away from her, hard at work de-feathering some large bird she'd killed.

Birdie looked up from her table and back to the woods at the sound of Evress's approach. When she saw Evress, her eyes opened wide as she put down her bird. A smile formed as she took one step toward Evress, but it faded again almost as quickly; then she stopped.

Sensing something was amiss, Evress approached tentatively. She offered a small smile of her own, but considering what she was here to talk about, she found herself also unable to maintain a smile for long.

"Hi, Birdie," Evress began. "Have you been well?"

"We're managing," Birdie responded. "Most folks are still getting used to their new lives, so not much has changed on that front. Losing everything you've ever known kind of takes some adjusting to, you know."

"Yeah, I do know," Evress said back, her expression apologetic.

"Do you?" Birdie asked, her face stoic. "Is that why I haven't seen you in over two weeks?"

"I'm sorry," Evress responded as she took another step closer. "It's just . . . a lot has happened."

Birdie sighed. "I'm sure it has, and I'm sure what Jax said to you last time hasn't helped things. Come on."

Birdie motioned for Evress to follow her, and she did.

The inside of the cottage was dark and quaint; the only light came from the open windows. Evress noted that Birdie had made the interior a bit more comfortable since the last time she'd visited by using various animal skins as carpets and cushions. It seemed Birdie really was finally starting to settle in.

"So, what made you decide to drop by?" Birdie asked as she sat down in a wooden chair. She then gestured for Evress to take a seat as well. "Things not going well entertaining Divine?"

Evress frowned, but sat down opposite Birdie regardless. She'd expected at least a moderately warm greeting, not hostility — not from Birdie.

"That's not what I'm doing," Evress countered. "I'm trying to make Doxlans' lives better where I can. I've replaced almost all of the Enforcers with individuals I've vetted myself, and Crovos has helped me find ways to make even immortals live more comfortably without breaking Sylvra's rules."

Birdie chuckled dryly as she placed a hand to her forehead. "Oh, Ev. Not once in a million years would I have thought I'd hear anything like that leaving your mouth. To think that you of all people would become a Master . . ."

"I'm doing the best I can," Evress returned. "I've made things better. I know I have! What more do you want me to do?"

Birdie smiled sadly. "Nothing. I believe you. I know you think you're doing your best, and you probably are. It's just hard knowing that you're living comfortably up in some tower while we all have to work to survive in a place where we know we're going to die."

A twinge of guilt shot through Evress's stomach. "I'll see if there's anything I can do to help you. I can't promise much, but I'm sure Sylvra will let me do something."

"It's fine," replied Birdie before smiling gently. "Honestly, I prefer living this way. I take care of me, and no one expects me to be the Radiant who has all the answers all the time. It's just knowing that when we die, the last bit of our Doxla will be gone forever — that's the real problem, and I get the feeling there's nothing you can do about that."

Evress looked quizzically at Birdie. "What do you mean?"

Birdie sighed and leaned back as far as she could in her chair. "You don't know? I guess the other Masters aren't telling you everything, then."

Birdie paused, presumably hoping for a response, but Evress simply waited for her to continue.

"Doxla ends with us," Birdie continued. "At least, the Doxla we came from does. Ever since getting sent here, no new children have survived childbirth. It's the same in every settlement we've made contact with. There's no other explanation. Your fellow Masters want us to die out, and at this rate we will."

Evress turned her eyes away from Birdie. "I see. I guess I shouldn't be surprised."

"That's it?" Birdie asked, raising an eyebrow. "That's all you have to say about our being driven to extinction."

Evress shifted uncomfortably in her seat. "It's not extinction that Sylvra's after. I'm sorry, but I can't say much. It's the only thing he's forbidden me from sharing with you. He doesn't want anyone — including the Enforcers — to know. I think he's afraid he'll be found out if you did."

"Right," said Birdie, leaning heavily on her arm, "because we're in the perfect position to tell the whole universe. Oh, wait. There aren't even Divine here."

Not appreciating Birdie's tone, Evress frowned. "Not now you can't, but you'll be able to one day. Your souls will live on. They'll go to the seitti realm." Evress shifted again. "It's probably all I should say on the matter. I'm sure he listens to everything I say."

Birdie just shook her head. "Whatever. It's not like any of us can do anything about it, regardless. Seems like you won't either."

Evress steamed at that remark. Birdie wasn't being fair to her. She was doing everything she could.

Birdie must have sensed that she'd gone too far, because the next thing she did was apologize. "I'm sorry, Ev. It's just that it's been two weeks. Two weeks! I know things have been a little tense, but when you disappear for that long, what am I supposed to think? I know you have your responsibilities, and not everyone has been exactly understanding, but . . ."

Birdie trailed off as she shook her head and put her hand on her face. After taking a deep breath, she continued.

". . . I'm just frustrated. Life here is comfortable enough, but I just wish I knew what was going on with you. I want to know that you're still you — that the Masters haven't changed you. I want to know that you're really doing the right thing. We all do."

Sighing, Evress stood up and moved her chair closer to Birdie. Sitting down once more, she placed her hand on Birdie's.

"I am. At least, I'm doing what's most right. Believe me, I'm still the same Ev that I was before. I still hate that Sylvra incites war against the immortals. I hate that one day, he will do to this new Doxla what he did to ours, but I've also seen how much worse other seitti are compared to him. If we somehow exposed him, we'd likely all end up in a seitti museum until the day our descendants get devoured by sentiments."

"Sentiments?" Birdie repeated. "What are sentiments?"

"They're creations of the seitti," Evress grimaced as she pulled her hand back to herself. "They were made to destroy all life that deviates from the laws of their society."

"That's ridiculous," replied Birdie. "If such things exist, then why are we still here?"

"Because life isn't supposed to exist here," Evress answered. "The Cosmic Graveyard is one of the few places that sentiments don't patrol. If other seitti come and take us away from Sylvra, they'll put us somewhere with sentiments and abandon us there. It would only be a matter of time until someone did something that lets them in."

"Correct me if I'm wrong," Birdie said while crossing her arms, "but didn't Syrus say his world's creator would make sure we'd be taken care of?"

"Syrus said a lot of things." Evress pulled her arms in close and furrowed her brow. "We trusted him, and he betrayed us."

"Syrus did everything he could to help us," Birdie interjected. "If Sylvra's tried convincing you otherwise, he's lying."

"Sylvra didn't convince me of anything," Evress met Birdie's eyes once more. "I saw it, Birdie. I saw what he did."

Birdie tilted her head. "Which was what, exactly?"

Trying her best not to get too emotional, Evress told Birdie everything about how Syrus had left them all as bait for the Masters so that their copies could escape. She told Birdie about speaking with some of the copies herself and how they didn't even care about what had happened.

"He abandoned us. He used us as tools just like every other Divine has ever done!"

To Evress's relief, Birdie didn't jump to Syrus's defense, but she was surprised to see that Birdie didn't seem all that upset either.

After pondering Evress's words for a moment, Birdie said, "So that's what's been going on."

A bit taken aback by Birdie's nonchalance, Evress prodded. "Doesn't it bother you?"

"Does it bother me that he made copies of us? I suppose so. He should have told us, but if he thought we would die, I can see why he didn't."

"That's it?" Evress got out of her chair and walked to the window where she gestured out of it. "He used us as bait! Us! Not the copies. He used *us!*"

Birdie sighed before getting up and joining Evress at the window with the flowers.

"I already told you that I don't like that he didn't tell us. I suppose I'm a little annoyed to be the one left behind as well, but you have to understand the sentiment around here. Everyone hates the Masters. At this very moment, Jax, Tallis, and Helcant are on an expedition to try and find the edge of the world to see if they can break out. If you told any of them what happened, they'd probably be happy to know there's still someone out there fighting."

Evress took a step back from Birdie and looked at her. "What about you? Are you happy about it?"

"Perhaps I would have been if you hadn't become a Master yourself. I honestly don't know what to think right now. I'd like to see the Masters brought to justice, but you keep telling me they have a good reason for what they're doing, as hard as that is to believe, especially since you won't even tell me what that reason is."

Evress looked away. If Birdie of all people wasn't convinced that Syrus was wrong, then what hope did she have of convincing anyone else?

"I'd better get back," Evress said, heading back to the door.

"Ev, wait," Birdie called after her.

Evress looked back.

"Be careful out there. I know what you're capable of with that anther stuff. Your copy is likely just as capable, so please be safe."

With a forced smile, Evress gave a subtle nod before stepping out of the door. The next moment, she was back at Lumine Tower once more.

* * * *

Not long after returning to her room, there was a knock on Evress's door. Opening it revealed Sylvra on the other side.

"I trust you had a pleasant visit with your friends?" he asked.

Evress frowned. She still didn't like that he was always spying on her.

"I'll take that as a negative," he said. "Though unfortunate, I have a new task for you. After my announcement a week ago, some Divine contacted me to report an unusual encounter in the Underworld. Apparently, there was an unusually powerful force protecting Conter Sul, including a naga wearing armor that belonged to the jungle naga tribe. I have only just learned the details of that encounter from one of my immortal contacts. Your copy was there to forge an alliance with the demons."

Her copy — Evress remembered from the bubble Sylvra had shown her that Jax and Lylia would be with her as well.

"Do you want me to track them down?" she asked.

"Crovos is still in charge of searching for your copies. I have already informed him of this lead, though after a week it is likely cold. No, I would like for you to head to the Underworld and undo what your copy has done."

With a snap of his fingers, a suit of demonic armor appeared beside him, and a small paper manifested in his hand.

"Put on this armor. You are to pose as your copy and claim that the entirety of the alliance and my announcement was a test to weed out any who would dare to oppose the Masters, then capture those whose names are written on this list. They are the ones most deeply involved in this little uprising, and they may know more about what our enemies are planning. I do not expect you to be able to find all of them, but that is acceptable. Capture who you can, then make a quest to hunt down the remainder. If any who are not on the list resist, kill them, and make a show of it. I want to do everything we can to discourage the demons from following through with their plans."

Great. He wanted her to pretend to be her copy again. "The last time we tried this, it didn't work out so well."

"We learned of where their base was in the Cosmic Graveyard. I would call that a success, would you not?"

Evress opted not to inform Sylvra that she would have been able to get that information regardless, and instead took the list from his hand. It was smaller than she'd expected.

"I suppose you have some way to find them," Evress stated. "I don't know who any of these people are."

"My contact, Nergos, will assist you in that regard," Sylvra answered. "He is waiting for you at the Underworld gate that lies beneath the Myco Fields. Unfortunately, I will not be able to join you, as the other group of Syrus's copies has also been very busy. The copy of your demon friend was spotted near Ghast Canyon. Apparently he left behind bits of anther scattered around the area. Though he has since slipped away, I must go and deal with the results of his actions."

Before Evress could say anything more, Sylvra turned away and vanished from her room.

She looked once again at the list in her hand. Only four names. With any luck, she'd capture them all on her own. The last thing that she wanted to do was make a quest that would send even more Divine to the Underworld and stretch tensions even further than they already were.

* * * *

Clad in the demon armor Sylvra had given her, Evress appeared at the center of the Myco Fields on their surface. She had no real reason to go there — her business was deep below ground — but her recent talk with Birdie had her longing for the days when things were simpler. The last time she'd been here, the world had still been black and white. Divine were saviors, immortals were villains, and everyone longed for the return of the Masters. Now, though, she almost wished she didn't know the truth.

Standing atop the soft, purple ground, she looked westward to the Windy Mountains where her journey to what she'd now become had more-or-less begun. If she hadn't met Birdie there, then she, Jax, and Gare would never have helped Syrus defeat Grandis. Apollyon would have devastated the world, and apparently the Masters would have returned earlier in response. She could have kept living her life in blissful ignorance, but that was something she could never go back to now.

With a sigh, Evress looked down at the sea of tiny mushrooms at her feet. She supposed she'd better get on with it. Using her teleportation tool and the map in her head, she transported herself deep underground to near one of the gates to the Underworld.

The heat from the Underworld met with the damp coolness of the underground Myco Fields and mixed to form a sauna. Streams of water flowed from the dark, purple fungus-lined caverns ever deeper toward the gate.

As she herself walked deeper into the Underworld, Evress was relieved not to see anyone else in the vicinity.

She eventually followed the streams to the great stone pillars marking the gate, where the water passed onto the barren rock to continue its steady journey until it ultimately poured into a pit of magma, producing an endless billow of steam.

Still no sign of anyone, Evress called out to Sylvra's contact. "Nergos? Are you here?"

A particularly tall and lanky demon with half a missing ear and a nasty scar across the middle of his face crawled out from a small crevice in the wall before dropping down before her. He smiled a toothy smile that was clearly missing some teeth.

"I am here," Nergos said, standing with a hunched-over slouch. "Master Evress, I presume?"

"Refer to me as Ev," she commanded as she switched to the authoritative persona she'd developed over the last few months. "That's the name of the individual I'm impersonating."

"How interesting," Nergos replied, eyeing her uncomfortably. "Your wish is my command, Ev. Shall I take you to the conspirators?"

"Lead the way," Evress stated.

Nergos bowed low to the ground. "Right this way," he gestured before leading Evress around a corner and into a narrow, dark corridor.

At the back of the corridor waited two hell-horses. Both Nergos and Evress mounted the steeds, and Nergos prodded his back toward the exit of the corridor.

"Two conspirators presently abide within Conter Sul," he stated. "I know not the location of the others at this moment."

Damn. That meant she likely would have to make a stupid quest after all.

"Which ones are missing?" Evress asked as she caught up with him.

"The ones known as Abeleth the Depraved and Pyrene the Burning," replied Nergos. "Those two lead the effort to spread plans of rebellion abroad."

"What about the others? What role do they play?"

"Meredith the Cleaver seeks to influence the aristocracy to join in her defiance. Belphor the Destroyer does the same but for the lower classes. However, they meet daily at the same locale every evening. That is where I now take you."

"What about you?" Evress asked as they passed over a jagged stone bridge that spanned a deep, seemingly bottomless rift. "I thought all demons hated the Masters."

"Loyalty to the Masters poses risk down here, it is true," Nergos stated as he pointed to the large scar on his face, "but for those of us who fear not pain, the rewards are even greater. I rather enjoy my yearly return to human form, complete with endless wealth at my fingertips. But of course, surely you must be aware of my arrangement with Master Sylvra."

"Sylvra doesn't usually share knowledge of his deals until he needs to," Evress deflected.

"Yes, I gathered such was his character, and of course you have not been a Master long enough for him to share much, have you?"

As much as she didn't appreciate the remark, Evress supposed she shouldn't have been surprised that Nergos knew that about her. She did her best to not show that she was bothered as they made their way to the gates of Conter Sul. The guards stopped them before they could enter, but upon revealing herself to be "Ev," they let them through.

Nergos led the way through the surprisingly busy streets. Evress had only thrice before visited an Underworld city back in the old Doxla, and none of them had looked like this — including the old Conter Sul. Here, thousands of demons went about their business. Gardens of strange plants bloomed near the outer walls, and large channels of water formed a web across the city. In her Doxla, the channels had been nearly dry, but here they were practically overflowing.

Deeper into the city they delved until at last they came to a small stone building just outside of the palace walls. Just as they arrived, the sound of a bell tower's gonging reached their ears.

"We are early," stated Nergos, "but that is good. Now you will see them when they approach."

"How long will we have to wait?" Evress asked.

"The palace supper has just concluded. Your quarry should not be long delayed."

"Well, we can't just wait here on these horses watching the building."

Evress looked around and spotted a large stack of barrels by the wall with just enough room to hide the horses behind.

"Over there," she said, and the two of them took up position out of sight.

After about fifteen minutes, a large demon entered into the building. Not long after that, a small demoness entered as well.

"Those are who you seek," stated Nergos. "Now, by your leave, I must go. I do not wish to have this face associated with what you are about to do. It would make learning the location of your other targets . . . difficult."

"As long as you're right about who they are, you can go," Evress said.

Nergos bowed. "It has been a pleasure doing business with you."

He then directed his hell-horse out from behind the barrels and back down the street.

With no further need for hers, Evress dismounted her steed and walked over to the small building. She could hear voices inside speaking excitedly about something, but she couldn't make out what. Seeing an opportunity to find out more about her copy, Evress gave herself an eavesdropping spell and used it to listen in.

Unfortunately, both for her and her soon-to-be prisoners, the only things that were discussed were who they'd succeeded or failed to convince to join them. They said nothing new of her copy's plan, nor of where she might be.

Once the conversation seemed to be reaching its end, Evress prepared herself mentally for what she had to do, then knocked on the door and did her best to get back into her "Ev" persona.

The door opened, revealing the demoness that Evress assumed was

Meredith. When Meredith's eyes landed on Evress's face, she looked a mixture of surprise, confusion, and pleased.

"Ev!" she exclaimed. "You have returned?"

Meredith then looked past Evress and to either side of her.

"Wait. Where are your companions? Has some ill befallen them?"

By now Belphor had joined Meredith — his expression somewhat more wary.

"Jax and Lylia served their purpose," Evress stated. "They will receive their reward soon enough."

She was now certain that these were the demons she'd been sent to apprehend, so she gave herself powerful binding spells to use should they try to escape.

Concern appeared on Meredith's face. "I do not understand. What do you refer to?"

Evress took two steps back from the door. "Please step outside. It will be easier for everyone if you don't resist."

Immediately, Belphor grabbed Meredith and pulled her back before slamming the door shut.

Not about to let this turn into a chase, Evress stepped forward and kicked the door off its hinges.

Belphor was waiting for her and lunged with his sword.

She let the blow bounce off of her before striking him with her binding spell.

Immobilized, Belphor collapsed to the ground. Meredith stood stunned, but her shock turned to outrage as she grabbed a knife from the table and threw it at Evress.

Again, Evress ignored the attack and incapacitated Meredith as well.

As she stepped over to grab Meredith by the arm, she heard her captive choke out, "Why? We trusted you!"

Belphor growled as well. "Wretched human. You will regret this!"

Evress didn't respond. Instead, she carried both Meredith and Belphor out into the street where she was greeted by a pair of guards who must have heard her break the door. When they saw her face, they drew their blades.

"Divine!" one of them shouted.

Not wanting the situation to escalate any further, Evress dropped both of them with her binding spell before either could attack.

By now, she'd attracted quite a bit of attention, but that was part of the plan anyway.

She removed her helmet for everyone to see her face. Several weaker-looking demons retreated at the sight. Some grabbed makeshift weapons, while others simply stood on guard — waiting.

Once she was sure she had the full attention of everyone on the street, she called her Master's armor to her, which instantly replaced the demon armor she'd been wearing. Standing up tall, she spoke in a magnified voice that the entire city would be able to hear.

"I am Evress, Master of Doxla. The woman that you know as Ev was merely a construct created to expose any who would dare try to oppose the will of the Masters."

As soon as the words left her mouth, whatever fight had been in the demons around her vanished, and Evress realized she perhaps had a chance to avoid needing to create an official quest that would upset these people's lives even further.

"These two have been found guilty of attempting to incite a rebellion and will be dealt with," she continued. "If you wish to prove that you are not a part of these plans, then capture those who are. Bring me Abeleth the Depraved and Pyrene the Burning, as well as all others who have joined them. Any who assist in this will be branded loyal to the Masters, but if I do not have them imprisoned by the time I return in seven days, then I will have no choice but to make it a quest for Divine to travel to the Underworld and purge it of insurrectionists. I truly hope it does not come to that."

Her speech complete, Evress teleported both herself and her two prisoners to the grassy prison world. Sylvra had neglected to tell her where to keep them, so she figured this place would do for now. Once there, she released Meredith and Belphor from their invisible binds.

"I'm sorry about this," she said, "but I can't let you start a rebellion against the Masters."

"We started nothing!" Belphor growled as he jumped to his feet and fire erupted down his back. "You are deceit! Your kind have only ever brought lies and suffering!"

"If you go to war with the Masters, your people will be slaughtered," Evress countered. "Is that what you want?"

Belphor thrust his finger at Evress. "You tricked us! You came to us as an outsider and promised we could win!"

That got Evress's attention. Sylvra hadn't asked her to perform an interrogation, but he never told her not to, either.

"Did I?" she prompted. "What exactly did I say?"

Belphor looked like he was about to explode. "You said you knew the Masters' weakness! You said—"

"Belphor, be silent!" Meredith shouted as she glared at Evress.

Belphor looked at Meredith, then back at Evress. His expression slowly shifted from outrage to something Evress wasn't sure she wanted to see.

"No, go ahead," Evress prodded, doing her best to sound cool and collected. "I don't have anything else to do. If yelling at me helps you feel better, then please continue."

"You would desire such, wouldn't you," Meredith growled, her gaze unmoving. "You are not Ev. You are just another deceiver — an impostor sent by the Masters to learn of those you fear. It will not work."

Evress tensed as she growled. "I am no impostor."

A smug smile began to tug at Meredith's lips. "How sweet this sight is. You, a Master, are afraid of nepacs. Whatever you do to me, I will die happy knowing that the real Ev will bring justice down upon you."

"She is *not* the real Ev!" Evress erupted.

No sooner had the words left her mouth than she realized the mistake she'd made. Whatever chance she'd had at convincing the demons that she was the Ev they'd spoken to had vanished, and the expressions on both Meredith and Belphor's faces showed that they knew that.

"Fine," Evress said after recomposing herself. "If you don't want to talk to me, then you can talk to Sylvra. I guarantee he won't be as friendly."

"He is welcome to do his worst," Meredith replied. "We no longer fear any Master."

With a frown, Evress stepped back and raised her hand. She wanted to create a room to imprison her captives, but she wasn't sure if she had enough anther to do that. Sylvra rarely entrusted her with much of the stuff at once.

Instead, she opted to place them in those little bubbles that she'd been put in when Sylvra had first captured her. They wouldn't be like the one that Sylvra had placed her in before to test her, however. She configured the anther to be completely unexploitable — not that she expected either demon to have even a clue as to how to break free, regardless. These bubbles would be true prisons.

Evress would tell Sylvra where they were the next time she saw him. For now, this would hold them. Sylvra would take care of them when he was ready.

Chapter 16

The early afternoon sun shined down into the clearing, reflecting brightly off of Crovos's blue-tinted armor. With Crovos standing only five feet away, Ev's instincts were torn between attacking and fleeing. The thought of facing another Master, let alone three, terrified Ev. Though she didn't recognize the two individuals flanking Crovos — a man on his left and woman on his right — they did accompany him, suggesting they were most likely Masters as well . . . Enforcers perhaps.

Her encounter with Amethine showed her that even Masters could be beaten back, but Amethine had been cocky, and they'd outnumbered her then. This time . . . well, Ev knew one thing. She wasn't going to simply lay down without a fight.

Ev put up an invisible barrier protecting her body to resist whatever these Masters might try. Hopefully it would be enough to buy her time to do something to hurt them.

Crovos moved, and Ev braced herself, but to her surprise, he didn't attack. Instead, he teleported the traitorous fairy between them out of the way as he constructed a small, transparent, blurry bubble around himself and Ev that sealed the two of them off from the outside world.

Confused but not at all about to let her guard down, Ev readied herself to strike — her memories of how to bypass Amethine's protections still fresh in her mind. If Crovos's defenses were similar, perhaps she stood a chance. Lylia, however — Ev had never shared with her what she'd learned. She only hoped that Lylia would be able to use her serpentine form to keep the others at bay. Before she could act, however, Crovos surprised her once again by speaking.

"You are Eveline, correct?"

Ev stood dumbstruck. How — of course. Tallis's group had been captured.

She realized her jaw was open and closed it, but she didn't respond. She knew Crovos would try something soon, and she'd be ready for it.

"You can relax," stated Crovos calmly, though his voice sounded muffled inside of the bubble. "I am not going to attack you unless I must."

"Sure you aren't," Ev replied. "How stupid do you think I am?"

From the corners of her eyes, she saw the distorted figures of the other two Masters positioned on either side of Lylia, but neither of them had attacked yet, either.

"Despite what you may believe, I do not wish to harm you," Crovos said. "I want to know what you are after. Perhaps we can come to an understanding."

"An *understanding?*" Ev bristled. "You destroyed my world and expect us to come to an understanding?"

"Your world may be gone, but your people live on," Crovos responded. "Even the millions who hid themselves deep in the Cosmic Graveyard — Sylvra found their settlement, but he did not destroy them. They have been moved to a new world where they may live out the rest of their lives in peace. If you come with me quietly, you may join them. No one else needs to get hurt."

Ev could feel the blood drain from her face. Sylvra had found the others? But how?

"I know you were able to defeat Amethine," Crovos continued, "but Sylvra is different. None of us can even come close to matching what he is capable of. If you continue to defy him, it will only end in ruin — for you and for everyone swept up in the conflict."

Crovos offered Ev his hand. "Come, relinquish the anther that you have stored within your body. I give you my word that no harm will come to you or your friends. I do not desire further bloodshed any more than you do."

Subtly, Ev turned her attention once more to Lylia and the other two Masters. Remarkably, they still remained at a standoff. In fact, though it was difficult to tell through the blurry bubble, it looked as if all three of them were watching the conversation between Ev and Crovos.

Ev turned her attention back to Crovos as she brushed up against the bubble. She couldn't help but notice Crovos tense just a bit as she did so.

"You said you wanted to know what I'm after," she told him as she sensed the antherial configuration of their container. "Why don't you tell me what you want first? You have the power to create worlds, yet you keep making Doxla again and again only to destroy it each time. Why? What the hell do you gain from any of this?"

To her surprise, Crovos seemed uncomfortable about the question. He lowered his hand.

"I wish I could give you your answer, but Sylvra's goals are his most guarded secret. Not even most Masters are aware of them."

"So what?" Ev retorted, not believing him for a second. "If you're just going to lock us away, why would he care what we know, or are you saying you don't know either and are just blindly following him?"

"Of course I know his goals," replied Crovos, though it was clear he was growing irritated. "Now please, submit. I offer you this chance out of respect for who you are, but I will do what I must if you force my hand."

Once more, Crovos extended his hand forward.

Ev stared at it as she considered her situation. Now that she'd analyzed it, she was sure she could break the barrier, but then what? She and Lylia didn't stand a chance against three Masters. They probably wouldn't even have enough time to open up any portals to escape through.

As she looked at Crovos, she could sense her time for making a choice grew short, so she seized on the only sign of weakness she'd seen from him.

Letting out a defeated sigh, Ev met Crovos's eyes with a tired gaze. "It doesn't look like I have a choice, does it? Could you at least tell me one more thing before we go?"

"That depends on what you ask," replied Crovos. It was clear that he, too, was on guard.

"I just want to know," she began, but then she slammed her fist into the wall of her prison.

An antherial shock of her own design rippled through the bubble and caused it to dissolve. Crovos reacted immediately, but Ev had already predicted that he would. She created an invisible wall that his own antherial attack crashed into as she pointed to the other two Masters to continue her thought.

"Do they know that Sylvra built our world in the Cosmic Graveyard?" she cried.

On the other side of the wall, Crovos's face went white. The sight gave Ev just the faintest glimmer of hope that this might actually work, so she pressed on.

"Do they know what he does with us when the Divine stop coming — how he harvests the nepacs and lets the worlds rot?"

Clearly frantic, Crovos crashed through the barrier only to find that Ev had erected another one inches away from herself. She didn't move as she continued.

"They don't, do they?" Ev glared. "How about that we're from another Doxla that he's already destroyed, and the only reason he didn't harvest us is because a Divine helped us escape into the Graveyard!"

"Enough!" Crovos shouted as he teleported behind her.

Before Ev could react, she found herself constrained using the same technique that Amethine had used against her. Crovos's hand clasped onto her shoulder and immediately broke through her inner barrier where it began siphoning her anther. She tried to break free, but before she should could do anything, her anther was gone. She was helpless.

Her only hope was Lylia, but as soon as Lylia made a move, the other Masters overpowered her and constrained her as well.

Crovos released his grip and spoke once more. "I'm afraid your misguided coup has come to an end. Whatever you think you know about Sylvra was clearly told to you in error."

Ev struggled with all of her might — her heart rate skyrocketing as the thought of failure pushed her to desperation — but it was pointless. She could hardly even breathe from the constrictive hold on her.

From behind her, she heard Crovos speak to the other Masters. "You may return to Lumine tower. I will take these two to a special location that Sylvra has prepared for them."

Tears of frustration and despair finally breeched Ev's eyelids and leaked down her cheeks. This was all her fault. Jax had tried to convince her to simply head to the rendezvous. Lylia had tried to warn her not to trust the fairies, but she'd gotten so caught up in trying to rally immortals against the Masters that she'd walked right into a trap and cost them everything.

"Go on," stated Crovos. "Now that they are restrained and free of anther, I will have no problem moving them."

Ev waited for them to vanish and leave her to Crovos, but . . . they didn't. Instead, they exchanged glances before the woman spoke up.

"Crovos, is what the girl said true?"

"Of course not," returned Crovos. "She is a nepac. She only believes those things because some troll of a Divine knowingly fed her harmful stories. That is why I do not wish to punish her. She is an innocent victim in all of this."

The two Enforcers exchanged looks once more but seemed somewhat reassured with that answer.

A series of frantic grunts escaped Ev's lips as she tried desperately to say more, but Crovos's constraints prevented her from vocalizing anything meaningful. Still, she caught the male Enforcer's attention. As unexpected as it was, the two Enforcers had quickly become her only hope.

"Maybe we should hear what she has to say," the man said. "If her claims are valid, then we could all face dire consequences.”

“Don’t be ridiculous,” Crovos returned, though it was clear from his voice that he was starting to sweat. “You authenticated Doxla’s location before ever coming here, didn’t you?”

“Well, yes,” replied the woman, “but locations can be spoofed. If she was actually in the Cosmic Graveyard like she claimed, she should be able to describe it.”

“Forget describing it,” added the man. “These two had raw anther. They could show us.”

“Do you even hear yourselves?” Crovos practically pleaded. “You’re talking about creating intelligent life in the Graveyard. It’s impossible!”

That response led to expressions on the Enforcers that gave Ev hope she might get out of this yet. If she could get two Masters on her side, then Sylvra was finished for sure!

“Why are you being so defensive about this?” the woman asked in an almost accusatory tone. “If she’s wrong, then there’s no harm in checking. I’m not losing privileges because we’ve been conned into helping with something illegal.”

“No more!” exclaimed Crovos. “I will not have my integrity insulted. Consider yourselves relieved of your roles and expelled from Doxla!”

The two Enforcers — and Ev’s last chance of escaping — vanished in an instant. The only faint glimmer of hope she had left was that Helcant would somehow finish their mission without her.

Crovos let out a frustrated sigh before stepping back into Ev’s field of vision.

“That was very clever,” he said. “Considering who you are, I shouldn’t have expected anything less, but I think it’s about time that I took you to your new —”

Without warning, Lylia slammed her shield into Crovos and sent him crashing into a large tree twenty feet away. She followed up by breaking Crovos’s constrictive field over Ev and, after a second’s hesitation, passing some of her anther into Ev.

“Lylia!” Ev cried in shock and relief.

“Surprise! Those Enforcers were sure nice to leave behind our anther,” Lylia flashed a quick smile before growing serious. “We will distract him while you devise an escape. We should be able to keep him at a distance.”

From the edge of the village, Crovos rose to his feet. Stretching out his right arm, he manifested a shining longsword in his hand. He stared down Ev, then

with a wave of his left hand, three copies of himself appeared by his side —
one focused on Ev and the other two looking directly at Lylia.

"Or not," Lylia peeped nervously.

The original Crovos charged at Ev while a duplicate leapt high into the air
towards her. The other duplicates threw themselves at Lylia using the same
strategy.

Ev drew her dagger as both she and Lylia braced for the attack.

Before any of the Crovoses reached them, the original launched what
looked like a normal spell at the ground in front of Ev. The spell exploded into
a wave of fog that covered the entire area.

Blinded, Ev jumped back and put up another antherial barrier around her.

Almost no sooner had she put the barrier in place then one of her attackers
crashed into it. She couldn't see him, but she heard the impact, and she knew
his next move would be to use his own anther to break her barrier. Before he
could do that, though, he'd have to catch her. Ev had never really tested just
how far her Radiant strength could push her, but she was going to find out.

Leaping as hard as she could, Ev jumped almost twelve feet straight up into
the air and above the fog that Crovos had created below. At the height of her
jump, she created a static barrier directly below her feet, which provided a
platform for her to stand on. Quickly, she applied another layer of protection
over her body. Crovos might be strong enough to break through it, but it was
still better than nothing.

Down below, the sound of steel clashing against steel told her that Lylia was
in trouble, but until something was done about that fog, Ev wasn't in any
position to help.

As she pondered a way to blow away the mist without using any more of
her limited anther, one of the Crovoses crashed hard into the bottom of her
platform and fell back out of sight. A second Crovos jumped up shortly after
and created his own platform beside Ev's. Since this one used anther, she
assumed it was the real Crovos standing before her now.

"It's not too late," Crovos said. "You can still lay down your weapons and
come with me. Sylvra can give you a soul. He doesn't want you to perish, and
neither do I. You could do so much good in your next life. If you die here, you
will simply vanish."

Ev swallowed but stood firm. Did he just offer her a soul? Did that mean he
knew she was a copy, or had Birdie been correct in her guess that no one in
Doxla had souls? Either way, it didn't matter. She had one purpose, and she

was going to see it through to the end no matter what.

"What the hell kind of offer is that?" Ev replied. "Give me a soul? Give me a break! Even if that's true, do you think I'd be stupid enough to accept something like that from the likes of Sylvra? I'd *rather* vanish than be another one of his pawns."

"Yet it seems you have no qualms with being a pawn of Syrus."

"Shut up!"

Ev dropped her dagger and reached for her bow. She was going to blast this creep into pieces!

Before she could reach her bow, Crovos moved. With his left hand, he shattered her barrier, then he swept his glowing sword from the platform up toward her chest.

Ev stumbled backward but couldn't avoid the blow altogether. Crovos's sword cleaved through her armor like it wasn't even there; its tip carved an inch deep into her chest and snapped the string of her bow, which fell into the fog below.

Clutching her wound, Ev fell backwards off of her platform. She created another platform just beneath the top of the fog for her to land on.

The sound of a loud crash told her one of the Crovos duplicates must have tried to strike her from below as she fell, but she had more urgent things to worry about as the original Crovos leapt down upon her.

Ev reacted by converting a bit of her anther into a wave of pure force that blasted him up into the sky. Using the short moment that would buy her, she healed the wound she'd received and pushed herself to her feet.

Before she could even create another barrier to protect herself, however, Crovos was back. He'd teleported behind her again — the only warning being the sensation of his anther before he struck.

Knowing she couldn't get away, Ev spun around and slammed herself into Crovos.

He managed to catch his footing before falling and retaliated by grabbing Ev by the shoulder.

No! She wasn't going to let him siphon her anther again!

In an act of desperation, Ev shifted all of her anther into her left hand. She could feel Crovos still taking it from her, but she only needed a little.

Recalling how she'd broken through Amethine's protections, she used her anther to form a more potent version of the same attack. She was nearly there when a searing pain shot up her side.

Ev gasped as she felt her last barrier fading when Crovos forced his sword through it and into her abdomen.

She was out of time. Even if she wasn't sure it was ready, she had to strike now.

Using every bit of strength she could muster, Ev drove her left fist into the side of Crovos's skull.

The effects of her anther rippled across his body as it erased the protections he had as a Master.

Crovos released his grip from Ev's shoulder as he stumbled, which gave her the opportunity to pull herself away from his blade.

Then, without warning, she felt a wave of modified anther wash over her as the entire world turned a hazy orange. Her entire body and especially her face burned, but the sensation passed as quickly as it had arrived. Whether the blast was Crovos's doing or someone else's, she couldn't be sure. Fortunately, however, the new layer of fog wasn't as thick as the stuff below her, and somehow, it even seemed to heal her slightly.

While she couldn't see far, she could still make out the foe before her. Blood began to drip from beneath Crovos's helmet, but she knew whatever damage she'd caused would already be healed. She needed to kill his body outright, if such a thing was even possible. Her own wound still bled profusely, but she could deal with that later. Right now, she needed to finish this before he restored his protections.

Using the last bit of her anther to form a short blade, Ev rushed Crovos. Her blade met his as he brought it down, with neither weapon able to cut through the other. She tried to push him back, but she found herself again frozen in his constrictive field.

"I'm afraid you have brought this upon yourself," Crovos said almost sympathetically through the haze. "It really is a pity."

Crovos raised his blade then stopped. He stared down — not at her, but at the glowing, blood-stained blade protruding from his chest.

Behind him, the barely visible figure of Lylia had risen up on her coils — glowing swords in each hand.

With a look that could only be described as sheer disbelief mixed with acceptance, Crovos met Ev's eyes once more just as Lylia used her other sword to slice his head cleanly from his body. She yanked the first sword out from his torso, and his body fell backwards into the denser fog below.

Lylia then used her own anther to free Ev from Crovos's imprisonment, after which Ev quickly healed herself before staring down at the mist in disbelief.

They'd done it. Even if she knew that Masters couldn't actually be killed, the fact remained that they'd actually defeated one in battle. But, the way he'd looked at her — despite the haze, she had seen it clearly. His expression had seemed so final. What was more, his body hadn't vanished upon death like it should have. It was almost as if they really had killed him, except Ev knew that was impossible. It had to be some sort of mind game he was playing on her to distract her while he prepared for his return.

Except, as a Master, Crovos should be able to return immediately.

At once, Ev was on guard again, but she saw no sign of Crovos, nor anyone else for that matter — save for Lylia, or course. Could it be? Could they actually have somehow killed him?

"We should make haste to leave this place," Lylia said to Ev. Her voice sounded different — almost pained, and she was clearly injured. "We are fairly certain another battle would not go well for us. We are nearly out of anther as it is."

Anther — that was right. Quickly, Ev used standard magic to heal Lylia before jumping down to the ground to search for Crovos's body. When she found it, she placed her hands on it to see if she could reclaim what he'd stolen.

Fortunately she could, and moreso, she was able to take his as well. However, she couldn't help but sense that his anther had clearly already been altered from its purest state, so she opted to leave it there. For all she knew, Crovos had corrupted it before his defeat so he could track her. The orange fog also seemed filled with anther, but it, too, felt tainted in some way.

Once her anther was back in her body, Ev addressed Lylia. "I'll work on making—"

Ev stopped herself. She clutched her throat as she realized her voice sounded different. Perhaps it was the fog, but she didn't have time to dwell on it now.

"I'll make more portals," she finished. "Grab the horses."

"Is this one certain making portals is wise?" Lylia asked.

"If no one else has attacked us after what we just did, I think it's safe enough."

Lylia didn't argue, and Ev activated the tool to make countless portals once more, using up very nearly all of the anther she'd recovered from Crovos.

Unlike the last time she'd used the portal tool, however, she this time added her own custom portal into the mix. She hoped it wouldn't be obvious that she'd specially made this extra one leading to the northwest, but they needed to get those wind wyrms. While she wasn't exactly sure about how far away they were, she was sure she could get them close enough.

Lylia was back with the horses almost as soon as Ev had made her portals, which she found impressive considering how bad the fog still was.

"I guess this mist doesn't bother you much," Ev stated.

"Not at all," replied Lylia. "It blocks light, but not heat!"

Ev nodded absently. She had a lot on her mind, but this wasn't the place to dwell on it.

"Let's go," Ev stated. "We need to hurry so we can get back to Jax and make our way to the rendezvous. No more help, though. We can't take any more risks than we already have."

Lylia nodded in agreement before picking up one of Crovos's glowing blades. Ev noticed that the blade didn't start glowing until Lylia actually picked it up.

"What are you doing?" Ev asked her.

"This is the blade of a Master," Lylia replied cheerfully. "Perhaps with this, Jax may also join us in our final battle."

Ev didn't like the idea of taking something of the Masters' with them, but seeing as how no one else had come for them yet, they were either already being tracked, or the Masters didn't keep tabs on one another.

Nodding her approval, Ev motioned Lylia through the portal. She picked up her dropped dagger and followed close behind. To her surprise, the orange haze waited for her on the other side of the portal as well, but that didn't really tell her that much about what had caused it. All she knew was that something big must be going on, and "big" wasn't something she imagined could be anything good.

Chapter 17

Upon returning from dealing with the demons, Evress was ready for a stiff drink — never mind that it wasn't even noon. Unfortunately for her, Amethine must have been waiting for her return, because no sooner had she arrived back in her room than Amethine summoned her.

Cursing under her breath, Evress teleported to Amethine's location up at the central control room at the very top of Lumine Tower.

The sight of the room immediately repulsed her. While there was nothing wrong with the rose and lavender-hued cloudscape that had replaced the normally starry-night sky that Sylvra preferred — and in fact Evress would have once considered the sight beautiful — the fact that she knew this was Amethine's preferred aesthetic made her want to wretch.

"What?" Evress asked tersely.

"Don't speak to me like that," Amethine snapped, clearly struggling to resist her usual insults. "Sylvra has another task for you."

"Then he can give it to me," Evress stated.

"He's busy," Amethine replied before fiddling with the controls of the nearest terminal.

An image of Ghast Canyon appeared in the air between the two of them. Its crooked, leafless plant life obscured the bottom of the canyon as it stretched in twisted knots across it.

"That demon friend of yours did more than leave behind anther," Amethine continued. "Apparently he left messages that convinced several Divine to conspire against us. Sylvra has gone to address that little problem before it spreads any further, so he wants you to find the demon and stop him."

Evress crossed her arms. "I thought Crovos—"

"Crovos is currently hunting the other 'you,'" Amethine stated. "You were last seen heading west from Tyranor's Domain, and he is investigating that. *I'm* still stuck guarding this tower, so that leaves you to go deal with your little friend."

"Those things are not my friends," Evress growled.

Amethine smirked. "Good. Then prove it by killing this one."

Evress stared with suspicion at Amethine. Even now, she wouldn't put it past the witch to try and trick her into getting into trouble. "Sylvra said he wants them alive."

The response she received back was pure condescension — like a bad teacher explaining something "obvious" to a child.

"That was *before* Divine started getting involved. Perhaps you aren't aware, but if he gets away and word continues to spread among the Divine of what we are doing, this entire world may as well be lost."

Evress blinked. She hadn't thought about that. If Divine wouldn't give prestige to Sylvra, then he had no reason to keep it going.

"Oh, finally sinking in, is it?" Amethine chided. "Then get moving. I've already sealed off the area that Sylvra thinks he's in. I *would* help you look . . ."

Amethine brushed her hand over the image of the canyon and moved the view deeper into it. She then looked Evress in the eye and smiled.

". . . but I'd much rather keep tabs on Crovos. If he does find the other you, well, I wouldn't miss *that* for anything."

Annoyed but not about to give Amethine the satisfaction of a response, Evress noted the location that Amethine showed her and teleported away.

She reappeared at the bottom of Ghast Canyon right where it connected to the valley of the Plaguefelled River, which sat southwest of Ars Summis. The place was — at the bottom, at least — just as ghastly as its name would imply. Behind her, a large, semi-transparent barrier stretched to the top of the Canyon, and behind that, the Plaguefelled River flowed. The ground around her lay completely dry and barren, save for the stray skeletons of whatever unfortunate creatures happened to fall in from above. Out of each side of the canyon reached giant, twisted, leafless "trees" that looked like fat, sickly vines. Each reached about two-thirds across the valley, and none touched any other, though their twisted "trunks" were thick enough to easily hide someone inside of their knots and grew plentifully enough to block most of the sunlight from above.

There was no sign of Helcant's copy, though Evress would have been quite surprised to have jumped straight to wherever he was hiding. If Sylvra hadn't found him, then the copy had likely found some tricky crevice somewhere to stow away in. The fact that the copies of Birdie and Umber were with him would likely make finding them easier, but in a place like this, Evress knew she had her work cut out for her.

Still, she had to do this. As much as she hated it, Amethine was right. If these copies weren't stopped soon, then all the good that Evress hoped to do with this world would be lost.

In fact, forget searching. Forget tact. The only things that should be in this place were monsters, those ugly trees, which she could restore, and Radiant-class Divine. Any Divine she came across, she could easily transport to safety. Everything else could burn, for all she cared.

After searching through her catalog of spells, she changed her spell set to include deathly freeze, incinerate, and force wave. That should prove more than adequate for both flushing out anyone hiding here and dealing with any monsters that might impede her progress.

Once that was done, Evress activated one of her Master's tools that she'd never used before — one that she'd honestly ever seen used only once, and that had been by Sylvra that first time she'd encountered him.

With a small bit of concentration, Evress floated up into the air. The sensation was odd at first, certainly, but she found that controlling her position was simple enough.

After taking a moment to make sure she was comfortable with the power of flight, Evress turned her mind back to the task at hand — finding Helcant and the other copies with him.

Now positioned about halfway up the canyon walls, Evress raised her hand towards the nearest tree, which she blasted with her deathly freeze spell.

The entire tree instantly iced over.

Evress followed up with the force wave, which rippled across the tree and caused the entire thing to shatter; its pieces clattered down to the ground below.

A number of ghoulish figures rose up from the ground in response. Some were confined to the ground, while other, more ghostly forms, streaked upwards toward her.

While Evress could easily have used her status to make the creatures ignore her, her hatred for monsters couldn't be ignored, and she figured a bit of catharsis wouldn't hurt.

Her incinerate spell made quick work of the ghasts and ghouls. Even the ghostly ones vanished under the might of her magic. She knew it was wasting time, but it felt good to have an excuse to purge a bunch of monsters for once.

Turning her attention back to the trees, Evress continued shattering them one at a time as she pressed deeper into the canyon. Progress was slow, but not too slow, and Ghast Canyon was probably only about five miles long. If

Helcant was here, she'd find him within the next few hours, and she'd find the copies of Birdie and Umber, too.

After about two hours of what had quickly become a slog, Evress finally spotted new movement on the ground.

Immediately she teleported down, ready to attack, but once she had a clear look at who she'd ambushed, she relaxed slightly.

Before her stood a group of eight very confused Divine. According to the names floating above their heads, each of them was ranked as fledgling Radiants. The titles of plain Lord and Lady told her as much.

"Master Evress?" said the one called Ferveon, who was clearly nervous. "Why are you here? Is there a problem?"

Evress tried to hide her frustration as she replied. "There is, but not with you."

Then remembering that Sylvra had recently put a bounty on the copies, she added, "One of the nepacs from Sylvra's announcement was spotted around here. Have you seen anything?"

The Divine exchanged glances with one another. To Evress's surprise, they seemed almost disapproving of her question.

"Well?" she pressed.

"We haven't," answered Ferveon, but he looked at her oddly. "Is that why you're destroying this valley? To find a nepac?"

"This nepac is dangerous," Evress shot back. "He has anther with him."

Ferveon and several of the others now looked at her like she was crazy.

"Don't you have a noise profile you can search for?" he asked. "Or, why don't you just do a facial scan? You clearly already know what these guys look like."

"I—" Evress searched for an answer. She may have had enough exposure to seitti civilization to know what a "facial scan" was, but she'd never heard of a "noise profile." She was a Master, though, and she couldn't let it seem like she didn't know anything that she clearly should have — especially not to a group of Divine.

"It isn't my decision," she answered, dodging the question. "Sylvra doesn't want to cause a panic. He wants me to keep the search quiet."

Ferveon shifted his eyes toward the huge pile of shattered, frozen plant matter behind Evress. "By destroying an entire valley," he stated dryly.

"Yes," Evress replied, trying to keep her voice cool. "A worldwide search would let everyone know, and I can repair any damage here as soon as I'm done."

Ferveon didn't seem entirely convinced, but to Evress's relief he didn't press the issue further.

"Fair enough, I guess," he said. "So, should we . . .?" Ferveon gestured first toward the pile of destruction and then back the way they'd come from.

"You can keep going," Evress replied, happy to put this conversation behind her. "Once you're clear, I'll continue my search. I'll remove the barrier around the Canyon when I'm through."

"Right," stated Ferveon. "We'll just hurry along then."

With a tilt of his head, Ferveon signaled the rest of his group to follow him, which they did. Once they were out of sight, Evress went right back to the tedium of clearing the canyon.

Progress remained slow, and by the time noon had come and gone, the thought that this was all a big waste of time slowly began to fill Evress's mind. That sentiment only grew when one hour later, she could see where Ghast Canyon opened up into a wide, dusty field — Amethine's barrier being the only separation. Evress had nearly reached the canyon's end, and there was still no sign of Helcant or any of the other copies.

Well, whatever. There were only a handful of trees left to check.

Freeze, crash. Freeze, crash. Down they went, one at a time, until—

Evress almost couldn't believe it. As one of the trees shattered apart, a scrawny figure tumbled out of it and hit the ground.

The copy of Helcant rolled away, but when he looked up and saw Evress, he stopped.

Immediately, Evress raised her guard. She knew she could handle Helcant in a straight fight, but he might not be alone. As quickly as she could, she shattered the remaining trees in the area. When no other figures emerged, she lowered herself to the ground where she stood before Syrus's creation. She switched out her incinerate spell for a binding one and approached.

"Well, well," growled Helcant. "The traitor appears once again."

"I don't have to explain myself to you, you fake," Evress shot back. "Give up now, or I will kill you."

She said that, but it was hard to feel it. The creature in front of her looked and sounded just like Helcant. Still, he was just a copy, and a dangerous one at that. She couldn't let herself get distracted by superficial similarities.

Helcant cackled and tilted his head. "Fake, am I? Perhaps. Birdie has revealed Syrus's secret to me, but what of it? I, at least, recall the villainy of the

Masters. What of you? What of the other me? Have you betrayed him as well?"

"The *real* Helcant is safe," Evress growled.

Helcant's smile vanished. "Where is he, then? Locked away, I assume, because *he* would not bend, unlike you."

Evress took a deep breath and looked Helcant in the eye. "You know what? You're absolutely correct. I never was able to convince him that what I'm doing was right."

Shooting her arm out, Evress tried to surprise Helcant with her binding attack, but he was ready for it. The nimble demon rolled out of the way and with a sweep of his arm sent a wave of erupting fire back at her.

Evress let the blast wash over her, knowing full well that she was immune to conventional damage. As the fire blazed around her, she prepared another spell of her own and aimed at the ground in front of Helcant.

A thick, glistening layer of ice covered the area, causing Helcant to slip and giving Evress the opportunity to successfully land her binding spell upon him.

Raging flames spread around him as he hit the ground, melting the ice, but it did nothing to free him.

Quickly but cautiously, Evress approached her captive to drain his anther, but just before she reached him, a portal opened up on the ground beneath him.

Helcant fell through into a misty, ruined landscape, and the portal closed as quickly as it had opened.

Evress cursed and stomped the ground where he'd vanished. She'd torn this entire place apart searching for Helcant's copy, and he'd escaped just as she was about to complete his capture?

No. Not yet. Not if she could help it. Recalling how the map of Doxla in her room had exploded with warnings and flashing dots back when the copies had first attacked, Evress quickly teleported back to her terminal to check and see if the same had occurred here.

To her absolute relief, two dots had appeared on her map, though they weren't flashing — presumably because Helcant had already closed the portal. Still, one was right at Ghast Canyon where she'd been, and the other was located at the top of a nearby mountain.

Evress was just about to teleport to Helcant's location when another pair of flashing dots appeared — one right on top of the mountain dot and another a great distance away in the middle of a swamp.

It was clear he was concerned he could be followed, but it was equally clear he had no idea how she could track him through portals.

Well, that suited her just fine. In fact, she could wait until he was done running before striking.

Typing a few commands into her terminal and sliding her fingers over the map, Evress removed the barrier around Ghast Canyon and placed a new one over the swampy region that Helcant had traveled to. She then activated a viewing terminal to look around where he'd opened the portal, but she saw nothing. Realizing that he could easily have made the second portal to trick her into thinking he'd gone there, she quickly placed a second barrier back over the mountain he'd traveled to before opening another viewing terminal over there.

Once again, she saw nothing, and despite knowing that she *had* to have him trapped, she started to get nervous.

The mountain ruins seemed utterly deserted. While there may have been plenty of walls and pillars strewn about, everything was more-or-less open, leaving very few places to hide. The swamp, on the other hand, was filled with tall reeds and drooping willows, as well as pulsating caverns that snaked through the scattered hills that rose up from the murky water. The heavy rains currently showering the area only made hiding even easier. If Helcant was anywhere, Evress had her money on his being there.

After taking another look around the area remotely and still seeing nothing, Evress knew she'd have to finish the search in person. She made one last change to her spell set — adding the incinerate spell back in to deal with all of the places that the fire-proof demon could be hiding — and teleported directly to where copy-Helcant's second portal had opened up to.

Thunder crashed overhead as Evress appeared in the middle of a muddy pool. The pool opened up into deeper water behind her, so that was one area she wouldn't need to check, at least. To her left and front, large, dripping willows blew in the wind. To her right was one of those fleshy caves that she'd rather not have to investigate, but she had a feeling that was where Helcant would be. Still, it wouldn't hurt to further narrow down her options first.

Raising her hand, Evress unleashed a maximally-powered incinerate on the trees around her.

All but the trunks of the trees immediately turned to ash while the rain burst into a wave of hot steam. The glowing embers of the trunks offered a fleeting bit of light to the area before being snuffed out by the rain.

As expected, there was still no sign of Helcant. He very well could have simply gone deeper into the trees, but Evress would work her way back to them eventually. For now, she'd perform a circular sweep of the area until she either found him or no further hiding places remained. It was annoying, but it was her fault for letting him get away. She would *not* make the same mistake a second time.

Stepping over to the nasty-looking cavern, Evress peered in to see slimy walls covered in some sort of orange, pulsating fungus. Tangled roots drooped down from ceiling to floor and obscured her vision. She had no idea what the stuff on the walls actually was, but she had few qualms about roasting the inside of the cavern to get rid of it and remove the cover provided by the roots.

Just as quickly as she had with the willows, Evress lit the entire cave ablaze. The slime fried and hardened as the roots turned to soot, leaving only smoke behind. Switching her ice spell for a wind one, Evress cleared the smoke from the cavern, which left it clear from one side of the hill to the other.

One more hiding spot down.

As she backed out of the cave, Evress called out. "You know this is pointless, right? You can't hide, and you can't stop what's happening. Even if you made it to Ars Summis, it's impossible to break into Sylvra's core systems."

Evress walked over to another bunch of trees and turned them into cinders. "All you're doing is making things worse. The more you fight, the more immortals suffer — not that I'd expect you to understand. Even the real Helcant refuses to accept the truth."

Water splashed behind her. Evress turned in time to see copy-Helcant leap up from the reeds and launch a swirling shimmer in her direction.

The antherial attack struck, but after a grand display of light and sound, nothing ultimately came of it. From the concern that subsequently appeared on Helcant's face, it was clear that wasn't the outcome he'd expected. He obviously hadn't figured out how to get past the special protections of the Masters.

Before he could dart away again, Evress hit him once more with her binding spell, but this time she teleported over to him as he fell. She wouldn't let him escape again.

Before the faux demon even hit the ground, Evress grabbed him and activated her antherial siphon.

Every last bit of anther drained from Helcant's body, which was surprisingly almost nothing. Had he used it all up in that attack, or had he somehow hidden it? No, that didn't make any sense either way. He had to have done something else with it. Sylvra had said Helcant had been scattering anther around. Perhaps he'd actually been so reckless with it as to have run out. Whatever the case, it wouldn't hurt to ask.

"Is that really all the anther you had left?" she asked him. "Were you so desperate to be a nuisance that you gave it all away?"

To her surprise, Helcant cackled in his nearly petrified state. "You claim to be Ev, yet you cannot even guess what I have done? How far you have fallen. It would disgust me, but I know your true self still lives free."

"I *am* the real me!" Evress nearly yelled as she lifted him up to look him in his face.

She wanted to lay into him about how he was a fake and how Syrus had abandoned her — how he was endangering Doxla by convincing Divine to defy Sylvra, but she knew it was pointless.

Instead, she just tossed him into a shallow pool of muck. She'd take him to the prison world and leave him for Sylvra to take care of when he had time.

Evress prepared to teleport herself and her captive there, but she stopped when she felt a wave of anther wash over her. In an instant, the entire world was covered with a hazy orange fog.

"What is this?" Evress asked, and she picked Helcant up once again, but she almost dropped him when she saw how different his face appeared. "Who did this? What are you all planning?"

Helcant looked back at her in shock, but his expression quickly turned defiant as he cackled through a pointy-teethed grin.

Frustrated, Evress teleported the two of them to the same place she'd imprisoned the other two demons that morning. She tossed copy-Helcant into an antherial bubble and made doubly certain that the entire thing was configured to be completely unexploitable. She even tested it herself to see if she could extract any anther from it. When she couldn't, she was satisfied, and she teleported back to her room to investigate what could have caused the orange fog.

What she found when she got there changed her attitude very quickly. The haze had even manifested in her own room, and worse, she now realized that it was filled with some sort of tainted anther. A small bit of relief returned when she realized that, try as she might, she couldn't use any of it. If she couldn't, then most likely Divine couldn't either, so that was good, but it didn't mean that it hadn't been tailored for usage by the remaining copies.

An odd feeling welled up inside of her — there was a sense of dread at what was to come, but a part of her couldn't help but wonder if maybe those stupid copies actually could pull off what they were trying to do.

No, that was ridiculous. No matter how much damage they did, they'd never be able to access Sylvra's core systems. It would all be pointless, and all they'd do is guarantee that this world would be discarded sooner than it otherwise would be. She had to stop them, and she had to do it soon.

Upon accessing her terminal, Evress's eyes opened wide at the alerts plastering the entire map. Flashing dots were everywhere — it was even worse than the first time the copies had broken into Doxla.

Evress scrambled to find the source of the problem, but there were far too many places to check. Even along the border of the world, there had to be thousands of places where Doxla had been exposed to the Cosmic Graveyard. She opened a view of each one, one at a time, but all she saw was abandoned rocky coast after abandoned rocky coast.

Her search was interrupted as Sylvra's booming voice caused her to jump out of her seat.

"Evress!" Sylvra yelled. "To me *now!*"

Evress fumbled for a second before realizing that Sylvra wasn't, in fact, in the room. In the six months she'd known him, not once had Sylvra raised his voice at her. Whatever had happened was serious, and she did not want to see what it was like to be on the receiving end of his anger.

As quickly as she could, Evress identified his location and teleported to him.

When she arrived, she spotted a pale-faced Amethine trembling in the corner. Without saying a word, Sylvra turned his head toward Evress. His face was stony, and his eyes gave her chills.

"Where is the demon?" Sylvra asked.

"I put him in that grassy world," she answered. "I didn't—"

"Can he escape?"

Evress shifted her eyes briefly to Amethine before answering again. "No."

"Are you sure?" Sylvra's voice was low and threatening.

Evress swallowed. Something was very wrong for her to be receiving this line of questioning. "I'm sure. Why are you asking? Did something happen?"

"Did something happen?" Sylvra enunciated every word as he turned the rest of his body to face Evress. "The entire world is covered in fog and corrupted anther. The question is not 'did something happen?' The question is 'who caused this?' Maybe you should be the one to answer that."

"I didn't have anything to do with this," Evress replied, growing defensive.

"No," returned Sylvra, "but you are the one who allowed the one called Tallis to escape."

Evress felt the blood drain from her face. "Tallis? He did this?"

With a few taps of his finger on the terminal by his side, Sylvra produced a view of the world border where Tallis stood trapped within a transparent bubble. He was trying to break free, but so far had clearly been unsuccessful. Gare was nowhere to be seen.

Evress swallowed, but she couldn't help but feel unfairly blamed for this. "I didn't let him go on purpose. I—"

"I do not want to hear excuses," Sylvra growled. "Because of you, we may very well lose this Doxla."

Warmth flooded into Evress's cheeks. It wasn't her fault that Tallis had gotten away! Out in the Cosmic Graveyard, they were on equal ground. How was she supposed to have stopped him from running away like he had?

Unfortunately, Sylvra wasn't done. He turned his attention back to Amethine and spoke in an even harsher tone, "And because of you, Crovos is dead."

The news hit Evress like a slap to the face. That couldn't be right. Crovos was the only one here who'd treated her like an equal; he was the only other Master who'd truly cared about the people of Doxla. How? Had those copies actually killed him?

Amethine's words returned to Evress as the painful realization set in. Amethine had said Crovos was tracking the copy-Ev. That meant she had to be involved in Crovos's death.

"What happened?" Evress asked in an accusatory tone that was directed at Amethine.

Amethine merely shrunk away from the question. A flash of anger crossed her face as she glanced at Evress, but it faded back to shame just as quickly.

Sylvra answered instead. "Amethine failed to monitor Crovos's battle after the appearance of the fog, choosing instead to seek its source. Her neglect cost him his life."

At that statement, Amethine spoke for the first time since Evress's arrival.

"He was about to win," she practically whimpered.

"Clearly, he was not," Sylvra shot back. He then turned to Evress. "Perhaps had he faced anyone else, the outcome would have been different, but Crovos was always sentimental. I suspect he showed your copy more mercy than he should have out of respect for you. Do *not* make the same mistake. These creatures are not your friends. They are soulless automatons created for the sole purpose of sabotaging everything we have worked toward."

"I know," returned Evress.

"Do you?" asked Sylvra. "Then why did you spare the demon?"

"It was a mistake," Evress answered. "I won't make it again."

Sylvra at last relaxed his gaze by the smallest degree. "I'm glad to hear it. In that case, I task you with erasing that one. Prove to me that you will not falter." Sylvra pointed to the image of copy-Tallis.

Evress turned her attention to the fake Tallis wasting his anther as he tried in vain to break Sylvra's bubble. Syrus had been willing to sacrifice her so those fakes could live, and now they'd killed the only person she considered a friend here. She *would* erase Syrus's creations, and she would show no mercy to them ever again.

Chapter 18

Ev and Lylia passed by several portals as they traveled through the orange haze that seemingly covered the entire world — each one reminding Ev of what they'd just done and somehow survived. The only reason she could see the portals at all was because of the light pouring through most of them. Combined with the dark clouds and rain pouring down around them, Ev could barely even make out Lylia's form to her right, though the glowing sword of Crovos was plainly visible in Lylia's left hand. The lack of visibility was in one sense comforting; whether true or not, she felt like it helped her hide from the Masters' eyes. She knew they had to be coming for her. Still, the presence of the haze was ultimately problematic. While she was fairly certain they'd arrived near the Spires of Mire — the home of harpies and wind wyrms alike — it was very difficult to even determine which direction they were headed.

"Are you sure we're going the right way?" Ev asked Lylia.

"Not in the slightest," Lylia chimed.

"Ugh, we need to get rid of this fog. How are we supposed to find the wind wyrms in—"

Ev stopped. She felt several strange waves of anther wash over her.

"What was that?" she asked.

Lylia appeared on guard. "It was difficult to tell, but we believe that was an attempted search."

At those words, Ev readied herself for a surprise attack, but as the seconds ticked by, nothing came. Relaxing slightly, Ev asked Lylia, "Are you sure that's what it was?"

Lylia tapped her chin. "Well, we thought as much, anyway."

Almost right after Lylia's response, the orange haze suddenly vanished. The ubiquitous, unusable anther that had accompanied it still remained, but the actual fog part was completely gone.

"Well," chirped Lylia. "Looks like that problem is solved, at least."

"What is going on?" Ev asked, then she noticed Lylia's face. It looked nothing like it had prior to the fight with Crovos. Her skin was lighter but older-looking, and Lylia's cheekbones looked thinner. Even her hair had changed color to be an orangish brown.

"Lylia? You — your face!"

"Yes?" Lylia tilted her head. "What about it?"

"It's completely different!"

Lylia placed a hand against her cheek and rubbed it. "Huh. Interesting. We wondered what that sensation was earlier."

Sensation? Wait, Ev recalled that she'd felt a burning sensation back when the orange haze had first appeared. That was also when both her and Lylia's voices had changed. Did that mean . . .?

In a panic, Ev quickly removed her gloves and patted her own face. It was hard to tell, but she had the terrible feeling that something was off.

"What about me?" she asked Lylia. "Did it get me, too?"

"This one looks fine," Lylia smiled. "Perhaps a smidgen older with the gray hair and wrinkles, but otherwise fine."

"*What?*" Ev yanked off her helmet and pulled a few strands of hair in front of her eyes.

She felt the blood drain from her face. Her hair wasn't just gray — it was nearly white. Even worse: her hands had become old and gnarled.

"Wha— How?" she fumbled for words. "Who did this to us!"

Lylia placed a hand against her cheek and tapped her finger as if deep in thought.

"We see no benefit to the Masters from this occurrence. It must have been one of our own. We certainly are not responsible, and neither Helcant nor Nictis are skilled in this type of anther usage." Lylia snapped her fingers. "It must have been our darling Tallis!"

"Tallis? But he was captured!"

"We don't know that for certain," Lylia corrected. "All we know is that Sylvra did not list him in his message. Perhaps Sylvra is simply unaware of Tallis, Gare, and Nictis."

Ev had to admit, she'd never thought of that. She supposed it was a possibility.

"But why would he make a giant fog that makes everyone old? What's the point?"

Lylia shrugged. "Perhaps to save us from that search? Our Tallis has always been very clever. He may have expected it to come."

"Sure, right. Well, if it was him and that's why he did it, then I guess we owe him," Ev stated while looking at the veins bulging from the back of her hand.

As old as she looked, she didn't feel any different. Her body seemed just as strong and healthy as ever. However, she also couldn't help but feel like she'd been violated. She'd been forcibly transformed into this new appearance, and as far as she knew, there was no way to reverse it.

As her disgust and outrage slowly turned to acceptance, she put her helmet and gloves back on before looking around the now significantly clearer landscape.

"At least we can see now. Maybe we can start making some actual progress in this place."

Progress would be easier said than done, however. The rain still beat down intensely, making it difficult to see more than thirty feet in any particular direction. The tall pillars of stone, which the "Spires" part of this place's name came from, surrounded them on all sides and with no particular pattern. The slopes they traveled along were rocky and crisscrossed with one another around the pillars, but deviating from the path even slightly would send them sliding down the muddy hillsides into greasy pits of muck from which there would be no escape.

"I guess we keep going up," Ev said after looking around.

"We would imagine so," replied Lylia. "Wind wyrms supposedly reside atop these pillars. Perhaps we will find a way to climb them if we keep ascending."

Ev tilted her gaze up at a nearby pillar, which stretched beyond the limits of her sight in the storm. It reminded her of the enormous tower she'd had to climb back in the Netherworld, though it was very much smaller than that one had been.

After what felt like hours of being pelted by endless drops of water, the storm finally let up. It was at this point that Ev realized that atop each pillar sat a large plateau, so large in fact that the plateaus nearly touched one another across pillars.

Another half-hour or so later, and Ev and Lylia finally wandered across a change in the scenery. The pillars and murky pits still surrounded them, but Ev couldn't help but notice that the pillars here were much shorter than they had been back at the start of their climb. The slopes down into the pits were also shallower than they had been lower down the mountain, but every other pit or so dropped off into a dark abyss rather than a muddy cesspool.

"Seems like we may be getting close," chirped Lylia.

"Any idea how to capture one?" Ev asked.

"Not a one. Perhaps we should ask a harpy?"

"Absolutely not," returned Ev.

"Why not?" asked Lylia. "They would probably help us."

"Or they could rat us out to the Masters like the fairies did."

"We find that unlikely," said Lylia. "Even if they would, they cannot speak to the Masters directly. They would need to contact Divine to pass on the message, and we have not seen any around here."

"That doesn't mean there aren't. The mountain's a big place, and harpies can fly. I'm not taking the chance."

Lylia shrugged. "If that is what this one wishes. Oh, look there. We both may have our first chance to capture a wind wyrm now."

Ahead of them waited a half-collapsed plateau at the top of a very short pillar. The hell-horses wouldn't be able to climb it, but it would provide a way for both Ev and Lylia to reach the top.

Once they'd arrived at the base of the rubble, the pair dismounted from their steeds and climbed up the broken rock.

At the top, the broken plateaus stretched out in all directions for as far as Ev could see. Some of the platforms were higher or lower than others, but all of them looked within reach; only small gaps that could be easily jumped separated them. Ev saw no sign of any harpies, but several large nests housing various creatures caught her eye. One of them not too far away particularly drew her attention with a white gleam in the sun.

"I think I see one," Ev told Lylia.

Lylia gestured with Crovos's sword. "Lead the way."

Cautiously, Ev stepped out to the edge of the plateau. The gap to the next platform was only about two feet, so she hopped right on over. Lylia didn't even need to do that and merely slid across. The next few gaps proved to be no more of a challenge than the first, and the pair soon found themselves on a platform adjacent to the one housing the wind wyrm's rocky nest. No sooner had Ev set one foot on the adjacent platform, however, than the wind wyrm lifted up into the air with a roar.

The twenty-foot serpentine monster circled in the sky above them, eyeing who had dared to disturb its rest. It clearly wasn't about to submit without a fight.

"Here's the plan," said Ev. "I'll distract it, and you see if you can climb on top of it."

Lylia looked up at the wyrm and back to Ev. "We have some doubts about this plan."

"Well, unless you've got a better one, this is what we have to work with."

Lylia held her gaze on Ev for another moment before planting Crovos's sword hilt-deep into the ground and getting into position.

Once Ev was sure that Lylia was ready, she fired a single arrow up at the wyrm, though she missed intentionally.

The wyrm responded exactly as she'd hoped and quickly dove down at the pair. It stopped a good ten feet above the platform and blasted Ev with a powerful gust of wind that sent her crashing backwards and nearly off of the platform. In doing so, however, it had come within Lylia's reach, and she used her coils to strike up at it before it could escape.

Now caught in Lylia's grasp, the wyrm thrashed about overhead before diving through the narrow gap between platforms. The maneuver allowed it to escape from Lylia's grip, and the next thing Ev knew, the ground below her shook as a loud crash reached her ears.

"What's it doing?" Ev asked as she rose to her feet.

A second crash gave her the answer. The platform they were on dropped out from under them, stopped as it hit something, then slid into the side of a neighboring pillar well below the level of the plateaus. The force of the collision threw Ev off of it and onto the path below. The landing knocked the wind clean out of her, and she had to roll to the side to avoid being crushed by a large boulder.

Fortunately, the collision didn't break the other pillar. Unfortunately, the collapsing platform wasn't done falling yet either. After about a second's worth of slow scraping, the platform slipped and continued its descent. When it finally hit the ground below, it sent Lylia crashing against one of the slippery slopes leading down to a pit of mire.

Ev watched helplessly as Lylia slid into the pit of muck at the bottom. The mostly still-intact platform slid after her but stopped short of covering the pit completely. Whatever was in that pit was clearly not normal mud, however, as the moment Lylia touched it, it stuck to her like a disgusting glue. Struggle as she might, Lylia couldn't break free, and she only sunk deeper as she tried to pull herself out.

"Don't move!" Ev called out. "It's only pulling you under faster!"

Lylia stopped struggling and looked up at Ev. She was still clearly sinking, so Ev knew she had to act quickly.

Looking around, there at first appeared to be nothing useful nearby, but then Ev noticed the hilt of Crovos's sword sticking out of the stone. If it was really as powerful as it seemed to be, then perhaps there was one way she could get Lylia out.

Sprinting to the side of the pit where the large platform had settled, Ev leapt onto what was left of it and ran to the sword. The moment she grabbed the hilt, she could feel its energy flow into her. With a tug, the blade emerged effortlessly from the stone.

Taking a few steps closer to the edge so she could look down at where she was relative to Lylia, Ev tried to gauge just how big the mud part of the pit actually was. Lylia was now up to her neck in the muck, however, so Ev knew she didn't have time to take exact measurements.

Sword in hand, Ev rushed to one side of the platform and swung downward. The blade cleaved effortlessly through the stone. Ev then dragged the half-buried weapon clear to the other side of the platform, and with a final push, she separated a twenty-foot-long slice of the downed plateau from the rest of it.

The slab of stone — slightly larger than the muddy region of the pit — dropped down and landed close to Lylia.

By now, Lylia's head had nearly gone under, and Ev knew she was out of time.

Sword in hand, Ev jumped down to the makeshift bridge and wedged the blade into the stone to use as an anchor. Reaching out, she was able to grab Lylia's hand from the mire. The mud clung to them both like glue, but with mostly stable ground beneath her, Ev was able to pull Lylia up enough for her to grab onto the bridge herself. Then, together, the two of them were eventually able to lift Lylia completely out of the mire and onto the bridge, though Lylia remained covered from head to tail in the disgusting glop.

"Many thanks," said Lylia tiredly as she tried to shake the mud from her arms.

"That was too close," said Ev, her heart racing. "I can't believe that wyrm broke the pillar like that."

"It was certainly a surprise," returned Lylia. She'd now resorted to scraping her arms along the ground to get the muck off of her.

Ev sighed. "At least we're safe. I guess we should work on climbing out of this pit now."

Lylia looked up at the bulk of the fallen platform still resting overhead.

"That should not be difficult. We can reach the ledge now that we are free."

Before Ev could respond, Lylia lifted up on her tail and grabbed onto the large platform. After pulling herself up, she dropped her tail back down for Ev to grab onto.

Ev retrieved the sword and held tight to Lylia as she was lifted out of the pit.

"Thanks," said Ev once she was back up with Lylia. "Any idea how we can stop the wind wyrms from doing that next time?"

Lylia tilted her head as she looked at Ev with a concerned expression. "We have none. If this one insists on a second attempt, however, perhaps we should ask for assistance from the harpies."

"No," Ev replied firmly. "I already said we aren't taking any more chances."

Lylia gestured at the broken pillar they'd fallen from. "This was *not* taking a chance?"

Ev felt her cheeks flush. It was true that they'd been lucky with how they'd fallen. If they'd both gotten stuck in the pit, she wasn't sure she'd have had enough anther to get them out of it.

Ev sighed in defeat. "Fine. I guess it wouldn't hurt to ask them. Any idea where they'd be?"

"Oh, that's easy," Lylia said with a smile. "They are right there!"

Ev spun to look where Lylia pointed behind her and was surprised to see no fewer than five harpies perched on the rim of the slope down into the pit. They all looked nearly identical to Ev's eyes — bodies like vultures with the heads of elderly women at the end of long, snake-like necks. Their faces all looked the same; the only real difference between them was the amount and length of the scraggly hair hanging from their scalps.

"Wha— how long have they been there?"

Lylia slid beside Ev. "We are uncertain. We weren't exactly engaged in our surroundings while we were trapped in the mud."

The harpies stared with wide eyes at Ev and Lylia, occasionally tilting their heads this way or that.

Knowing it was too late to avoid a confrontation, Ev took a few steps toward the bird-women.

"Hello," she said. "We hope we didn't cause any trouble here. We were just trying to capture a wind wyrm, and we didn't expect it to knock down the pillar."

The central harpy — one with particularly sparse and matted hair —

lowered her head as she stared directly at Ev. After a moment of silence, the bird-lady spread her wings and flitted over to the fallen platform. Landing just out of reach of Ev's sword, the harpy stared up at Ev's face before letting out a shriek.

"Human!" she shouted. "Human in demon's armor!"

The other harpies took to the air and surrounded Ev. Lylia responded by swiftly placing herself between Ev and the bulk of the airborne creatures. Her quick movement caused most of the harpies to retreat a short distance, but the one on the ground didn't budge. Instead, she shifted her gaze to Lylia with the same wide-eyed expression she'd held the entire time.

"Human and naga," the harpy shrilled. "They work together?"

Ev seized on her chance to apply calm to the situation. "That's right. Lylia and I are friends. We don't mean harm. We're just trying to capture some wind wyrms so we can be on our way."

The grounded harpy looked back at Ev once more, tilting her head this way and that as she stared intensely. She then looked back to Lylia, then to Ev yet again.

"Faces are different, but alliance is same. Forbidden! Demon armor . . . demon assistance? Yes! Unnatural strength. Strange sword. Defiance! Unknown by Masters? Impossible, or is it? Sisters! Assist in judgment!"

The other four harpies all landed beside the center one and immediately entered into a fevered, high-pitched discussion. Between the shrillness of their voices and the fact that they all seemed to be talking over one another, Ev wasn't able to make out a single word they were saying.

She tried to interject, but her attempts fell on deaf ears. She looked to Lylia, but Lylia merely shrugged.

After a few moments the cacophony subsided, and the center harpy once again turned her wide eyes to Ev.

"You defy Masters. Servants of rebel Divine?"

"Servants? N-no, we are just passing through," Ev stammered.

The center harpy tilted her head as the others began clucking in whispers to one another. Ev felt a bead of sweat forming on her brow. She may have been willing to ask for help, but she did not want anyone associating them with making efforts against the Masters.

Lylia leaned in close to whisper in Ev's ear. "We suggest honesty. Harpies are very good at detecting lies."

Ev turned her head to Lylia. "But I'm not lying! We aren't anyone's servants.”

Center harpy tilted her head in the opposite direction. “Not servants? You defy Masters alone?”

“I—” Ev stopped herself. There was no point in hiding anything. A single scream from one of the harpies would alert all others for miles around, and these had already concluded that she was indeed working against the Masters.

Taking a breath, Ev looked down at the little bird-woman before her. “We are not alone. There are many who have seen the Masters for what they really are, and we stand together with them.”

Center harpy examined Ev’s face for a moment before lowering her gaze to Crovos’s sword. “No Divine? What sword then is this? Never seen before.”

Ev doubted the harpies would believe her if she told them the truth about the sword, and she wasn’t sure that she wanted to share that information regardless.

“It’s true that we did have help from a Divine in the past,” she said. “He taught us how to fight the Masters — how to break the rules of the world that they put in place. He has since been banished, but the Masters can’t track nepacs, and we know how to defeat them. If we can get to Ars Summis, we can take Doxla back from their control.”

Lylia chimed in from behind. “And we may have more help from other Divine in the future. A dragon told us where to find them.”

Furious murmurs punctuated by the occasional shriek erupted amongst the harpies. After another unintelligible debate and numerous wide-eyed glances, the center harpy spoke once more.

“Speak truly human. Were you shown by Master Sylvra in sky-lights?”

Ev could only assume the harpy was referring to that message Sylvra had sent out back when she was in the Underworld. If so, then the answer was, “Yes.”

A final round of debate broke out between the harpies. When it at last subsided, the center one turned to Ev once more.

“Wait here. We shall help.”

With that, the harpies lifted up and flew away. Where to, Ev didn’t know, but the last time she’d been told to wait, Crovos had shown up instead.

“Let’s get out of here,” she said to Lylia.

“If we leave, we may never obtain a wind wyrm,” Lylia replied.

“And if we stay, we might be done for.”

“Perhaps,” said Lylia, “but we think they are trustworthy. We doubt we could leave without being seen, regardless."

Ev wanted to argue, but Lylia did have a point. If the harpies intended on betraying them, they were likely being watched right now.

"Alright," she said reluctantly. "We'll stay."

Every second of the wait was unbearable. Ev couldn't help but feel they were waiting for the net to fall. Fortunately, she didn't have to wait long, and when the harpies returned without any undesirable accompaniment, she finally relaxed just the smallest amount.

The main harpy landed with a small flute in her mouth. She hopped forward and dropped the instrument at Ev's feet.

"Take this," the harpy said. "It calms wind wyrms. Use it to free us from this curse."

Ev picked up the slightly wet flute and looked back down at the main harpy. "Thank you. We will, or we'll die trying."

The harpy bowed her head before taking off once more. The other harpies dropped what looked like large reins and bridles at their feet before joining the first as they flew out of sight, leaving Ev and Lylia alone on the fallen platform.

"See?" Lylia trilled almost obnoxiously. "This one should not let one bad experience prevent her from trusting others."

"That's not . . ." Ev trailed off. That was exactly what had been happening.

"Let's just get some wyrms," she said, and she led the way back to the pillar they'd first climbed up on, with Lylia humming a little tune right behind her.

Atop the plateaus once more, Ev searched for another wind wyrm nest. It really didn't take that long to find. As she approached it, she gripped the flute tightly in her hands. The harpies hadn't told her to play any particular melody, so she hoped simply the sound of the flute was all that it would take.

When the wyrm noticed their approach, it flew up into the sky and circled them just as the previous one had.

Ev placed the flute to her lips and blew into it. A melodious note echoed out across the area, and the great flying serpent ceased its restless circling. Instead, it hovered in place, looking down at the one who had blown on the flute.

Ev blew into the flute once more — this time twiddling her fingers over the holes to play a nonsensical tune.

Though it didn't sound all that good to her, the wyrm seemed almost entranced. Slowly, it lowered back down to the platform before Ev.

Cautiously, Ev stepped toward the great beast. The wyrm watched her movements with its eyes but otherwise remained still. Carefully, Ev reached out her hand to touch the wyrm's glistening white scales. They were cool and smooth to the touch, and memories of Birdie's old zodiac mount came flooding back.

This was a feeling that Ev hadn't felt in a long time — communing with the non-monster creatures of the world. Well, she supposed a wind wyrm was sort of a monster, but it wasn't like the kind that existed only to cause destruction.

Lylia slid up beside her with one of the bridles in hand. "This one seems happy."

Ev nodded. She had to admit that she did feel pretty good.

"That is excellent," Lylia smiled. "Let us prepare this one for riding. We look forward to acquiring a second."

"Yeah, me too," replied Ev. "Then we can finally head back to get Jax."

* * * *

With two wind wyrms under their control, it only took a day and a half to fly to the northern reaches of Tyranor's Domain. When Ev and Lylia finally arrived where they were supposed to join up with Jax, however, they were met only with empty, ashen soil and scalding streams of glowing lava. The barren fields at the bottom of the volcano stretched on for miles before the first sign of trees could be seen in the distance.

"He's not here," said Ev. She supposed it wasn't too surprising since they hadn't exactly planned on a set time, but his absence still concerned her.

"Perhaps this one's brother is waiting in the forest over there," said Lylia. "That one always did seem a tad hot-headed for this much heat."

"Yeah," responded Ev. "It wouldn't hurt to look."

Ev directed her wind wyrm to fly over to the forest. In all honesty, she didn't have much hope of finding Jax. She'd been betrayed by immortals, and he had gone to contact actual Divine. She wanted to believe that the dragon's words had been true — that there were Divine who would aid them, but if even some immortals were against them, what hope was there of that?

About halfway to the forest, Lylia pulled her wyrm to a halt.

"Be alert," she said. "We have company."

"What?" Ev looked up from her thoughts in time to see a lone pegasus fly out from the trees in their direction.

Ev instinctively reached for her bow, but after a moment's thought she left it where it was.

"Act natural," she told Lylia. "Pretend it doesn't bother us."

"Is this one certain that is wise?" Lylia asked.

"If it's a Divine, they can still report us if we split them. Attacking would only confirm that we are who we are."

Lylia seemed unsure about that, but she acquiesced. Ev directed her wind wyrm down to the ground, and Lylia did the same. The rider had of course already seen them, and he or she shifted their course to fly directly towards Ev and Lylia.

"Oh, dear," remarked Lylia as she pulled her wyrm to a stop just above the ashen soil.

"Stay calm," Ev stated as she, too, pulled back her mount's reins.

Ev couldn't help but tense up as the pegasus drew closer, but once she got a better look at the rider on its back, she began to relax. The rider was wearing demon armor, so it must have been Jax. She didn't know where Jax would have gotten a pegasus, but it would not be an unwelcome turn of events.

The pegasus landed about twenty feet away, where the rider dismounted and began to approach.

Ev hopped off of her wyrm as well, but when the rider was only ten feet away, she and he both stopped.

The face of the man was *not* that of her brother. It was younger, thinner, and much paler. She knew it was probable that Jax had also been affected by the orange fog, but she wasn't going to take another step closer until she was sure.

"Jax?" she asked.

"Maybe," was the man's reply. "Who's asking?"

"Someone born in Maristol," Ev answered.

"I think you'll have to give me more than that."

"Maybe you should tell me who you are first, then."

The man stared at her, and Ev glared back. She knew it had to be Jax, but she couldn't bring herself to take the chance — not after the fairies' betrayal. Besides, he had approached them, and Ev had Lylia with her. It should be more obvious who she was than who he was.

"Oh! Oh!" Lylia shouted excitedly. "We have knowledge that might help! We are an ancient naga warrior who once guarded the sacred temple of 'the dummy stone,' but one day the stone was taken by two humans, and now they only stand around all day asking each other who they are despite them already knowing. Enlightening, yes?"

Ev felt her cheeks flush. After making a sideways glance at an annoyed Lylia, she looked back at her brother and tried again.

"Jax?"

Jax's pale cheeks had turned pink after Lylia's reprimand. He shifted uncomfortably as he answered.

"Yeah. Ev?"

Ev nodded.

"Great!" shouted Lylia. "Now, isn't it better when we aren't all ignoring what's directly in front of us?"

"Hey," Ev shot back, "he was riding a pegasus! He could have been a Divine who'd stolen that armor."

"Yeah," Jax replied while rubbing the back of his neck. "One of the Divine offered it to me when I told him how far we needed to go."

"Divine?" Ev nearly shouted. "Divine know where we're going?"

"Well, yeah," Jax looked back at her oddly. "You wanted us to work together, right?"

Ev grabbed at her helmet as she turned around and stepped away from Jax. Of course, he was right. That was what he'd set out to do, but now that he'd done it, had they jeopardized their entire mission?

"Uh, you okay?" Jax asked. "You're acting like you're not happy about this."

Ev laughed nervously. "Happy? Of course I'm happy. Why wouldn't I be happy that you told a bunch of Divine all of our plans?"

Jax crossed his arms and cocked his head. "Again, that's what I was supposed to do. Why is this suddenly such a problem? Did something happen?"

"Did something *happen?*" Ev spun on him. "I'll tell you what happened. We were betrayed! The water elementals wouldn't help us, and the fairies told some Divine where we were, and then we were attacked by Crovos!"

"Oh, wow. I'm sorry, Ev," Jax replied, but then realization suddenly appeared in his eyes. "Wait, did you say Crovos? Are you okay?"

"Yup!" chimed Lylia. "And we both brought this one a present. Here you go!"

Lylia tossed Crovos's sword in Jax's direction. The sword stopped glowing as soon as it left her hand and clanged when it hit the ground at Jax's feet.

"A sword?" Jax picked up the blade, which sprung back to life in his hand.

"Not just any sword," Lylia teased. "This is the weapon of Crovos himself."

"What!" Jax shouted. "How in Doxla did you manage to get this?"

"Oh, we killed him," Lylia shrugged absently.

"You *killed* him? How is that even possible?"

Lylia shrugged again.

Jax turned to Ev. "Is that true? Did you actually kill a Master?"

Ev shook her head. "I don't know. All I know is that his body didn't vanish like a Divine's, and he didn't come back after he fell."

"And no one else has come for us, either," added Lylia.

Jax stared at Ev and Lylia, seemingly at a loss for words. After a moment of awkward silence, he held up the glowing sword and examined it.

"Well, I guess either way, it proves we can beat them," he said, slicing the blade through the air as he tested it out. "Perhaps that's just what we need to show the world that we can do this."

"No," stated Ev.

"What do you mean, 'no'?" said Jax with a frown. "It was your idea to rally more people to our cause."

"And we've done that," returned Ev, "but we almost lost everything because I tried asking the fairies for help."

"We did tell you not to trust the fairies," Lylia stated from atop her wyrm. "The harpies still assisted us."

Ev didn't respond at first. Lylia was correct, and Ev knew it, but she still didn't want to try again.

"It doesn't matter," she said at last. "We can't afford any more risks. Besides, the demons have already agreed to help us, and we have less than two weeks to reach the rendezvous. If Helcant, Tallis, or Nictis are still out there, then we need to meet up with them to coordinate our assault."

"Alright, Ev," Jax sighed. "I don't have any objections to that. Lead the way."

Ev nodded to Jax and mounted her wyrm. Jax discarded his old sword and carefully sheathed his new one, then climbed back atop his pegasus. Ev looked to Lylia for signs of disapproval, but Lylia also seemed on board with the plan.

That was a relief. Ev was more than ready to head to the rendezvous. Yes, she wanted to bring the fight to the Masters and bring justice upon them, but she also needed to know if the others were okay. It had been over a week since she'd last seen Birdie, and she couldn't help but be worried. Deep down, she knew that nothing mattered more than stopping the Masters, but maybe some things mattered nearly as much.

Chapter 19

Fully refilled on anther by Sylvra, Evress focused on the location where copy-Tallis yet tried again and again to break through Sylvra's containment. Vainly and repeatedly he struck the barrier with various antherial blasts, but nothing penetrated.

Evress scowled. These creations of Syrus had already taken Crovos from her. They would *not* be the reason this Doxla ended early — not while she was responsible for it.

In a flash, she teleported directly behind the fake Tallis; she would drain his anther before he even realized he was under attack. Her arm thrust toward his back, but before it connected, she was struck with blow after blow from all directions; blinding lights pierced through her Master's enchantments as she staggered back in pain. She realized too late that the "attacks" he'd been making against his bubble had in fact been setting up a trap, and she'd jumped right into it.

Barely visible through the orange haze and onslaught of light, Evress saw Tallis move. Before she could react, a powerful blow sent her crashing to the ground as she clutched at her rapidly healing wounds. Tallis's attack had utterly shattered the armor around her chest, but it, too, quickly mended itself.

Tallis moved again, but by now the onslaught of lights had ceased, and she was able to concentrate enough to teleport behind him once more. Again, she tried to grab him, but again he was ready.

A portal opened up directly between the two of them, and her arm passed harmlessly through to the other side.

Evress quickly retracted her arm before Tallis could close the portal back on it, then readied herself for whatever tricks he tried next.

Tallis glared at her, eyeing her armor and her tiara in particular. "So, this is what you've become. You didn't just join the Masters. You are one. You're literally everything we've spent the last fifteen years trying to save ourselves from."

"You didn't even exist fifteen years ago," Evress shot back. "You aren't Tallis, and none of you know what I know! All you're doing is causing this world to end sooner. Even if you get to Ars Summis, you can't get into Sylvra's systems. It's impossible, and you'd only succeed in handing Doxla over to another seitti if you could!"

"Maybe you're right," replied Tallis, "but that doesn't mean we shouldn't try. Come on, Ev. I know there must be a part of you that remembers what we're fighting for."

"Where's Gare?" Evress demanded. She wasn't going to waste her breath arguing with a fake.

Tallis sighed, then shrugged. "Sorry, but I seem to have misplaced him. Maybe he's with the real Ev — the one who hasn't sold out her friends and family to suck on the Masters' teats."

Once more, Evress teleported behind Tallis, but instead of attempting to grab him, she formed an antherial blade and arced it through the air.

He brought up another portal between them, but when Evress's blade struck it, the entire thing exploded, leaving a swirling hole in space that seemingly led to nowhere. The blast sent Evress flying backward, but when she looked up, it was clear that Tallis had taken far more damage than she had even prior to her regeneration kicking in. Still, he was back on his feet in no time, and the two of them once again stared each other down.

"So that's how it is, huh?" he asked after wiping the blood from his mouth. "I gotta say, I kind of knew this would be my final stand. I just didn't expect that you, of all people, would be the one to try and put me down."

Evress ignored him, instead forming another antherial blade. It was time to end this.

"So you really are beyond reason," Tallis said. "I didn't want to believe it, but I suppose I can't deny it anymore. You brought this on yourself, traitor."

With a frightful glare, Tallis shot his arm out in her direction.

Evress sidestepped the ball of anther he'd thrown at her, then charged forward.

Tallis responded by pointing his hand at the ground and summoning a large spire of earth directly beneath her. The attack sent Evress flying, and she cursed that she hadn't considered the possibility that he'd restored his magic since his return. A portal of Tallis's making opened up and swallowed her, but she teleported back to the battlefield a short distance in front of where Tallis had been.

An explosion rang out behind her from the direction that Tallis's ball of anther had flown, and she caught him sprinting towards a hole that he'd broken in Sylvra's bubble. She couldn't be sure because of the fog, but she suspected he was heading for the world border.

"Not this time!" Evress yelled, and once again she teleported to appear right in front of him.

She immediately felt an enormous amount of anther surrounding her. At first she was worried she'd fallen for another of Tallis's traps, but then she realized that the anther was raw, which meant there was likely a hole in the world border nearby.

Tallis pointed his hand at the ground once more, but before he could cast another spell, Evress activated one of the tools Sylvra had given her long ago. In an instant, all of Tallis's magic was drained from his body, which prevented his attack.

Taking advantage of his surprise, Evress again swung her blade.

Tallis erected a barrier just before it connected, causing another sparkling explosion as her attack struck. To Evress's shock, he then followed up by reshaping his barrier into a spike, then crashing into and impaling her in the chest. Before she could even process the pain shooting through her, she found herself being lifted up into yet another portal directly above her.

Evress panicked as she realized what Tallis was about to do. With all of the concentration she could muster, she put up a barrier to protect herself against the portal as Tallis tried to close it around her neck.

The spike in her chest expanded, and she nearly passed out from the pain. By some miracle, she was able to retain consciousness, though she almost wished she hadn't. Her barrier began to crack, and with every last bit of effort she could manage, Evress was able to focus long enough to teleport off of the spike and a good distance away from Tallis.

Almost immediately, the pain subsided as her body healed itself. She was shaken, however. Tallis was far more capable than she'd expected he would be, and Sylvra — damn him! She'd nearly died, and he'd done nothing! Was he even watching their fight?

She supposed it didn't matter. Right now, she needed to defeat this copy, and she knew exactly how. Now beside the world border, Evress saw what she'd expected — a massive gash leading to the Cosmic Graveyard. As long as that was there, it would be impossible for her to drain Tallis of his anther, since he'd just as quickly restore it.

Well, if he was going to take advantage of that, then so would she. Absorbing as much of the raw anther as she could, Evress prepared to engage

Tallis once more.

The fake ran towards her, and she could tell from his expression that he was concentrating — most likely configuring a new attack in hopes of getting past her, but she wouldn't give him the chance.

Evress raised her hand and let loose an attack that she hadn't used since her fight with Xaltus several months ago.

Thousands of invisible strands shot out and spread in a chain reaction that completely covered Tallis. A brief flash of realization appeared on his face, but it was too late. In an instant, the copy of Tallis was ripped apart before exploding in a raging inferno. The orange haze vanished with him, and she could see clearly once again.

The deed at last complete, Evress lowered her hand and took several deep breaths. She couldn't believe how close she'd come to dying. And fake or not, the thing she'd just killed had the face of a man she'd only months ago called "friend."

Evress swallowed. It was okay. What had happened couldn't be helped. He never should have been created; his mission was pointless, and it was only hurting the very world that she was trying to help as best she could. Of course he'd tried to kill her. Of course she had to kill him.

Upon taking one last look around at the damage done — a swirling vortex in space and a gaping hole leading out into the void, Evress teleported back to Lumine Tower. She knew she should try and fix it, but she didn't particularly feel like staying here anymore. She'd done what Sylvra had wanted.

Once she was back at the tower, however, she realized that it may have been a wiser decision to stay at the border a little longer. Sylvra was absolutely fuming, and the moment he laid eyes on her, he laid into her.

"It seems you failed to disclose to me the full extent of your Syrus's teachings, Evress."

Evress had no idea what this was about, but she wasn't in the mood to be blamed for anything else. "I told you everything you ever asked me about."

"Is that so? Then how is it that you neglected to mention that Syrus taught you about genetics and pattern recognition?"

"What in the world are you talking about?" returned Evress. "He never taught me about anything like that."

Sylvra took a step closer to her. "I just searched all of Doxla for your face, your DNA, and your noise profile, and the only result each time was you. That copy you just destroyed did something to hide the remaining copies, and a native Doxlan would not know about any of those topics if they were not taught by a Divine."

"You asked me what Syrus taught me," Evress defended. "You never asked what he taught the others. Besides, you're the one who said you didn't want to use anther to search for them."

"Clearly, that was a lapse in judgment," Sylvra growled. His expression then softened. "You did well in disposing of that threat. However, I must ask that you leave me be while I reassess our approach to dealing with this menace."

"You saw that?" Evress scowled. "You saw me almost die and didn't help me!"

"Don't be a fool," Sylvra growled. "Why do you think you were able to concentrate enough to use anther with a hole in your chest? My anther flows through you, and my will with it. Speaking of which . . ."

Sylvra held out his hand. "I believe that you have absorbed some raw anther. Please relinquish that to me."

"Why?" Evress asked.

"You have no need of it," was Sylvra's response. "I will provide you with whatever anther you need when you need it. It is too much of a risk for even you to carry such loose power within you."

Evress met eyes with Sylvra, who's expression rapidly grew impatient when she delayed. Reluctantly, she clasped his hand, which allowed him to siphon the raw anther away from her.

"Thank you," he said once he was done. "Now, leave me."

Gladly, Evress thought, and she headed directly to her room. Once there, she paced aimlessly as her thoughts raced over the events of this horrible day.

Crovos was dead. Her own copy had been the one to kill him. Tallis had returned and caused havoc, and Sylvra not only blamed her for that but had forced her to kill him. Gare was missing, and now they couldn't find the other copies even using anther to search. All of Doxla was likely in chaos, and if they couldn't stop Syrus's creations soon, Sylvra would almost certainly abandon the world early.

Eventually, Evress found herself in front of a mirror. Her eyes were drawn to the emerald-green armor — the tiara Sylvra had given her still sitting bright atop her head despite the ferocity of her battle with copy-Tallis. For the first time since Crovos had taken her to his little village of avians, she had to question if she'd really made the right choice.

She knew she was doing the right thing; she'd seen for herself what would happen to her people if Sylvra *was* somehow stopped. They'd all either end up under the control of some other seitti, or they'd be placed in the so-called "Preserves," where there was a good chance they'd all die to those sentiment things she'd talked with Birdie about. For as much as she hated how Sylvra ran Doxla, at least here she could do something about it. If another seitti took over, she'd be helpless when they inevitably abused it in their own way.

No, it wasn't a question of if she was doing the right thing. It was a question of if she could keep doing it. It would be so much simpler to give up her status and abilities and go spend the rest of her days with Birdie and the others. But, could she even do that now? Would Sylvra even let her at this point? Would the others accept her back if she tried?

Tiredly, Evress removed her little crown and held it in her hands. She knew now what she needed. With a simple thought, she sent the crown and the rest of her armor away. She then changed into her old pants and tunic.

Whether what she was about to do was a good idea or not, she'd find out soon enough. With Crovos gone, there was only one other person she could still talk to as a friend, and that's exactly where she was going.

* * * *

Back in the tiny world that Sylvra had placed her friends in, Evress headed straight towards Birdie's cottage at the edge of the woods. Fortunately, Birdie wasn't out hunting this time; she was out back putting minimal effort into her laundry while talking to Umber. Before Evress could announce herself, Birdie called to her without even looking her way.

"Back again already?" she said as she pulled down a pair of wrinkled pants. "After our last hiatus, I wasn't expecting you back for at least another week."

"Birdie, please. I really need to talk to you."

Birdie sighed and wiped her hands on her shirt before turning to face Evress. One look at her, however, and Birdie's expression became one of concern.

"What happened?"

Evress hesitated. She wasn't exactly comfortable talking about this with Umber present, but thankfully Umber seemed to pick up on that.

"Perhaps I should leave the two of you alone," he stated.

Birdie gave him the go-ahead, and Umber started around to the other side of the cottage.

241

"Thanks," Evress mumbled, and Umber gave her a slight nod in response.

Once he'd left, Evress opened up about everything. She told Birdie about the fake Helcant and Tallis; about Crovos, Amethine, and Sylvra; and about all the damage that the copies had caused.

"I don't know what to do," she concluded with tears in her eyes. "I can't think of any way to stop them, and I feel like a monster for trying. He looked just like him, even though I know he wasn't."

Birdie stared at Evress for a moment before sighing and approaching her. She placed a hand on Evress's shoulder, which Evress leaned into.

"Ev," said Birdie softly yet sternly, "you need to get out of there."

"Get out?" replied Evress. "How? I can't!"

"Ev," Birdie said again. "Your copy killed a Master, and Tallis's copy altered the entire world before almost killing you. Copies or not, these people clearly know what they're doing, and they'll be coming for you as long as you're with Sylvra."

Evress looked away from Birdie before she answered. "It doesn't matter. He'd never let me leave. Not now. Not after everything that's happened."

"And you're okay with that? You're okay with him controlling you?"

"Of course not!" Evress pulled away from Birdie. "But I don't have a choice!"

"Don't you?" Birdie pressed. "It sounds to me like these copies even have Sylvra worried. If he's worried, then that means they can win."

Evress couldn't believe what she was hearing. Birdie was actually suggesting she turn against Sylvra.

"You're wrong," Evress said somberly. "He's worried because he might lose this Doxla. That's all. No one can beat him. He's the only one who can access his core systems and communicate with other seitti."

"Are you sure? There might be a way—"

"No!" Evress shouted with clenched fists. "It's not possible, and it wouldn't matter even if it was. We'd just end up with some other seitti lording over us, and we'd be even more powerless than we already are!"

Birdie crossed her arms and cocked her head. "Maybe so, but it sounds like Syrus's seitti would be a hell of a lot better to be stuck with than Sylvra."

"Syrus betrayed us, and even *he* said that Aurum doesn't care what happens to us. How would someone like that be better than Sylvra?"

Birdie frowned. "You asked me for my advice, or did I misunderstand it when you said you don't know what to do?"

Flustered, Evress walked away from Birdie before turning back and approaching her again. "I did, but — I *know* . . ."

Evress placed her hand to her forehead as she struggled to collect her thoughts. "That's not what I came to you for. I just need to know that I'm not alone — that there's still someone I can come to who'll tell me that it's all going to be okay."

When she didn't hear a response, Evress looked up at Birdie once more. Her throat tightened at the look of sorrow in Birdie's eyes.

"I can have that, can't I?" she pleaded to Birdie.

Birdie averted her gaze and sighed. "Ev, I just found out this morning that copies of us have been carrying on a fight we've been fighting for the past fifteen years and that you're trying to stop them. I haven't even had time to process that, and now you're telling me those same copies have succeeded in standing as equals against the Masters. Even still, you'd rather follow Sylvra into a battle against them that could be your last than go back to what we had before."

She finally looked back at Evress. "How can you honestly expect me to say that I support this?"

Evress swallowed. She'd known coming back here so soon had been a risk, but she'd hoped Birdie could at least understand — even if she didn't agree — why Evress had to protect Doxla from these copies.

"I see," Evress said, trying her best to hide her hurt. "Then I should let you get back to work."

"Ev, I just—"

"It's fine," Evress interrupted with lowered eyes. "I'll be back when this is over. If I'm not, then it means I didn't make it."

"Ev, please wait."

Evress met Birdie's eyes one final time. "I'm sorry, but I have to do this. Goodbye, Birdie."

Before Birdie could say anything more, Evress returned to her room in Lumine tower. With no one left to turn to, she fell onto her bed and let her tears soak into her pillow. Their cold wetness would be her only comfort as she let sleep ferry her away from this nightmare, if only until she was thrust back into it with the coming dawn.

Chapter 20

At long last, after nearly four days of flying, Ev, Jax, and Lylia arrived at the Shrine of Merius — a series of three glistening towers rising high out of the center of a swirling lake. They'd arrived at high noon, and the thick mists that normally cloaked the shrine had evaporated for a spell. They would surely return, but their absence gave the trio the chance to scout out the area from the skies.

No fewer than seven camps lined the lake, though all but two of them were empty. Most likely, the Divine they belonged to had already entered the Shrine, or perhaps they had fallen to the rough waters surrounding it. Either way made little difference to Ev. They were supposed to meet the others at the southernmost tip of the lake, and that area appeared free of any troublesome onlookers.

Not wanting to fall into another ambush, Ev gave the southern forest multiple passes. On her final and lowest flyover, she spotted a single large man lurking behind the trees nearest the water's edge. Friend or foe, she couldn't be sure, but she felt safe enough to land her wyrm in a clearing located a few hundred yards away.

Jax was the first to dismount as he called back, "You two stay here. I'll go see who that guy was."

Ev didn't argue. If the others had had their faces changed the same way she had, then the only way to find out who was who was to talk to them.

She wished Jax good luck, then waited patiently for his return, though she was ready to take off at a moment's notice should the need arise.

She didn't have to wait long, however, as only ten minutes later, Jax had returned with the large man carrying an equally large bag in tow. When Ev saw him up close, her whole body flooded with relief. His face was unfamiliar, but the way he walked, talked, and laughed as he spoke to Jax — she knew without a doubt who he was.

"Gare?" she called as she dismounted from the wyrm before rushing over to him. "You're okay!"

Before even thinking about it, she threw her arms around the big guy. Gare returned a tentative pat, but sounded unsure as he spoke.

"Ev? Is that you?"

Ev quickly released Gare and backed away; she'd forgotten for a moment just how different she also looked now.

"Yeah," she replied, now just a tad embarrassed.

"Ha!" Gare belted out. "Wow. I guess Tallis's magic thingy really did its trick."

Ev looked back at Lylia, who gave her a face that said "I told you so." She then turned her attention back to Gare once more.

"So he did do it," she said. "But why?"

"He was afraid Sylvra would be able to find everyone if he didn't," Gare replied, confirming Lylia's suggestion from earlier. "Said that if he knew how to find people, then Sylvra could too, so he acted first. Looks like it did a real number on you, though, huh?"

Ev frowned at that remark, which Gare quickly tried to amend.

"Hey, at least you didn't end up like this guy," he said while jutting his thumb towards Jax. "And here I thought he couldn't get any worse."

"Speak for yourself," Jax retorted. "You look like a pig got kicked in the face by a horse. Have you even seen your nostrils?"

Gare brought his hand up to his face and touched his nose. "Oh. Guess that explains why I could smell you before I saw you. And here I thought it was 'cause you'd started a protest against bathing or something."

Jax cracked a grin. "Oh, no, I did that, too. Figured I'd try living like you for a change."

With a hearty laugh, Gare popped Jax on the shoulder, causing Ev to smile as well. It was so nice to see one of her friends okay. Still, only having Gare here made her worried. He wasn't supposed to be traveling alone.

"It's good to see you Gare," she said, "but, where *is* Tallis? Where's Nictis?"

"Yes!" Lylia slid over immediately. "Where is Tallis?"

Immediately, Gare's mood dimmed, and he shook his head sorrowfully. "I suppose I'd better start from the beginning. Nictis didn't make it. We got attacked by Sylvra right after Tallis tried to make us Radiants. He put us all in this grassy place, and then — I still can't believe what happened next."

Gare looked between an expectant Ev, Jax, and Lylia. He sighed.

"Look, what I'm about to say will sound crazy, but I saw it myself. Somehow, there's another Ev out there, and she's helping Sylvra."

Ev's face went white. It couldn't be. "Wh-what?" she asked.

Jax seemed far less fazed. "Come off it, Gare. Whatever you saw, it was probably some trick by Sylvra to mess with you."

"I saw what I saw," insisted Gare. "I even talked to her. Unless the Masters somehow read all of our minds, she was the real thing."

"Listen to what you're saying," said an increasingly angry Jax. "How is it possible for there to be another Ev? It's not, and Ev would never help the Masters! Tell him, Ev!"

Jax looked at Ev, but she didn't respond. She felt faint. When Amethine had attacked, she'd spoken to Ev like they'd known one another. When Crovos had accosted her, he'd said he respected who she was. As impossible as it seemed, she knew that it had to be true. Somehow, her original self had survived, and she'd allied with the Masters.

"Why?" she barely whispered.

Jax was taken aback. "Why? What do you mean, 'why'?"

Ev looked up at Gare. "Why is she helping them?"

Both Jax and Gare stared at her — but Jax was the first to respond.

"Ev, come on. You don't actually believe there's another you, do you?"

Solemnly, Ev looked Jax in the eyes as she answered. "I already knew."

Jax looked like he'd been slapped.

"You . . . you did?" asked Gare.

Words returned to Jax before she could respond. "Ev, what happened? What did you do?"

"I didn't," she replied, balling her hands into fists. "It was Syrus. He . . . made copies of us."

At first Jax stammered for words, but then his face turned red. "Um, excuse me, Ev, but what the hell! You *knew* that? You knew and didn't tell us?"

Ev felt her own anger rising. "What did you want me to tell you, Jax? That Syrus made copies of everyone, so the Masters would think they got us after we escaped? That he's just as big of a monster as every other Divine? None of them were supposed to survive. There wasn't supposed to be another me still alive!"

"Well, sounds like that worked out just great, didn't it? Now we not only have to deal with the Masters, but a bunch of angry copies of ourselves!"

"Uh, actually, it sounded like . . ." Gare began, but he stopped when Ev shot him a pleading look and subtle shake of her head.

"Actually, what?" said Jax with a glare.

"Uh, well," Gare paused for a second before continuing as he clearly struggled to find an answer that wouldn't cause any more trouble, "the thing is, we think it might just be the other Ev that's helping them."

Thankfully, Jax seemed to buy that answer, allowing Ev to breath just a bit easier. After how much she'd struggled with the revelation, she didn't want Jax to also learn that *they* were in fact the copies.

"What makes you think that?" Jax asked.

"Well," Gare rubbed the back of his head, "it's just the things she said. It sounded like she decided to join Sylvra on her own when she found out what he was doing."

Jax was livid. "Oh, you mean using our worlds as playthings just to throw them away when he's done with them?"

"No, bud, it's more than that," Gare responded. "I'm not sure I really understand it, but I'll tell you what she told Tallis and me."

Gare then went on to explain about how Sylvra was turning surviving nepacs into seitti with the help of some group called AnAnCol. For the most part, Ev, Jax, and Lylia simply let him talk, with Ev remaining particularly silent. Gare never revealed that they were the copies, but that didn't do anything to change the fact that Ev knew the truth. It was her original self that had chosen to join Sylvra, and she — a copy created by Syrus — was the one who still opposed them. What was worse — she understood why her original would do that. Syrus, a servant of the seitti, had betrayed her, and Sylvra, in his own twisted way, was trying to create a new generation of seitti that would have compassion on the nepacs that they ruled over.

Once Gare was finished, Jax shook his head. "That's it? That's his goal?"

"I mean—" shrugged Gare.

"That's stupid," Jax interrupted.

Though she knew she shouldn't have been, Ev was shocked at his immediate dismissal of Sylvra's motivations.

Jax continued. "I might not know much about seitti or prifae or any of that stuff, but I know bullshit when I hear it."

Jax looked from Gare to Lylia to Ev. "Even if he did make copies of us, Syrus never lied to us. He told us that most seitti treat their worlds better than the Masters treated ours, and after talking with those Divine who said they'd help us, I know he was telling the truth. Sylvra might claim to be fighting for the 'greater good,' but there's definitely something else going on here."

"Agreed," said Lylia. "Our conversations with Syrus have led us to believe that most seitti are rather conceited, but few would intentionally harm the people of their own worlds as Sylvra has. Even if Sylvra does do as he claims, we fail to see how his additional seitti would make any significant difference in the greater scheme of things."

Lylia made a good point. Still, Ev couldn't help but wonder about her other self. Sylvra must have done something to convince her original to join him — unless it really was simply a matter of broken trust from Syrus's betrayal. She supposed it didn't matter, however. There was no turning back from this path they traveled, and no matter what the other Ev might believe, this Ev knew that stopping Sylvra was the only way to save, not only this Doxla, but potentially countless others from suffering under his reign.

In agreement with both Jax and Lylia, Ev nodded, but she still wanted to know more. Addressing Gare, she asked him, "What did you say that group Sylvra is working with was called? AnAnCol?"

With a nod, Gare replied, "Yeah, I think that's what she called it."

Ev looked to Jax, who had the same idea she did. "Sounds like something we should ask our Divine friends about when they get here."

"Whoa, hold up," replied a shocked Gare. "When you said Divine were helping you, you were serious?"

"Yeah, I was," said Jax with a touch of pride. "They should be here in a week. They've got some rules about how we have to talk to them, but we can worry about that later."

"That's right," said Ev before turning back to Gare. "You still haven't told us how you got back here."

"Or where's our darling Tallis," Lylia added, her expression pained.

Sadly, Gare looked up at her. "I'm sorry, but I don't think he made it either."

Lylia's expression slowly shifted from heartbroken to angry. "What happened to him?"

Gare took a deep breath before answering. "After we escaped from the other Ev, Tallis started working on making tools to counter everything he thought she would know how to do. He knew it would take time to use them all, though, and he knew we wouldn't be able to avoid being found if he used them, so he made a big fog to hide me while I used a portal to get here.

"He stayed behind. Said that if he was going down anyway, he wanted to at least try and convince the other Ev that she was wrong. For all I know, Sylvra never even gave him the chance."

Lylia looked sorrowfully at the ground, but she said nothing else. Ev couldn't think of any words to comfort her, either, so the four of them simply stood in silence until Gare spoke again.

"Oh, and I just remembered. He also gave me these things for you."

Gently placing the bag he'd brought in front of them, Gare removed the rope holding it shut to reveal a number of large, glassy dark orbs. Smokey swirls with a luminescent shimmer pressed against the surface of the glass.

Ev bent down to pick up one of the balls. Despite its appearance, she couldn't sense any anther from it.

"What are they?" she asked.

"Most of them are balls of anther," Gare answered. "Tallis spent a week trying to figure out how how to contain the stuff like that. He said you just need to break 'em to let it out; each one's supposed to be enough to fill you up pretty good. He also made a couple of them special."

Carefully, Gare dug through the orbs until he pulled out a small red one. "Here's one of them. He was trying to find a way to copy himself, but it, uh, didn't really work out. The copies kept dying, and he gave up after the second one. Can't say I blame him, but he thought maybe the two of you could figure it out."

Gare handed the orb to Ev, who stared at it in disbelief. He'd actually tried to make *more* copies of them? She wasn't sure if that was harder to believe, or the fact that he'd failed was harder. They'd both duplicated food countless times. Sure, apples weren't people, but could it really be that different? Ev was tempted to take a look at what Tallis had created right then and there just to see where it had gone wrong.

Jax, for one, seemed uncomfortable with the whole idea. "Why would he think we'd want to make copies of ourselves? It didn't exactly work out when Syrus did it."

"Didn't it?" Lylia said from behind. "We never would have made it this far if he hadn't. While we all may have an unexpected new enemy because of it, Syrus did succeed in tricking the Masters into thinking they'd won. Such a trick might even be able to work twice."

"Yeah," said Gare. "That's what Tallis was thinking. Here, Lylia. This is the other special one. He made it just for you after he gave up on the copying thing."

Lylia took the swirling green orb from Gare and held it in her hands. "What is it?"

Gare shrugged. "I dunno. He told me it was none of my business and just to make sure you got it — said if anyone could figure out how to make it work, you could."

"Oh," said Lylia. "Well, we are grateful."

Gare nodded, then looked to Jax. "So, now what? Are we just camping out, or . . .?"

"I think so," Jax answered. "We still have a little over a week before everyone is supposed to be here. Ev?"

"Yeah," she nodded. There really was nothing else to do for now but wait, and maybe take a closer look at the red orb that Tallis had made for her.

* * * *

Late in the evening a few days later, Ev sat busy feeling through Tallis's copying tool once again while Jax patrolled the area for intruders. No matter how many times she examined it, she couldn't figure out what he might have done wrong. What he'd come up with was essentially the same thing she'd done to copy that apple, which told her that there must be something different about copying people. Could they actually have souls after all? Was that what was missing? It had to be either that, or there was something about how they scanned the original to make a copy. Perhaps they hadn't been making perfect copies all along, and only nearly-perfect. It didn't seem that far of a stretch to think that countless minor errors in the process could add up to be fatal for a living thing.

She glanced over at Lylia, who was still entranced by the green orb that Tallis had made for her specifically. The one time that Ev had asked about what was in it, Lylia had only responded with "something precious." Whatever it was, it was clearly important to her, so Ev decided to let her be.

No sooner did Ev go back to her own orb, however, than her ears detected a rustling in the leaves. Across from her at the edge of camp, two figures emerged from the woods.

At once, Ev jumped to her feet. If these people had snuck up on them, then either Jax was slacking, or they'd purposefully slipped by him. Her bow lay unstrung and unusable at the moment, but she was confident enough in her skill with a knife to be able to take on any potential foe.

"Hold it right there!" she yelled, brandishing her dagger.

Lylia and Gare responded to her cry by grabbing their weapons as well, and Ev could hear Jax tromping toward them through the brush. The man and woman before them both froze and put up their hands.

"What are you doing here?" Ev demanded.

The woman, at first staring at Lylia, shifted her attention to Ev, cocked her head, and smiled. "Just looking for a special friend of mine. She, her headstrong brother, and a way-too-nice snake lady were all supposed to meet us here. I don't suppose you've seen them, have you?"

"B-Birdie?" Ev responded as she lowered her blade. "Is that really you?"

Birdie lowered her hands and shrugged. "Apparently. Blond doesn't really suit me, and is the rest really as bad as Umber says it is?" she added while pointing to her face.

"Oh, n-no. You look great! Certainly better than what happened to me, anyway."

"Aw, pff. You look fine, Ev," Birdie replied as she looked sideways at Jax, who'd arrived by now. "And let me guess: the former captain of the Shadow Guard, here to save the day?"

Jax briefly gave Birdie an annoyed look before breaking into a smile. "Yeah, yeah, it's good to see you, too."

Before any more words could be exchanged, Ev rushed over to Birdie and squeezed her tightly.

"I was so worried about you," Ev said upon letting go.

"Why? I told you I'd be here, didn't I?" Birdie replied as she flipped a lock of hair away from Ev's eye.

Ev smiled. "Yeah, you did." She then turned to Umber. "Hey, Umber. It's good to see you, too."

"Likewise," relied Umber, "though we see that we are missing some in number."

Ev looked back at the others behind her; the absences of Tallis and Nictis were all too apparent.

"A lot has happened. Not everyone made it." Turning back to Birdie, Ev asked, "What about you? Where's Helcant?"

Birdie sighed and shook her head. "We don't know. After we saw — oh! Ev, there's something really important that I have to tell you."

Grabbing Ev by the shoulders, Birdie leaned in close to speak quietly. "Do you recall that conversation we had about us being copies?"

Looking at Birdie, Ev sighed. "Let me guess. You saw the other me, didn't you?"

Ev couldn't remember the last time she'd seen Birdie look so surprised.

"You knew?" Birdie asked.

"Yeah," Ev nodded softly. "Apparently Gare ran into her, too."

She then relayed to Birdie everything that Gare had told them, as well as their thoughts on it all.

"So that's what's going on," Birdie stated while looking down in thought. Returning her eyes to Ev's, she asked softly. "How are you feeling about all this? Are you okay?"

With a small smile and a slight shrug, Ev replied, "I'd be lying if I said I was, but you don't have to worry about me. Other me or not, I'll fight against Sylvra until the end. Now, what were you saying happened to Helcant?"

After taking a deep breath, Birdie replied. "Right. Well, after we saw the other you, I told Helcant and Umber everything you had told me. Helcant began to worry that more of us would have joined Sylvra, and he wanted to try and recruit Divine to our cause in case they had. His plan was to leave messages for them encased in anther, and since he was the only one who could, he went off on his own while Umber and I worked on bringing immortals to our cause. Helcant also gave me a little something for you as well."

Flipping her backpack around to her front, Birdie extracted a large, golden shimmer. If Helcant had made it himself, he would have had to have used up nearly half of his anther just for that alone.

Eyes wide, Ev took the shimmer from Birdie. "What is it?"

"He got the idea from that big announcement Sylvra made. Apparently this'll do the same thing, and Helcant was damn sure no one would be able to track us down if we use it. He thought we could send out a call to arms on the day that we strike — both to rally our allies and show the Divine what the Masters really are."

That could very well be useful, Ev thought, though she had to wonder whether or not the amount of anther he'd put into making it was necessary.

"I think that's a good idea," she said. "At the very least, the world deserves to know why things are the way they are."

Jax, apparently, disagreed. "Except if we use it, the Masters will know when we're about to strike. Wasn't the whole point of everything we've done to prepare an assault that they won't be ready for?"

"I think we've already proved that they aren't ready for us," Ev said confidently as she turned to him. Between Birdie, Umber, and Gare's return; the offer of assistance from the demons, Divine, and potentially others from Birdie and Umber's efforts; and the gifts that Tallis and Helcant had created for them, Ev finally felt that they really stood a chance at getting to those core systems.

She continued, looking at Gare, Umber, then Birdie in turn. "We've already taken one of them down, fought back another, and even gotten two Enforcers banished just by telling them the truth. A message might tell them we're coming, but they already know that. Let them know we're coming. It won't save them once we've exposed what they really are to the whole world."

"Well said!" cheered Gare.

With a look of surprise, Birdie put up a hand. "Whoa, wait a minute. What do you mean when you say you've 'taken one of them down'?"

Ev told Birdie about their encounter with Crovos and how his body hadn't vanished on defeat.

"And we got his sword!" exclaimed Lylia, to which Jax proudly revealed his new glowing blade.

From Birdie's expression, Ev could see that she was processing that information. After a moment, she looked at Umber, as if the two of them shared the same thought.

Umber spoke first. "You said the Enforcers vanished in the same manner as Divine."

Ev wasn't sure where he was going with this. "That's right. Why?"

After Birdie and Umber exchanged another look, Birdie answered. "Crovos was a nepac."

Ev's eyes widened in shock.

"A nepac?" asked Jax. "What are you talking about? He was a Master!"

"And?" replied Birdie, turning her attention to him. "If Sylvra recruited the other Ev, then how is it unreasonable to believe he's made other nepacs into Masters?"

Jax had no response to that, but Gare did. "If that's the case, then that's great news! It means that any of them we beat that don't vanish — they're gone for good!"

Even more confidence welled up inside of Ev. "You're right. And if Crovos could banish Enforcers, maybe we could do the same. Syrus showed us how to banish Divine, after all."

Birdie cautioned Ev on that one. "We'd still have to hit them with that degradation tool of his, which we don't have."

"Right," said Ev, having forgotten about that, "and we can't make degradation without being found out. I guess we'll just have to hold off on making that until the battle actually starts. We'd have to hold off the Enforcers the old fashioned way until then."

"We can work out a plan for them once the Divine show up," said Jax. "Just remember: we can't actually talk out loud around them. The Masters' systems listen to everything they say, so we'll have to work around that."

"We'll follow your lead," said Ev.

Jax grinned. "And we'll follow you to victory."

* * * *

The night before the Divine were set to arrive, Umber and Lylia had volunteered to take the first watch. While no one was particularly concerned that they'd be caught at this point, they still chose to err toward the side of caution.

Embers from the evening's fire still crackled and flickered dimly in the center of their small clearing. Nearby, Jax and Gare reclined practically shoulder to shoulder against the same large tree. They'd piled up twigs and leaves between its roots to form a pair of makeshift beds. Ev and Birdie had done the same by a smaller tree. Umber's bed sat alone and empty, and Lylia hadn't bothered to ever build one. Instead, she'd opted to sleep out of sight up in the treetops, just in case any wandering adventurers happened to sneak past their watch in the night.

Upon taking a final swig from his canteen, Jax said to the group, "So this is it. Tomorrow's the day we could finally end this."

"Tomorrow's the day we meet the Divine," corrected Birdie. "I somehow doubt we'll attack the same day that we make a plan."

"Maybe we won't; maybe we will," said Jax with a shrug. "Either way, it's happening soon. It's kind of hard to believe when you think about it."

"You can say that again," said Gare. "To think we started off worshiping the Masters, and now we're going to try and take them down. Fifteen years ago we'd have been laughed out of town for even thinking that."

"Fifteen years ago, we could barely take on a revenant," Jax smirked. "Now look at us. We've fought and beaten multiple Radiants."

"Yeah," nodded Gare. "I guess in a way, we kind of owe Dezeroth for attacking Marisol. If he hadn't done that, we never would have learned the truth about Grandis and the 'Dark Radiant,' eh, Birdie?"

A small chuckle slipped from Birdie's throat. "I dunno. I was kind of planning on stealing my Heart back anyway. I'm sure I could have made it past the entire Light Guard and Grandis before Apollyon returned. Then you'd have found out either way."

"What are you talking about?" asked Jax. "I thought you didn't know that you were the Dark Radiant."

"Oh, I didn't, but I still knew you had something that I wanted. I was drawn to my Heart even without knowing what it was. Why do you think I was following you after you escaped from Marisol?"

"Whoa, wait," said Gare. "You were following us?"

"Of course," Birdie shrugged. "I knew my way around those mountains. It wasn't that hard, especially since I just had to show Dezeroth's forces that I was a shade, and they let me go on my way."

"So, let me get this straight," said Jax. "You somehow followed us through a cave with a collapsed entrance, on a horse, and we didn't notice. And, you thought you could steal the Heart on your own?"

Birdie laughed, then cleared her throat. "Well, actually, once I'd seen how many of you there were, I'd planned on letting the bublobs get you, so I could swoop in and take it from them, but," Birdie looked over at Ev with a smile, "I had a change of heart. I couldn't let someone who even cares about tiny lizards get eaten alive by monsters."

"You're messing with me," Jax said. When his answer was nothing more than a smile, he addressed Ev instead. "She's kidding, right?"

Ev simply smiled as well and shook her head. Birdie had already confessed that story to her before.

Jax turned his attention back to Birdie. After a moment's silence, he also cracked a grin. "Heh. I guess that just means my first impression of you was right after all, wasn't it?"

Birdie shrugged. "Yeah. More or less."

"Well," said Gare, seemingly unfazed by the revelation, "regardless of how we started out, we made a good team in the end, eh?"

"Yeah, we did," said Ev, clasping Birdie's hand in hers.

With a soft smile, Birdie squeezed Ev's hand in return.

Ev smiled back, then looked over to Jax and Gare. It hurt to think that there was a very good chance that this could be their last quiet moment together, but at the same time, she couldn't think of anyone else she'd rather have her final moments of peace with. She knew she shouldn't think that way, but she also knew this would likely be a one-way trip. Whether the others knew as well or not, she couldn't be sure, but there was no guarantee that they would survive even if they succeeded.

Their goal was to send a message to Syrus from Sylvra's core systems. If they could do that, then Syrus would know Sylvra's true identity, and seitti authorities would be able to track him down, but Ev knew better than to kid herself. Syrus would have to relay that information to his seitti creator, and from there on to seitti authorities who would then need to step in before it was too late. The likelihood of that happening before Sylvra erased them all — Ev had no idea. All she knew was that if she and her friends didn't succeed, then the tragedy that befell her Doxla would repeat endlessly.

Tomorrow. Tomorrow they would have a plan. Tomorrow they would speak to Divine, who could hopefully shed a bit more light on what they would actually face. Maybe, just maybe, they could even help them make it through to the end.

* * * *

Early the next morning, Jax went out with Gare to meet the Divine, who were supposed to arrive from the south. When they returned, a group of five heavily armed Divine trailed behind him, all of them engaged in what sounded like a conversation about what they would do with some haul of treasure. Ev couldn't help but tense at the sight, but deep down she knew that they weren't her enemies. If they were, then the Masters would already have been here.

As the group approached, Jax rushed forward and handed Ev a sheet of paper with the words "This is how we must speak" written on it.

Ev nodded silently, then motioned for the Divine to approach a tree stump that they'd smoothed into a table using Jax's new sword.

Only two of the Divine stepped forward. The other three remained back where they continued their conversation. The two that had joined Ev also continued to speak to one another, but they'd switched their discussion to one regarding the perils of infiltrating the Shrine of Merius.

One of the two who had approached her placed a paper down on the stump and began to write on it with a piece of charcoal — all while continuing to talk to his companion.

"I am Solas. Pardon our talking, but we must take no chances. The Masters always listen, and Jax has told us your tale."

Solas offered a second piece of charcoal to Ev, who responded by writing, "I understand. I am Ev."

Solas extended his hand, which Ev tentatively shook.

"You are the leader," Solas wrote. "What do you know? What is your plan?"

As uncomfortable as Ev was divulging that information, at this point she was already committed. She told the Divine everything that she knew about the Masters and their systems, up until the point that their paper had been saturated with black dust.

At that point, the Divine — fully entranced with the words Ev had written — gestured for one of the others to bring more paper. Once it had arrived, Ev filled out that sheet as well, then another, until she wrote down the word "Anincol."

At that instant, Solas went silent and tapped on the paper for Ev to stop.

Surprised by the interruption, she did.

Solas then gestured wildly for the other Divine to gather around. When they did, he rewrote what she had written, this time spelled "AnAnCol." Whatever the other Divine had been talking about was forgotten, as not a word was spoken while they exchanged glances with one another. The silence was revealing enough for Ev — the expressions on their faces telling her that this tiny detail had far more significance than she ever would have imagined.

Placing the charcoal to the paper once again, she asked, "What is AnAnCol?"

Solas looked to her, cleared his throat, and made a comment about a group of birds fighting on the ground. That got the other Divine talking again, but it was clear from their tone of voice that whatever AnAnCol was had them shaken.

After several failed attempts to write even the first word of his answer, Solas finally wrote, "It is difficult to explain in detail. Their goals lie at the heart of what makes a seitti a seitti and worlds such as yours exist. To tell you everything would be against our laws and would likely not be something you wish to learn."

Angrily, Ev scribbled down, "I don't care. We deserve to know why our worlds are used the way they are. We deserve to know why we are treated like cattle and pawns in a game. We are not animals! We're people, too!"

Once more, Solas fell silent, as did his conversation partner. The two of them exchanged looks before Solas's partner finally sighed, shook her head, and shrugged. This in turn caused Solas to sigh, and reluctantly, he put his charcoal to the paper once more.

"You are treated as such because that is what you are. Your worlds, your very reality is false. It is all created by seitti for the sole purpose of living out our fantasies. Companions, experiences, pleasure, whatever we desire we can create. We are limited only by the permissions we are granted — permissions dependent on our standing in the systems that bind even us, for even we live in a false reality. In truth, most of us were also created as you were, but the few of us who were not come from the true reality, or at least that is what we have been taught to believe. Those original seitti are the last remnants of a civilization whose technology grew to the point where it consumed them. Now, they, we, and the worlds we create — we are all merely ideas brought to life in a great, ever-growing machine."

At this point, Solas stopped and looked at Ev. If he was hoping for a reaction, he would have been disappointed.

At the moment, Ev wasn't really sure how to feel about this revelation. If true, then that meant the fact that she was a copy was irrelevant. She had never been real to begin with. None of them had — not even seitti themselves.

Yet, at the same time, she couldn't help but wonder. Did it even matter? Her thoughts returned to her conversation with Birdie at the Throne of Ascendance. From there, she thought back to last night. She'd again held Birdie's hand in her own, and it felt as real as it ever had.

Perhaps her world was false. Perhaps everything was merely some "idea" in a machine, but it was real to her, and the Masters were a threat to it and everyone — no, every*thing* that she cared about, and apparently even more.

With resolve in her eyes, Ev flipped the paper over and wrote on its back the same question she'd asked before. "What is AnAnCol?"

She stared at Solas as she awaited his response. He seemed surprised by this, but after gazing into Ev's eyes, his expression softened.

"AnAnCol is the Anonymous Anarchist Collective. It is an organization that has found flaws in the system that holds us all and seeks to exploit those flaws to ultimately destroy it. They aim to force a return to the true reality, if that is even possible, because they believe that doing so will allow them to recreate the reality that we now live in. They hate the regulations placed upon them by the current system, and they believe seitti should be free to do as we please without oversight.

"If Sylvra is involved with them, then he must be stopped at all costs. AnAnCol will never succeed in their goals, but every seitti indoctrinated into their way of thinking has the potential to ruin trillions of lives in pursuit of their cause. The fact that they are stealing what you call souls proves as much."

Solas's phrasing told Ev what she already knew — that none of them actually had souls, at least not in the manner that she had believed. But she was curious. What sort of 'soul' could the thought of a machine even have?

"What is a soul, then?" she asked.

Hesitating only briefly, Solas wrote down his answer. "It is a registration. It is a promise that one will not be forgotten by the machine after death. AnAnCol has found a way to corrupt registrations, however, and can copy the minds of others into existing registrations, but they cannot do so en masse. This erases whoever was remembered before. That they would do this shows exactly what kind of people they really are."

After reading Solas's explanation, Ev stood up and went to her bag at the edge of camp. When she returned, she placed the bag of dark orbs by the table, then handed the small red one to Solas.

"I know how to stop him," she wrote on the paper, "but we'll need your help."

Solas watched silently as Ev detailed out her strategy for breaking into Lumine Tower. His eyes opened wide when he saw her mention how Syrus had shown her how to use degradation to banish Divine. When she finished, he looked at the orb she had given him. After a moment of studying it, he smiled.

"Tell us Syrus's true name," he wrote. "We will send him a message to be ready."

"Rusalka," Ev wrote. "He is a prifae from a world called Veravis, created by Varidis Aurum."

"Do you have his contact key?" Solas asked.

Silently, Ev made a copy of the antherial key that Syrus had given her.

Solas took the key, nodded his thanks, then gathered up all but one of the papers. On that last paper, he wrote, "We will help you prepare. We will return with what you asked for, but it may take some time to develop the protections you require. Don't worry. The Masters should not be able to detect our usage of anther unless it directly affects their systems. We will not be found, and we will not betray you if we are."

He then handed back the red orb, and Ev could tell that it had been slightly altered, and exactly in the one area that she'd suspected could have caused errors in the copying. When she looked at him, he again smiled. His fellow Divine then collected all but twelve of the dark orbs.

The exchange complete, the Divine headed back into the woods. Once they were gone, Jax and Birdie approached Ev.

"So, what now?" asked Birdie.

"Now?" Ev replied. She held up the red orb in front of Birdie. "Now we end this."

Chapter 21

Over two weeks had passed since Evress had destroyed Tallis's copy — two weeks since she'd last spoken to Birdie, or really pretty much anyone. The atmosphere at Lumine Tower had been solemn and tense. The only task that Evress had been given was to search for any sign of her copy, but the trail had gone cold. It was as if the copies had gone into hiding after killing Crovos, but Evress knew that couldn't be the case.

After interrogating the fairies who'd witnessed the battle, it was clear that an assault against Ars Summis was inevitable. Worse: some of the fairies had been inspired by seeing Crovos fall and had left to spread the word to other immortals. That was news that Sylvra hadn't taken well, and Evress dreaded to find out what he had summoned her for in response.

Appearing in the main control room at the top of Lumine Tower, Evress spotted Amethine next to Sylvra at his personal terminal. Neither of them looked happy, but "not happy" was certainly better than angry.

"You called for me?" Evress asked Sylvra.

"Indeed," stated Sylvra as he motioned her over. When she arrived, he pointed to his terminal. "We are losing Divine at a rapid pace. The demon's messages seem to have found an audience."

"What does that mean?" asked Evress, though she feared that she already knew the answer.

Amethine snapped at her. "What do you think it means? Word is obviously spreading through the Divine from outside of Doxla. This world is useless!"

"Incorrect," stated Sylvra. "These Divine are useless. This Doxla can still be salvaged if we erase the immortals who know the truth."

"Erase?" repeated Evress. "How many?"

Sylvra barely turned his eyes in her direction. "However many we must. It is either that, or this world will indeed be lost."

Evress wanted to protest, but she remained silent. Sylvra no longer took her objections kindly.

"That said," he continued, "we are still earning a significant amount of prestige from the Divine who remain. For that reason, our plan of action is as follows."

Sylvra turned his attention fully to Evress. "You and I shall hunt down every nepac with forbidden knowledge and erase them. The sooner this is done, the fewer we will need to dispose of."

Evress said nothing, not that Sylvra gave her the chance before addressing Amethine.

"You will do what you do best. Investigate the other realms to find the ideal audience for us to attract next. Make absolutely *certain* it is a realm with minimal connections to our current clientele. As soon as our incoming prestige drops to fifty percent of its current rate, we will banish all Divine, tell the nepacs that these Divine were corrupt, give them a decade or so to forget the details, and then we will open up to our new patrons. Understood?"

"Perfectly," replied Amethine.

"Good," stated Sylvra before turning back to Evress. "Then let us begin. Take me to the location of the fairies who witnessed Crovos's fall."

Evress suppressed a growl. He was perfectly capable of transporting them himself. Considering what he was about to make her do, he could at least have the courtesy to be responsible for travel.

Nonetheless, she obliged, and the two of them appeared in the center of the fairy village.

No sooner did they arrive, then the fairies flitted away to cover — all of them except for the one named Belle Sweet, who instead tentatively flew over to Evress.

"M-Master Evress," she squeaked. "How good of you to return. And M-Master Sylvra, to what do I owe this honor?"

Sylvra smiled down at the winged woman. "We are here—"

"Doxla! Hear my words!"

Sylvra's face turned pale at the booming voice exploding all around them, but that was nothing compared to the utter horror Evress felt when she looked up and saw the image of an old woman in the sky shouting down at them all.

"The Masters are not invincible. They can be brought down like any other! Crovos has already been slain! To all of you who wish to fight back against their tyranny, now is the time! In fifteen minutes, we will open gateways to Ars Summis, destroy its guardian, and remove its protections. Aid us, and together we will make them pay for their crimes!

"Oh, and to the one that chose to join Sylvra rather than oppose him, I can only hope that you don't actually know what he does with the nepacs he harvests, because if you do, then you are a monster. I think you and I both know how I feel about monsters, so you know exactly what I'll do to you when we attack."

The woman then seemingly looked directly at Evress as she added, "See you soon."

With those parting words, the image in the sky vanished, and Evress found herself back at Lumine Tower before she could even process what had happened. It took her a moment to realize that she'd been brought back by Sylvra, who had already rushed over to his terminal. After frantically tapping away at the keys, he slammed his palms down with such force that the terminal cracked before rapidly pulling itself back together.

His faced etched in such fury that both Evress and Amethine backed away from him, Sylvra glared at Evress.

"Well," he said in a terrifyingly calm tone, "it would seem that we have found your counterpart."

"I can stop her," Evress stated nervously.

"See to it that you do," Sylvra replied. He then stood up straight. "Recall all of the Enforcers. Tell them to focus on protecting the systems of Ars Summis. We will hold this room."

"But shouldn't we—" Evress began.

"I *said* we will hold this room," Sylvra interrupted. "They will come to us."

Amethine of all people protested. "We should stop them now. If they reach the terminals—"

"They can do nothing," replied Sylvra, though he was clearly growing agitated. "They do not have permission, and they will never have permission to access them. Either they are fools who think they can, or their strategy is to drive the Divine from Doxla, which is something we will already do ourselves. We wait here."

Though she didn't look happy about it, Amethine obeyed, and she took up a position as far away from Evress as she could manage.

Evress, on the other hand, sidled up to a terminal of her own. First, she used it to relay Sylvra's message to the Enforcers, but then she told it to show her various locations in and around Ars Summis. Whatever her copy was up to, she doubted it was as simple as Sylvra believed, and she fully intended to find out what it was.

Time passed slowly as Evress waited for the assault to begin, and every second put her further on edge. The copies had already caused so much damage. Sylvra already intended to kill who knew how many immortals. After this? He might even decide to abandon the world entirely. Everything she'd worked toward would be gone.

Yet, Birdie's words still haunted her. These copies were carrying on the fight that she'd once fought, and they'd gone farther than Evress would ever have thought possible. A part of her almost hoped that they somehow would succeed, but then she remembered what fate awaited Doxla if they did. It would be erased, and its survivors would be lucky to even have a world to live in, let alone one where seitti did not control their lives even moreso than Sylvra already did.

Her thoughts abruptly ended with an explosion of activity on her screens. Countless portals opened up all across Ars Summis. Most of them sat dormant, but others unleashed hoards of immortals — primarily demons, harpies, and shades — into the streets. At first the intruders all stood frozen amongst utterly horrified Divine — unable to act because of the city's anti-nepac defenses — but after only seconds the city's protections vanished, and the standoff turned into a slaughter, as nearly none of the Divine in the main streets were Radiants capable of dealing with high-level foes such as demons. Countless Hearts littered the streets. At first, the Divine resurrected almost immediately on top of their dropped Hearts, but before they could reclaim them, the helpless Divine would be struck down again and again until most of them gave up and outright vanished.

Throughout it all, Sylvra neither acted nor spoke as he stared at the reports flashing on his screen, but Evress used her terminal to search through the city for any sign of her doppelganger. As the war raged on below, however, she saw no sign of any of the copies. Instead, the immortals pressed ever deeper into the city, eventually drawing out even the Radiants from in and around Lumine Tower. Not long after the Radiants engaged the invading force, however, an explosion reverberated all the way up into the control room.

"What was that?" Evress shouted.

"Ignore it," commanded Sylvra as he opened a tear in reality, which Evress recognized by the shimmer it produced as some form of degradation.

A second explosion shook the tower, and Evress switched her view to its base. With the Radiants now engaged with the immortals, Evress saw that the copies had moved in. Even though their appearances had changed, Evress could recognize herself and Lylia immediately. It was also obvious who Jax and Gare were from their choice of weapons — the sight of Crovos's sword in

Jax's hand renewing her hatred of these copies — which meant that the other two humans were Umber and Birdie, respectively. More concerning than them, however, were the five unfamiliar demons who were clearly using anther to break through the tower's self-repair capabilities.

"They're trying to bring down the tower!" Evress called.

"Stay *here!*" Sylvra ordered before sending a signal to the Enforcers to deal with the problem.

At once, the entirety of the Enforcers teleported to the tower base. Almost as quickly, it became apparent that they were outmatched. The copies were immune to most of the tools that the Enforcers possessed, which immediately skewed the battle in the copies' favor. Jax and Lylia somehow cut right through the Enforcers while Gare and Umber focused on breaking the supports of the tower. The other Ev, meanwhile, concentrated on each fallen Enforcer and banished them from Doxla while Birdie stayed close to her casting some spell.

How? How could they be winning? They weren't even struggling! It made no sense! Except . . .

Looking more closely, Evress swore she could see the assisting demons directing anther between the remaining Enforcers and the copies. Simple usage of anther such as breaking protections was one thing, but nullifying the tools of the Master was something that would require years of training to master. She suddenly realized what spell Birdie was casting.

"Sylvra!" Evress called. "Those demons aren't immortals. They're Divine!"

Pulling up a new display at that announcement, Sylvra narrowed his eyes. "So they are."

He quickly tapped a few keys on his terminal, and the demons below vanished from sight, as did every other Divine in Ars Summis. Only two Enforcers remained, but it was too late to save them. Lylia used her tail to hold one in place until she skewered him with her antherially augmented spear, while Jax used Crovos's blade to cleave right through the other's enchantments. Their Hearts vanished almost as quickly as they did.

Looking at Jax's smug expression on her screen, Evress clenched her fingers tight around the terminal. In only minutes, the copies had already decimated Ars Summis. They'd banished all of the Enforcers that she'd personally chosen, and she'd just stood there and let it happen!

Another explosion rocked the tower, and this time it listed slightly.

Evress spun toward Sylvra. "We have to do something! They'll destroy everything!"

"The kid is right," Amethine agreed. "We should end this now. We don't know what they're planning. We can't risk it!"

Another blast. More leaning. It was clear that Sylvra wasn't able to keep up with repairing the damage happening downstairs.

"Do as you please," Sylvra stated at last, and with a wave of his hand, Evress felt herself filling up with his own special brand of anther.

She also felt something that she hadn't before. He'd placed some new sort of antherial protection inside of her, and after only a moment's inspection she realized that it would block any form of indirect antherial contact.

Amethine took a step toward Evress. "Let's go."

Giving a nod, Evress looked at her screen one more time to identify the perfect place to strike. It would be six on two, so she would need to amend those odds immediately. She gave herself illusion magic, and as she glared at her false counterpart, she knew exactly who she had to remove first.

Spotting a place out of sight of the copies, Evress teleported both herself and Amethine down to the base of the tower. Before anyone noticed her, she shot out a wave of antherial strands directly at the other Ev.

Ev reacted almost immediately by putting up a barrier. The back of her head then morphed into her front, and Evress realized she'd been tricked by another of Birdie's illusions. She braced herself for a counterattack, but all she received were words.

"There you are," Ev stated with daggers in her eyes.

In a flash, Amethine appeared directly behind Ev, but before she could strike, she was blasted by Jax and sent flying.

"Go!" he yelled. "We'll take care of these two!"

At his command, Lylia opened a portal that dropped all of the copies save for Jax and Ev directly into Sylvra's control room. The last thing Evress saw before the portal closed was the lot of them engaging Sylvra.

"Really?" cackled Amethine. "*That's* your plan? Sylvra will make shorter work of them than we will of you."

"That would sound impressive," said Jax as he squared off against Amethine. "Only problem is, we'll be the ones beating you."

Amethine manifested several antherial spheres in the air around her that she promptly hurled toward Jax. To both her and Evress's surprise, however, Jax raised an antherial barrier of his own before countering with a blast of light that sent Amethine flying through a large window. Throughout the exchange, Ev simply stared at Evress. It wasn't until Jax had chased after

Amethine that she spoke again.

"Surprised?" Ev taunted. "Turns out even Jax can use anther when given the right tools by Divine. How long do you think Sylvra will last against four anthermancers?"

"That's all you care about, isn't it?" Evress spat. "Syrus's puppet. You're a soulless automaton. You don't care about what happens to this world. You don't care that he betrayed us, nor about the forty million others he made copies of!"

Evress used illusion magic of her own to form a sphere of blinding light around Ev's head, then she formed an antherial blade and lunged.

As expected, Ev put another barrier around herself as she tried to dispel the illusion.

Instead of striking it, Evress placed her hand on the barrier to read its exact nature and see how she might bypass it entirely.

No sooner had she touched it however, than the barrier exploded outward. The force embedded her into Lumine Tower's rapidly repairing walls, but otherwise she was unharmed.

Pulling herself free of the metal, Evress leered at her copy. Ev had already dispelled the illusion and had even readied her bow with an arrow. The arrow glowed with an iridescent shimmer, indicating that it had been augmented with some sort of antherial tool.

"Maybe I am a puppet," said Ev, "but so are you. You let Sylvra control you, and for what? To help AnAnCol steal the souls of others for nepacs? Do you even know what they're really after?"

"I don't care what they're after!" replied Evress. "I've seen how seitti treat their worlds. At least here I can do something!"

"Syrus told us that most seitti care for their worlds. Are you honestly going to believe Sylvra over him?"

Evress gripped her blade tightly in her hand. "Considering that Sylvra wasn't the one who left me to die, I'm going to say *yes!*"

Raising her blade high into the air, Evress teleported just as Ev unleashed a rain of arrows that tore through the tower wall. Now above her copy, Evress threw her blade against Ev's barrier with all her might. Just before the blade struck, she created a barrier of her own and anchored it so that it wouldn't budge under any force.

Once again, Ev's barrier burst outward, but when it collided with Evress's, the both of them shattered.

Evress landed directly behind Ev. She pulled back her arm, and as soon as Ev started to turn around, Evress teleported once more to the other side of Ev. There, she thrust her hand forward and connected with her copy.

Ev jerked away, but it was too late. Evress had managed to siphon a sizable amount of the copy's anther. From the defiance still etched into her face, however, Ev almost seemed unfazed by the shift in the battle.

"This ends here," Evress stated as she formed another blade.

Ev reciprocated by forming an antherial blade of her own. "Kill me then. Just know that if I die, another message will be sent out across the world. Every single nepac will know exactly what Sylvra's trying to do. They'll know all about AnAnCol, and they'll be useless to Sylvra. What do you think he'll do to them then?"

Evress went white. "No! You can't!"

Ev flashed a brief smirk. "That's what I thought. You know he's a monster. You're me, after all."

"Syrus is just as much a monster as Sylvra!" screamed Evress. "Don't stand there and act like you're better than me! If you send that message, then you're the one dooming all those people!"

"I know what Syrus did was horrible, but this is bigger than us," the copy said. "Ev, you know you can't trust Sylvra. Do you think he even trusts you? He's controlling you, and he probably has ways to stop you if you ever even think about crossing him. He'll never let you truly protect Doxla. You have to realize that!"

Slowly, Evress lowered her blade. As much as it hurt, she knew that her copy spoke the truth.

"It doesn't matter. I've seen how Sylvra accesses his core systems, and only he can do it. It's not possible to beat him. Working with him is the only way to help Doxla. Please don't send that message."

"It goes out when I die," her copy stated. "If you don't want it sent, then help me win this."

Evress looked down at the shimmering weapon in her hand. There was no way around it. At least after Doxla was abandoned, its inhabitants would be allowed to live out the rest of their lives in peace.

Evress dissolved her blade, and her copy slightly lowered her own. Then, before her copy could respond, Evress teleported to Ev and drained her of her remaining anther.

Ev struck Evress with all of her strength, but without anther, she was ultimately powerless.

With one final swift motion, Evress threw her copy against the wall before unleashing a wave of destruction that utterly disintegrated the other Ev. A part of her hated doing it, but she knew that she had no choice. This was the only way forward.

Panting, Evress closed her eyes. In the distance, she heard the copy's voice echoing throughout the city — every syllable a death knell for the world. She listened as it revealed Sylvra's plans, knowledge about seitti and other Divine, and how AnAnCol—"

Evress opened her eyes in shock. She couldn't have heard right. No, it had to be a lie. AnAnCol was helping Sylvra make new seitti who cared about other worlds. They weren't trying to make seitti completely unaccountable for their actions. They couldn't be!

The sound of footsteps behind her drew Evress's attention. Amethine had returned, and she looked very pleased with herself.

"Seems like I was wrong about you," stated Amethine with a disgusting smile. "Maybe you do have what it takes to be a Master."

"I did what had to be done," Evress replied quietly.

"Oh, is that why you look so unhappy? And here I thought it might be because you learned the truth about AnAnCol."

A chill washed over Evress.

Amethine's smile widened. "I do hope that won't be a problem for you. It would be such a burden for me to be the only Administrator serving alongside Sylvra."

Evress swallowed, but she wouldn't allow herself to appear intimidated. "Of course it won't. What AnAnCol does isn't my concern. I only care about what happens to Doxla."

"Is that so?" replied Amethine. "Then let us return to Sylvra and inform him that the vermin have been disposed of."

Amethine vanished from the room. Not wishing to give her any time to speak with Sylvra alone, Evress followed.

Back in the control room, it was as if nothing had ever happened. The place was pristine, the borders of the room displayed Sylvra's peaceful starry sky, and there was no sign of any of the copies that had attacked Sylvra. The man himself stood working stoically at his personal terminal, seemingly unfazed by the attack. Amethine had already made her way over to him.

"All threats have been eliminated," she said. "It's a shame that the nepacs now know of AnAnCol, however. I suppose this world really is lost, now."

"So it would seem," stated Sylvra absently.

Amethine leaned on the terminal next to his. "Shall we erase this world and move on, then?"

Evress stepped forward in protest. "You can't be serious! Just because we have to abandon this world doesn't mean we have to destroy it!"

Sylvra stopped what he was doing and glared at Amethine. He then sighed and turned his attention to Evress.

"We have no hope of passing any of these nepacs on to AnAnCol. Allowing them to live is a risk that yields no reward."

Evress couldn't believe what she was hearing. "But they're harmless! I can watch them. I can make sure they don't discover degradation or anther or anything else that might make them dangerous!"

"I have made my decision," declared Sylvra as he gazed directly into Evress's eyes. "This world will be put to rest. Do I make myself clear, Evress?"

From behind Sylvra, Amethine flashed a wicked smile.

Evress felt herself trembling. Her copy had been right all along. Now, there was nothing she could do. Nothing, unless . . .

Evress lowered her head defeatedly. "As you wish, Sylvra."

After a moment of silence between them, Sylvra appeared satisfied. He turned his attention back to the terminal and resumed his work. As he moved his fingers, Evress watched his display closely, fully aware that Amethine's eyes were on her just as intently. She'd only have one chance to act. One brief moment to maybe, possibly, finally protect this world from its fate.

Eventually, Sylvra placed his hand on the display and channeled his anther into it. A second display opened up.

This was the moment Evress was waiting for. Sylvra had accessed his core systems.

Immediately, Evress shot out her arm, but instead of unleashing a wave of destruction, she found herself frozen in place.

No. No! He'd expected this!

"My, my. How disappointing," Sylvra stated without looking at her. Behind him, Amethine's eyes lit up with evil glee.

"Please, allow me," she cooed.

Sylvra sighed. "Very well, but be quick about it."

As Amethine stepped around Sylvra, Evress struggled to find some way to free herself. The anther that Sylvra had provided now bound her in place. She tried to expel it, but it refused to obey her. But, she did have one thing she could use.

The anther she'd drained from her copy. Maybe she could push Sylvra's anther out with that!

Evress focused with all of her might to use her stolen anther against Sylvra's, but as Amethine drew closer and closer, it became ever clearer that Sylvra fought back against her. She couldn't get his anther out!

Amethine stopped just out of reach of Evress's hand.

"I'm going to enjoy this," Amethine purred as she began channeling anther into her arm.

No! It couldn't end like this! She just had to focus . . .

Sudden movement. A flash of light from behind Sylvra accompanied by an explosion that struck him in the back.

"What!" Sylvra roared, turning back to whoever had attacked him.

Immediately, Evress felt his will weaken, and with all of her concentration, she blasted his anther from her body and rid herself of every tool and enchantment he had ever given her. The shock wave sent an off-guard Amethine staggering backward, which gave Evress just enough of an opening to drive an antherial blade straight through that witch's heart.

Amethine shrieked as she clawed at Evress, but Evress wasn't about to give her even a chance to fight back.

With a mighty roar, Evress tore her blade upward and twisted it violently as it passed through Amethine's skull.

The Master's enchantments healed the wound instantly, but it couldn't repair everything. Amethine's shriek turned to a gurgle as her eyes glazed over. Twitching violently, she fell to the ground as a brain dead husk.

Not willing to even chance that Amethine might somehow recover, Evress raised her hand and blasted the rest of Amethine away with a destruction wave. When the light cleared, she found herself face to face with . . . her copy?

"W-what?" Evress stammered. "B-but—"

"No time to explain," Ev said, and from the battle between Sylvra and the other copies raging behind her, Evress could see why.

"Will you help us?" Ev asked.

"I . . ." Evress hesitated, but she knew that she had no choice. It was either stop Sylvra, or Doxla would be utterly destroyed.

"Yes," she answered.

"Then take this," Ev handed Evress a copy of Syrus's antherial key. "You know what to do with it."

Absorbing the key into herself, Evress nodded. "What about you?"

"We watched when he fought our copies, so we know how he fights," Ev replied as she turned toward the battle. "We'll keep him off of you, no matter what it takes."

Ev then erupted in a shimmering glow, and Evress realized just how much she'd underestimated Syrus's copies as she noticed that all of the other copies already had that same glow.

"*Enough!*" Sylvra erupted in the midst of the battle.

Evress looked just in time to see Sylvra vanish from sight. She had no idea where he went, but she had a very bad feeling about it.

"Get on that terminal!" Ev yelled at her. "We won't get another chance!"

Before Evress could respond, Ev disappeared as well, and so did Jax, Lylia, and Gare. Only Birdie and Umber stayed behind.

"Please hurry," Birdie said as she offered Evress some antherial tools she didn't recognize. "We'll do our best to protect you, but I'm not sure how long we'll last against Sylvra. Those things will hopefully get you through to the end in case we can't."

Though wary, Evress knew this wasn't the time to question her own safety. She activated the tools, and as much as she wanted to study what the effects were, she knew that she didn't have time. Instead, Evress rushed over to Sylvra's terminal. When she saw the display for his core systems, her heart sank. She'd never gotten a good look at them before, and while it wasn't completely foreign to her, it wouldn't be easy figuring out how to send a message from here.

As Evress went to work, she felt she couldn't remain silent. "Birdie, in case we don't make it, I just wanted to say I'm sorry."

"How about we worry about apologies later," Birdie said.

"Agreed," added Umber. "Besides, we are the ones who intentionally drove Sylvra to desire this world's destruction. None of us are free of guilt in this war. At least your path has led you to greater familiarity with his systems than any of us could have ever had."

Evress supposed Umber was correct, but unless she could figure this out, all of it would amount to nothing. She only hoped that her copy — no, her other self — would be able hold Sylvra off long enough for her to make amends for everything she had done.

Chapter 22

"We'll keep him off of you," Ev called back to her original self — now called "Evress," apparently, "no matter what it takes."

Ev then activated all of the defensive tools that the Divine had helped her create. They'd assured her that these tools would protect her against all of the common methods that a seitti might use to incapacitate an opponent. She hoped they were right, because the copies who'd fought against Sylvra earlier had been taken down in less than a minute without them.

"*Enough!*" Sylvra erupted in the midst of the battle behind her.

Sylvra then vanished from sight. Ev expected him to return at any moment; after all, this was the only place where he could stop them from accessing his core systems, but she also had a feeling that something was off. Using another tool that the Divine had given her to help track teleportation, she saw that he had traveled all the way to the top of the sky over Doxla, right next to the world border. Whatever he was doing, Ev knew she had to stop him.

"Get on that terminal!" Ev yelled back to her counterpart. "We won't get another chance!"

Ev then teleported everyone save for Evress, Birdie, and Umber up to where Sylvra waited for them. They immediately dropped back down, but the downward acceleration activated a tool that created platforms beneath them.

In the center of them all, Sylvra scowled. "Truly, you are impressive, Eveline. It's a shame that I will not have one of you serving me. With your talents, I could have finally run multiple Doxla's simultaneously."

Ev didn't know why he was wasting time talking, but she could certainly run with that. Every second she could buy her other self was critical.

"Why are you so obsessed with Doxla?" she asked. "Why keep creating the same world over and over?"

Sylvra smirked cruelly. "I'm afraid you won't distract me, Eveline. I only offered those final words out of respect for one with talent nearly as great as my own. Now, though, I'm afraid all of you must die."

As quick as lightning, Sylvra slammed his fist into the sky above him. Instantly, the sky vanished and the world went dark as the world border shattered from horizon to horizon.

Instinctively, Evress and Lylia both used the anther now pouring in all around them to create light, warmth, and air for the group. If Sylvra thought that little stunt would be enough to stop them . . .

Wait. Ev's stomach turned over as she realized what he was really after.

His hand still outstretched, Sylvra pulled in anther from the Cosmic Graveyard. Clenching his fist, he sent out a chain reaction through it that set the sky ablaze in a raging inferno. The light should have blinded Ev, but the protections that the Divine had provided thankfully dampened both the light and heat equally well. Still, Ev dreaded what other power Sylvra might wield now that he held unlimited access to anther.

While the air broiled around her, Ev drew her bow and aimed it where she'd last seen Sylvra. She doubted it would do much, but she readied it with the same attack that her copy had tried to use against Evress. As soon as the light faded and Ev knew she had her target in her sights, she unleashed a rain of arrows augmented with both piercing and enchantment-breaking bolts.

The enchantment-breaking bolts exploded on impact and removed Sylvra's Master's protections, while the piercing ones shot through him as if he were paper. At the end of the volley, what was left of Sylvra's body dropped lifelessly to the ground below.

As surprised as she was at the effectiveness of her attack, Ev knew full well that wouldn't be the end of it. She braced herself for whatever might come next. Then, without warning, she felt herself jerked back by some unseen force only for Sylvra to reappear with his shimmering hand directly where Ev's head had been a fraction of a second prior. Upon seeing that his attack had failed, Sylvra's face contorted with rage.

Ev swallowed as she realized that she would have been dead twice over if not for the tools that the Divine had given her. It was only a matter of time until Sylvra tried something that the Divine hadn't thought of, and as soon as he did, it would be over.

Two explosions struck Sylvra in the back as both Jax and Lylia fired off beams of light. Sylvra's enchantments had clearly been restored, however, as the attacks didn't even garner a flinch.

In retaliation, Sylvra warped back into the center of the group. His face red with fury, he thrust his arm upwards. A wave of blackness erupted from his hand and washed over everyone.

Darkness swallowed Ev. All sound ceased save for the beating of her own heart. She felt like she was floating, but when she took a breath, she found she couldn't breathe!

Ev tried not to give in to panic. She still sensed anther all around her, and she'd come too far to let it all end like this.

Her first thought was to try and put fresh air directly into her lungs, but even if she could, that wouldn't help the others. No, she needed a way to counteract what Sylvra was doing, but she had nothing to help her figure out what that even was!

Wait. "Nothing." That was it! Sylvra was trying to suffocate them by erasing everything around them!

Ev wasn't sure if she could counteract his will, but she was damn sure going to try. Channeling the anther both within and around her, Ev used the small bubble of space she was sure still existed within the field of her protections as a template and forced it back out into the void that Sylvra had created.

At first she wasn't sure if it was working, but then a deafening crash and blinding flash brought the world back into sight, where Ev saw that Lylia had joined her in helping reverse Sylvra's attack.

Surprise gave way to frustration as Sylvra's face turned even redder. In an instant, he was on top of Ev once more. Again, her body jerked away from him on its own, but this time it encountered at first resistance, then a crushing pressure from all sides as her every limb was frozen tightly against her body.

"Not this time," Sylvra growled as he clasped a single hand around her neck.

"Ev!" Jax yelled as he fired another blast of light in vain.

Sylvra had her firmly in his grasp, yet he didn't attack. That meant he had to be probing the protections that the Divine had given her. Unable to move, she did the only thing she could to get away.

Ev teleported out of his grip and closer to the others, only to find his hand once again on her throat almost immediately. The binds he'd placed on her tightened further after her maneuver, so much so that she feared they would soon crush through her defenses. The only glimmer of hope was that Sylvra grew ever more frustrated, telling Ev that he had yet to find any way to circumvent the Divines' gifts.

"Agh!" Sylvra howled in pain as he found his arm one hand lighter, courtesy of Gare's shimmering ax.

Seizing on the distraction, Ev finally overpowered her binds and broke free. She lunged at Sylvra with an antherial dagger only for him to reappear behind her and strike her with such force as to send her bouncing across the platforms in the sky. The blow left her dazed, but more concerningly . . . he'd hit her! He'd figured out some of their protections after all!

Ev quickly looked back towards the battle to see Gare laying unconscious on his platform and Sylvra unaccounted for. She spun back around to check behind her, but the Master was nowhere to be seen.

The horrible realization of where he must have gone setting in, Ev called out, "Back to the tower!"

Not even bothering to teleport the others with her, Ev arrived just in time to see Sylvra throw Birdie across the room and slam Umber clean through the floor, which quickly repaired itself.

Evress was completely undefended.

"No!" Ev yelled as she teleported between him and her other self.

No sooner had she reappeared than Sylvra himself warped. Before she could react, she found herself sliding across the floor after receiving yet another blow to the back. By the time she recovered enough to even lift her head, it was too late. Evress lay crumpled against the starry wall, and Sylvra smugly tapped a single finger from his now-regrown hand against the terminal.

The look of victory that appeared on his face slowly vanished, however, and he pressed his finger down again. Twice more. He slammed his fist down on the machine.

"What did you do!" he roared at Evress.

Sylvra teleported to Evress and picked her up by the throat, only to drop her again and spin around in horror.

Ev stood up, hoping that they'd finally won, but then Sylvra waved his hand.

The room shifted slightly. All of the terminals rotated clockwise by ninety degrees, and the Evress against the wall vanished as another one appeared at Sylvra's actual terminal.

Ev almost smiled as she realized Birdie's deception, but now Evress truly was exposed. If she didn't act—

Sylvra teleported.

Without even thinking, Ev warped beside Evress and put up a barrier just in time to catch Sylvra's fist halfway through.

A familiar battle cry then reached her ears as Jax and Lylia reappeared in the room — Jax already on the attack.

Sylvra's eyes opened wide as Jax landed a blow from behind. Crovos's blade cut clean through Sylvra's legs, which caused the Master to topple to the ground — his hand still trapped in the barrier.

"Let's see how long it takes you to recover from that," Jax taunted.

In a flash of light, Sylvra vanished and reappeared — completely healed — face-to-face with Jax.

Jax jumped back and swept his sword upward, but Sylvra shattered it into pieces with a burst of energy. He then struck Jax with an even more powerful blast so savage that Ev feared the worst regardless of what protections the Divine may have given them. That fear only compounded when her brother punched into the wall so hard that the starry sky flickered before Jax fell limply to the ground.

Sylvra then attacked Lylia before she could land a single blow. In seconds, the naga was slammed repeatedly into the floor until she lay in a motionless heap.

When Sylvra turned his gaze once more to Ev, she couldn't help but back up against the terminal where Evress continued to work frantically.

"Tell me you've almost got it," Ev pleaded.

"I think," began Evress, "I just need to—"

Sylvra slammed his hand against Ev's barrier. Ev retaliated by blasting her barrier outward, but Sylvra held his ground.

His eyes stared directly into hers — the look of a monster who knew he at last had his prey — as her barrier cracked against his will.

Ev pressed her hands against the barrier and poured every last ounce of her focus into holding this final wall together, but try as she might, the cracks only spread.

"Ev, hurry!" she called to Evress.

"I'm trying!"

The barrier shattered.

In a single motion, Sylvra battered Ev to the side as he stepped toward Evress.

Ev leapt forward to attack but found herself once more trapped in his invisible binds.

Sylvra merely tossed her aside as he reached for Evress.

His hand only inches away from her, a cloud of darkness suddenly enveloped him.

Again, Ev felt her binds weaken as Sylvra roared in rage. She broke free at the same time that the Master blindly swept his arm in Evress's direction. The attack knocked Evress away from the terminal, but just as Sylvra dispelled the darkness, Ev tackled him through a portal that she opened right beside him.

The two of them grappled against the wall near where Birdie had cast her spell, with Sylvra quickly overpowering Ev up until Birdie raked her shimmering dagger across his eyes. Ev tried to use the opening to invoke her own version of antherial binding, but at that point Sylvra absolutely erupted.

Mimicking Ev's own explosive barrier, Sylvra sent out a shock that blasted both her and Birdie away from him. Before Ev could recover, he struck her brutally on the back of the head.

For a brief moment, Ev's world went dark. When she opened her eyes, the room lay silent save for the sound of Sylvra's footsteps approaching her. She tried to turn her head to see him, but she couldn't. She couldn't move a single muscle under his binds.

Sylvra stopped right beside her and dropped the still body of Evress such that she landed face-to-face with Ev.

"I'm sorry," Evress whispered. "I tried."

Ev closed her eyes. They'd come so close. They'd given everything they had. If only Helcant, Tallis, and Nictis had survived, maybe they could have won. If only they'd made more copies of themselves when Sylvra shattered the world border, then they could have held him off longer. But they hadn't. The thought had never even occurred to her until now, when it was already too late.

Ev opened her eyes again. "It's okay. We all did."

Seemingly savoring his victory, Sylvra at last spoke. "And now you at last see how powerless nepacs truly are against seitti. You could have helped me change that. We could have brought down their empire together, but you chose to side with the few over the many. You are both disappointments. Your failure will be your final legacy as I erase you with the rest of this pointless world."

Ev heard Sylvra turn and walk calmly away from them back toward his terminal. She closed her eyes once again. At least the end would be painless.

But, as she awaited the inevitable darkness, the sound of her own laughter reached her ears.

Ev opened her eyes to see Evress smiling. Sylvra must have also heard, because his footsteps ceased.

"Our legacy won't be failure, Sylvra," said Evress. "The only failure was mine in stalling you long enough that we'd still be alive to see you brought to justice, but whether we see it or not doesn't change a thing."

Looking Ev in the eye, Evress gave a comforting smile. "They know."

Ev gasped. She didn't know whether to laugh or cry, but tears filled her eyes all the same.

Even without seeing him, the panic in Sylvra was palpable. Ev could hear him feverishly tapping away on his terminal.

"NO!" Sylvra screamed. "*What have you done?* Y-you, you . . ."

Sylvra trailed off as he put his full focus on his terminal. The binds on Ev loosened almost completely, allowing both her and Evress to free themselves with ease.

Back on her feet once more, Ev was happy to see that both Jax and Birdie had begun to stir. If these were to be their final moments, they'd love to see that they'd not only beaten Sylvra, but broken him.

Panting and heaving, Sylvra spun back toward Ev and Evress. "You've cost me everything. *Everything!* I'll kill you! I'll erase *everyone!*"

Sylvra slammed his hand onto his display and channeled his anther into it. The lights of the control room flickered. The walls began to crumble.

"Nothing will be left! Nothing! You will get *nothing* for what you've done to me this day!"

Ev stepped forward defiantly. "You're wrong, Sylvra. We get peace."

"And freedom!" called Birdie.

"And justice!" yelled Jax.

"And most important of all," Evress said as she stood next to Ev, "we get rid of you."

Sylvra screamed in rage. The world around them vanished. The five of them floated in a black void of nothingness, but something was off. This wasn't the Cosmic Graveyard. All of Ev's anther had vanished from within her, and she could sense absolutely none nearby. Yet, even without light, she could still see everyone clearly, and Sylvra looked absolutely terrified.

Three strange figures suddenly flashed into existence nearby. The first — a short, four-armed, tentacled individual — Ev recognized as Syrus in his true prifae form. The other two Ev had no clue about. One of the strangers looked like a smaller, glowing, gossamer-winged version of Syrus with wisps of shadow bleeding out from their iridescent skin. The third entity could only be described as an enormous, headless, legless beetle that towered well over all of them and was surrounded by luminous golden orbs.

A golden orb slid across the body of the beetle and pointed at Sylvra. Then, in a low, booming voice that was more a feeling than a sound, the beetle spoke.

"Griseo Cornu. You have abused the privileges granted to you and stand accused of supporting AnAnCol. You are now banned from use of the Cosmic Graveyard and shall remain so until investigations into your actions are complete."

"*What?*" Jax yelled at the giant creature. A second golden orb slid across the beetle and pointed at Jax, who stood tall as he continued. "That's it? He destroys our worlds and harvests our people, and all he gets is a glorified timeout?"

"Jax," Birdie hissed. "Maybe *don't* antagonize the only thing that can punish Sylvra."

"Or what?" Jax replied. "What's he gonna do? Erase us more than Sylvra already would have? Sylvra's a monster! And he was totally working with that AnAnCol group!"

The beetle hummed in a note so low that Ev couldn't hear it, but she felt its vibrations nonetheless. "You speak with conviction. Do you have proof of your claim?"

"I—" Jax started.

"He doesn't," said Evress, "but I do! Just look into Sylvra's systems. He funneled all of his prestige to AnAnCol."

"The girl lies," protested Sylvra, though he was clearly sweating. "I have nothing to hide. Check my activities."

"That will not be necessary," the beetle droned, and with its words a third orb appeared and pointed toward Evress. A strange light poured forth and surrounded her, lasting only a second, before all three orbs and several others shifted their focus to Sylvra.

"The girl's memories are clear. You are guilty."

In the span of a single second Sylvra's face went from white to red to purple as his gaze shifted from the beetle, to Ev, then to Evress. Ev braced herself for one final attack from the Master, but all she got was a pathetic display.

Sylvra clawed at his face as he dropped to his knees and let out a primal scream. Seemingly unamused, the beetle's orbs flashed brightly for a brief instant, and Sylvra vanished into sparkling dust. Ev could only hope that truly was the end of him.

Three orbs then focused on Ev and Evress together and Jax and Birdie separately. "My involvement here is complete. I leave your fates to Varidis Aurum."

The orbs shifted to the fairy-like prifae — apparently Aurum — who looked up at the beetle for a few seconds. After some silent exchange, Aurum nodded to the beetle, and the towering entity disappeared.

Almost as quickly, the complete blackness around them gave way to orange and purple clouds illuminated by bright stars off in the distance. A glassy floor materialized beneath their feet, and Syrus changed his appearance to his usual human one.

With Syrus trailing closely behind, Aurum floated over to the group. They offered a smile, but Ev had trouble fully reading Aurum's expression, what with their eyes consisting of little more than four glowing slits.

"Well, then," Aurum said in a voice that sounded like a man, woman, and whispering darkness all speaking in unison, "I'm certain you all must be curious as to what happens next. Would that be correct?"

Ev glanced over at Evress, who seemed particularly pensive.

"Yes, please," Ev said to Aurum. "With Sylvra gone, what's going to happen to us? What's going to happen to everyone from the worlds he created?"

Jax stepped forward angrily. "And what happened to Sylvra? If he isn't executed for his crimes—"

Aurum laughed and held up a hand. "Easy there, Jax. What happens to Sylvra is beyond my control. Though his fate does depend on his level of involvement with AnAnCol, I expect he'll be stripped of his seitti status and banished from our realm, and/or placed in a state of limbo for near eternity. Would that be satisfactory?"

Jax frowned, but he seemed placated. "I guess it has to be. Wait, how do you know my name?"

"Well, it wasn't exactly my choice." Aurum pointed a thumb in the direction that the giant beetle had been. "Les Aeter wanted me to also see Ev's memories. Apparently, they thought it important that I understand what exactly has transpired.

"In retrospect, I suppose I agree, but now knowing what I know, I think that the two of you," Aurum pointed to Ev and Evress, "probably have some things you should talk about, both with each other and with old Syrus here."

Ev looked between Evress and Syrus. Neither of them appeared particularly comfortable with that suggestion.

"We'll have time to talk later," Ev said. "We just want to know what's going to happen to us now."

Aurum shrugged. "That's honestly up to you. Each and every nepac will be given the choice to either live in one of my worlds or to try and resume the lives that you had in a world mirroring Doxla somewhere in the Preserves."

"In other words," Evress stated, "we either obey you, or we're left to the mercy of sentiments."

At that, Syrus finally spoke up from beside Aurum. "It's not like that. The Preserves are safe as long as you don't try to break out of your world, and Aurum isn't like Sylvra. They are Veravis's supreme authority in name only."

Crossing her arms, Birdie addressed Syrus. "Is that so? Based on what you told us about Aurum before, I find that hard to believe."

Aurum looked from Syrus to Birdie. "I believe what Syrus means to say is that I no longer play any major role in direct governance of my empire, thankfully. There are laws you would have to follow, of course, but that would be true of pretty much anywhere. I can even provide you with your own world, which I highly recommend. I can't imagine most Doxlans would be comfortable inserting themselves into a society that is thousands of years more advanced than their own. That said, the choice is ultimately yours."

Ev, Evress, Jax, and Birdie all exchanged glances. Through all the intensity of the past several months, Ev honestly hadn't thought much about what would come next.

"Do we have to decide now?" Ev asked.

"Of course not," Aurum replied. "You haven't even seen what either option actually entails. Due to these rather unusual circumstances, I have been given permission to manage a world in the Preserves for one month. It's not exactly something that I want to do, but I'm curious enough about how this will all turn out to put up with it."

Aurum cocked a head and flipped one of their hands absently. "You and the other nepacs will be taken there. I will provide you and everyone else from your worlds with whatever information you desire regarding Veravis. You will have until the month is up to make your decision."

"I see," said Ev quietly. "Thank you."

Aurum nodded, and in a flash, Ev found herself standing in the middle of a grassy field. All around her were mountains covered in glowing pines, and she realized that this field was Ars Summis, except the entire city was missing, and the sky was back where it belonged. Ev couldn't explain how she knew it, but this had to be the world in the Preserves.

Syrus and Aurum were nowhere to be seen, but Umber, Gare, and Lylia were there with them, and thankfully they all seemed completely unharmed. Even the army of immortals was present, but the Divine were gone, and Ev knew that they would not return.

"Whoa," said Gare as he looked around. "What happened?"

"What happened?" Ev repeated with a smile. "What happened is we did it. We won."

Chapter 23

Nearly a month had passed since Sylvra's defeat — a month since Ev had last spoken to either her copy or Syrus, and a month since she'd given up her identity as Evress. With the help of Aurum, she'd been reunited with her versions of her friends and family. This Preserves world turned out to be an amalgamation of all of the worlds that Sylvra had created — at least the ones that had anyone living in them — plus a little extra to hold it all together. Some magic and all of the systems that boosted the strength of nepacs had been removed, as had all of the monsters, and immortals were no longer immortal. The weather had been stabilized as well; there was little danger of this world decaying as her own Doxla had. To Ev, this place was as ideal as any could be.

Jax, however, disagreed, and he'd dragged not only Fauna but the entire group over to Birdie's cottage to help him argue his point on the front lawn.

"Ev, no one else wants to live in the Preserves," he pleaded in the evening sun. "Most immortals want to live in Aurum's world so they can be human again, and we want to go with them. You'll be here all alone if you stay."

Birdie placed an arm over Ev's shoulder as she came to Ev's defense. "Not *all* alone, Jax."

"Birdie, you're not helping," retorted Jax. "Ev, please. Aurum's going to take us away any minute. We'll never see each other again."

"If you want us to stay together, then maybe you should stay here," returned Ev.

Her mind was already made up, and she was tired of having this same discussion every single day.

"Ugh," cried Jax in frustration before turning to his wife. "Help me out here."

"What do you want me to say?" asked Fauna. "Jax, we've all tried. I don't think any of us can change her mind."

Frustrated and defeated, Jax turned back to Ev. "But why? Aurum's world is supposed to be exactly like this one. Why are you so dead set against it?"

"Because here," Ev replied, looking at the faces around her, "we are free.

Isn't that what we always wanted? To be free from control of seitti and all the other Divine?"

Jax took a step toward Ev. "But Aurum gave us his word that he wouldn't intervene outside of stopping wars. He even said we could always go to a different world in the Preserves if we decide that we really don't like it there."

"That's beside the point," Ev stated. "Jax, I was Sylvra's puppet. For six months, my life was controlled by a seitti, and before that, I was used and discarded by Syrus, a prifae."

"But—" Jax began.

"Even if Aurum does let us be," Ev continued, "they're still ultimately in control of our fate. All they'd have to do is just wake up one day and decide to be rid of us, and we'd be powerless to stop it."

Ev shook her head. "I'm sorry, Jax, but I can't live with that hanging over my head. Please understand."

Jax lowered his eyes. It seemed as if Ev had finally gotten through to him.

"Okay," he said last. "If this is really what you want."

"It is," replied Ev.

Jax looked over at his wife, who nodded back at him.

"In that case," he said, "we're staying, too."

"What?" Ev blurted in surprise. "Jax, no. You want to go to Aurum's world."

"Maybe," he replied, "but I wasn't there for you when you needed me before. I'm not making that mistake again."

Fauna put her arm around Jax's. "We've already discussed it. We agreed that if you wouldn't come, then we'd stay."

Ev found herself at a loss for words. "You— are you sure?"

Gare pounded his chest. "Of course we are. We couldn't leave you behind after everything we've been through."

"Gare? You too?" Ev asked, now even more surprised.

Gare nodded as he pulled his wife and daughter in close beside him. It was almost overwhelming; she couldn't believe that they'd all give up going to Aurum's world just to support her; she felt guilty, but at the same time, she appreciated it to no end.

Still unsure of how to feel, Ev looked at the other faces around her. "Are all of you staying?"

"Not a chance!" announced Helcant with a grin. "Now that we once more are mortal, Nictis and I wish to live our last years free from the curse of the

Masters."

Nictis nodded in agreement. "We also wish to avoid the inevitable wars that will arise now that the world order has so drastically changed."

"And Lylia and I want to learn more from Syrus," added Tallis. "We know there's so much more he can teach us, and we can't do that here."

"Besides," chimed Lylia, "it will be so interesting so see new kinds of creatures."

"I will stay," stated Umber. "I have no preference either way. Both worlds would offer a new experience for me."

Birdie responded with a smirk as she cocked her head. "I kind of hoped you'd be sticking around."

Umber gave a slight smile and nodded.

"Well," began Ev with a touch of both relief and guilt, "I mean, if you're sure, then that would mean the world to me."

"We're certain," said Jax with a smile.

Returning the smile, Ev moved in and hugged her brother tightly.

"Thank you," she said.

For the next fifteen minutes, those leaving and those staying said their farewells to one another. Perhaps it was because they'd spent most of the last year apart, perhaps it was because she and Birdie weren't going to be left alone after all, but Ev didn't feel particularly sad about their imminent departure. If anything, she felt at peace. Though she had yet to forgive herself for the horrible things she'd done as Evress, everyone here had. Knowing that they parted on good terms was comforting, and though she'd miss them, she hoped they'd find the life they longed for on the other side.

"So," said a strange voice as the farewells drew to a close, "I take it that you're ready to go?"

Ev turned to see Syrus standing next to . . . a man? The person's face was as androgynous as their voice, and Ev realized that must be the human form of Aurum.

Tallis stepped forward and spoke for the group. "We are, but—"

"—only you, Lylia, Helcant, and Nictis are leaving," Aurum finished for him.

"You were listening?" Ev asked, a bit put off.

Aurum shrugged. "Enough to pick up on the context. So, are you ready?"

The departing group all looked back at those staying. Ev was fairly certain they'd all said all that they had to say, and it seemed the others felt the same.

Tallis turned back to Aurum once more and nodded. The next instant, he and the others were gone. Ev expected Syrus and Aurum to vanish as well, but they remained and stared silently at Ev.

"Yes? Is there something else?" she asked.

Aurum didn't answer, but they did push Syrus forward. Clearly uncomfortable, Syrus slowly approached Ev.

"Ev," he said, "we will likely never speak again. As such, there is something I must say to you."

Ev didn't like where this was going. She'd avoided speaking to Syrus for a whole month, and she didn't want to break that silence now.

"It's okay," replied Ev with a shrug in the hopes of avoiding a prolonged conversation. "I know why you did what you did. You were right. The lives of a few million were nothing compared to what Sylvra was trying to do."

Syrus diverted his gaze, but he continued. "That's not what I wanted to say. I wanted to apologize."

"You don't need to," returned Ev, now also looking away.

"Yes, I do," said Syrus. "I've already spoken to everyone else, but not you, because I know I hurt you more than any other.

"If I don't say what I've come to say now, I'll never get the chance to. I . . . I didn't know what Sylvra was doing. I thought he'd kill everyone, and I thought —"

Syrus sighed. "Clearly I thought wrong. I should have told you from the beginning. I don't expect forgiveness, but I want you to know that I truly am sorry. To you, and to everyone else, too."

Clenching her fists, Ev turned further away. She didn't want Syrus to see the tears forming in her eyes. After a moment, she was able to take a deep breath and calm herself enough to reply.

"Like I said, it's okay. If I'd known then what I know now, I would have done the same thing."

Syrus looked like he expected her to say more, but Ev had nothing more to say. After a moment, he bowed his head.

"I see. Well, I thank you for giving me the chance to speak." Syrus then looked to everyone else present, lingering particularly on Birdie. "I suppose this is goodbye, then. For what it's worth, I will miss you. Though I know I may not have always shown it, there are few whom I've cared about as much as all of you. Do take care, my friends."

Syrus bowed his head once more, and with that, he too vanished, yet

Aurum still remained. Approaching Ev, Aurum spoke to her directly.

"May we speak in private for a moment?"

Right. She supposed she should have expected this. Ev took a step forward before looking back at Jax and Birdie. "I won't be long."

"Ev," said Jax, "what's this about?"

"It's nothing," she replied.

Birdie crossed her arms. "Uh-huh. Well, we'll be here, then."

Ev gave a slight smile before following Aurum far enough away to be out of earshot.

"While it's clear that you have declined two of my offers," Aurum began, "there is one more to which I believe I've not received an answer."

"I'm going to have to say 'no' to that one, too," Ev said.

"As you wish," replied Aurum with a shrug. "If you don't want to speak to her, that's your business, but she'd like you to know that she does want to speak to you. She also wants you to know that she has no hard feelings regarding your time working for Sylvra."

"Does she?" Ev asked. "Does she know that I'm the one who killed her Tallis?"

"Eh," Aurum wiggled a hand. "I wouldn't say 'killed' so much as 'altered,' and yes, she does."

"'Altered'?" Ev repeated. "What are you talking about? I erased him!"

"True," replied Aurum. "The new Tallis is not the same one that you destroyed, but you didn't quite destroy him as completely as you might think. Prior to your fight, their Tallis attempted — to a questionable degree of success — to preserve his memories in anther. Your Tallis has since allowed me to study him so that my sineform friends and I could use those memories to bring a version of the Tallis you destroyed back to life. That development, plus your crucial role in stopping Sylvra, has alleviated nearly all ill will towards you from your copies."

That was possible? Ev could hardly believe it. It was almost enough to make her want to see for herself if Aurum spoke the truth, but ultimately, she couldn't bring herself to face the copies.

"Can you tell me one thing?" she asked.

Aurum nodded.

"The other me. Did she accept your other offers?"

"Yes."

"That's good," Ev said. "I hope she does well."

"I'm sure she will," returned Aurum with a slight tilt of the head. "I'll inform her that you don't wish to meet. Be well, Ev. I truly do wish you the best."

At last, Aurum also disappeared, and Ev looked back at the others.

This would be her life now. No more Divine, no Radiants, no monsters. No more seitti. Only a small cottage in a small town in the middle of the woods. Just her and Birdie and Umber, and now Jax, Gare, and their families, too.

Ev knew it wouldn't be easy. After everything that had happened, this new world would likely be in chaos as its people adjusted to all the changes, but that was fine. They'd chart their own path, free from the influence of higher powers who had nothing at stake.

Taking a deep breath of cool, evening air, Ev smiled. This was certainly not the outcome she'd expected or even hoped for, but as she watched everyone talking happily in front of the cottage, she knew there was nothing more that she wanted.

* * * *

Up on the courtyard wall of Contur Sul's palace, Ev and Birdie sat watching the water flow along a nearby aqueduct as they awaited Syrus and Aurum to come and retrieve them. The Underworld wasn't exactly Ev's first choice of interim shelter, but they'd become heroes to the demons who lived here, and they didn't exactly have anywhere else to go. Besides, Abeleth and Meredith had gone out of their way to make the group as comfortable as possible, even going so far as to convince Queen Ibilis to provide them private suites in the palace.

Speaking of whom, Ev spotted the two of them walking in the courtyard below and waved. They waved back before continuing on their way — most likely finalizing their affairs before leaving the Underworld forever.

With a frustrated sigh, Birdie addressed Ev. "Where are they? They were supposed to meet us here."

"I guess they got distracted," said Ev as she stood up. "Maybe we should go find them."

Birdie also stood up, but before they left, she spoke again.

"Oh, there they are," said Birdie, and Ev followed her line of sight to spot Jax leading the others through the courtyard gates down below.

Ev smiled when she saw them — Jax and Gare laughing and joking with their families. Lylia practically hung onto Tallis's shoulders the whole time; she'd been a tad overprotective of him since she'd helped Aurum bring him back to life, but Tallis didn't seem to mind. Even Nictis looked happy as she spoke to Helcant, which was rare for her, and Umber, though off to the side a bit, seemed pleased as he looked up to the wall where Ev and Birdie were.

"I guess we should head on down," Ev said to Birdie.

"If we have to," Birdie replied. "They're the late ones. I think they should come up here."

Ev smiled and tugged on Birdie's arm. "Come on."

Birdie smiled, too, and together they made their way down the stairs to the center of the courtyard.

"There you are," Jax said with spread arms and a wide grin. "Don't you know how to be on time?"

Ev shrugged. "I guess it must just run in the family."

Jax chuckled. "Yeah, well, sorry we're late. How long do you think it will be before Syrus gets here?"

"Hopefully not long," Ev said. "As nice as it's been here, I'm kind of looking forward to traveling to a new world."

"You are not the only one who is eager," exclaimed Helcant. "We shall at long last be human again!"

Birdie waved her hand dismissively. "Forget human. I'll get to be a shade again. Sort of."

Umber spoke up. "You have decided to be transformed into a noctlus?"

Birdie nodded. "Yeah. I kind of miss shapeshifting, but shade magic doesn't exist in most of Veravis. Noctlus sounded like the best of the options Syrus suggested. It'll be weird being made of goo, but I get the feeling it will be somewhere between human life and shade life, so I'm sure I'll manage. What about you?"

Umber looked down at his hand. "Perhaps one day. However, I do not feel ready to explore Veravis beyond the world we are being given. A transformation back into a shade is sufficient for me."

Birdie nodded. "Fair enough."

"So, what about everyone else?" Ev asked cheerfully, "I take it everyone is ready to go?"

"We're here, aren't we?" replied Jax. "The only one we're waiting on now is Syrus."

"Perhaps you should recheck your surroundings," called Syrus from a short distance away.

"Syrus!" Ev exclaimed in surprise. "How long have you been there?"

"Approximately fifteen seconds," Syrus stated.

"Good timing, then," said Jax. "So, are you going to take us, or how exactly does this work?"

"I'm afraid we will have to wait for Aurum," Syrus answered. "I will, of course, be happy to keep you company until then, if you wish."

"Um, sure?" replied Ev.

To be honest, she still wasn't completely comfortable around Syrus, but she'd done her best to put it behind her. They all would likely have ended up unwitting pawns of Sylvra's schemes if it wasn't for him, after all. Besides, she'd accepted Aurum's offer to study how seitti actually use anther — apparently direct usage of the raw stuff wasn't exactly common — and she knew she'd be seeing a lot of Syrus if she did so.

"Where is Aurum, anyway?" Ev asked.

"Speaking with your other self, I believe," replied Syrus.

"Oh," said Ev. After a brief pause, she asked, "Do you know what our other selves are planning to do?"

"Most of them will remain here in the Preserves. Only their Helcant, Nictis, Tallis, and Lylia will join us in Veravis."

Ev nodded in understanding. If they weren't all going, then that made the most sense for how they would have split up.

A minute or so later, Aurum finally appeared. When Ev's other self wasn't with them, she knew that the two of them would never get the chance she'd hoped to sort out their differences. There was so much she wanted to say, but she also wasn't surprised. They were the same person, after all. If their roles had been reversed, Ev knew that she, too, would prefer to move on completely without ever looking back.

Aurum gave a very brief glance over everyone present. "Well then, it looks like everyone's ready, yes?"

Ev stepped forward with Birdie and Jax by her side. "We are."

With a smile, Aurum glanced over at Syrus. "In that case, Syrus, why don't you do the honors?"

With a smile and a nod, Syrus answered, "Gladly."

The next thing Ev knew, they were back on the surface near a small town on the side of a mountain, but something was different. No one else was around, and she sensed something odd. A new flavor of anther?

"Welcome to your new home," said Syrus with an outstretched hand. "We'll coordinate the transfer of everyone else in a few hours, but I wanted to give the lot of you a chance to adjust yourselves, especially since some of you will be given unique privileges," he added with a knowing look toward Ev.

"Wow," said Gare as he looked out over the landscape. "To think that this is a completely different world . . ."

Jax joined his friend in admiring the view. "You know, technically we were already in a different world."

"What's that anther I sense?" asked Ev. She attracted the attention of both Lylia and Tallis with her question.

Syrus turned his head to Ev. "Oh, that was my suggestion. It's just a way to make this world a bit more like the rest of Veravis, for once its civilization is ready. I don't expect Aurum will ever allow unrestricted travel between this place and the rest of Veravis—"

"—I won't," interjected Aurum.

"—but they have said they are open to letting individuals move between worlds on a case-by-case basis. I thought that this exposure might help ease any such future transitions. Plus, it will probably make your studies easier on you."

Tallis crossed his arms and smiled. "And I guess that's the real reason for it, huh?"

Syrus shook his head. "No, I truly do hope that there will be travel between worlds. I loved Doxla, and I'm sure there are many other Veravisians who would as well, just as I'm sure there are many Doxlans who would love to see other bits of Veravis."

"Oh!" exclaimed Lylia. "Speaking of which, may we see it now? We are very much curious to see the land of your origin."

Syrus replied sheepishly, "That isn't exactly possible quite—"

"Certainly," interrupted Aurum, who then nudged Syrus and whispered something to him. Shock appeared on Syrus's face, but then he smiled as Aurum give a quick poke to Syrus's shoulder, and Ev noticed a small shimmer get transfered into Syrus.

"Yes," Syrus said. "For the five of you who expressed interest, we can go right now if you wish, but," he added as he looked at Jax's wife, "perhaps only for a moment,"

"Yes, please!" exclaimed Tallis as Lylia bounced excitedly.

Jax shrugged after Fauna gave him the go-ahead. "I guess so."

"I'm good if Ev is," said Birdie. "I'm rather curious to see how she looks covered in fur."

Ev blushed, but she wasn't going to let embarrassment slow her down. Her choice to become a caprigee had not come lightly. Dianites looked far more human, but caprigee had attunement to Veravisian magic that surpassed even prifae, which she thought would be a helpful quality to have in her studies.

"I'm ready," she said.

"Alright then," replied Syrus. "In that case, let me make sure I have your chosen forms correct. Dianite, levian, noctlus, caprigee, and caprigee, correct?" he said as he pointed to Jax, Lylia, Birdie, Tallis, then Ev in turn.

Everyone nodded, and Syrus smiled.

The world flashed white. When Ev opened her eyes, she stood in a world completely foreign to her, in a body unfamiliar to her, surrounded by creatures, machines, and architecture that she'd never seen before. Yet, for all the strangeness, and though their appearances were completely different, Ev felt at peace.

They'd overcome the Masters. They'd given Doxlans a chance to live free. Though the worlds were different, the people were the same, and that included the people standing by her side right now.

This was the dawn of not only a new day, but a new era, and as Birdie worked to fashion her new amorphous form into a human-like shape and Jax joked about how Lylia now looked even more like a snake, Ev smiled.

Whatever the future held in store, she knew they'd face it together. Whatever challenge would come her way, she was ready.

They were ready.

For more information about upcoming books in this
series and others, check out D. S. Kogler's website at

dskogler-books.com

While you're there, be sure to sign up for the mailing list
as well!